Children of the Lamp

BOOK FOUR

THE DAY OF THE DJINN WARRIORS

Children of the Lamp

BOOK FOUR

THE DAY OF THE DJINN WARRIORS

P. B. KERR

SCHOLASTIC INC.

NEW YORK TORONTO LONDON AUCKLAND SYDNEY
MEXICO CITY NEW DELHI HONG KONG BUENOS AIRES

For Charlie and Naomi Kerr

ISBN-13: 978-0-439-93216-5
ISBN-10: 0-439-93216-5

12 11 10 9 8 7 6 5 4 3 2 1   8 9 10 11 12 13/0

Printed in the U.S.A.   40

First paperback printing, December 2008

CHAPTER 1

METHUSALEH

Before leaving New York for Iraq to take up her new position as Blue Djinn of Babylon, the most powerful djinn in the world, Layla Gaunt put a Methusaleh binding on her husband, Edward, to stop her twin children, John and Philippa, from following her. Now, Methusaleh is the oldest person mentioned in the Bible. And, as you might expect, a Methusaleh binding causes a person to age and become extremely old very rapidly.

Mrs. Gaunt wouldn't normally have subjected her husband to such a terrible fate. She had designed the binding only to operate in the absence of the twins. Mrs. Gaunt's binding was only meant to prevent the twins from gallivanting off to Babylon in pursuit of her. Mr. Gaunt would never have aged quickly at all if his children had been at home. But at the time she made the binding Mrs. Gaunt had no idea that the two figures she thought were her twin children were in fact a pair of perfect imitations, created by an angel named

Afriel, to cover up the fact that the real children were in Nepal and India on an adventure. As a result, by the time the twins did finally return to their East 77th Street home, their poor father was a very old man indeed.

Ancient didn't begin to describe how he looked when they first saw him again. Human beings — for unlike his wife or his children, Edward Gaunt was a mere mundane, which is to say a mere mortal, and not a djinn — who look as old as he did are usually inside a coffin. Confined to a wheelchair because his spindle-thin legs were now too weak to support him, and wearing a tartan shawl against the cold of the New York spring, it was hard to connect Mr. Gaunt with the father the twins had once known. Indeed, he seemed hardly human at all and more like something from a creaky old horror film.

John thought his father looked about eighty. In fact, he had aged so much that he now looked as he would have if he had been 250. Mr. Gaunt was easily the oldest-looking human being that has ever existed since Methusaleh himself.

Nimrod, another powerful djinn, and uncle to John and Philippa, was of the opinion that so long as the twins stayed close to their father, Mrs. Gaunt's binding would no longer operate: "After a while," he said, "this binding will reverse itself and your father will start to get younger again. The important thing is that you remain with him, here in New York. I shall, of course, stay with you instead of going home to London."

Mr. Rakshasas, also a djinn and quite aged himself, being at least 150 years old — for djinn live much longer than humans — agreed with Nimrod that the binding would reverse itself. Addressing the twins from inside the antique brass lamp in which he lived, he advised them to consult Jenny Sachertorte, a djinn doctor. "Sure," he said in his gentle Irish accent, "she'll be able to tell you how some of the more inconvenient effects of the binding might be made less distressing to poor Mr. Gaunt. There's no remedy for being an old man quite like the care of a younger woman."

But Jenny Sachertorte was unable to come and, speaking on the telephone, suggested that Nimrod retain the services of a djinn nurse called Marion Morrison. "She's an Eremite," said Dr. Sachertorte. "You know, one of those djinn who have dedicated their lives to the benefit of deserving humans. She specializes in helping people who have been the subject of malicious djinn bindings or who have made unfortunate wishes. I'll get a message to her, only it might take a while. I believe she's in the Amazon jungle working with some unfortunate natives who found themselves cursed by a monkey's paw."

"This *is* rather urgent, Jenny," insisted Nimrod

"I know, I know," said Dr. Sachertorte. "But I have to be with Dybbuk right now." Dybbuk was her mischievous djinn son, and friend to John and Philippa. "He needs me, Nimrod. Especially now that he's found out who his real father is."

Jenny Sachertorte was a good djinn. So was Dybbuk. At least he had been good until now. Recently, however, poor Dybbuk discovered that his real father was Iblis, the most evil djinn in the world, and leader of the Ifrit, the wickedest of the six djinn tribes. There was some genuine concern among those djinn on the side of good that, unless Dybbuk was handled very carefully, he might easily go to the bad.

"I understand," said Nimrod. "Say no more, dear lady. Dybbuk must come first, I agree. I shall await the arrival of Marion Morrison here in New York."

Meanwhile, until the djinn nurse arrived, the family was obliged to entrust Mr. Gaunt to the care of the family housekeeper, Mrs. Trump. And guessing that she would now have her hands full looking after Mr. Gaunt, Nimrod decided to send for Groanin, his English butler.

"Poor old Groanin," said Philippa. "Doesn't he hate New York?"

"He loathes everything about it," said Nimrod, "but that can't be helped. I think Mrs. Trump has urgent need of his help."

A former beauty queen, Mrs. Trump was a kind soul, not to mention a wealthy one. The previous year she had won millions of dollars in the New York State Lotto. She remained oblivious of the fact that she owed her good fortune to a wish she made in the earshot of Philippa, who, naturally, had granted it. Despite her riches, Mrs. Trump continued in the service of the Gaunts as their devoted servant. She was especially fond of the children and of the gorgeous Mrs. Gaunt. But Mrs. Trump soon found her patience severely tried by Mr. Gaunt's demanding behavior, as she herself explained to Nimrod and the children: "He is very exasperating," she said. "Sometimes, by the time I get all the way up to his room he's completely forgotten what it was he wanted. Then, about a minute or two after I've left, he remembers what it was after all, and rings the bell again. I don't mind telling you I'm absolutely exhausted."

"Poor Mrs. Trump," said John.

He and his sister had tried to help Mrs. Trump to look after their increasingly cantankerous father, but the old man would only be waited on by Mrs. Trump. This was because he persisted in believing the housekeeper was his wife, Mrs. Gaunt. It was true, there were a few similarities between these two women. Especially of late. Since winning her fortune, Mrs. Trump was much improved to look at. She had been to a dentist to have her missing tooth replaced. She wore nicer clothes. All in all, Mrs. Trump had become an attractive woman again. But she still lacked Mrs. Gaunt's obvious glamour and personality.

Not that Mr. Gaunt, with failing eyesight and hearing, noticed any of this. And nobody guessed that this case of mistaken identity was based entirely on the simple coincidence that Mrs. Trump wore the same perfume as Mrs. Gaunt. There was nothing wrong with the old man's sense of smell. So he called her "darling" or "honey" and sometimes "baby" and insisted that she hold his hand.

It was a situation Mrs. Trump found embarrassing. She was able to excuse Mr. Gaunt's peculiar condition and conduct only because she accepted Nimrod's explanation that he was suffering from a rare but reversible genetic disease, as well as Nimrod's assurances that a special nurse would soon be arriving at the house to take care of the old man. It was just as well that she had already become used to strange things happening at number 7 East 77th Street. Indeed, so often did strange things happen in the Gaunt household that many of these no longer seemed strange at all.

"That nurse can't get here soon enough," said Mrs. Trump at the end of another long day. "If tomorrow's anything like today, I'll need a nurse myself."

These words proved oddly prophetic. The next morning, Mr. Gaunt clumsily managed to break the string of pearls Mrs. Trump wore underneath her uniform. This was Mrs. Trump's most treasured possession, which was why she never took the necklace off, not even when she was cooking, vacuuming, or dusting knickknacks.

Crawling across the bedroom floor on her hands and knees, Mrs. Trump recovered nearly all of her pearls. But three rolled under the door and across the landing where, minutes later, she stepped on them, slipped, and fell down a whole flight of stairs with a crash that sounded like a whole building collapsing.

John and Philippa ran into the hall to find Mrs. Trump lying unconscious on the floor. Nimrod called an ambulance and Mrs. Trump was taken around the block to the Kildare

Hospital on 78th Street. But after surgery, she still remained unconscious.

Her surgeon, Dr. Saul Hudson, met Nimrod and the twins with a face that was as grave and full of foreboding as Salem Cemetery.

"I'm afraid we've done all we can," he said. "It's up to her what kind of recovery she makes. But right now she's not responding to any kind of stimulation. And the longer she remains unconscious, the more worried I'm going to be. I'm sorry not to have better news for you."

"Can we see her, Dr. Hudson?" asked John.

"Of course."

Dr. Hudson led them to Mrs. Trump's bedside and then left them alone. Her head was now swathed in bandages and her face was the color of volcanic ash. She was in a private room with a window overlooking the Gaunts' own backyard. For a long time no one said anything.

"I think it's nice that you can see our house from here," Philippa said eventually. "Mrs. Trump would like that."

"I'm sure she would," agreed Nimrod.

"Is there nothing we can do for her?" John asked Nimrod. "I mean using djinn power?"

"I'm afraid not," said Nimrod. "I wouldn't know where to start. Brains are complex things and it's never a good idea for a djinn to go messing around with one. That's how Frankenstein got started."

"If only Mom were here," said Philippa. She smiled sheepishly at Nimrod. "Oh, I didn't mean that I don't think you're up to dealing with all this, Uncle Nimrod. You are. I know you are. It's just that I miss her and I'd feel a lot better if she was here with us now."

"Light my lamp if I don't agree with you," said Nimrod. "Your mother, my sister, is a very capable woman."

The twins stayed at Mrs. Trump's bedside, holding her hands and talking to her. She remained unconscious. Nimrod waited with them, trying for their sake to seem optimistic about Mrs. Trump's chances of making a full recovery. But he knew that they knew that things were not looking good for the housekeeper. After a while, John got up and went to the window. Looking out across the hospital's small garden, and his own backyard, he thought he saw something at his father's bedroom window. And then, a second or two later, a man's outline at one of the lower floor windows.

"That's strange," he said.

Nimrod joined him at the window. "See something, did you?"

"Something or someone," said John. "There's no one else at home. Unless you count Monty." Monty was their cat. He was an unusual cat in that for many years he had been a human female named Monica Retch. Until Mrs. Gaunt had turned her into a cat. "But I don't think it was him."

"I hope everything's all right," said Philippa. "I don't think I could take another disaster right now."

"We'd better go home," said Nimrod. "Besides, there's nothing we can do here."

CHAPTER 2

THE WAR OF PHILIPPA'S EAR

Instead of another disaster waiting for them at home, they found Mr. Groanin in the kitchen polishing silver and making tea. Since gaining a second arm (for a long time, Groanin had existed with just one) Groanin had taken to always doing two things at once, such as hugging two children to his ample stomach instead of just one.

"I flew in from London this morning," he explained. "The front door wasn't locked. So I let myself in and made myself useful, as you can see."

The twins were delighted to have Groanin with them. He might have been the gloomiest butler ever to pick up a tea tray or a dust cloth, but somehow he always managed to make them feel cheerier.

"It's good to see you kids again," he said in his loud Manchester accent. "I said, it's good to see you again. Even if it is in such unhappy circumstances as these. Blimey! With cheese as hard as yours, you could start your own flipping workhouse."

The twins winced as Groanin's words trampled all over their raw feelings like a pair of enormous hobnailed boots. Still, they knew the butler's heart was in the right place even if his mouth was sometimes somewhere else.

"I hope it's true that accidents come in threes, and that's the end of it," he said. "I say, I hope that's the end of it. And that some of your ill luck doesn't rub off on me."

"Do shut up, Groanin," said Nimrod.

Philippa fixed a smile to her face and hugged Groanin tighter in the hope that she might stop the butler's runaway train of thought.

"Thank you for coming, Mr. Groanin," said Philippa.

"Don't mention it, miss," he said. "Besides, I had nothing better to do. And City is hardly playing its best right now." Manchester City was the name of the soccer team Groanin supported.

"Same old Groanin," said John.

Minutes later, the doorbell rang and Groanin, being a true butler, quickly removed his apron, put on his coat, and shimmered away to answer it.

"There's an American person to see you," he said, upon his equally smooth return. "A somewhat unusual-looking lady who says that she is expected and that her name is Miss Marion Morrison."

"You'd better show her into the library," said Nimrod.

Marion Morrison was indeed unusual. She was a tall, fat, old woman with a husky voice and two beady gray eyes that she was able to control so that she could look in two different directions at the same time. Her short, reddish-gray hair resembled rusted steel wool. She wore a red shirt, a pair of tan pants, a leather vest, and cowboy boots. In one fist she held a huge bean sandwich and in the other a mug of steaming black coffee.

"Howdy," she said. "You must be Nimrod," she said with one eye on the twins. "And you must be John and Philippa Gaunt," she said with the other eye on Nimrod. "Heard a lot about you kids. Mostly good." After a noisy slurp of coffee, she added, "Fixed myself some supper. Hope you don't mind. Been riding a whirlwind all day to get here and I'm a little unraveled."

"Did you have a good flight?" Philippa inquired politely.

"I'm here, ain't I?" Marion Morrison grinned and took a large bite out of her sandwich. "That's as good as it gets, I reckon."

To Groanin's fastidious horror several of the beans from her sandwich fell onto the expensive library rug, and her cowboy boots seemed quite muddy for someone who had been on a whirlwind all day. By the door was her bedroll and some saddlebags, as if she had just dismounted from a horse.

"Jenny Sachertorte said you are a djinn nurse," said Nimrod.

"To djinn, maybe," said the strange-looking woman. "But to humans, I'm a lot more than just a nurse. Doctor, healer, medicine woman. Mundanes have called me all of those things." She sipped her coffee noisily again, and then threw the dregs onto the fire. "Now where's the patient? If he's been hit with a Methusaleh, time's not on our side, so let's mount up."

Nimrod and the twins took their strange visitor upstairs and by the time they'd reached Mr. Gaunt's bedroom, she had finished her huge sandwich. Entering the room she held up her hands like a scrubbed-up surgeon, and they crackled with a thin blue flame for a moment as she allowed a small quantity of djinn power to escape from her body and destroy the dirt and bacteria on them. The flame was powerful enough to singe the edges of her shirt cuffs.

John, who'd never before seen this, felt his jaw drop a little.

"'S'a matter, son?" she said. "Ain't you ever seen anyone washing their hands afore?"

"Er, not with djinn power," he said.

"Better than soap and water, by a long ways," she said. "Never much liked the feeling of water on my skin. Seems unnatural for a djinn to go near water if you ask me." Planting her enormous backside on Mr. Gaunt's bed, she eyed him gently. "Hi there, old-timer," she said.

Mr. Gaunt looked myopically straight past his new nurse and into thin air. "Who's there?" he said, cupping one incredibly hairy and elephantine ear with a shaking hand. "Pardon?"

"He's a little deaf," explained Philippa.

"Mmm-hmmm. Old-timer doesn't see so good, neither."

"He's not exactly an old-timer," said John. "If you don't mind me saying so, Mrs. Morrison. He's really only fifty. Which is old enough for a human, I guess. But not that old. Not as old as he looks, anyway. And he's not normally as can-tankerous as he seems right now. He's really very nice, for a father."

With one eye on her patient, the djinn nurse fixed the other on John and smiled approvingly. "It's good that you say so," she said. "Man's lucky to have a boy like you. Fact is, even grown men need kindness and understanding. I reckon it'll take two or three months for him to make a full recovery. Until then, we can relieve some of the worse symptoms of old age. And by the way, it's not Mrs., and never Marion. Call me M. Or Doc."

"Pardon?" said Mr. Gaunt.

"Now tell me all about the binding," she said.

Nimrod explained the nature and timing of the binding and the fact that the children were supposed to have acted as inhibitors. Doc listened and then placed a finger inside one of Mr. Gaunt's ears and another in one of his nostrils to take his temperature. Her eye lingered upon a bonsai tree that stood on top of the chest of drawers on the far side of the bedroom. It was a Japanese maple tree, just twenty-seven inches high.

"Is that there bonsai tree the genuine article, from the Far East? Or a piece of junk from a mail-order catalogue?"

"It's the real thing, all right," said Philippa. "It was a birthday present to my mom from my dad. He bought it in Hong Kong."

Marion got up and looked more closely at the tree. "So this dirt is one hundred percent Chinese?"

"I guess so," said Philippa. "Are you interested in bonsai trees?"

"Nope," she said. "Can't stand them."

Marion helped herself to a small amount of earth from the bonsai plant, smelled it, tasted it, spat it out, and then nodded. A second later, she wrenched the ancient little tree out of its pot and threw it into the corner of the room.

"Hey," said Philippa. "That tree cost twenty thousand dollars!"

"I don't guess the size of people's wallets has got anything to do with their brains." She spat onto a handful of the earth and then heated the mixture in her hands with djinn power to make a kind of clay that she proceeded to smear onto Mr. Gaunt's eyelids.

"This'll improve his vision some," she said. "Enough so he can read a newspaper or watch TV."

She heated the remainder of the clay in her palm some more until it was a very fine powder. This she blew into Mr. Gaunt's two hairy ear passages and up his nose.

"And that will fix his hearing so he can listen to the radio."

"How does that work?" asked Philippa.

"Djinn saliva," said Marion. "It contains healing properties. At least it does for humans. And mixed with Chinese earth it becomes a very powerful material that has an endless number of apparently supernatural properties." Marion grinned. "It was a real stroke of luck, finding that bonsai here. I was running short of Chinese dirt." She picked up the planter and poured the rest of the earth into a plastic bag she produced from her hip pocket. "I'll put the rest in my saddlebags, if you don't mind, in lieu of my fee."

"I never knew that," said Nimrod. "About djinn saliva and earth."

"Ain't you ever heard of Adam?" said Marion.

"Adam?"

"Feller made of dirt in the Bible. That's what the name means. From the ground."

Nimrod nodded. "Yes, of course," he said.

"You're not Layla," Mr. Gaunt told Marion, suddenly piping up. It seemed his eyesight was already much restored.

"Take it easy, old-timer," said Marion. "I'm a healer. We're trying to fix you up, here."

"Perhaps you could also heal Mrs. Trump," said Philippa, and proceeded to explain what had happened to their beloved housekeeper.

"Mrs. Trump?" said Mr. Gaunt. "Why? What's happened to her? And where's my wife? Where's Layla?"

"Take it easy, Dad," John told his father. "Lie still. This lady is here to help you."

"In the morning I'll mosey 'round and take a look at her," Doc told Philippa. "Only heads are complicated."

On her way out of Mr. Gaunt's bedroom, Marion bent down and picked up something off the floor. It was a pearl. She looked at it for a moment and then, before anyone could stop her, popped the pearl into her mouth and crunched it noisily, like a nut, something no human set of teeth could ever have done.

"You eat pearls?" said John.

"Sure do," said Marion. "If you're a djinn they're good for you. Union of fire and water. The third eye, some call them. One of the eight treasures, they are for sure. A pearl is the crystallization of light, transcendent wisdom, spiritual consciousness, and the essence of the universe." She grinned. "'Sides, they taste good."

Later on that evening, after Marion and Mr. Groanin had gone to bed, and following a long conversation with Mr. Rakshasas, Nimrod summoned the children to the library. "We've been talking it over," he said, "and we think there might just be a way to bring your mother back home."

As usual, he was wearing a red suit, and as he stood next to Mr. Rakshasas, who was wearing a white one, these two djinn looked like the flag of Indonesia, which, as anyone knows, is a red stripe on top of a white one. Both of them were sitting very close to the fire — almost too close — but being djinn, of course, who are made of fire, they were as comfortable there as two pieces of hot, buttered toast.

"How?" asked Philippa, who had quite given up hope of ever really seeing her mother again for, as she knew only too well, becoming the Blue Djinn of Babylon involved putting yourself beyond good and evil and listening only to the cold hard voice of pure logic, like some awful math professor. Only in this way, it was believed, could the Blue Djinn act as the supreme judge between the three good tribes of djinn and the three evil tribes. And only in this way, it was generally held, could a balance of power exist between them. Philippa took off her suddenly steamy glasses and polished them furiously. Just the thought of never seeing her mother again had brought a tear to her eye.

"'Tis only an idea, mind," said Mr. Rakshasas. "And it certainly wouldn't do to go building all your hopes on Dingle Beach. Not until we've asked himself. And, for that matter, herself. Which will be no walk in Phoenix Park, I'm thinking."

"Himself?" repeated John. "Herself? Who do you mean? Cut to the chase will you, Mr. Rakshasas?"

"Dybbuk," said Nimrod. "And his sister, Faustina. We shall need their help."

"But didn't Faustina lose her body somewhere in England," said Philippa, "after you exorcised her spirit from the prime minister?"

"That's almost right," said Nimrod. "When Guru Masamjhasara, or Dr. Warnakulasuriya, as he was then known, took a sample of blood from the prime minister, he unwittingly prevented Faustina from reclaiming her body again.

At least not without the help of another djinn. A tiny part of her spirit was lost forever with that blood sample."

"I don't understand how she can help," said Philippa.

"Me neither," said John.

"If we could somehow reunite her body with her spirit," said Nimrod, "there's a very good chance that she could become the Blue Djinn instead of your mother."

" 'Twas always intended that Faustina should be the Blue Djinn one day," said Mr. Rakshasas. "She was the anointed one. But sure, losing her own body banjaxed all that and no mistake."

"But is it possible?" said Philippa. "To reunite her body and soul in the way you describe?"

"Well, yes," said Nimrod. "Provided one knows where to look for the soul. And I didn't until you told me, Philippa."

"Me?"

"Didn't you say that when you went to Bannermann's Island, you heard the voice of an invisible girl whispering in your ear?"

Bannermann's Island, in New York's Hudson River, was where Dybbuk's aunt Felicia lived in splendid but nonetheless creepy isolation.

"Yes," said Philippa. "Just for a moment, anyway. And I felt something brush past me. Like a trailing cobweb. Are you saying Faustina's spirit is hanging out there?"

"When Dybbuk was in danger, he fled to Bannermann's Island because he felt safe there," said John. "I'll bet Faustina felt the same way."

"But I thought that if you were out of your body for too long, you risked drifting off into space," said Philippa. "That's what you told us back in Egypt, anyway."

"That's true," said Nimrod. "But only if you can't get to a place that's familiar to you. An old haunt, if you'll pardon the expression. If you can find such a place, your spirit can hang on indefinitely. For Faustina, that would very likely be a place like Bannermann's Island."

"So all we have to do is go to Bannermann's and reunite her body with her soul," said Philippa.

"That's not as simple as it sounds," said Mr. Rakshasas.

"Somehow I knew it wouldn't be," John groaned.

"It will be necessary for someone to enter the ethereal world as a transubstantiated being," said Nimrod. "That person will have to leave his or her own body behind and go through a portal in the wall of the other world to speak to Faustina."

"What kind of a portal?" asked Philippa.

"An ancient temple," said Nimrod. "Egyptian, Mayan, Babylonian. That's really what they were designed for in the first place."

"I'm thinking Egyptian is best," said Mr. Rakshasas. "That way we'll get a Ka servant to take care of any sinister characters that we might meet."

"Who's going to do it?" asked John.

"It will have to be someone of her own age, whom Faustina will trust," said Nimrod.

"Dybbuk," said John.

"Yes," said Nimrod. "That's what I thought."

"He'll do it," said John. "He'll have to do it. After all, Faustina is his sister."

"Perhaps." Mr. Rakshasas sighed. "But I'm thinking he'll require some careful persuasion. Every foot is slow on an unknown path."

"Of course he'll do it," insisted John. And for once he decided to answer Mr. Rakshasas in kind with a proverb: "After all, blood is thicker than water."

"Yes," Mr. Rakshasas said in a way that made John think he wasn't sure at all. "Honey is sweet, but it takes a brave man to lick it off a beehive."

"Mr. Rakshasas is right, John," said Nimrod. "Kid gloves will be required to handle the poor chap. Dybbuk's still recovering from the shock of learning who and what he is. But there's not much time. In less than thirty days it will be too late for Faustina to do anything to take your mother's place. I shall leave tonight and speak to him tomorrow."

John was about to suggest that it might be best if he went along with Nimrod because he and Dybbuk were friends. But then John remembered his father, and the Methusaleh binding.

"I agree," said Nimrod, for while he couldn't read minds, he was very good at reading what was written on a boy's face. "It might be a good idea to have you along, just to reinforce our case."

"But how?" he asked Nimrod. "We have to stay here, don't we? Me and Phil. Otherwise Dad's going to start aging again."

"There might be a way," said Mr. Rakshasas, who, as the author of the *Shorter Baghdad Rules*, was an expert on what djinn could and could not do. "A *Posse Commodata*. That means a loan of power. Most djinn are reluctant to loan their power to another djinn since it requires an uncommon degree of trust. But I'm thinking that shouldn't be a problem between twins. The binding is only affected by the proximity of djinn power, not your body, John."

"All right then," said John. "How do I do it? How do I give Phil all my power?"

"Don't be a goose in a hurry to a fox's den, young fellow me lad," said Mr. Rakshasas. "Giving another djinn all your power is not something done lightly. What's more, *Posse Commodata* is not always to someone's taste. Before and after. The only way for one djinn to loan power to another is for that djinn to summon all his internal heat and then breathe into that other djinn's ear."

"Breathe into her ear?"

"For about sixty seconds," said Mr. Rakshasas.

John looked at his sister's ear and grimaced with disgust. "No way. You cannot be serious. I mean, if it was anyone else but her. That's disgusting."

"Believe me, the feeling's mutual, bro," Philippa said, coolly. "The thought of having your slobbery mouth on any part of me is totally gross."

"What's gross about it?" asked Mr. Rakshasas.

"For one thing, she's my sister," protested John.

"And for another, he's my brother."

"It's just not the sort of thing brothers and sisters do," said John. "Blow in each other's ears."

"We're not doing it."

Nimrod and Mr. Rakshasas stayed quiet and let the twins make their protestations of revulsion and disgust, knowing, as the children did themselves, that in spite of these spiteful words, they were going to have to do it. And after a while, when John and Philippa had stopped yelling and making faces at each other, they both looked at the two older djinn feeling a little embarrassed at this display of youthful petulance.

"Sorry for sounding off like that," said John.

"Me, too," said Philippa. "I don't know what came over me."

"As you get older," said Mr. Rakshasas, "you'll learn that silence is the fence around the field where the wisdom is stacked." He smiled calmly. "In life, you must learn to take the little potato with the big potato."

"What do I have to do?" John asked, not entirely sure he understood what Mr. Rakshasas was talking about.

Nimrod directed Philippa to lie down on the floor and then told John to put his fingers around his sister's ear. "Now then, John, take a deep breath and press your mouth over her whole ear, just as if you were trying to eat it. Then you must breathe deeply into it, until I tell you to stop."

"I hope your ears are clean," said John.

"Cleaner than yours, I bet," said Philippa.

John looked at Nimrod and raised his eyebrows, as if asking him to recognize this latest provocation.

"Come on, you idiot," said Philippa, and closed her eyes.

Holding his sister's ear, John bent forward.

"Ugh," said Philippa. "His breath. It feels really hot."

"That's the whole idea, Philippa," explained Nimrod.

As soon as John had finished, Philippa rolled quickly away and wiped her ear with her forearm. "Ugh. That was really horrible. Like having a lamprey attached to my ear."

The distaste John felt at having pressed his mouth against his sister's ear was quite overtaken by a dreadful feeling of mortal ordinariness. It was as if a small part of him had died. He stood up, sat down again almost immediately, and hung his head in his hands. "What's a lamprey?" he whispered.

"A jawless fish," she said cruelly, "with a toothed, funnel-like sucking mouth. A little like an eel."

John smiled wearily.

"How do you feel?" Nimrod asked the boy.

"Wasted," said John.

"And you, Philippa?" asked Nimrod. "How do you feel?"

"Twice as strong," she said. "Like I just plugged myself into the electricity and then had a cup of really strong coffee."

"I think it worked," said Nimrod.

"Is this what it feels like to be mundane?" said John.

"How *does* it feel?" asked Philippa, placing a concerned, sisterly hand on his shoulder, and already regretting some of the nasty things she'd said to him.

"Like I just came in last in the New York City Marathon and, somewhere along the way, managed to lose something very, very valuable. Like a limb. I feel like I'm coming down with some kind of virus."

"Sure, you never miss the water until the well runs dry," said Mr. Rakshasas.

"That's for sure," said John. He took a deep breath and stood up. "When do we leave?"

"Now," said Nimrod. "There's really no time to lose."

They went out of the house, and into New York's Central Park, which, late at night, is mostly deserted. There, in an open patch of ground, Nimrod whipped up a powerful but invisible tornado that was marked only by a discarded newspaper swirling around the base of the vortex. In a matter of a few seconds, he and John started to rise up on top of this column of air as if they had been summoned to appear before some celestial court. Philippa and Mr. Rakshasas watched them until they were almost fifty feet in the air, at which point, Nimrod turned the funnel of wind westward and, at a speed of almost 261 mph — an F5 on the Enhanced Fujita-Pearson Tornado Intensity Scale — they disappeared into the Manhattan night sky.

CHAPTER 3

MYSTIFIER

Dybbuk wanted to meet his real father.

That's normal, isn't it? Iblis might be the wickedest djinn in the world, but I'm still his son. What could be wrong with me wanting to meet the guy? Every kid wants to meet his old man, even if he is a sort of monster.

At the same time, however, he knew his mother, Jenny Sachertorte, would never permit such a thing. For one thing, she was frightened of Iblis. Most sensible people were. And for another, she would worry that meeting Iblis would only tempt Dybbuk somehow to go bad.

I don't know what she's worrying about. It's not like I'm wicked or anything, like him. Sure, I do something wild now and again. What kid doesn't? But that doesn't make me a bad person. Maybe, if he met me, that might help Iblis not to be bad himself anymore. It could be that not having had me around all his life has just made him worse.

Dybbuk knew where his father was to be found. Every djinn knew that it was the Ifrit who controlled Las Vegas, not the Mafia, like most humans thought. And Vegas wasn't actually very far away from Palm Springs where Dybbuk lived. It was just a question of getting there. But how was he ever to persuade his mother to let him go? Since his arrival back from India, she was keeping a pretty close eye on him. What was worse, she'd made him swear an oath that he wouldn't start any whirlwinds and fly off somewhere on his own. He was grounded.

Dybbuk always laughed when he heard kids at his school use that word, "grounded," as if it meant something. Unlike them of course, he really was grounded. He could always have caught a bus to Vegas, but Dybbuk was much too lazy ever to do something like that. He hated buses. Was even a little frightened of them, and of the smelly, aggressive people who were often on them. Then there was the claustrophobia he felt on a bus. This is normal for any djinn, who hate all enclosed spaces except their own lamps.

So Dybbuk stayed home and hatched a plan that would get him to Vegas legitimately.

There were times when Dybbuk could play his mother like a guitar. He knew just how to pick her up, tune her a little, and then strum the strings to hear the tune he wanted. He knew exactly what to do to make her say the sort of thing she always said. So he walked around the house with a face like thunder, saying nothing very much and staring into space. Meanwhile, she baked him his favorite kind of curried cake, let him watch unsuitable DVDs, gave him his allowance, and she even gave him a new PlayStation game. But still he kept on with the face. And finally, she cracked. She

snatched a bowl of cereal out of his fingers that he'd chosen to eat instead of her cake, and hurled it against the
kitchen wall.

"Dybbuk," she yelled. Only when she was really angry did
she call him by his given name instead of calling him Buck,
which was the name he preferred. "You're trying my patience.
I bake you a cake. I get you a game. And still you walk around
looking like a long streak of misery. Isn't there anything that
would cheer you up?"

Now I've got her.

"Isn't there anything I can do that's going to put a smile
on your gloomy face?"

He nodded. "Sure," he said. "I want to go to Las Vegas."

Jenny Sachertorte's eyes narrowed with suspicion. "Vegas?
What do you want to go there for? You're too young to gam-
ble and too old for the Chocolate Factory tour. Besides, no
good djinn ever goes to Vegas without a good deal of caution.
You know the place is run by the Ifrit."

"Forget it," he groaned like a bassoon, and rolled his eyes
in his head.

"No, no, no," she said. "If it might make you happy, we'll
go to Vegas. Just tell me why you want to go. Is it the lights?"

"I hate the lights," said Dybbuk. "They look so dumb
and tacky."

"What then?"

"I want to see Adam Apollonius."

Adam Apollonius was the most famous illusionist and
magician in America. He was also the author of several

self-promoting publicity stunts, such as his famous strait-jacketed skydiving escape, and his blindfolded climb up the exterior of the Sears Tower in Chicago. Dybbuk had a poster of him on his bedroom wall.

"I don't understand the fascination," said his mother. "You know it's all just an illusion. Any djinn can do that magic stuff for real. So what is it with this guy?"

"I dunno." Dybbuk yawned. "I guess it's just that he makes it look cooler than we do. Besides, I like the fact that it's an illusion. Like you say, we can do it for real. I guess that makes it seem kind of ordinary. And he makes a show out of it, doesn't keep it all a weird secret the way we do."

"You know why we keep it a secret," said Jenny Sachertorte. "It's to protect ourselves."

Dybbuk's yawn grew larger. "Yeah, I know." He shrugged. "Look, you asked what might make me happy. I told you. But it's no big deal. Forget about it, okay?"

"No, we'll go," she agreed. "It might be fun at that."

Dybbuk congratulated himself on the success of his plan.

I can hardly be in Las Vegas without my father knowing about it. He's bound to seek me out. Surely. And it's not like I want him to do anything. All I want to do is talk to the guy. To hang out with him for a few hours.

He smiled.

"There, that's better," said Dybbuk's mother. "I just want what's going to make you happy, honey."

Iblis had always expected his youngest son to show up in Las Vegas at some time or other. Indeed, for many years he had been counting on it, although perhaps not quite as soon as this. And it was just good luck for Iblis — which of course is bad luck for the rest of us — that Dybbuk and his mother should have shown up in the gambling capital of the world just a few hours after Iblis had been mauled by a pair of black djinn tigers. Mauled severely enough to necessitate abandoning his previous body and seeking out a new one. He had been going about this tedious process when he felt himself suddenly touched by his son's presence — the minute Dybbuk got off the plane at McCarran International Airport and stepped onto the desert tarmac. This was also a bit of good luck for Iblis. In his physical human shape, he might never have felt the boy's presence at all. A physical shape makes a djinn less sensitive to cosmic vibrations. But in his temporary existence as pure spirit it was much easier for him to detect his son's arrival in Las Vegas — something Jenny Sachertorte could never have supposed.

Moving at the speed of light, Iblis flew through the dry Nevada air like an invisible missile locked onto its unwitting target. He found the boy and his mother at the baggage carousel, recognizing Jenny Sachertorte immediately in her scarlet, rhinestone pantsuit. The boy was tall, good-looking, and obviously charismatic. *Just like his father,* Iblis told himself conceitedly. And it took only a matter of a few brief seconds for him to occupy Dybbuk's mind and discover the secrets of his young heart. With an ethereal, occult smile, Iblis realized that an ingenious plan he had been waiting for almost thirteen years to act upon was now ready to put into immediate effect.

As quickly as he had taken possession of Dybbuk's body, Iblis was gone again, before Jenny Sachertorte — or, indeed, Dybbuk himself — was really aware that the spirit shape of the evil djinn had even been near them.

"What's the matter?" she asked Dybbuk. "You looked blank for a moment."

"Did I?"

"Yes. I asked you to grab that suitcase and it was like you hadn't heard me."

"I didn't hear you. My ears. I'm still recovering from being in that plane. I hate planes almost as much as I hate buses."

"It'll pass. Take another claustrophobia pill."

"I still don't know why we took a plane at all, instead of traveling by whirlwind."

"We're here, aren't we? Stop complaining. Besides, I don't want us drawing attention to ourselves by using djinn power. You hear me, Buck? This town is full of Ifrit and if they sense us using djinn power we might find ourselves in trouble. Okay?"

"Okay, okay."

They took a taxi to the Winter Palace Hotel and checked into a two-bedroom, rooftop suite with a spectacular view of Las Vegas. After dinner, they went to Adam Apollonius's show, where they had the best seats in the house. Apollonius himself was a tall, thin man with a little goatee, an earring, and a lot of tattoos. Jenny Sachertorte thought he looked and sounded like an English soccer star.

The show was in two halves. In the first half, Apollonius made a variety of bears — polar bears and grizzly bears — - appear and disappear from different parts of the auditorium. He also turned himself into a real silverback gorilla and then back again before having himself beheaded by a man wielding a giant ax who proceeded to walk around the stage carrying the magician's still-talking head. (For those who disliked Adam Apollonius, this was usually the best bit in the show.)

Dr. Sachertorte tried not to look bored, but of course she was. By contrast, Dybbuk looked like he was entranced. In the intermission they got some drinks, and she asked if Dybbuk minded her not coming back for the second half.

"I don't mind," said Dybbuk.

In the second half, Apollonius made an elephant disappear from the stage, which, even to Dybbuk's djinn eyes, looked pretty impressive. Then Apollonius said he wanted a volunteer from the audience to help him with his signature magic trick: the Magic Bullet Catch. He selected Dybbuk to come up onstage. And Dybbuk was, of course, delighted. He loved guns almost as much as he liked magic.

The Bullet Catch, in which a marked bullet is fired at the magician who catches it in his teeth, is the most dangerous trick in magic and has taken the lives of more than a dozen performers. Apollonius, who did nothing by halves, invited Dybbuk to fire a rifle at his head. Before Dybbuk could decide exactly how Apollonius was going to work the trick, the magician had ordered a loud drumroll from the orchestra, and invited his volunteer assistant to pull the trigger.

A split second later, the magician shouted at Dybbuk to stop. Too late. The gun fired and Adam Apollonius, who must have thought he had been shot, cried aloud and then rolled on the floor. The audience stood up as one. There were shouts and screams. Someone rushed onto the stage. Horrified, Dybbuk threw down the gun and ran forward to the apparently stricken magician.

A moment later, Apollonius jumped up again, grinning triumphantly, with a rifle bullet clearly visible between his teeth. He handed the bullet to Dybbuk, who verified that it was indeed the very same one marked by him earlier, and then bowed to the huge applause that shook the whole auditorium. Taking hold of Dybbuk's hand, Apollonius invited the excited young djinn first to take a bow himself, and then to join him backstage.

Dybbuk was beside himself with pleasure and delight at meeting with his hero.

"For a minute back there, I thought I'd actually shot you," confessed Dybbuk when they were alone in the magician's dressing room.

"All part of the act, old boy," said Apollonius. "The idea that there's been some kind of accident gets the audience excited. They love the idea that I might have been killed."

"Just like the great Houdini, huh?"

"You know about magic, kid?"

"Houdini was the greatest," said Dybbuk. "But you're pretty good."

Apollonius tried to look modest, and failed. "What about you, kid? Do you do any magic yourself?"

"Sure."

Infected with the bright lights of Las Vegas and the excitement of a lavish stage show, Dybbuk wanted to impress his glamorous host and, despite the warning his mother had given him about using djinn power, he decided to show Apollonius something the magician would probably think was just a bit of close-up magic instead of the real thing. Dybbuk extended his arm, pulled up his sleeve the way real magicians did on TV, and showed Apollonius his open palm and then the back of his hand. Dybbuk whispered his focus word. And when he showed Apollonius his palm again there was a chocolate bar in his hand.

"Pretty good," said Apollonius.

"May I borrow your handkerchief, sir?" Dybbuk asked politely.

Apollonius tugged his handkerchief out of his breast pocket and, as requested, covered the chocolate bar in Dybbuk's hand. Dybbuk whispered his focus word again and then lifted the handkerchief away to reveal the chocolate bar had disappeared. Apollonius started to applaud.

"How old are you, sonny?" he asked.

"Nearly thirteen, sir."

"That's the best close-up illusion I think I've ever seen," said the man. "And believe me, I've seen the best. Show me another."

"Let me see here," mumbled Dybbuk, and thought for a moment. "How about a little levitation?"

He'd seen street magicians on TV levitating a few inches off the ground. It was a trick done with a couple of powerful magnets in the heels of their shoes; you just slipped one shoe off, let it stick to the other, and then lifted one foot in the air. Usually the magicians cheated a little with the TV camera so that you only saw one side of the magician's body. But somehow it always looked impressive.

Maybe if he could make a very small whirlwind underneath his feet he could lift himself that way. He'd never really tried it before but, to his surprise, it worked. What was more, it looked a lot more convincing than anything ever seen on TV; Dybbuk rose all of twelve inches into the air, hovering there for several seconds before slowly coming down to earth again.

"Amazing," said Apollonius. "I've never seen anyone do a levitation trick that's as good as that. How do you do it?"

Dybbuk shrugged modestly. "Practice," he said.

"Thirteen years old and you're doing close-up tricks that take years to perfect. Years." He shook his head in genuine awe. "What's your best trick? The climax of your act."

"The Indian Rope Trick."

"Did you bring the rope?"

"It's in the auditorium," said Dybbuk. "I left it there, under my seat." Even as he spoke he was putting a long length of thick rope under his seat, with djinn power.

"You came prepared, didn't you?"

They went back onstage, in front of the now empty auditorium. Dybbuk got the rope and then laid it in a careful coil on the stage, like a sleeping python. Then, at the very moment when Apollonius was examining the rope, Dybbuk conjured a flute from the air.

"How'd you do that?" asked Apollonius.

"Practice."

Dybbuk sat down and started to play and slowly the rope began to rise. Apollonius watched, apparently amazed as the rope straightened and rose up into the lights above the stage. "Is there some kind of wire in the rope, is that it?"

Dybbuk put down the flute and went up the rope like a monkey, and when he was near the top, he began to transubstantiate, which looked like smoke covering his disappearance.

"Where are you?" called Apollonius. "Where did you go?"

Dybbuk let the rope drop back down to the stage and while Apollonius was busy examining that, he transported the smoke carrying all of his atoms to the back of the auditorium, where he reassembled himself and then called out to the famous magician.

"Here I am."

Dybbuk walked back to the stage, where Apollonius was still shaking his head.

"I've never seen anything like that. In all my years of magic. I mean, you make the Indian Rope Trick look like the real thing."

Dybbuk grinned. He was enjoying himself.

"You've got it all, kid," said Apollonius. "You're young, good-looking, you've got more talent than I've ever seen. How would you like your own TV show?"

"I don't think so," said Dybbuk, conscious now that, perhaps, he had gone a little too far.

Apollonius laughed. "What do you mean, you don't think so? You're a natural. A star. And I can make it happen. Believe me, in a few weeks you could be the most famous face in America. I can make you more famous than fame itself."

Dybbuk was still shaking his head. His mother was going to kill him.

Apollonius thought Dybbuk was still being modest. "No kidding. I'm serious. You're what magic has been crying out for. A magician who's as big as any pop star. Maybe bigger. We're going to make a fortune. And the girls are going to love you, Buck. The girls are going to worship you, my boy."

That got Dybbuk's attention. "Girls?"

"Sure, girls. Lots of girls. You like girls?"

"Oh sure, but . . ." The "but" was on account of the fact that Dybbuk was a little shy of girls. With girls it was so easy to get things wrong. There had been a girl named Lisa of whom he'd been very fond. She'd made a wish and because Dybbuk had dearly wanted her wish to come true for her, he'd made it happen. He wished he hadn't. But he had. Lisa had wished that Teddy Grosvenor, who was a boy at their school in Palm Springs, "would just disappear." And Dybbuk had learned the hard truth of what Mr. Rakshasas was always saying: "A wish is a dish that's a lot like a fish — once it's been eaten it's harder to throw back."

"Girls," said Apollonius. "You'd better get used to the idea of hundreds of them screaming outside your hotel and camped in front of the gates of your Hollywood home. Sending you their pictures and locks of their hair. Greeting your arrival at airports all over the country. Fainting with excitement when you autograph their hands. Crying because you said hello to them."

"Hundreds?"

"Thousands."

Dybbuk nodded. All thoughts of meeting his father were now gone from his mind. He knew who he wanted to meet. He wanted to meet girls. *Thousands of them.*

Halfway across America, Nimrod called Jenny Sachertorte on a cell phone from inside his whirlwind.

"Nimrod," she said. "I was just going to bed. What's happening? Has Marion Morrison shown up yet?"

"Yes, yes, dear lady, everything's fine on that score," said Nimrod. "How's Dybbuk?"

"Oh, he's fine, I think."

"John and I are on our way to Palm Springs to see him on a mission of mercy," said Nimrod.

"Well, we're not there. We're in Las Vegas. At the Winter Palace. For a weekend break. Dybbuk wanted to see a show. I think it's really cheered him up." Her tone hardened a little. "Is he in trouble again? What kind of mission of mercy?"

"Light my lamp, no. Nothing like that. Perhaps I'd better tell you when I see you both." He looked at his watch. "Shall we say at breakfast? Tomorrow morning? In your hotel?"

A few hours' flying time brought them within sight of Las Vegas. In the Nevada night it looked like some huge and exotic species of electric jellyfish floating in a jet-black sea. Nimrod landed them in the huge parking lot of the Marriott Winter Palace — a luxury hotel that was the image of the famous royal palace in St. Petersburg, Russia. They checked in and went straight to bed, tired and a little windswept after their long flight.

In the morning, they went down to breakfast in the Pompeii Room and found Dybbuk and Jenny Sachertorte sitting quietly and staring down at their cereal. It was plain from their faces that they had argued about something.

"Hey, Buck," John said brightly, and tapped him on the shoulder with his fist playfully. "How are you doing, buddy?"

Dybbuk ignored him.

"Look, I'll come straight to the point," said Nimrod, and explained in detail his plan to reunite Faustina with her body and, in the process, enable her to fulfill her destiny, which was to become the Blue Djinn of Babylon.

Jenny Sachertorte, who was, of course, Faustina's mother,

started to cry. "Do you really think it's possible, Nimrod? To bring Faustina back? After all these years?"

"Yes," he said. "But there's no time to lose. Dybbuk here will have to go to Egypt with us and —"

"I'm afraid that won't be possible," Dybbuk said coldly. "I have other plans."

"Well, look," said John. "We don't have to leave right away. I mean if you want to stay here in Vegas another day, I'm sure that's possible."

"You don't understand," said Dybbuk. "When I say I have other plans, I have other plans — *for the rest of my life.* I've been offered my own television show. And I'm not about to drop a chance like that just to go off with you on another pointless journey. Faustina's gone. Get used to it." He looked unpleasantly at his mother. "All of you."

He got up from the table and walked away. Nimrod looked at John and nodded that he should go after him.

John threw down his napkin and followed his old friend into the Hall of Hercules, which was full of slot machines and hundreds of people filling them urgently with coins.

"She's your sister, Buck," he said, catching up with him. "You *have* to do it."

"My sister's dead," he said.

"No, she's not," said John. "She's lost, that's all. You can find her. You can't just abandon her."

"Don't think I haven't guessed why you're doing this, pal," said Dybbuk. "You think you can bring your mother back from Babylon by having Faustina take her place as Blue Djinn. Well, I'm not doing it."

"But it's what Faustina wanted, apparently," John insisted. "Look, ask your mother if you don't believe me."

"To ask her, I'd have to speak to her, and I don't want to do that in case she tries to put a binding on me. Or Nimrod."

"Nimrod wouldn't do that," said John.

"Wouldn't he?" Dybbuk hardly looked convinced of this. "Look, nothing personal, but I really think it'd be better if we don't see each other anymore. I'm going to be famous. And I don't want anyone from my old life interfering, get it?"

John was disappointed in his old friend. "What kind of TV show is it going to be, anyway?" he asked.

"Street magic," said Dybbuk.

"You mean tricking gullible mundanes with stupid bits of sleight of hand."

"Good-bye, John," said Dybbuk. "If you ever see me again, just pretend you don't know me."

"I don't know you now," said John. He shook his head and walked away. But he hadn't gone very far when he saw someone he recognized.

It was Finlay McCreeby. Finlay was the son of Virgil McCreeby, a magus and sorcerer to whom John had once been obliged to grant three wishes. One of these wishes had resulted in John turning poor Finlay into a peregrine falcon. Fortunately, John had been able to return Finlay back to his original human shape eventually, and Finlay had gone off with Edwiges the Wandering Djinn to exploit one of her gambling systems and make enough money to put himself through school. John found Finlay wandering through the hotel lobby. At least John thought it was him; Finlay looked a lot taller than he remembered.

"Finlay, what are you doing here?"

"Trying to avoid security," said Finlay. "I'm too young to be playing the machines. They'll throw me out if they find me."

"What happened to the roulette system?"

"Oh, the system was fine," said Finlay. "But Edwiges kept on trying to be a mother to me. She meant well, but after a while I had to get away."

"What about school?"

"I've got a place at a boarding school in England," said Finlay. "It's all paid for, in advance. By Edwiges. I'll say that for her, she was very kind. But until school starts I'm just killing time. It's not so easy gambling when you're a kid. To be honest, I'm kind of looking for a job. Just to tide me over. Until school starts."

John had a brain wave. "I'll give you a job." He glanced around and saw Dybbuk on the other side of the Hall of Hercules. "You see that boy over there? The one with the rock T-shirt and the motorcycle boots?"

"Gloomy face, longish dark hair?"

John nodded. "That's the one."

"What about him?"

"I want you to follow him," said John. "Find out who he sees, who he meets, where he goes."

"I get it," said Finlay. "Like a private detective."

"Exactly." John took out his wallet and handed over all his money. "There," he said. "That should cover your expenses for a few days. To keep in touch, just call the house in New York. We're in the phone book."

"Thanks, John," said Finlay. "I appreciate it. By the way, what's the kid's name? The one I'm following."

"Dybbuk Sachertorte," said John. "And he's not a kid exactly. He's a djinn."

Finlay grinned. "With a name like that? It's probably just as well."

CHAPTER 4

MIRACLE ON MADISON AVENUE

Where one accident occurs another two usually follow. To think otherwise is to misunderstand the three-sided nature of Luck, which is a force in the universe, just like mass and time. The great scientist Albert Einstein never quite grasped the importance of Luck, as he himself admitted when he said that he could not believe "that God plays dice with the universe." And he might just as well have written the equation $L = mc^2$ as the one for which he is more famous.

As some will know, djinn are the only beings on earth that can influence Luck, for good or bad. But even djinn can have accidents. Especially when they are tired and distracted, like Philippa, who was worried about her parents, and Mrs. Trump. And this is how Philippa, walking around the corner to the hospital to visit Mrs. Trump, came to step in front of a bus.

The bus, a number 4, heading north up Madison Avenue, was moving fast and there was no obvious reason why Philippa didn't hear it coming. Ordinarily she probably would have been killed. Manhattan buses are notoriously unforgiving of the people who step in front of them. Especially the number 4. (In Chinese, four is a very unlucky number, being the same word for death, which is why you will seldom see Chinese people on a number 4 heading north up Madison Avenue.) Luckily for her, Philippa was not run down and killed. A policeman on a horse who was passing by galloped forward, grabbed her by the collar, hauled her clear of the oncoming bus, and saved her life.

"What the heck d'you think you're doing?" he yelled when she was standing safely on the sidewalk again. "You could have been killed." The policeman had a face that was the shape and color of a brick, being square and red and hard.

"I'm sorry," said Philippa, her legs turning to Jell-O as she began to understand the narrow margin of her escape. She sat down in the doorway of an expensive French restaurant.

"You would have been," yelled the policeman. He got off his horse, secured it to a streetlight, and then yelled at her some more. "You would have been, little Miss Death Wish." He pulled out his pen and ticket book. "I'm going to give you a ticket, because that way you'll remember to look where you're going."

It's not always the nicest person who saves your life. Or the one who is the most deserving of great good fortune.

Nevertheless, Philippa knew that it was now her solemn obligation as a good djinn to reward this policeman in the traditional, time-honored way.

"And I'm going to give you something," said Philippa.

"You are, huh?" said the cop. "Like what?"

"Three wishes," she said.

"Three wishes?" He smiled. "I wish I had three wishes. I really do. You've no idea. I suppose you're a genie, is that it?"

"Something like that. By the way, you still have three wishes. That first wish you made gives us a logical fallacy of causation. You can't wish for something you already have because I can't give you what I've already given you. But if you're prepared to waste one wish I can prove that you really do have three wishes, officer. Although of course by then you'll only have two wishes."

"I wish I knew what you're talking about, kid," said the policeman . . .

"FABULONGOSHOOMARVELISHLYWONDERPIPICAL!"

. . . And suddenly the policeman did know what Philippa was talking about. "Holy mackerel," he said. "You really are a djinn."

"You saved my life," said Philippa. "I'm obliged to you. And even though you're a bit of a jerk, if you don't mind me saying so, I have to grant you three wishes. Or to be more precise, two, since you've made one wish already. Only be careful now. With a mouth like yours, it would be all too easy to put your foot in it and squander the other two, 'wishing' that you knew what to do. Believe me, I've seen it happen."

The policeman took off his helmet and scratched his head. "You're right," he said. "I'm a jerk. I wish I wasn't but what can you do? It comes from having to deal with a lot of other jerks. Sometimes this job brings out the worst in me."

"Not anymore," said Philippa, and, muttering her focus word, granted the policeman's wish.

Immediately, the cop's face took on a less bricklike aspect, becoming a little less square, a little less red, and little less hard. He even managed a smile, which was something his facial muscles hadn't achieved in several bad-tempered years of law enforcement.

"Two down, one to go," said Philippa.

"Hey," said the cop. "You know what? I do feel kind of different. Like maybe I'm not such a bad guy after all."

"That's because you're not," said Philippa. "You're a nice guy. A very nice guy. Probably you always were that nice guy underneath. I can tell because it didn't require much power to bring that out."

The cop patted Daisy, his horse, affectionately. He hadn't always been nice to Daisy. There had been times when he'd ridden her a little too hard. And it was now he remembered why he'd become a mounted policeman in the first place. Because he loved horses. And not just horses. He loved all animals. Just thinking about how much love he had for animals brought a tear to his piggy eyes.

"You know something, little girl?" he said, and uttered a loud sigh. "I hate the way people mistreat living creatures." He nodded at the menu in the window of the restaurant where they were still standing. "I mean, just look at the stuff people eat in this city. Some of it is just so cruel to animals." As he spoke, tears started to roll down his fat face. "You want to know my third wish? I wish no one in New York could eat pâté de foie gras. That's what I wish. That no one could eat pâté de foie gras."

Philippa glanced at the menu, saw pâté de foie gras listed among the hors d'oeuvres — which is French for starter courses — and considered for a moment how she might make the cop's unselfish, animal-loving wish come true. She had no idea how many people in Manhattan liked eating pâté de foie gras. What was more, even feeling as powerful as she did now, she hadn't a clue as to how she might affect the tastes of hundreds, possibly thousands of New Yorkers. But a wish granted was a wish granted. And she decided to grant the policeman's third and last wish in the easiest, most straightforward way possible: by causing the city's entire supply of pâté de foie gras simply to disappear. Within seconds of her uttering her focus word, there was not a bit of pâté de foie gras nor a mention of it to be found anywhere in New York.

"There," she said, tapping the menu in the window triumphantly. "Just as you asked. It's gone. No one in New York can eat pâté de foie gras. Satisfied?"

The cop nodded. "Yeah," he said. "Thanks a lot, little girl."

"No, thank you," she said, "for saving my life."

"You take care, now." And then, with a big smile on his face, the cop mounted his horse and rode away in the direction of the park.

Philippa felt as if she had done a good deed. But instead of congratulating herself for helping to make someone a better person, she might have done better to have remembered that all use of djinn power in the mundane world has a random and unpredictable effect, even when that power has been used for something as apparently benign as saving the enlarged livers of a few French geese — for that is what pâté de foie gras is made of. And if djinn are sometimes reluctant to give ordinary people three wishes it's not because they're mean and stingy, it's because they have learned to appreciate that granting wishes to human beings has unseen, unpredictable consequences. Even a wish that's made with a kind intent. It's the one aspect to being a djinn that young djinn take the longest time to learn. Sometimes it's a hard lesson, too. As Mr. Rakshasas was fond of saying, "Having a wish is like lighting a fire. It's reasonable to assume that the smoke might make someone cough."

There's an old nursery rhyme that explains how small things can have large consequences. It goes:

For want of a nail, the shoe was lost.
For want of a shoe, the horse was lost.
For want of a horse, the rider was lost.
For want of a rider, the battle was lost.

For want of a battle, the kingdom was lost.
And all for the want of a nail.

Now, because of this wish Philippa had granted the police officer, a chain of events was set off, and one thing led to another; it's probably just as well that Philippa never ever connected the dreadful thing with the third wish she gave that New York policeman.

The djinn have a word for this kind of misfortune: *Kismet*, from the Persian *qismat*. According to the *Shorter Baghdad Rules*, it means "that which is destined."

Safely back home again, Philippa switched on the TV and tried to relax. But she couldn't help noticing that a lot of her favorite TV shows had been taken off the air. According to the TV news, this was because a Las Vegas–based TV company called LZ kid TV had been aggressively buying up all the best TV shows and simply putting the tapes in a vault where no one could see them.

"Best place for 'em if you ask me," said Mr. Groanin. "Some of them shows you kids watch on TV are tripe. I say, some of them TV shows you seem to like so much are just tripe."

Philippa switched off the TV. "Well then, let's go out," she said.

"What about your dad?" asked Groanin, who wasn't keen on going anywhere in Manhattan.

"Doc will look after him. He's already getting better."

"It's a miracle what that woman can do," said Groanin, who liked Marion Morrison more than he ever would have admitted to Philippa.

"I know," she said. "Let's go to the Metropolitan Museum. They have one of those famous terra-cotta warriors on loan from China. I've been meaning to go and look at it for a while. Besides, the Met is full of really cool things. You'll like it."

"I doubt it," said Groanin, reaching for his coat. "If you recall, miss, I had a bad experience in a museum once. A tiger tore off me arm. Still, I'm game, if you are."

The Metropolitan Museum on Fifth Avenue was a few blocks from the Gaunt house on East 77th Street. From the front, it looks like a sort of giant-size temple, with tall columns and a flight of steps as wide as a football field. But the museum was closed because of a twenty-four-hour strike by museum attendants, and the steps were crowded with people carrying placards and shouting loudly about something. Philippa and Mr. Groanin stayed for a moment to read the placards with slogans such as METROPOLITAN MUSEUM OF FEAR, NO GO IN GHOSTLY GALLERIES, POLTERMET, and NIGHT VISITORS MEANS NO VISITORS.

A few minutes' conversation with one of the attendants revealed that they were on strike because, he said, the Met was haunted. Several of them had reported seeing and hearing ghosts in the Sackler Wing and in the Chinese art galleries on the second floor.

"I'd say they were just after more money," said Groanin as he and Philippa went back home again. "My guess is that one of those blokes what works at the Met read this." He showed Philippa a copy of the previous day's *Daily Telegraph*, and drew her attention to a front-page headline that read, SPOOKS SPELL STRIKES AT BRITISH MUSEUM. "Very likely someone read that and thought it sounded like a good way of getting more money out of them as pay their wages."

Philippa read the story in Groanin's newspaper as they walked. "I'm not so sure," she said. "This means something. But I'm not sure what."

When Philippa and Groanin got home, they found John and Nimrod had returned from Las Vegas. They were huddled in the library with Mr. Rakshasas, discussing everything that had happened at the Winter Palace Hotel.

"So what happens now?" asked Philippa when her brother and her uncle had finished explaining their lack of success. "We've wasted two days trying to get Dybbuk on board."

"All is not lost," said Nimrod. "Accompanied by Mr. Rakshasas, for whom the ethereal world is more comfortable at his age, one of you children will have to go after Faustina instead of Dybbuk."

John looked at Philippa. "Remind me a little," he said. "What exactly is the ethereal world?"

"'Tis the spirit world, John," said Mr. Rakshasas. "The world of ghosts and phantoms and assorted apparitions."

"Oh, *that* world." John shivered uncomfortably. He didn't like ghosts, and meeting the ghost of the Pharaoh Akhenaten had done nothing to change his opinion of them. Ghosts were creepy. Especially the ones that went around haunting places and scaring people.

Philippa, who liked the idea of ghosts even less than her brother, was just about to volunteer, nevertheless, when Groanin spoke. "The spirit world can be frightening, even when you're a djinn," said Groanin. "Especially when you can't actually rely on using djinn power in there yourself."

There was a longish silence.

"Did I mention that?" said Nimrod. "No, perhaps I didn't. Djinn power is severely limited in the ethereal world. Oh, you can move stuff about a bit. Take possession of someone. Rattle a chain, open a door — not that you'd need to, of course. But your focus word will be useless, I'm afraid."

"We may enter the spirit world only as spirit," added Mr. Rakshasas. "But djinn power is not something of that world."

"Quite simply you can't practice mind over matter where there is no matter," said Nimrod. "But in some ways more can be achieved. You'll find time moves much more slowly in the spirit world."

For a moment, neither one of the children said anything. But eventually, sensing his twin sister's greater fear of ghosts,

John spoke up. "I guess it had better be me that goes," he said finally.

"Good lad," said Mr. Rakshasas. "Sure, it's true what they say: What you're afraid to hear you'd better say first yourself. But we'll look after each other, I'm thinking."

"Very well, then," said Nimrod, continuing. "You, Philippa, will accompany Groanin and me to London, where we will attempt to locate Faustina's body, and then bring it back here to be reunited with her spirit."

"Wait a minute," said Philippa. "I thought you said you *knew* where her body was. You said it was in a private clinic for sick djinn."

"I did," said Nimrod. "But it isn't. It seems that there was some kind of clerical error. This is common enough in British hospitals. Believe me, they're always mislaying patients and bodies, not to mention people's organs. The ambulance forgot to pick her up, apparently. So, it seems her body is still where Faustina left it. In Madame Tussaud's."

"The wax museum?" said Groanin.

"That's right."

"Ugh," he said. "I don't like the sound of that. Waxworks are creepy sorts of places. Ghosts and such like. Worse, probably. When I were a lad, Tussaud's used to pay a man a thousand pounds if he dared to spend the night in the Chamber of Horrors. Them as did went off their heads. Or had their hair turned white from the sheer terror of it."

"Thank you, Groanin," Nimrod said crisply. "That will do."

"There's something else I don't understand," said Philippa. "If John's going to the spirit world to look for Faustina, how can I go to London with you guys? What about Dad? Don't we have to stay near him to counter the effects of Mother's Methusaleh binding?"

"It's very simple," said Nimrod. "You're going to give John all your power. And he's going to leave his body here at home. He'll only need a little bit of djinn power to come out of his body. The rest will remain here, near your father. This will counter the binding, as you say."

Philippa made a face. "You mean I've got to breathe into his ear now?"

"I'm afraid so," said Nimrod.

"Don't think I'm looking forward to it, either," said John. "I think I'd rather see Akhenaten's ghost than let you taste my ear."

"Now, now," said Mr. Rakshasas. "They are short of news those that speak ill of their own blood."

"Okay, bro, I'm sorry," said Philippa. "Look, I'm really grateful to you for going to the spirit world instead of me. And I've been thinking, you won't have to go all the way back to Cairo to enter the ethereal world through an Egyptian temple portal. You can do it right here in New York. At the Met. They have a temple there — the Temple of Dendur."

"Light my lamp," said Nimrod, "of course. It's the only Egyptian temple in the Western Hemisphere. A gift to the United States from the people of Egypt in 1965."

"Except that the museum is closed right now," added Philippa. "Mr. Groanin and I tried to go there earlier today."

"Closed?"

"The museum attendants are on strike," she explained. "They said that it's because the building is haunted. According to the guy we spoke to, the ghostly activity seems to be located in the Sackler Wing and in the Chinese art galleries on the second floor."

"The same thing would appear to have happened in London, sir," added Groanin, showing Nimrod his newspaper. "And in Paris and Berlin, also."

"Interesting," Nimrod said thoughtfully. "Perhaps John and Mr. Rakshasas will be able to find out more when they go to the Sackler Wing."

"The Sackler Wing?" repeated John.

"That's where the Temple of Dendur is located," said Philippa. "At the Met."

"When shall we start?" John asked.

"Now, of course," said Nimrod.

"Aye," said Mr. Rakshasas. "There's no time like the present. Except when you're dead."

John gulped. "Will we see real dead people in the spirit world?"

"Not as such, no," said Mr. Rakshasas. "The dead look real enough to one another in the spirit world. But they aren't people. Not anymore. Which is why they tell no tales. Sure, there's many a thing that's been learned after a trip to the cemetery."

CHAPTER 5

THE KA SERVANT OF DENDUR

Philippa returned John's power, and at the same time, transferred her own power to him by blowing in his ear.

Then, John said his good-byes to her, to Nimrod, and to Groanin, after which, accompanied by Mr. Rakshasas, he went up to his room, lay down on the bed, and, leaving almost all of his power inside his body, set about trying to raise his spirit up to the ceiling.

For a moment it was like growing taller, much taller, except that when he looked down, he found himself staring at a tallish, good-looking, dark-haired boy he hardly recognized. For a moment, he thought it was Dybbuk. And it was another split second before he realized with a jolt that he was looking at himself.

"Sure, you're doing just fine," said a voice beside him. It was Mr. Rakshasas, of course, whom he couldn't see but, oddly enough, whom he could smell quite distinctly. His body was now seated in John's favorite armchair. "Would you like to hold hands or do think you're old enough to try without?"

"I think I'll try without," said John, who disliked holding hands with anyone.

"Mostly we'll get along quite invisibly," said the kindly old djinn. "But if we get lost, stand somewhere cold so that I can see you a bit and I'll come and find you. Only try not to do it where there are people about, or they'll think you're a ghost."

"Okay."

"If you start to panic about being a free spirit, or feel like you're starting to suffer from astral-sickness, then just slip into a mundane's body for five minutes and have a rest. Sure, it'll give that person a nice déjà vu moment, so don't worry about it."

"What's a déjà vu moment?"

"When someone has the illusion of having previously experienced something that they're actually doing for the first time."

"Right."

"But it's only in the physical world that we'll feel like ghosts. Once we enter the portal, it'll be like we're real again. I'll be able to see you and you'll be able to see me. Not to mention other spirits we might encounter along the way."

"That's what I'm worried about."

They floated down the stairs, through the front door of the house — without opening it, of course — and headed toward Central Park. At Mr. Rakshasas's suggestion they traveled about ten feet off the ground, so they wouldn't go through any people, which also made it seem easier to cross the street.

On Fifth Avenue, they turned right and floated along to the Metropolitan Museum where the striking attendants were still assembled on the steps. John had the sense that Mr. Rakshasas moved much more easily as a spirit than as a body. Much faster, too. He didn't know how much faster until, floating up the steps, he saw several horrified attendants pointing through the glass doors of the 81st Street entrance. And arriving at the door himself, he saw what they had already seen — the faint shape of Mr. Rakshasas floating, ghostlike, across the huge expanse of marble floor. John guessed what had happened. It was a warmish day outside and, despite the Met being closed, the air-conditioning was on. The cooler air inside the museum had made Mr. Rakshasas almost visible.

"Get that TV crew up here," yelled one of the attendants. "There's a ghost heading toward the membership desk."

John watched as, quite unaware of the excitement he had caused, Mr. Rakshasas disappeared behind the membership desk, heading north to the Egyptian galleries and the Sackler Wing. And wishing to avoid being filmed by the TV crews that were now pointing their cameras through the glass doors — he was sure that they had just missed filming Mr. Rakshasas — John decided to seek another way into the Met.

Floating above the heads of the people now peering through the doors in the hopes of seeing a real ghost, John went around the other side of the museum and flew up a level and in through a tall sloping window. Once inside the museum he floated through the Chinese galleries and was just about to head downstairs to the Sackler Wing when he noticed that one of the museum's glass cases had been smashed and the exhibit removed. Curious, he stopped for a moment to read the description card and saw that a priceless collection of jade once displayed there had apparently been stolen. And it occurred to John that the theft might have had something to do with the ghosts that were supposedly haunting the museum. None of that seemed important now. He had to catch up with Mr. Rakshasas.

On the floor below he found the Sackler Wing of the museum and a small sandstone temple that was not unlike ones John had seen in Egypt. Except that the temple was itself in an enormous modern hall, and surrounded by a little lake of water. A glance at the information on the wall of the hall confirmed what John suspected: This was the Temple of Dendur.

Imagining that Mr. Rakshasas must already be here, John called out to him. "Mr. Rakshasas?" he said. "It's me, John. Where are you?"

To his surprise, there was no reply. John called out again and, standing almost immediately over an air-conditioning unit in the floor, made himself less invisible. It was curious to see himself in this way — there and yet not there. Like a reflection in a pool.

"Mr. Rakshasas?" he said, a little louder this time. "Here I am."

"Quiet, John, quiet," whispered Mr. Rakshasas.

Instinctively, John looked around and saw nothing. He felt Mr. Rakshasas pull him away from the air conditioner and saw his own body fade to nothing as his spirit grew warmer again.

"What is it?" he whispered to the figure he now felt but couldn't see standing next to him.

"Sure, I don't know," whispered Mr. Rakshasas. "But I'm thinking it's something strange, right enough. Ssssh. Look. Look there, John."

Through the south door of the Sackler Wing came a strange figure, about seven feet tall, wearing gray knee-length robes, "fish-scale" body armor, a small chin beard, an elaborate topknot hairdo, and carrying a long sword. It was a man, and yet not a man, for the brighter gray of the figure's expressionless face and the way his empty eyes never moved made John think that it was only the image of a human being. The figure's movements were hardly natural, either, but jerky, as if he was not used to walking or to swinging his powerful arms, so that he resembled a very ancient kind of robot. Given this, John might have expected to hear footsteps on the polished marble floor; but the strange-looking man moved quite silently, almost as if he wasn't there at all. The figure walked straight past the recessed doorway where John and Mr. Rakshasas were standing, and a strong smell of damp earth pricked their invisible nostrils, as if they were seeing something that had been buried for a very long time.

"What is it?" whispered John.

The creature stopped and stared as if searching for the source of the noise. Clearly, there was nothing wrong with the thing's hearing, and John wondered what it might have done with the sword if it had seen them. It waited for almost a minute, staring at but not seeing them with its peculiar blank eyes, before continuing slowly on its way until it reached the museum wall, where it stopped and then disappeared around the corner.

"Whatever that was," said John, "I don't think it was friendly, do you?"

"I do not," said Mr. Rakshasas.

Growing cooler again, they became more visible.

"Over here," said a voice.

Looking across the gigantic hall, they saw another figure beckoning to them from the doorway of the Temple of Dendur. But this one couldn't have looked more different from the frightening creature they had just seen. This one was wearing the costume of a Victorian gentleman.

"Quick," he called. "Before he comes back again."

John and Mr. Rakshasas crossed over to the temple, and as they stepped between the two columns on the exterior, they both immediately took on their physical appearances again. John breathed a sigh of relief, pleased to see the return of his own body — or at least the shape of his own body. Even if it was in black and white instead of color.

"Well, that's a relief," he said. "Being invisible is a lot harder than it looks. If you know what I mean. But why are we in black and white?"

"Because only the living world is in color," said Mr. Rakshasas. "It's color that makes life worth living, I'm thinking."

"That makes sense, I guess," said John.

Mr. Rakshasas pointed out some of the carvings on the temple walls. The ankh — the symbol of life — the lotus blossoms bound with papyrus, and the various hieroglyphs that described the gods of the afterlife that had once been worshipped here: Isis, Osiris, and their son, Horus. "We're here," he said simply. "This is the gateway to the world of spirit. Now where's that fellow gone? The one who called out to us."

"Here, sirs," said a voice, and through a false door in the temple stepped a fat, balding little man with bad stumpy teeth, a squeaky, foreign sort of voice, and wearing a rather dirty white suit. He bowed very gravely. "Leo Politi at your service, sirs. I'm the Ka servant for this temple."

"The what?" asked John.

"Every ancient Egyptian temple had its Ka servant," said Mr. Rakshasas. "In death, he was responsible for serving the spirits — the Ka — of those who entered the temple. But sure, I never heard of an Italian doing it. And certainly not one who, from the look of his shirt and tie, has only been dead for the blink of an eye."

"I'm Greek, actually," said Leo. "From Cyprus. But you're right about the other thing, sirs. I've only been dead since 1872."

John was a little surprised by the little man. Leo Politi didn't much look like a ghost, but that's what he was.

"If you don't mind my asking," said Mr. Rakshasas. "How did someone who's been dead for less than one hundred and fifty years become the Ka servant of a two-thousand-year-old Egyptian temple?"

"I went to Egypt to negotiate a contract to supply Turkish delight to the Egyptian royal family," said Leo. "On my day off I went to see this temple and, in a bored moment, like others before me, I carved my name on the wall. Here it is. See?"

Leo pointed to the spot on the wall of the temple where the name POLITI was still clearly visible.

"But, in order to do it I erased the hieroglyphs of an important Egyptian priest, who was the previous Ka servant of this temple, thus condemning myself to replace him in eternity. Soon after that, I was bitten by a mosquito, died, and then found myself here. I've been with the temple ever since. When it was still in Egypt, things weren't so bad. But since this temple was given to the Americans, things have been very quiet. No new dead people for me to guide. Just tourists. You are my first new dead people in years. Tell me, sirs, have you been dead long?"

John frowned. "Who said anything about being — ?"

"Not long," said Mr. Rakshasas, interrupting John, and shooting him a look that was meant to persuade him to keep his mouth shut on that subject. "But tell us, Leo. What's the story with the fellow with the sword?"

"I think maybe he is an exhibit," said Leo. "But I am not sure. He marches up and down as you can see, sirs. You'd better make sure he doesn't see you. He's not very friendly. I think it's what he's supposed to do: scare the attendants. Since he arrived, this whole museum has been in turmoil. The museum now has several ghosts."

"Ghosts?" asked Mr. Rakshasas.

"In the museum, sirs, yes," said Leo. "At night they are especially noisy."

"That explains why those guys outside are on strike," said John.

"It is true, sirs," said Leo. "These ghosts have driven away all of those fat attendant fellows."

"But what caused this to happen?" asked Mr. Rakshasas. "Where did these ghosts come from, Leo?"

"I don't know for sure, sir," said Leo. "But I think from inside the fellow with the sword."

"Inside him?" repeated Mr. Rakshasas. "How extraordinary."

"Shhh, here he comes again. If he sees you, you must both run away. Only don't worry about me. He will leave me alone. Because of the Ka servant's curse, I am obliged to stay here, whether I like it or not."

Leo pushed John and Mr. Rakshasas up against the false door so that the creature with the sword would not see them. As before he moved slowly, silently, and like something automatic.

"Those clothes he's wearing," observed John. "And all that armor. He doesn't look every Egyptian to me."

As before, the strange figure halted in front of the north wall of the Sackler Wing, then turned abruptly and marched around the corner.

Leo breathed a sigh of relief and wiped the sweat from his smooth round face with a grubby white handkerchief. "There. He's gone."

"What will happen to us if we don't run away, Leo?" asked John.

"Those who get too near, he simply absorbs," said Leo. "He soaks them up. Like a sponge. Really, I saw him do it. I think he is trying to absorb all of those he released earlier on."

"Now why would he do a thing like that?" asked Mr. Rakshasas.

"That I cannot explain, sirs," said Leo. "But of late there has been a great deal I cannot explain. More so than at any other time since I became the Ka servant of Dendur."

"Such as?" asked John.

"Before these ghosts appeared in the museum and scared off all those fat attendants, I'm thinking there was a kind of earthquake. In the spirit world. That's the best way I can describe it."

"An earthquake?"

Leo nodded. "The spirit world shook, most violently. After that, things in the world of spirit were very quiet for a while. It was like no one was there. And then the man with the sword came and the hauntings began. To be honest with you, sirs, when it first started happening, I was a little relieved that I wasn't on my own. That there were indeed other spirits around. Until that moment I had started to think I was the only ghost left around here. And that scared me."

"I can imagine," said John.

"Now then, sirs," said Leo. "Where would you like me to guide you? To the Underworld? To Purgatory? Or have you a mind to haunt someone yourselves, perhaps? An ungrateful relation. A nasty boss. An unfaithful wife. In which case I can direct you straight to their home. Myself, I think I should love to haunt someone."

"We would like to go Bannermann's Island," said John. "On the Hudson River, just north of here, in upstate New York. Do you know it?"

"Fortunately, there is almost nothing I don't know," said Leo. "One of the few benefits of being dead is that suddenly you seem to know everything. Well, perhaps not everything. But a lot more than you did before. Of course this is what makes it so easy for living people to be duped by mischievous spirits in séances and things like that."

"Aye, that's right enough to be sure," said Mr. Rakshasas. "You never know who you're talking to when you're holding hands in the dark."

"We'd better get going," said Leo. "We've a longish journey ahead of us."

Leo pushed the false door, which turned out to be a false door only in the real world. And being an experienced guide meant that he was ready with an explanation for this phenomenon: "In the spirit world this is one of the points through which a deceased person's soul could magically pass between this world and the afterlife," he said, ushering them through. "This would have been understood by the Egyptians, of course. Although not so well today. But you are welcome, sirs. Welcome to the place the Egyptians called the Kingdom of the West. Welcome to the afterlife."

CHAPTER 6

THE HOUSE OF WAX

A whirlwind carried Philippa, Nimrod, and Mr. Groanin to London, and the back garden of Nimrod's house at number 7 Stanhope Terrace, Kensington.

"I used to think I could never get used to traveling like that," moaned Groanin as Philippa and Nimrod went into the large house ahead of him. "Not anymore. Flying by airplane is quite spoiled for me now. Lines for check-in, did you pack this yourself, X-ray machines, biometric scanners, and Lord knows what else. It's too much to think about. I've come to the conclusion that the best thing a man can be in this world is a fool — a handsome fool."

"Then it sounds to me like you're halfway to being a very happy man," Nimrod said.

Groanin muttered something under his breath and went off to prepare dinner.

"Nimrod," scolded Philippa. "That was rude."

"Unkind, maybe," admitted Nimrod. "But it's for his own good. Groanin's not been himself lately. He is only ever happiest when he's moaning about something. Just now was the first time in ten years that Groanin has ever said anything good about traveling by whirlwind."

They ate some dinner and when it was dark, Groanin got the Rolls-Royce to drive the three of them to Madame Tussaud's. In front of the entrance was an even larger electric-blue Rolls-Royce and out of this stepped a small, wiry-looking man with the most criminal-looking face Philippa had ever seen. He had a sloping forehead with lots of wrinkles, protruding ears with diamond stud earrings, and more tattoos than a beach in Florida. The little man touched his forelock as he approached Nimrod.

"Hello, sir," he said in a quiet Cockney accent.

"Hello, Silman," said Nimrod. "Silman, this is my niece, Philippa."

"How d'you do, miss?"

"Philippa, this is the great Silman Franco, recently returned to these shores after a long stay in southern Spain. And very welcome, too."

"You're too kind, sir," Franco said modestly. "Too kind."

"Over the years, Silman has performed many valuable services for our tribe," said Nimrod. "He does jobs that, sometimes, for one reason or another, we'd rather not do ourselves. Snooping, sleuthing, ferreting, scouting, burgling, breaking and entering, and shadowing. There's nothing nefarious, illegal, or criminal that's beyond him."

"Anything to help you, sir, Mr. Nimrod."

"Silman's a good honest rogue that you can trust," said Nimrod.

"All thanks to you, sir," said Franco, bowing again.

"Have you brought it?"

"I have, sir; I have." Silman Franco reached into his silk jacket pocket, withdrew a small, hard, leather case about the size of a matchbox, and handed it to Nimrod.

"Years ago," Nimrod told Philippa, "I was obliged to grant Silman three wishes. One of these was that I should create a special key of his own special design."

Nimrod opened the box to reveal a human skeleton that was no longer than a paper clip and not much thicker. He put the tiny set of bones in his fist and breathed on it, as if it were tiny dice. When he opened his hand, the skeleton stood up and stretched like someone who had been asleep for a very long time.

"Wakey, wakey," said Silman, chuckling. "Rise and shine, my beauty."

"Ugh," said Philippa. "What is that?"

"A skeleton key," said Nimrod.

Philippa watched, more than a little horrified as Nimrod held his hand next to the keyhole on the front door of the wax museum and the skeleton marched across his palm and disappeared inside.

"There's no need to pick a lock with this remarkable little fellow in your pocket," said Nimrod. "He does it all for you. Pushes the pins, moves the levers, pulls the bolts."

"That's right, Mr. Nimrod," said Silman. "There's nothing he can't open."

A few seconds passed, and sure enough, Philippa heard the sound of the door lock opening. A moment later, the little skeleton was climbing back into his leather box, and Silman was through the door as quickly as a greased ferret, to shut off the alarms. Before Philippa could say "Mission Impossible" he was back again, grinning triumphantly.

"There you go, Mr. Nimrod," he said.

"Thank you, Silman," said Nimrod. "If you wouldn't mind waiting here, just in case you're needed again."

Silman touched his forelock. "Right you are, sir. I'll wait in the car."

Switching on his flashlight, Nimrod led the way into the wax museum, followed closely by Philippa and Groanin.

Groanin was right, thought Philippa, pointing her own flashlight around the exhibition as she and Groanin followed Nimrod through the darkened building. It was creepy inside the museum. Everywhere you went it was like there were people staring at you. A few of them she recognized immediately, of course. The president. The British prime minister. The British royal family. Some movie stars. One or two of these wax dummies looked extremely realistic. But several almost made her laugh they were so bad. *Almost.* There was something about the wax museum at night that discouraged laughter. And as usual it was Groanin who managed to put into words the sense of fear Philippa felt at being inside such a place after dark.

"It's said that Madame Tussaud learned her trade in Paris," he whispered, "from making models of the severed heads of them who'd been guillotined during the French Revolution. That would be creepy enough. But I can't help but feeling that, perhaps, some of these wax figures are just the corpses of real dead people covered in wax. That it's why they're so lifelike, some of them. And have you noticed the way their eyes seem to follow you around?"

"I've been trying not to notice that, actually," confessed Philippa. "And why are you whispering?"

"I was wondering that myself," said Nimrod.

"Well, it's like when you're in a crypt or a cemetery," said Groanin. "I always think that a ghost is more likely to come here and hang around the image of how someone used to be than the box of bones that ends up in a grave. Especially some of those murderers downstairs that's been hanged or did themselves in."

"Do shut up, Groanin," said Nimrod, and opening a door, led the way down a narrow corridor. "You're making my niece nervous."

"No, I'm fine," said Philippa, but quickened her step so as to avoid being left behind in the darkness.

"There are several old storerooms somewhere down here, where the old dummies are kept," explained Nimrod. "And it's in one of these where Faustina left her body when her spirit took off to possess the prime minister. On shelf thirteen in storeroom thirteen to be precise."

"Unlucky for some," said Groanin.

"But it's been more than ten years since I was down here," said Nimrod. "And my bearings are a little bit rusty."

They went down a long winding staircase into a deep and rather damp basement. Nimrod walked to the end of a corridor and opened another door. "Ah, this is it, I think," he said, and brushing aside several cobwebs, went inside and switched on the electric light.

Philippa glanced around the storeroom in wonder. The chair in the corner was perhaps the one normal thing in the room. There were several rows of once famous heads, as if Madame Tussaud had collected them from the basket in front of a more recently active guillotine, and some larger racks where dummies had been stored separately. And there was a box of hands and a box of eyes.

"How could she do it?" said Philippa. "How could Faustina ever leave her body somewhere like this? I'd have been petrified just coming in here."

"Faustina was not like most female djinn of her age," said Nimrod. While he spoke, Nimrod advanced into the back of the storeroom where, on wide metal shelves, there lay hundreds of dummies. "She was a solitary child. Serious. Given to melancholy. Even a little cold-blooded. All of them excellent reasons why she was ideally suited to becoming the Blue

Djinn of Babylon. Besides, one of these old dummies is Ronald Reagan. My information was that Faustina always rather admired Ronnie in a granddaughterly way, and I suppose she must have thought it might be nice to stay on the same shelf as Reagan for a while. Because that's where I found her the first time I came down here."

"You mean the guy who used to be president of the United States?" said Philippa, only vaguely remembering him now.

"That's right," said Nimrod. "And here he is."

Nimrod advanced on a man in a suit who was still grinning genially from the shelf where he was lying. But next to him on the shelf was an obviously empty space.

"Not anymore," said Groanin.

"She was right here," said Nimrod. "I'm certain of it."

"Perhaps that ambulance came and took her after all," suggested Philippa.

"No, no," insisted Nimrod. "I told you, Philippa, I checked with the hospital. Besides, this has happened relatively recently. Look at the dust on this shelf. Clearly, a figure has been lying here until just a few months ago, I'd say. The figure of a young person, too. Look how much shorter this outline is than that of President Reagan."

"You don't suppose they took her to be melted down, thinking she was made of wax?" said Groanin. He walked down to the end of the freestanding shelves and pointed his flashlight into the shadows.

"What a horrible thought," observed Philippa.

"But why her and not these others?" said Nimrod. "There are wax figures in this room that have been here much longer than Faustina. No, Groanin, Faustina's body has been stolen, I'm quite certain of it."

"Who would steal her body?" asked Philippa. "And why?"

"Perhaps there are more than one that are gone," said Groanin. "Look at this."

Nimrod and Philippa followed him to the end of the shelf. Clearly visible on the shelves were two more dusty outlines, where other wax figures had previously lain. "Yes, you're right, Groanin," said Nimrod.

Groanin bent down and picked up something off the floor. It was a small strip of peel-and-stick adhesive. And on it was a fingerprint. "Hello," he said. "What have we here?" He shone his flashlight across the floor and found another similar strip, only this one was still unpeeled. "Looks to me like the police have been here, sir," he said. "The crime scene people from Scotland Yard. This is an evidence strip. For fingerprints."

"In which case," said Philippa, "the theft of three wax-museum dummies may well have been noticed and reported."

"Well done, Groanin," said Nimrod. "Very likely there will be a record of a police report upstairs in the office. Let's go and see, shall we?"

Up in the museum office, Philippa tried to see what she could discover using the office computer while Nimrod and

Groanin searched through the filing cabinets. It didn't take long for them to find the clues they were looking for.

"Here's something," said Nimrod. "It would seem that a disgruntled employee named Cristina Buonaserra was dismissed on suspicion of theft three months ago."

Nimrod brandished a sheet of paper in front of Groanin, who made a note of the name and then began a search of another cabinet.

"She was suspected of having stolen three wax dummies," continued Nimrod. "It doesn't say who the dummies were. But one of them must have been Faustina. The dummies were never recovered. Soon after being dismissed, Miss Buonaserra left the country and went to live in Italy. *Italy*. Oh, Lord. We'll never find her in time now. She could be anywhere."

"Ahem. Not necessarily, sir," announced Groanin. "This is Miss Buonaserra's file, sir. Her next of kin is listed as living in Italy. It seems she has a brother who is a priest. Or more precisely, the abbot of the Carthusian Monastery in Malpensa, just outside the town of Eboli."

"Malpensa," said Philippa, typing a search word on the computer keyboard.

"Malpensa's a town in the south," said Nimrod.

"I'll bet she went to see him," said Groanin.

"Eureka," said Philippa, sitting back from the computer screen. "I've found it. The Convento di Carthusi in Malpensa. Oh, gross! This has to be the place where she went. Look!"

On the screen was a picture of what looked like an underground cemetery consisting of tunnels and rooms with platforms and shelves for coffins and sarcophagi. But what was really strange was that all of the dead people were mummified and laid out like exhibits in a museum. Some of the corpses had long ago lost all their flesh and were little better than skeletons, while others looked as if they were only asleep.

"Gross," repeated Philippa.

"They're catacombs," said Nimrod, looking over Philippa's shoulder. "Underneath the monastery. Where people are preserved and put when they die instead of being buried. It's an old Italian tradition."

The pride of the catacombs, as shown on the Web site, was the corpse of a still perfectly preserved girl of about twelve years old who had died in 1920 and whom the local people called "the Sleeping Beauty." The girl was displayed in an open glass case, and with the pink ribbons in her still-lustrous hair, she did indeed look like something from a fairy tale. But there was something about this young girl that seemed vaguely familiar to Philippa. For a moment she was struck by the odd resemblance to Dybbuk, of all people. And then Philippa remembered the portrait on the wall of the house on Bannermann's Island — the same island where John and Mr. Rakshasas were now heading. That was where she'd seen this girl before. It was the girl in the portrait. This young girl wasn't dead at all. *It was Faustina.*

CHAPTER 7

MEN IN BLACK

It's strange," said Leo Politi, the Ka servant of the Temple of Dendur. "But you two ghosts aren't like any dead people I've ever had to guide through the spirit world before."

"Really?" said John. "Why do you say that?"

"Most people are very confused about what has happened to them," said Leo. "So confused that they don't suspect the great change they have undergone."

"How do you mean?" asked John.

"I mean they don't have any idea that they are dead," said Leo. "No sooner are they out of their earthly form than they try to live their lives along the old familiar lines. And then they get angry when living people ignore them. The Egyptians knew that. It's why they created their temples and the institution of the Ka servant. So that there would be someone to gently explain to the spirit what had happened to them. Of course, these days people have no idea where to go when they die. Certainly, they wouldn't dream of coming to the

79

Metropolitan Museum of Art in New York and the Temple of Dendur. But you two ghosts seem to know what you are, what you're doing, and where you want to go."

"Sure, it's no use carrying an umbrella if you've holes in your shoes," said Mr. Rakshasas. "We know where we are, Leo, and we're not the kind to complain about it. You must take the little potato with the big potato."

The three of them were sitting on a bus heading down to Grand Central Station to catch a train up the Hudson River. John had noticed that none of the other passengers paid them any attention. Like they weren't there at all. *Like they were ghosts.* Leo was right about that. Apart from that, John thought the spirit world seemed much like the physical one. Except that everything was in black and white. Even the living appeared to be black and white on this side of a temple portal. But he was beginning to think that entering the ethereal world, as Nimrod called it, through the temple had been a waste of time.

John leaned toward Mr. Rakshasas and whispered, "If it's just a question of getting on a bus and a train, then surely we could have done this by ourselves. I know the way to Bannermann's Island. Why did we need to go to that temple, and why do we need Leo?"

"For one thing," said Mr. Rakshasas, "we can see ourselves now, when we couldn't before, which is useful. And we'll be able to see Faustina, which will be useful, too. Being invisible is a great disadvantage when you're trying to have a chat with someone."

"Yes, I hadn't thought of that," whispered John.

"Here's another," continued Mr. Rakshasas. "A Ka servant is like any other tour guide in that he knows one or two things that we don't. Such as which of these people we're looking at is dead and which of them are properly alive. And of these folk who are dead, he knows those who are to be trusted and those who are not. Sure, there's many a wolf that's tried to pass himself off as an old granny. Which is another way of saying that he's a bit more than just a guide, John. He has power in this world which we do not."

"You mean he's like a bodyguard?"

"Since neither of us has a body right now," said Mr. Rakshasas, "that's not quite it. He's more like a guardian angel. Except that he's not an angel, of course. I'm not entirely sure how it works. Let's just hope we don't find out the hard way."

John agreed. Being little more than a ghost himself, he was beginning to think a ghost was something he could probably deal with; but what Mr. Rakshasas had called "*something else*," well, that *was* something else.

At Grand Central they boarded the same train to Newburgh Bay that John and Philippa had traveled on the first time they'd been to Bannermann's Island, just a few weeks before. It was getting dark by the time they arrived at the Newburgh Bay Boating Club, where John had told Leo they could probably borrow a canoe to get to Bannermann's Island. And while Leo went to look for a canoe, John and Mr. Rakshasas wandered over to the old boathouse. From the outside it looked exactly the same, but the old boatman who lived there seemed younger than John remembered. Younger but somehow sadder, too. As if some calamity had befallen him. What was more, John had the distinct feeling that the boatman could see them, although he knew that was hardly possible. Living people could only see ghosts in what were exceptional circumstances.

They watched the boatman from outside the open kitchen door for a moment as he made himself some tea. Then, muttering to himself, he went through the door and into the living room, slamming the door noisily behind him. John wanted to see if he still had Dybbuk's friend's cat, Hendrix, and so, not thinking that this could do any harm, they followed him through the closed door and into the boathouse.

The house seemed very still and quiet and not at all cozy, like the last time John had been there. Of Hendrix the cat, there was no sign. A grandfather clock stood silently in the hall. There were cobwebs on the curtainless windows. And most of the furniture was covered in dust sheets. It was a coolish evening but there was no fire in the living room grate, which struck John as a little unusual. But not as unusual as the two men who were seated at a table in the living room.

The men were both wearing shiny black suits and black shirts, and had black beards and black eyes; in their hands were black books and black beads. Even their socks were black. One of them had a small black valise, like a doctor's bag, at his feet, and the other a railroad schedule in his top pocket, as if they had stepped off an earlier train. John decided there was something about these two that he did not like, and it wasn't just the strong smell of incense that came off their clothes.

Without speaking to either one of them, the boatman sat down in a rocking chair and started to rock himself, and while he rocked, he hummed. As soon as he did this, the two strange men jumped a little as if something had startled them. One looked at the other and nodded gravely. Then they opened their books on the table and started to read aloud and in turn, at which point the boatman in the rocking chair started to moan quietly to himself as if he had a stomachache.

"What's the matter with him?" whispered John.

As soon as John spoke, one of the men at the table began to read more loudly and the other to splash the room with water from a little bottle he held in his hand, which seemed only to prompt the boatman's moaning to become rather more doglike.

The volume of their reading aloud increased a second time. Not that it made much of a difference to John, who couldn't understand a word. The books they were reading from seemed be in a language that was familiar to him and yet not. Then, still reading, the two men stood up, and John noticed something about them he hadn't seen before. They were scared. But of what?

"Can you understand what they're saying?" he asked Mr. Rakshasas.

"It's Latin," shouted Mr. Rakshasas, for by now the reading was loud enough to make listening uncomfortable.

The noise had summoned Leo into the house. For a moment he stood in the doorway, with a look of increasing horror upon his pudgy face. "Come on," he said. "We have to leave. *Now.* Don't you get it? They're exorcists."

"Gee, what kind?" asked John.

"Does it matter?" yelled a very agitated Leo. "If we don't leave something terrible will happen. That's what exorcists do. They drive the ghosts out of a place."

Before he could say another word, however, the boatman in the rocking chair screamed loudly and ran through the window. And it was only when the window didn't break into a dozen pieces that John, with a sense of profound shock, realized the boatman was a ghost.

"He's dead," said John.

"That's right," said Mr. Rakshasas. "Only I don't think he's admitted it to himself. He's confused. The way Leo said people get confused after they die."

But if John had thought the boatman was the only ghost in that old boathouse he was very mistaken. As John and Mr. Rakshasas entered the corridor, heading for the back door, yet more ghosts appeared from other floors and rooms. Older ghosts. Ancient spirits. Ghosts who had haunted that part of the Hudson River valley for perhaps hundreds of years. Ghosts who were now yelling and screaming and in a state of some considerable distress to be gone from the house before the two exorcists could bring down some extra calamity upon their heads.

"I don't understand it," shouted Leo. "There shouldn't be so many ghosts in one house. It doesn't make sense. It's like they've all been hiding from something in here."

John tried to get out of the way of these panicking ghosts, but there was no time. One of them, frantic to get out of the boathouse, ran straight through John, so that for a brief moment he was running for his life, too, which was a horrible sensation, and he heard himself cry out to Mr. Rakshasas. At the same time he had a blinding flash of the horror — the *horror* that this other ghostly being had suffered before its death 350-odd years before, and the misery it had endured ever since.

The first time this happened it lasted only a moment. The second time it happened, it seemed to last forever. . . .

He was running through the damp forest for his life. The early morning spring air of the Hudson River valley was thick with the smell of gunpowder, wet underbrush, and the whoops of warlike Mohican Indians who had come upon the little party of Dutch fur-trappers out of nowhere. The Indians' weapons were crude but effective: war clubs, bows and arrows, and tomahawks. Some of his party had fired their flintlock guns, but for most of them there had simply been no time, and insufficient distance to get off a shot. And now he himself was sprinting for his life although in which direction, he had no idea. The important thing was just to get away. To escape. To get far enough away from the Mohicans so that he could hide and then, under cover of darkness, find his way back to the fort again. His being just a boy would count for very little with the Mohicans. He ducked quickly under a tree branch and leaped over a small stream. Momentarily, he lost his footing and fell, but let himself roll on his back several times as he hit the ground, crashing down a steep slope, regaining his feet at speed, and then hurdling a fallen log with the agility of a running fox. Something hit the log behind him and he heard the shrieking, birdlike war cry of an Indian in close pursuit, letting the others know where he was and to come and help chase down the "white eyes." They were closing in on him and all he could think about was the date. The twelfth of May, 1640. It was his fifteenth birthday. Would he ever have another? Would he ever see his mother in Amsterdam again? Crashing through some bushes, he found himself at the steaming bank of the great Hudson River. There was no point in trying to cross the glassy smooth water. It was much too wide. Besides, he couldn't swim. Which way to run? Upriver or downriver? In the mud of the riverbank, he slipped, crawled under a bush, waded through some water, and then ran around the trunk of a thick tree straight into the outstretched, muscular arms of a large, painted Mohican. The strong-smelling Indian grabbed him by the wrist, grinning a wolfish smile made whiter by the black daub that covered the whole of his shaven head, and then clubbed him on the head with a piece of brightly colored wood shaped like a pistol, which left him lying stunned on the ground. Looking up at the treetops, the half-naked Indian let out a series of triumphant piercing cries, and dragged him up the riverbank like a sack of potatoes, where he tied the seated boy quickly to a tall fir tree with thin strips of animal hide. Other Mohicans quickly arrived, howling loudly like a pack of excited timber wolves, their heads painted black like his captor, so that these almost seemed to have been stuck on the wrong bodies by some playful child. One of the Indians lit a fire. Another found a hollow log and started to beat on it rhythmically like a drum and to chant a tuneless song. Sensing the extreme desperation of his situation, he looked up at the blue, cloudless sky and began to say his prayers. . . .

CHAPTER 8

WEDNESDAY'S ANGEL

They had flown by whirlwind to a field outside Malpensa, which is located in the heel of the boot that is the map of Italy. And once there, using an ambulance that Nimrod had created using djinn power and with which they hoped to remove Faustina's body, they drove up a steep hill and into town.

Philippa thought that Malpensa was a curious little place. Built on the top of a high cliff, it looked as if it were growing out of the rock like a tree or a bush. Inside the town, the buildings were in a poor state of repair from the earth tremors that occasionally affected this part of the world. Fearful of the effect one of these might have on their already weakened houses, most of the people in the town now chose to live in the area's extensive network of caves, like so many bears and bats.

Quite a few of the larger, more important buildings, such as the town hall and the police station, were now propped up by enormous timbers or surrounded by great cages of scaffolding so that parts of Malpensa looked as if extremely large and fierce animals were caged there.

"Easy to see why this place got its name," observed Philippa.

"Oh?" said Groanin. "What exactly does 'Malpensa' mean, anyway?"

"Bad thought," she said.

"It does have a certain air of disaster about it," said Groanin.

The Carthusian catacombs were located in a small church in the Piazza Carthusi, on the edge of the town, opposite a soccer field where, underneath floodlights, a soccer game being watched by the whole population — approximately 825 people — was in noisy progress.

"How is it," moaned Groanin, "that we always seem to visit these horrible places at night?"

"These catacombs are Malpensa's only real tourist attraction," said Nimrod. "So we've not much choice to come any other time. According to the guidebook, the place has as many as a hundred visitors a day in summer."

"There's no accounting for what folks want to do and see on their holidays," said Groanin.

"Besides," added Philippa. "I don't think they're going to just let us walk out of the catacombs with one of their main exhibits in broad daylight, do you?"

"I admit," said Groanin, "body snatching is something that's probably best left to nighttime. Although I could easily wish otherwise."

The church door was not locked. They went inside and picked their way between some timbers that were propping up the walls. Several dozen candles burned in an enormous candelabra that hung from the ceiling on a metal trestle in a little chapel. Nimrod brought three candles from a pile stacked, like so many cigars, under the trestle, lit them, and then handed one to Philippa and one to his butler. At the back of the church, behind the altar, a crudely printed sign pointed out the way to the catacombs.

Nimrod had borrowed Silman Franco's skeleton key for the trip to Italy and he now fed this into the keyhole of a saucer-size padlock that secured the iron gate to the catacombs. The padlock now opened, Groanin hauled the heavy gate open and stood aside while Nimrod and Philippa went down the steps. Of course, he was quite happy to afford them this courtesy, being someone who was more than a little afraid of the dark — and of ghosts, in particular. Not to mention dozens of dead bodies.

He gave a little shudder as the first group of bodies met his eyes. Near enough to touch, these were displayed like the chief treasures in some weird collector's private museum. Laid out on shelves or propped up against the whitewashed wall, some were very well preserved, perfect in every feature, with hair and eyes, while some were little better than skeletons, with hands and jaws missing. There were dead babies and children, too, since death has little respect for youth. Groanin thought these especially sad and there were several whose little faces brought a tear to his eye. At the same time, he thought it easy to see why someone might have been unscrupulous enough to steal three wax-museum dummies and use them to replace some of the corpses in the catacombs. For the place reminded him most of a wax museum.

"Blimey, O'Reilly," he said. "Just look at all these stiffs. There's thousands of them. It's like the Houses of Parliament in here."

Philippa sniffed the air loudly, yet there was no trace of any odor.

"By heck!" exclaimed Groanin. "This one's been dead since 1599. Strange to think that all of these folk had lives, families, and jobs, like we do. Gives me a funny feeling. Like it won't be long before I'm ready to be mounted on a wall myself."

"That's a cheerful thought," said Nimrod, and clapped Groanin happily on the back.

"Are you telling me that tourists really come down here?" Groanin asked Nimrod. "It's not exactly Disneyland, is it?"

"Not exactly," said Philippa, and pointed to another sign. "But it does say, 'This way to the Sleeping Beauty.'"

Turning the corner, they found themselves in a room with just one corpse: Lying on top of a glass case, just like the heroine in some cheesy cartoon, was the perfectly preserved body of a girl of about the same age as Philippa. It was Faustina.

"According to the guidebook, the Sleeping Beauty that was in here died in 1920," said Nimrod. "I wouldn't mind betting that the original decomposed and they needed to obtain a quick replacement. Most likely they buried the original and then pinched Faustina from the wax museum."

"That's a shocking thing to do," murmured Groanin.

But more shocking to Philippa were the clothes Faustina was wearing. "Oh, my God — look at those clothes she's got on," said Philippa. "They're so old-fashioned. I wouldn't be seen dead dressed like that."

"Then it's just as well for Faustina that she's merely in a state of suspended animation," said Nimrod.

"And what happened to her hair?" said Philippa.

"My guess is that tourists have been snipping bits of it off, for souvenirs," said Nimrod.

Groanin glanced around nervously as he heard something rustle in the darkness. The overwhelming sense of death and decay was beginning to penetrate the marrow in his bones. "Come on, sir," he said. "I think this place must have mice or rats or something. Zap her inside a Coke bottle or whatever you're planning to do with her and let's get out of here."

Nimrod muttered his focus word. But Faustina did not disappear. Instead, a stretcher appeared underneath Faustina's body. "What?" groaned Groanin. "You mean we've got to carry her?"

"I'm afraid so, Groanin," said Nimrod. "It would be dangerous to transubstantiate a djinn whose spirit has left her body." He put down his candle and took hold of the bottom end of the stretcher. "Come on. Grab hold."

Handing his candle to Philippa, Groanin took hold of the front end and, lifting Faustina up, they carried her back along the corridor.

"Don't walk so fast with them candles," Groanin told Philippa. "You're leaving us behind here in the darkness."

Philippa stopped to allow the two men to catch up. The candles cast a warm gentle light over Faustina so that she really did resemble some kind of Sleeping Beauty. "She looks like an angel," she said.

"I don't think so," said a deep and, in the darkness, very masculine-sounding voice.

Groanin yelped and almost dropped the stretcher holding Faustina, and Philippa had to stifle a little scream.

A big burly man wearing an ill-fitting white suit stepped into the candlelight. On his head, which was like a bowling ball, his fair hair was short and uncombed and his face unshaven. His shoulders were as broad as one of the beams propping up the church.

"She doesn't look like any angel I've ever seen," said the man. "And I've met the whole team. Good and bad." He chuckled in a subterranean sort of way and glanced down at Faustina. "Nothing like. Too skinny for one thing. And a girl, for another."

"Am I right in thinking you're an angel yourself?" said Nimrod.

"That's right," said the angel. "The name's Sam."

"Sam?" Groanin sounded disbelieving. "Whoever heard of an angel called Sam?"

"And who said you couldn't be an angel if you're a girl?" demanded Philippa.

The angel advanced on Groanin and Philippa, with his heavily stubbled jaw arriving slightly ahead of him.

"I wouldn't antagonize him if I were you," advised Nimrod. "I imagine he's here to guard something."

"Sam," he repeated. "It's short for Samael. And just so you know, being an angel is man's work. Always has been."

"I'm sure it is," said Groanin.

"Just so as you know," said Sam. "I'm the angel ruling Wednesday. And I get a bit fed up with all those pictures of angels that make us all look like a bunch of wet girls with big soppy eyes and hairless faces."

"Um," said Groanin, "if you don't mind me saying so, today's Thursday."

"Yeah, well, maybe it is," said Sam. "But I've still got to come when I'm summoned. Your boss, the djinn, is right, see? For hundreds of years I've been coming here at the request of the monks who run this place, to guard it against intruders." He nodded at the stretcher bearing Faustina. "So I'd put her down if I were you."

Nimrod and Groanin placed the stretcher on the floor.

"No offense," asked Nimrod. "But are you sure about that?"

"What do you mean, djinn?"

"Are you sure you're guarding the whole place, or someone in particular? After all, a lot of the people who are in here were nobody of any real importance." He pointed at Faustina. "This djinn girl isn't even dead."

"Then why's she in here?" growled Sam.

"She misplaced her body, that's all," said Nimrod. "We're taking it out of here so it can be reunited with her spirit."

"That doesn't alter the fact that I'm supposed to look after this place. So she stays here. End of story."

"Did they ask you specifically to guard her?" asked Nimrod.

"Ask me to guard some slip of a girl?" asked Sam. "I should say not. Being an angel is man's work."

"Yes, you said that," said Nimrod. "Look here, you said you've been looking after this place for hundreds of years. But our friend's only been filling in here as the Sleeping Beauty for a matter of months."

"And the real Sleeping Beauty's only been here since 1920," added Philippa.

"So they couldn't possibly have meant for someone as important as you to look after her," said Nimrod. "They must have hoped you would look after someone else. A saint's bones, perhaps. St. Bruno, for example."

"It doesn't make any difference, pal," said Sam. "You're not getting her. Not without a fight." His eyes brightened and he grinned a big gap-toothed sort of smile. "That's supposing any of you has got the guts for a fight."

"Not a very fair contest," said Nimrod. "Everyone knows that an angel is more powerful than a djinn. Let alone a human."

"No, no," said Sam. "I wouldn't need angel power to beat any of you lot. Djinn or human. All I need is muscle."

"You seem to have plenty of that," said Nimrod.

"So how about it?"

"You wouldn't be the Samael who wrestled Jacob in the Book of Genesis?" asked Philippa.

"Maybe," Sam said defensively. "What of it?"

"All right then," said Philippa. "We accept your silly challenge. If you agree not to use your powers as an angel, Mr. Groanin here will wrestle you, won't you, Groanin?"

"Me?" Groanin's jaw dropped. "Fight him? Have you gone mad, miss?"

"I had the same thought myself," admitted Sam.

"And if he wins, we get to take our friend out of here," said Philippa. "Deal?"

"Could I have a word with you, miss?" whispered Groanin.

Sam's grin had widened by a couple of feet. "Deal," he told Philippa. "But it'll have to be a proper wrestling match. With a ring and a referee and a crowd. Not like that fight with Jacob. That was just the two of us in the desert at night. Not much fun in that. And not much incentive to win. I like a crowd, I do."

"Yes, I can see that," said Nimrod, glancing around the catacombs.

"I don't mean in here," said Sam. "I mean somewhere you get a decent crowd. Somewhere proper. Like when you see wrestling on the telly. Madison Square Garden. In New York. Agreed?"

"Oh, agreed," said Philippa.

"I like you," Sam told Philippa. "You're all right. For a girl, that is. But you" — Sam pointed a thick stubby forefinger at Groanin — "I'm going to rip your head off and use it for a paperweight."

Sam snapped his fingers and they found themselves transported into a wrestling ring in Madison Square Garden, in front of a crowd of twenty thousand spectators. There were vendors selling programs and hot dogs, newspapermen and photographers at the ringside; there were even large blond-haired women, dripping with diamonds, who were holding up signs with Sam's name on them.

"Blimey!" said Groanin. "This feels as real as a rainy weekend in Manchester."

"It is real," said Nimrod, who was hardly surprised to see such a display of absolute power as to see it done so easily and so well. And this served to remind him that in spite of his stubbly chin and rather coarse manners, Sam was an angel after all, and a very powerful one at that. "At least it's real for now. Reality is something that's easily made by an angel."

A loud fanfare of music and several bright spotlights greeted Sam's arrival upon a stage at the back of the audience. He held up his arms in a gesture confident of eventual victory. The fight was about to begin.

CHAPTER 9

FAUSTINA'S ZOMBIE

"John, wake up."

John opened his eyes. He was sitting on the ground, leaning against a tree, and looking at Mr. Rakshasas and Leo Politi, who were kneeling in front of him anxiously. Then he remembered the Mohicans and scrambled to his feet, full of fear and the still vividly painful memory of what he imagined had just happened to him.

"Take it easy, lad," said Mr. Rakshasas. "You're all right now."

"That was horrible," he gasped, running both hands nervously through his hair, as if checking that it was still attached to his head. "Horrible. I was back in 1640. I was some Dutch boy running through the forest who was being chased by Indians. And it was . . . horrible."

"We were in that boathouse," explained Mr. Rakshasas. "Do you remember? There was an exorcism. And when all the spirits fled the house, one of them must have got himself mixed up with your spirit for a while. I daresay that you just relived everything that had happened to that poor young fellow and which probably made him the ghost he is now."

"Those Indians," said John. Feeling faint at the very thought of it, he sat down again and tried to rid his mind of the memories that still filled it.

"You take it easy for a minute. Sure, there were many terrible things done on both sides, I'm thinking. Human nature is a terrible thing when there's ignorance and stupidity involved."

"It wasn't real," said John. "But it still feels like it was."

"Seeing is believing," said Mr. Rakshasas. "But feeling is the God's own truth, right enough."

"Perhaps now would be a good time for you to explain how it is that you were the only two among the spirits in that house, myself included, who were not in a hurry to be gone when an exorcism was in progress," Leo said stiffly. "It's my opinion that neither one of you is dead at all. For if you were, you could hardly have stayed there."

"Fair enough," said Mr. Rakshasas. "You're right. We're neither one of us dead, I'm glad to say. And I'm right sorry for the deception, Leo, for you're a decent fellow. We're djinn, and we're on a mission of mercy."

"You mean like genies?" said Leo.

"The very same. And before you ask, I can't give you three wishes because for one thing you're dead, and for another, djinn power doesn't work in the spirit world." He paused and then added, "Tell me, Leo, are you a good judge of people?"

"I think I'm a good judge of people, I trust, sir," said Leo.

"That's a fine answer," said Mr. Rakshasas. "If you help us, Leo, we'll do our best to help you when we're back on the other side. Won't we, John? You have our word on it. So that you can stop being the Ka servant of that temple back in Manhattan. What do you say?"

"I say all right," said Leo. "I haven't got anything to lose. After a hundred and thirty years, I've had enough of being a guide."

"You said that you thought many of those spirits were hiding in that house. From what exactly?"

"It's like this," said Leo. "Normally, there are thousands of spirits around. But those were the first spirits we've seen since entering the portal. And what's more, they were hiding."

"From what?"

"I don't know. Is it important?"

"It might be." Mr. Rakshasas shrugged. "Where's that canoe?"

Leo took them to the canoe. And while they paddled their way up the Hudson River, John and Mr. Rakshasas told him a little about Faustina and a little bit more about being a djinn.

"To have the power to give someone three wishes must be a tremendous responsibility," said Leo. "But to have three wishes given to you would also require great intelligence to handle well. It is perhaps not always good to receive exactly what you want."

"Sure, with wisdom like that, you could be a djinn yourself, Leo."

They reached Bannermann's Island in the early hours of the morning. Gray dawn was breaking and the creepy-looking gray house in the center of the island was at its most still and quiet, and just as John remembered it. More or less. The grave where he and Dybbuk had buried Felicia's butler, Max, was now marked by an ape-shaped headstone.

They went into the living room where the remains of a fire were still smoldering in the fireplace, and sat down underneath the black-and-white oil painting of Faustina. To John's eye, she looked even more like Dybbuk than he remembered. Willful and mischievous. It was hard to believe that the last time he had been in the room she might have been there, too. Invisibly. In spirit. Watching them.

"Do you think we should call out to her?" John asked Mr. Rakshasas.

"If she's here, she'll come. Remember, it's the quiet pig that eats the meal." Mr. Rakshasas leaned back on the sofa and then yawned. "This was always a fine room for waiting in."

But they did not have to wait long.

"Who are you?" said a voice. "And would you mind telling me what you're doing here?"

Faustina was taller than John had supposed from her portrait, and much lovelier. John thought she looked exactly like what she had been on the day her spirit had lifted out of her djinn body: a twelve-year-old girl. And yet he knew that it was twenty-four years since she had been born. Did that make her twenty-four years old? Or just twelve? He very much hoped the latter and felt his heart miss a beat as he stood up and looked into her gray eyes for the first time.

"My name's John," he said a little awkwardly. "I'm a friend of your brother, Dybbuk."

"You've been here before, haven't you?"

"Yes. A few weeks ago."

"I thought I recognized you."

"We've come to bring you back home," he said. "So you can regain possession of your body."

Faustina let out a breath and sat down heavily, opposite her three visitors.

"Don't you," John asked anxiously, "want to go home?"

"Always," she said. "At first, I prayed that someone would come and find me and take me home. But no one came." Faustina started to cry. "No one came."

"We've come now," said John. And he proceeded to tell her how Nimrod and Philippa had gone to London to recover her body from the wax museum, where she had left it while taking possession of the British prime minister.

Eventually, when Faustina had stopped crying, she wiped her eyes, blew her nose, and said, "I don't see how you can help. I tried to get back into my body before. But I just couldn't."

"That's because the Indian doctor who was summoned to treat the prime minister took a small sample of his blood," explained John. "Some of that blood contained a few grams of your own spirit. Which meant there was part of you missing when you tried to regain control of your own body. But it's going to be okay now. My uncle Nimrod has got a sample of your mother's blood and we're going to use that instead."

"D'you really think that'll work?" she asked.

"Sure, we wouldn't be here now if we thought we were after a tartan-colored unicorn," said Mr. Rakshasas.

"This is Mr. Rakshasas," said John. "He's a very wise djinn. Although sometimes the wisdom is a little hard to understand."

"That's the way with wisdom when you're young." Mr. Rakshasas smiled at Faustina and nodded.

"And this is our friend Leo Politi. He's been our guide through the spirit world. Leo knows everything about the world of spirits."

"I wouldn't say 'everything,'" said Leo, a little embarrassed. He bowed very politely. "But I *am* a proper ghost."

"Well then. Perhaps I *can* go home," she said. "Even if it's for only a short time."

"What do you mean?" asked John, who was already blinded by Faustina's beauty and had quite forgotten the reason why he and Mr. Rakshasas had come to find her in the first place.

"I'm going to be the next Blue Djinn of Babylon," said Faustina. "That was always my destiny. When Ayesha dies, I'm going to take her place. Isn't that right, Mr. Rakshasas?"

"Aye, it is. And it's news I have for you," said Mr. Rakshasas. "Ayesha, blessed be her name, is dead."

"I see," said Faustina. "That explains why you've come to get me." She shrugged sadly. "I guess I'm needed now, when before, I wasn't."

"That's not quite true," said John. "We didn't know where to find your spirit until very recently. It was only after I came here the first time, with my sister and your brother, that we guessed where you were to be found."

"So she *did* hear me then. Your sister."

"Yes."

"Tell me, who did Ayesha appoint as Blue Djinn in my absence?"

John hesitated to say. He knew that telling her the truth would only confirm Faustina's suspicion that there was a hidden motive behind her rescue. But he also knew he could hardly lie about such a thing. And to her of all people. John thought Faustina was much too pretty to be deceived about anything.

"My mother," he said.

"Ah," she said. "That explains why it was *you* who came to get me, John. You need me to prevent your mother from leaving you and your sister. Isn't that right?"

"That's true," John said unhappily. "At least it was true until I met you."

Faustina smiled courageously, which seemed to touch John deep inside his own brave heart; he was already certain that there was nothing he would not have done for her.

Leo looked at Mr. Rakshasas, who smiled back at him; both of these older men recognized what had happened between these two young ones, even if they didn't realize it themselves.

A little awkwardly, as if conscious that he was breaking a kind of spell that hung in the air, Mr. Rakshasas said, "You'll never cook a pancake by tossing it over in your head, so I'm thinking we'd better be making a move."

"Wait," said Faustina. "Before we go back to the physical world, there's something important I have to tell you, which we might need Leo's help to understand. I'm not sure what exactly, but something very strange has been happening in the spirit world."

"There is always something strange happening in the world of spirit," said Leo awkwardly, a little unwilling to contradict this lovely young girl. "Indeed, I should go so far as to say that 'strange' is the one word that perfectly characterizes the spirit world."

"What I meant to say was that this is something stranger than the merely strange. This is something abnormal and bizarre. It may even be something evil.

"In the last twelve years I've learned to know my way around the spirit world and to recognize the *merely* strange." Faustina glanced at Leo as if challenging him to disagree with her definition. "I've met poltergeists, banshees, ethereal beings, wraiths, specters, even a demon or two. As you have no doubt gathered for yourselves, the spirit world looks a lot like the physical one. But just a couple of weeks ago something happened that I just can't explain. I was walking around the gardens here when this enormous power started to drag me along like some huge magnetic force. And amazingly quickly, too. I had no idea where I was going. Only that it was quite irresistible. At the same time, I was aware of all these spirits running in the opposite direction. Away from their usual haunts. And that they were being pursued by these strange-looking men. It was only later on that I managed to get a good look at them."

"That's what I was telling you about back at the museum," Leo told John and Mr. Rakshasas, excitedly.

"At the time I didn't see them very well," said Faustina. "Indeed, the power was so strong that I may even have blacked out for a while. I have no idea how long it lasted. Perhaps several hours. When it finally stopped, I didn't have the first clue where I was. No idea at all. Except that I was in a huge underground cavern with a great sea made of liquid silver that surrounded a humongous green pyramid."

"An underground green pyramid," said Mr. Rakshasas. "Sure, I never heard of such a thing."

"There were lots of these men I mentioned earlier who were working around this pyramid," continued Faustina. "Although I'm not too sure what they were doing. I didn't hang around there for long. Especially when I realized they weren't men at all. They just looked like men. In fact, I think they were zombies."

"Zombies?" exclaimed John. "You mean like dead people walking around?"

"Sort of," agreed Faustina. "They weren't dead. And they weren't alive, either. It's like they were living *and* dead. So I guess they must have been zombies. But to be honest, I'm only calling them that because there was a man there — I don't know who he was — who used that word. At least that's what I think he said. Fortunately, they didn't see me because these zombies looked none too friendly. Anyway, I wandered around for a while trying to find some way out of the cavern. Eventually, I did find my way out, of course. And you can imagine my surprise when I discovered I was in China."

"China?" said John. "You're kidding."

"To be exact, I was in Xian," said Faustina. "The capital of ancient China."

"So how did you get back?" asked John.

Faustina shrugged. "I got myself to the local airport," she said. "It took me ages to get back here."

"A strange tale indeed," admitted Mr. Rakshasas.

"That's it. Except to say that everyone seems to have left the world of spirit. I think the zombies consumed all the spirits they could find. You're the first I've seen since that day. I wondered if Leo, being a Ka servant 'n' all, could maybe tell me what might have happened."

"I have no explanation for what happened," said Leo. "And I do not know anyone else but you, Miss Faustina, who ended up in China. For everyone else, I think it was as if the spirit world had been affected by some sort of cataclysmic natural disaster. Every spirit and ghost was chased from its usual haunt by these creatures you spoke of. I think maybe there were many spirits who were absorbed that day. Who were absorbed and possibly destroyed forever. If I hadn't been cursed to stay at the Temple of Dendur as the Ka servant I, too, might have been destroyed, like the rest of them."

"But is that possible?" asked John. "To destroy a ghost? I mean, how can you kill something that's already dead?"

"There are ways," said Leo. "An exorcism is one way, although most ghosts are much too sensible to hang around and just let themselves be destroyed. They run away. Just like those ghosts did back at the boathouse."

Mr. Rakshasas nodded. "It's time we were leaving," he said. "We've a good deal of traveling to do to get back to the Temple of Dendur."

They set off without further delay, canoeing back to Newburgh in the breaking morning light and then boarding an early commuter train that was bound for New York City. While the train rocked along, Mr. Rakshasas told Faustina what would happen when they got back to the temple in the museum.

"The three of us will go back to John's house," he said. "Sure, with any luck, Nimrod and Philippa will have already arrived back from London with your body, Faustina. As soon as we're all tucked up and snug in our human shapes again, you can decide your next course of action while the rest of us figure out what to do about Leo's little problem."

"Thank you, Mr. Rakshasas," said Faustina. "I can't tell you how grateful I am to you and to John. Most of all, I am really looking forward to there being some color in my life again."

It was midmorning by the time they reached the Metropolitan Museum again, where the attendants' strike was still in progress, but they thought no more about it until they reached the door of the Temple of Dendur, which would have allowed the three djinn to leave the spirit world and reenter the living world of physical matter. There a rude shock awaited them, for, blocking the door, was the same gray, strange-looking figure with the sword. He was positioned with his back to the door, as if on the lookout for something.

"That is one of those creeps I saw in China in that underground cavern," whispered Faustina. "That's one of the zombies I was telling you about."

"Can we get past him?" John asked Leo.

"I don't think so," Leo whispered back. "Not without being attacked and absorbed. Like those others I told you about when we were here before."

"What are we going to do?" said John. "We can't get back into our bodies again unless we leave through a temple."

"If only we knew what this fellow wanted," said Mr. Rakshasas. "Perhaps I should try to talk to him."

"I wouldn't advise it," warned Leo.

"Maybe I can reason with him," said Mr. Rakshasas.

"Honestly," said Leo, "I think you'd be making a fatal mistake."

"Who is this guy?" John shook his head with anger and frustration. They were so near home and yet, while this figure remained in their way, blocking the door to the temple, they were still so far.

CHAPTER 10

HEAD-TO-HEAD

There were twenty thousand people in Madison Square Garden, and it seemed to Nimrod and Philippa that most of them were on Sam's side, for they had greeted his arrival in the ring with deafening cheers.

Groanin climbed into the ring to a chorus of loud whistles and boos, some coins, and several pieces of an orange peel.

"Pay no attention to them," said Philippa as she and Nimrod followed Groanin to his corner. "Sam just wants them here to scare you."

"Look here, Miss Philippa, why ever did you say I'd fight him? I'm no wrestler. You know that." Groanin pointed at Sam, who was flexing his not inconsiderable shoulder muscles for the entertainment of the crowd. "He knows that, too, which is worse."

"Of course," said Philippa. "He's expecting to wipe the floor with you. To tie you in knots and use your head as a paperweight. Like he said. Only you have a secret weapon he won't be ready for."

"What secret weapon?" demanded Groanin.

"Your new arm, of course," said Philippa. "The one we gave you back in India to replace the one you'd lost. It's much stronger than a normal human arm. That's what he won't be expecting."

"She's right," said Nimrod. "I'd forgotten about that. Sam thinks you're just a normal human."

"And don't forget," added Philippa, "that when Samael fought Jacob in the Bible, the result was a draw. And think about this: Jacob wasn't even the strong one. That was his brother, Esau. Jacob was the smooth one."

"Well done, Philippa," said Nimrod. "I'd forgotten that, too."

"I hope you two are right," said Groanin, and threw off his cape. "After all, it's my head he's planning to use as a paperweight."

As well as transporting them all miraculously to Madison Square Garden, Sam had made sure that he and Groanin were wearing suitably theatrical costumes. Sam himself was wearing a splendid white, diamond-encrusted cape and a matching spandex leotard. He looked every inch the good guy. It was equally clear, however, that Sam had meant Groanin to look exactly like the villain of the contest: Groanin was wearing a black spandex leotard and a necklace of white skulls around his neck. There were even little skulls on the laces of his black wrestling boots.

Groanin advanced to the center of the ring and shook hands with his grinning opponent. He went back to his corner trying to smile with confidence, but it came off looking thuggish and sinister. A piece of orange peel hit him on the back of the head. The bell rang to begin the contest.

"Good luck, Groanin," said Nimrod, and pushed him out of his corner. "You'll need it."

Sam held out his hand. Groanin took it politely, only to find himself tossed through the air like a boy backflipping into a pond on a hot summer's day. Philippa and Nimrod closed their eyes for a moment as Groanin landed flat on the canvas with a crash that was louder than a grand piano falling out of a sixth-floor window, and lay still.

The referee began to count. Sam was already walking triumphantly around the ring acknowledging the cheers of the crowd. Philippa and Nimrod each opened one eye. And eventually, but rather reluctantly, so did Groanin.

"Get up, Groanin," yelled Nimrod. "Or you'll be counted out."

"Yes, sir," said Groanin, and, like a drunken man, he staggered to his feet only to be booed loudly and then felled again by a mighty forearm smash from Sam.

"Sam's not exactly what I'd call angelic," observed Nimrod, "is he? But he seems to understand how to please an American audience."

Philippa, who was hating every moment of this contest, shook her head and rubbed the tears from her eyes. Watching Groanin thrown around like a rag doll was awful to her, especially as it had been she who had volunteered him for the fight. And yet Philippa still thought Groanin could defeat Sam. She leaned forward under the rope and yelled at the prostrate butler, "Use your arm, Groanin. The next time that big ape takes a swing at you, block it with your arm."

Groanin struggled to his feet and Sam, cocky now, and thinking he might finish the contest quickly, started to bring his elbow down hard on top of Groanin's shoulders, like a sledgehammer. Except that before the blow landed, Groanin lifted his arm over his head, to protect himself.

It was as if Sam had hit his elbow against an iron bar. Grimacing with pain, he lurched around the ring holding his arm against his body, and howling, almost as if he had broken it. He hadn't, but it was certainly badly bruised.

"Now pick him up and throw him," yelled Philippa.

Once again Groanin did as she had suggested and, with his more powerful arm, sent Sam flying vertically through the air. The angel landed on the canvas with the sound of a huge door slamming shut in some giant's castle. The crowd went mad.

"Now get him around the neck," yelled Philippa, "and pin his shoulders on the canvas until the ref counts three."

Groanin grappled the burly angel to the canvas and pressed him down with all his strength.

"One . . ." said the ref, and slammed the canvas with the flat of his hand.

"I do believe Groanin is going to win this," observed Nimrod.

"Two . . ." said the ref, and slammed the canvas again.

Sam made a superhuman effort to lift himself up but there was nothing he could do against the huge strength of Groanin's arm. Then, with an almighty gasp, his whole body seemed to go limp and he conceded defeat.

"Three!"

Groanin had won. The ref lifted his arm in the air.

"The winner!" he yelled.

Philippa grabbed Nimrod and hugged him. "He did it!" she cried. "He did it!"

They climbed into the ring and while Philippa hugged the butler, Nimrod lifted his other arm in triumph. "Well done, Groanin," he said. "I didn't know you had it in you."

"Thank you, sir."

Sam stayed down for a moment, then rolled onto his ample stomach and shook his head in disbelief before banging his fist angrily on the canvas.

"I hope he's only angry with himself," said Nimrod. "It doesn't do to upset an angel. Just look what happened in Egypt. Not to mention Sodom and Gomorrah. Angels can be sore losers."

Groanin blinked some sweat out of his eyes and when he looked at Philippa again they were all transported back to the Carthusian catacombs in Malpensa. He was wearing his normal butler's clothes again, and Sam was seated on a shelf between two corpses, looking thoroughly miserable.

Philippa put her hand on the angel's shoulder. "Never mind, Sam," she said, and tried to think of something nice to say. "I liked your costume. It was very . . . angelic."

"I'm not much of an angel," he said, "if I can't trounce some poncy English butler in a wrestling match."

"Never underestimate an English butler," said Nimrod. "They are the janissaries of civilization."

"I don't even know where St. Bruno is," said Sam with a loud sigh. "You know? The chap whose bones I'm supposed to be looking after? You were right about that. All the labels got mixed up back in 1750, see? And I kind of lost track of him. I'm a hopeless failure."

"I think I might be able to help you there," said Nimrod. He picked up one of the still-burning candles and walked back down the corpse-lined corridor. "Most of these chaps are monks, from the look of them."

Nimrod stopped in front of one of the older-looking skeletons.

"But this one is especially interesting," he said. "He's holding a skull in his hands. That usually means something important. And look here. That piece of rusting metal on top of his head. If I'm not mistaken it's supposed to be a little crown of seven stars. *A crown.* That means something important, too."

Sam stood up, a smile spreading on his big face. "Are you sure?"

At that precise moment, the skeleton's head fell onto the floor like a coconut dropping from a tree.

"I'd say old Bruno just gave you the nod on that one, Sam," said Groanin.

Nimrod picked up the ancient skull and wiped some of the dust off it. "Someone's written something on his head," he said, putting on his glasses. "It's a bit faint. '*Sancti Brunonis Confessoris, qui Ordinis Carthusianorum fuit Institutor.*'" Nimrod tossed Sam the skull. "No doubt about it, Sam old chap. This fellow is St. Bruno, all right."

"St. Bruno," said Sam, cradling the skull. "You've found him."

Nimrod wiped his hands on the handkerchief Groanin now handed him.

"How can I thank you?" said Sam. There were tears of gratitude in his eyes. "I thought I'd never find him again."

"Well, you can start by letting us take our friend out of here," said Nimrod.

"Of course you can," said Sam. "We had a deal. Your butler won the fight fair and square."

Nimrod and Groanin went back up the corridor and picked up the stretcher bearing Faustina.

"If there's ever anything you need," said Sam. "Anything. Just call me. And I'll be there."

"That's good to know," said Nimrod.

"Yeah, you're an angel," said Philippa.

CHAPTER 11

FAUSTINA'S ZOMBIE II

He doesn't look much like a zombie to me," objected John.

They remained in the temple, unable to travel through its all-important doorway, now blocked by the figure with the sword, and into the living physical world of color. He stood with his back to them, facing the Sackler Wing of the museum, as if his purpose was to prevent anybody or indeed any spirit from using the temple to enter the ethereal world.

"I think you've been watching too many movies," John told Faustina.

"Oh? And what's a zombie supposed to look like?" she asked.

"A mindless, shambling, decaying human corpse with a hunger for human flesh," said John. "Everyone knows that."

"Now who sounds like he's been watching too many movies?" said Faustina.

"This guy doesn't look like a corpse," said John. "And he sure doesn't want to eat people."

"When I used the word 'zombie,' it was the shambling, mindless qualities I had in mind," said Faustina. "Hey, you might make a decent zombie yourself, John."

John could see he wasn't about to get the better of Faustina in an argument. To that extent she reminded him a lot of his own sister.

"Perhaps he's a ghost zombie," she said. "And instead of consuming human flesh, he consumes ghosts and spirits. That's what you said, isn't it, Leo? That he absorbs spirits?"

"That is correct, miss," said Leo.

"Ridiculous," said John. "I never heard of such a thing."

"Sure, if you want to hear a pointless argument," said Mr. Rakshasas, "just listen to the cat and dog having a conversation." He chuckled quietly. "Whatever he is, this fellow is in our way. As I see it, we either have to find another temple through which to enter the spirit world, or find a way around our friend here."

"There's not another temple like this in the whole of North America," said John.

"Isn't there one in South America?" asked Faustina. "Or maybe Central America?"

"Perhaps," said Mr. Rakshasas. "The question is, can we afford to take the time to get all the way down there and then come all the way back here to collect our bodies?"

"He's right," said John.

"Yes, I'd forgotten you're in a hurry to get rid of me," Faustina told John.

"You're bolting your door with a boiled carrot, Faustina," said Mr. Rakshasas. "So why bother to make us break it down?"

Faustina was silent for a moment. "One of us should probably distract him," she said. *The zombie.* She looked at John and squared her jaw as if defying him to disagree with her again. "So that the other two can make a getaway."

"I'll do it," said John. "It's only right that it should be me. After all, I'm the quickest."

Mr. Rakshasas sighed and laid a hand on John's shoulder.

"Prudence dictates that it might be inconvenient if you were absorbed by this zombie fellow. *I'll go.*"

Mr. Rakshasas raised his hand to stop John's objection.

"It must be so, John," he said. "You see, it's not just your life you're putting at risk. It's Philippa's, too. Ask yourself this: How would she get her power back from your body if you weren't there to help her do it?"

Recognizing the wisdom of what the old djinn had said, John nodded. "You will be careful, won't you?"

"Sure, I'll be careful," said Mr. Rakshasas. Under his breath he added, "But if you go mowing the grass in the middle of a horse race, there's always a risk you'll get trampled on." He pointed into the dark shadows of the temple doorway. "You two hide in there," he told John and Faustina. "And then when I've got him distracted, make a run for it."

"Good luck," said John.

"The boy will do his best for you," Mr. Rakshasas told the Ka servant of the temple.

"What did he mean by that?" John asked Faustina when they were hidden in the shadows.

Faustina shrugged. "You know better than I do what he's like." She bit her lip and it was plain that she understood what John still did not: that Mr. Rakshasas did not expect to survive his encounter with the zombie. "I don't understand half of what he says."

John smiled and got ready to run.

Mr. Rakshasas was already standing immediately behind the zombie. He spat on his hands and rubbed them together in anticipation. Then he cleared his throat, and said, "Would you mind getting out of me way, you great big ugly lummox, you?"

The creature shifted on each foot and, as it turned slowly to face Mr. Rakshasas with its staring, doll-like eyes, John was obliged to admit to himself that it looked more like a zombie than anything else he could think of. Only now that he saw it more closely, he could hardly fail to recognize that the creature's narrow eyes, high cheekbones, and drooping Charlie Chan mustache marked it as being Chinese. A

Chinese zombie. Well, why not? China must have zombies, just like everywhere else.

The zombie's eyes may have remained blank but they seemed to function well enough, for the creature lunged at Mr. Rakshasas with one big arm and sought to grab him. Mr. Rakshasas ducked under the arm and hobbled quickly out of the temple and into the museum. The creature turned and pursued him.

"Come on," said John. "Let's go."

John took Faustina's hand and they ran out of the temple and down the steps onto the marble floor of the Sackler Wing, disappearing as they entered the physical world. As they ran, they shouted at the zombie, hoping to distract it and draw it away from the pursuit of Mr. Rakshasas. But the creature did not even look around, for there was nothing to see, of course, and much faster than before it was advancing upon the old djinn who, quite on purpose, had run through the cold water in front of the temple and then a current of air-conditioning in order to remain tantalizingly visible to his pursuer.

Suddenly, the zombie seemed to accelerate, almost as if some kind of electrical current were carrying it forward. At the same time, Mr. Rakshasas stopped to catch his breath and look around. John cried out with horror at what he saw was about to happen.

"Mr. Rakshasas, look out!" he yelled.

The next second, the zombie collided with the old djinn.

But it did not knock him over. Nor did it pass harmlessly through the spirit of Mr. Rakshasas. One moment the thin, half-visible shape of Mr. Rakshasas was almost there, and then it was not. He disappeared completely, as if absorbed by the zombie, which continued on its way for several more feet and then walked around the corner.

John and Faustina stopped running and waited to see if Mr. Rakshasas would make himself nearly visible again. When he did not, John and Faustina shouted his name several times. Minutes passed and nothing happened.

"It was just like Leo said. He got absorbed by that thing."

Still holding hands, they crossed the floor and went back up the steps to the Temple of Dendur where they could see Leo staring anxiously out of the door and into the museum. As they came between the pillars of the temple, John and Faustina became visible again.

"You should go," Leo told them. "In case that zombie comes back again."

"We can't go without him," insisted John.

"It's what Mr. Rakshasas would have wanted," said Leo. "He knew what he was doing. That's why he did it. So you two children could get away."

John shook his head. "This can't be happening," he said unhappily. "I don't believe it. Not Mr. Rakshasas."

Faustina squeezed his hand and then put her arms around John's neck. "Leo's right, John," she said. "We have to go, and go now. Before it comes back and does the same thing to us that it did to Mr. Rakshasas."

"You don't understand," said John. "He's my friend. I can't leave my friend."

"It's too late, John," she said. "He's gone. Mr. Rakshasas is dead."

CHAPTER 12

THE VOICE OF THE SILENCE

Nimrod and Groanin carried Faustina's body to the ambulance and laid her carefully in the back. Groanin slipped behind the wheel and quickly started the engine while Nimrod and Philippa got into the front alongside him. "Where to, sir?" he asked. "Some quiet field? A rooftop? Somewhere you can get a nice whirlwind started."

"Groanin, your new enthusiasm for traveling by whirlwind is most unsettling," said Nimrod. He took out his cell phone and called New York. Marion Morrison answered and reported that while Mr. Gaunt was continuing to make good progress, there had been no change in the condition of Mrs. Trump, who remained in a coma. And there was still no sign of John and Mr. Rakshasas. Nimrod thanked her and then hung up.

"We need to get into contact with John and Mr. Rakshasas and find out where they are and what's happening," he said. "I need Mr. Rakshasas to bring Faustina's spirit out here to

Italy. For one thing, it will save us going all the way back to New York. For another, Italy's more than halfway to Babylon. Let's not forget, time is getting short. It's been almost three weeks since your mother left New York."

"How are we going to get in contact with them?" asked Philippa.

"The same way mundanes do when they want to contact the spirit world," said Nimrod. "Through a séance."

"A séance?" said Groanin. "You mean all the mumbo jumbo with moving wine glasses and canasta cards is true?"

"Some of it," said Nimrod. "The most important thing is to choose a good medium. Which makes it very fortunate for us that we're in Italy. The best medium in the world lives in Rome. Come on, Groanin. That's where we're going. Rome. The eternal city."

"What's a medium?" Philippa asked Nimrod.

"A medium is a person thought to have the power to communicate with the spirits of the dead or with agents of another world or dimension. Also called a psychic."

"Pyscho more like," muttered Groanin, steering the car down the mountain road. "A lot of silly people meddling with stuff they don't understand, if you ask me. I thought you didn't hold with all of that malarkey, sir."

"Ordinarily I don't, Groanin," admitted Nimrod. "But this is a special case. Besides, Madame Theodora Sofi is no ordinary medium. Her powers are quite genuine. Which is hardly a surprise. At the age of eighteen she went to Tibet to study for seven years with the brothers."

"What brothers?" asked Philippa.

"The true authors of the Tibetan Book of the Dead," said Nimrod. "Some monks and lamas who know more about the afterlife than any other mundanes that have ever lived. They taught her everything they knew. She has given her whole life to spiritualism."

It took several hours for Groanin to drive the ambulance to Rome from Malpensa. Arriving at the outskirts of the great city, Groanin asked Nimrod for Madame Sofi's address.

"She hasn't got one," said Nimrod. "Theo's the only person in Rome who doesn't need an address."

"How does that happen?" asked Groanin.

"Because she famously lives in the only pyramid in Rome," said Nimrod. "All we have to do is ask where it is." Rolling down the window, Nimrod leaned out of the ambulance and, in his perfect Italian, asked a policeman on a motorcycle for directions. The policeman, who had a large red mustache, pointed up the street and then bent his hand left, and when he had finished speaking, he saluted Nimrod smartly.

Groanin drove on.

"How does Madame Sofi come to be living in a pyramid, anyway?" Philippa asked her uncle. "Is it a real one?"

"Real enough," said Nimrod. "It was built in 12 B.C. as the tomb of some rich Roman praetor called Cestius, who fancied a family sepulcher with a difference. Madame Sofi's the first person ever to live in it, though. It's not everyone's cup of tea, living in a pyramid."

"I should say not," said Groanin. "Makes the furniture difficult to choose, I'd have thought. But won't she want something in return for helping us? Three wishes, I mean. That always ends in trouble."

"She had three wishes, the last time I saw her. How do you suppose she came to be living in a pyramid?"

At last they caught sight of the pyramid. Compared to the Egyptian pyramids, which she had seen the previous year, Philippa thought the Roman Pyramid of Cestius was a little too pointed. Like an over-sharpened pencil. Made of white marble and exactly one hundred feet tall, it was, however, in an excellent state of repair, as if recently completed by some trendy modern architect, like the one in Paris.

They found Madame Theodora Sofi awaiting their arrival at her triangular front door, a fact that Philippa and Groanin couldn't help but feel impressed by, given that Nimrod hadn't actually telephoned the great medium to tell her they were coming.

She was a tall Italian woman with a long sinuous neck, a voluptuous head of red hair, a big nose, and tinted glasses that seemed to be as large as television screens.

"I felt you coming here about ten minutes ago," said Madame Sofi. "By the way, did you speak to a policeman on a motorcycle en route? A man with a large red mustache?"

"However did you know that?" asked Groanin.

"I am Theo Sofi," she said rather grandly as if that were the only explanation necessary.

They went inside the pyramid. There were no windows but the interior was oddly cool and bright, as if there were some secret means of conducting sunlight and fresh air into the pyramid, which was just as well because the place was full of cats.

Nimrod introduced his niece and his butler.

But Madame Sofi was more eager to be about her business than to talk. "You have come because you want to speak to some people on the other side, yes?"

"Yes," said Nimrod. He was about to speak again when Madame Sofi started to cry. "Why, what is the matter, dear lady?"

Madame Sofi removed her glasses and dabbed at her eyes with a handkerchief. "What you ask may not be possible," she said. "Either I have lost my gift or something is very wrong on the other side. I have tried to speak to the spirits many times these last few weeks. But with little or no success. It's almost as if there's no one there. Like nothing I have ever felt before."

"Whatever do you mean — no one there?" asked Nimrod.

"Just exactly what I say." She blew her nose and put the handkerchief up her sleeve. "Normally, the clamor of voices on the other side is very loud. Now there is only silence. The spirits I usually speak to, here in Rome, are no longer there."

"That's strange," said Nimrod.

"Isn't it? And yet, until recently, the museums and ancient temples in the city were all reporting an increased amount of paranormal activity. The attendants wouldn't go near them. They went on strike."

"It's the same in New York," said Philippa.

"Which was great news for burglars of course," said Madame Sofi.

"Really?" said Nimrod. "How do you mean?"

"During the strike," explained Madame Sofi, "many of the museums in Italy were robbed. Strange. But always it was the same thing stolen. Jade."

"Jade?" said Nimrod. "That's interesting."

"Precious stones mean nothing to me," said Madame Sofi.

Philippa thought this was a little rich given the diamond necklace Madame Sofi was wearing around her long neck.

"Without the spirits to speak to, I have nothing," said Madame Sofi. "I've even been to the Forum. To try to speak to some of the oldest spirits in Rome, but I couldn't get through to them. It's almost as if they were afraid to speak to me." She shrugged. "Or not there at all."

"The people I wish to contact are not actually dead," said Nimrod. "They're disembodied djinn. My nephew, John, and my friend, Mr. Rakshasas, whom you've met, I think."

"They won't hear us," she said matter-of-factly. "Not being dead themselves, they will be unused to the world of spirit. But if they were sensible enough to enter the spirit world through a portal. A temple perhaps . . ."

"They did," said Philippa. "The Temple of Dendur. In New York. It's an Egyptian temple to the goddess Minerva, built by the Roman Emperor Augustus."

"In which case they will certainly have tried to pick up a spirit guide. All Egyptian temples have a Ka servant. We must try to contact him. The Ka servant's ears will be well-tuned to the other side, if he still exists."

Madame Sofi ushered them into a wide room and invited them to sit around a table. They sat down and, at Madame Sofi's invitation, held hands. She placed a piece of black lace on her head, removed her outsized glasses, closed her eyes, and started to breathe deeply through her largish nose. Minutes passed and, after a while, Philippa was quite convinced that Madame Sofi was asleep. She looked at Groanin and tried not to smile as he made a face.

After a while the medium straightened a little and said, "I'm speaking to the Ka servant of the Temple of Dendur. Formerly of Aswan in Egypt and now in Manhattan, New York. If you can hear me, O spirit guide, please speak to us. I am here with some friends of Mr. Rakshasas and John Gaunt, who are anxious to speak to them."

Another minute passed and gradually Philippa became aware of a long thin current of sound, which was like someone had switched on an invisible radio. The sound appeared to be coming from Madame Sofi's open mouth. A second or two later, she felt her hair stand on end as a foreign-sounding voice came drifting slowly out of Madame Sofi's mouth, as though arriving from a long silence on a very high mountaintop in a country that was very far away. But Madame Sofi's lips did not move.

"This is the Ka servant of Dendur," said the voice. "My name is Leo Politi. I have the nephew of Nimrod by my side, and his friend, Faustina. We are at the temple in the museum in New York."

"It's them," squealed Philippa. "Thank goodness they're all right."

"This is wonderful." Madame Sofi tightened her grip on Nimrod's hand. Once again there were tears in her eyes, only these were tears of happiness. "Go ahead," she said in her own voice. "Speak to him. He will hear you through my ears."

John and Faustina had been leaving the temple a second time when Leo touched his ear with his plump hand and asked them to wait a moment. "There's a voice coming through from the other side," he said. "A medium who's with your uncle and your sister."

"I can't hear anything." John let out a sigh and shook his head gloomily. After what had happened to Mr. Rakshasas he thought his senses must have been numbed. Which seemed hardly surprising. At the same time he felt a huge sense of relief to hear from Nimrod. Surely he would know what to do.

"Ssssh," said Leo. "Your ears are not yet tuned to the world of spirit. That's why you can't hear anything. I shall be your medium. Wait a few moments, then speak, and they will hear through me."

Leo closed his eyes and, taking a deep breath, appeared to enter a light trance. His mouth sagged open and a sound came out. A strange, unnerving sound that John instinctively knew came from a source that was not Leo. At first John thought it was like the sound of a dentist's spit sucker. Gradually, as the volume of the noise increased, it became a cappuccino machine. Then a vacuum cleaner. And finally a still silence came carrying a human voice he recognized.

John glanced around. "Better keep an eye out in case that zombie comes back," he told Faustina.

"John?" Nimrod's voice was coming out of Leo's motionless mouth. "Can you hear me?"

"I can hear you," yelled John, for in truth the voice in the silence was very faint and he thought he'd better speak up, just in case it was the same at the other end. Wherever that might be. "Thank goodness you, er . . . called."

"Is Faustina with you?"

"Yes, she's here."

"And Mr. Rakshasas? I need to speak to him if I can, please, John."

"No," said John. "Something happened to him. A sort of zombie absorbed him. He's disappeared." He felt a lump in his throat and tried to control the grief that threatened to choke him.

"Absorbed him? How?"

"I don't know. It was here in the museum. There's this zombie that looks like some kind of ancient Chinese warrior that's scaring the other ghosts here away. And if it catches up with them, it absorbs them. That's what it looks like, anyway. And that's what happened to Mr. Rakshasas." John swallowed some more grief. "I don't know if he's alive or dead, Uncle Nimrod."

"A Chinese zombie, you say?" said Nimrod. "I never heard of such a thing."

"I'm not making it up. One minute he was there and the next he was gone."

"Listen to me, John," said Nimrod. "I want you and Faustina to go home and check on his body. It might be that he had a good reason to leave you and has gone there. To get back into his own body."

"What if he's not there? What if he's dead? And how on earth will I tell? I don't know about this stuff. I don't know how I'm going to be able to tell if he's all right."

"If he's not at home there's nothing you can do. Without his spirit, you can't help him. You'll have to leave his body there. Then I want you and Faustina to get yourselves on a plane and come here to Italy. But don't forget to leave your own body at home, John. Remember there's a Methusaleh binding on your father that's still active. If your body and your djinn power leave New York, he'll start to age again."

"All right," John said dully. "We're both to go to Italy. But why Italy? I thought you were in London."

"Change of plan," said Nimrod. "Faustina's body was in Italy. Tell her it's fine. And that it's just as she left it."

"Where in Italy?" asked John.

There was a long silence.

"John," said Nimrod. "Why did you say that the zombie was Chinese?"

John told him about the spirit world tsunami and how Faustina had found herself in Xian, the old Chinese capital, and how the museum zombie was the same as the zombies she'd seen there.

"To be honest, she's not exactly sure about the word 'zombie,'" added John. "She thinks she heard someone use that word. But it could be something else."

"All right, John," said Nimrod. "Listen carefully; I want you and Faustina to go to Venice. We'll be waiting for you at the Gravelli Palace Hotel. Something very odd is happening in the ethereal world and I think we'd better find out what it is and quick."

"Venice?" repeated John. "Why Venice?"

"Because Venice has one of the best libraries of antiquarian books about China in the world. I need to try to find out more about this zombie of yours."

"John," shouted Faustina. "We've got company."

John glanced around and saw the Chinese zombie was already striding mechanically across the museum floor toward them.

"Got to go, Uncle," John yelled to Nimrod. "Faustina's zombie is back again. See you in Venice, I hope."

He grabbed her hand and they ran for their lives.

CHAPTER 13

THE BOY WONDER

Since leaving Las Vegas with Adam Apollonius, Dybbuk had been having the time of his young life in New York City. The British-born Apollonius had dedicated himself and most of the people who worked for him to making Dybbuk the star of his own live TV magic special, entitled *The Boy Wonder*.

"First we're going to give you a complete makeover," explained Apollonius. "So that you look like the star you're so obviously going to be."

"Before we get to that," said Dybbuk, "I want to change my name. I hate my name. I've always hated it."

"I thought Dybbuk sounded rather good, actually," said Apollonius. "It means —"

"I know what it means," said Dybbuk. "And I hate it. I want to be called something else."

"Well then, it had better be a name that seems appropriately magical, hadn't it?" Apollonius laughed. "David somebody. Half the magicians in the world seemed to be called David these days, don't you think."

"I hate the name David." Dybbuk shook his head. "I like your name."

"Sorry, kid, but I'm using it."

"I meant I'd like a name *like* that. Something with a bit of flair."

Apollonius thought for a moment. "How about 'Jonathan Tarot'?" he said. "That's tarot as in the tarot cards that are sometimes used by people to foretell the future. Nonsense, of course, but a name full of magical meaning, don't you agree?"

"Jonathan Tarot," said Dybbuk. "I like it."

"Then, Jonathan Tarot it is, my boy." Apollonius clapped his hands together and rubbed them expectantly. "And what about your new look?"

"My look?"

"You know. How you see yourself."

Dybbuk had never really paid much attention to how he saw himself. He rarely combed his hair, which was slightly long and seldom washed. He nearly always wore a T-shirt, a pair of black jeans, and motorcycle boots. Beyond that he didn't ever think about his hair and clothes, except in the sense that he saw other people, hated what they wore, and pitied them.

"Maybe you'd like to look like me?" suggested Apollonius, vainly stroking his little chin beard and then fingering his earring.

Onstage and on TV, Apollonius usually wore short-sleeved white smocks, which he said he wore so that people could see he wasn't hiding anything up his sleeves. Dybbuk thought these made Apollonius look more like a dentist or a chef than a magician. He smiled politely and shook his head.

"Actually, I do have an idea of my own," he said. "I'd like to look like Elvis Presley when he played Las Vegas. I want to wear one of those shimmering, rhinestone-encrusted white eagle costumes with the big collars and the fringes and the cape and the white boots."

"Don't you think that Elvis is a bit too 1970s?" asked Apollonius.

"That look's cool again," said Dybbuk. "So are the seventies." In truth he didn't know if this was true or not and he didn't much care either way. Dybbuk was sufficiently savvy to know that grown-ups generally backed down when kids started telling them what was cool and what was not. "No one was ever as cool as Elvis," he added.

Apollonius shrugged. "If you say so, kid," he said. "Elvis it is."

So Dybbuk had a thousand-dollar haircut from New York's top hairdresser, the surprisingly bald Jon Bread, and ended up with his jet-black hair looking like something that had been drawn on top of his head by a manga comic artist, with a proper quiff and a shine that would not have disgraced a Cadillac. Just like Elvis. Dybbuk loved his new hair and spent an hour or two practicing a matching sneer that was pure rock 'n' roll.

Then a man arrived from a store in Hollywood with a selection of Elvis-style jumpsuits in a variety of colors. Most of these were bedecked with metal and jewels and beads and weighed a lot, but when he put one on, Dybbuk felt like a king. This was hardly a surprise as only a king could have afforded one. Each suit cost fifty thousand dollars. Dybbuk especially liked the belts, each of which had a buckle that was as big as a saucer.

Meanwhile, Dybbuk had been working on devising ways of using djinn power that might be mistaken for illusions and magic tricks, albeit spectacular ones. He looked at films of famous magicians, and sought to imitate what they had done, while at the same time going one better. Or even two or three better. And soon he had a repertoire of so-called illusions that Adam Apollonius declared was the most impressive he had ever seen. The close-up stuff was easy, of course. But Dybbuk had wanted something more remarkable than just making an apple appear from underneath a silk handkerchief on his hand. Or a kitten disappear from inside his shirt.

"I've been thinking," he told Apollonius. "We need something really amazing to end the TV special, right?"

"I thought you were going to do the Indian Rope Trick."

"I've got something better," said Dybbuk. "I call it my Goldfinger Trick. It's inspired by the James Bond movie."

"Goldfinger," said Apollonius. "I like that."

"It's really quite simple. I get locked inside an Aston Martin car that just happens to be in a car crusher. I escape from the car unseen by the cameras before the car gets crushed, of course, and under the noses of a couple of hundred soldiers, secretly make my way inside the U.S. Bullion Depository."

The U.S. Bullion Depository is a fortified vault building located near Fort Knox, Kentucky, which is used to store the majority of the United States' gold holdings. The vault that stores the gold has granite walls and is protected by a door that weighs twenty-five tons.

"Once inside the vault, I steal a bar of gold," continued Dybbuk, "which has been specially stamped by the United States Mint, of course, maybe set off the alarms just so that they know I'm in there, and then appear on the roof holding the bar in my hand."

"You're kidding," said Apollonius.

"I can do it," said Dybbuk.

"Yes, but how?"

Dybbuk smiled his secret smile. "Practice."

"Seriously, kid. Level with me. What's the trick?"

"Do I ask how you do your tricks?"

"No," Apollonius answered carefully. "But what you're proposing is a little different from making a polar bear disappear inside a theater. You're working outside. You'll need trick photography and that's expensive."

"Would Harry Houdini have used trick photography?" asked Dybbuk. "I think not. For starters, there wasn't any trick photography back then. And for another, he was the best. He was the best because he did the impossible. That's what I propose to do. The impossible. On second thought, maybe that's what we should call the trick. 'Mission Impossible.'"

"I have to admire your nerve, kid," said Apollonius. "But —"

"No buts," said Dybbuk. "Believe me, I can do this."

"Oh, I don't doubt you can do it," said Apollonius. "It's just that I wish I knew how. Can't you tell me? I promise not to reveal how you do it. You know I'd be kicked out of the Magic Circle if I did."

"What's the Magic Circle?" asked Dybbuk.

"Like a trade union for magicians and conjurers," answered Adam.

Dybbuk thought for a moment. "I'd like to tell you," he said cleverly. "Really, I would. But haven't you noticed how it is when you learn how simply an illusion is performed, it doesn't seem like magic anymore? Think about it. Wouldn't you prefer to live with the idea of the magic rather than knowing all the dirty little tricks I use to do my stuff?"

"So these are proper tricks?" said Apollonius.

Dybbuk smiled. "Of course," he said. "Do you think I'm some kind of alien?"

Apollonius smiled. "Maybe. I dunno. All I know is that for thirteen years old, you really are the boy wonder." He shook his head. "Kids are going to go wild for you," he added. "Especially the girls."

Dybbuk smiled.

Jonathan Tarot's incredible feats of magic were viewed with universal astonishment when the TV special went on the air. And with the exception of those lucky humans who had ever received three wishes from a good djinn, everyone who saw the show agreed that they had never seen a magic show quite as good as Tarot's. No illusionist had ever made a coin appear in *someone else's* hand, or bent a fork with the power of his mind *within ten seconds*. Jonathan Tarot levitating himself a good twelve inches off a New York sidewalk had provoked gasps of amazement, as had his extensive repertoire of card "tricks," the best of which was when he turned every card in a pack into a picture of the girl to whom he had been showing the trick. But the greatest praise had been for the Mission Impossible Trick, which Tarot performed so well that several people had fainted when the Aston Martin had been crushed, while the U.S. Bullion Depository was now conducting an investigation into how its security measures had been so easily breached.

Adam Apollonius had not exaggerated the effect that Jonathan Tarot's first appearance on TV would have on the world. Kids watching the special did go wild for him. Especially the girls. Indeed, "wild" was a word that hardly did

justice to Tarot's newfound celebrity. In short, Tarot's live
TV special made him what people in show business used to
call "an overnight sensation." A recording of the show was
screened two nights in a row, with the second repeat drawing
an incredible fifty million young viewers, outperforming all
other TV shows. Of course, it helped that there was so little
to watch elsewhere on TV with many of the most popular TV
shows having been mysteriously taken off the air. But no one
ever thought to connect the two.

Jonathan Tarot was invited on several late-night television talk shows and asked to perform yet more live magic and
impossible escapes. On one show, he stood in a plastic gar-
bage bag and, by transubstantiating just his legs, created the
illusion that his body had caught fire. On another show, he
walked out of the Ed Sullivan Theater on Broadway and performed a sensational live escape after having been handcuffed
and locked in the trunk of a New York City police car that
was parked outside. But the best of these stunts was when he
had disappeared from an elevator in the GE building, located
in New York's Rockefeller Plaza, as it traveled between the
first and the sixty-ninth floors, only to reappear a few
seconds later on the roof of the building.

Apollonius smacked the newspaper he had been reading
with the back of his hand. "Listen to this," he said. " 'Last
week, no one had ever heard of thirteen-year-old Jonathan
Tarot. This week, the sensational young illusionist and
escape artist is the most famous boy in America and is as

well-known as any pop idol or movie star. What is even better is that, unlike these others, Tarot has genuine talent, and it is to be hoped he will become a positive role model and good influence on children all over the world.'" Apollonius let out a laugh. "That's you they're talking about, kid. How about that? Isn't it amazing, Jonathan?"

"I guess so," admitted Jonathan. (No one, not even Adam Apollonius, was allowed to call him "Dybbuk" anymore.)

"Do you want to be a good influence on children all over the world?"

Jonathan shrugged. "I dunno. I guess so. Why not?"

Apollonius grinned. "Well, that's great, son," he said. "That's great. Because you *can* be an influence. Like no one else in history. With your humongous talent and the enormous power of television, we can do anything we want."

"If you say so, Adam."

"I do say so." Apollonius rubbed his hands enthusiastically. "I've got such plans for you, my boy. We're going to make money and then we're going to make history."

"Great."

"Tell me. How do you do it, kid?"

"Practice," said Jonathan patiently.

He didn't blame Adam Apollonius for asking. Not in the least. In Jonathan's eyes it seemed entirely natural that Apollonius would want to know his secrets, given that he was a professional magician himself. It would have been weird if he had not been curious as to how Jonathan's tricks were performed.

144

Apollonius also knew this very well. Indeed, it was the reason why he asked Jonathan about the tricks: to deflect any suspicions the boy might have of him. Because the plain fact of the matter was that Apollonius already knew the secret of how the boy performed his magic tricks. He knew exactly who and what Jonathan Tarot was. How could he not? Dybbuk was his own misbegotten son. The body of Adam Apollonius was possessed by none other than the spirit of Iblis the Ifrit. And, as usual, the evil djinn was planning something suitably horrible.

CHAPTER 14

TWO'S COMPANY . . .

Reaching his house on East 77ᵗʰ Street, John suddenly felt ill. It was like someone had placed him on the rolling deck of a ship at sea in a storm. His balance was gone. He could hardly stand and had to crawl through his own front door. Every time he fixed his eyes on some stationary object, it would start to wander away on its own accord. If he hadn't known better, he would have said he was drunk. Or drugged.

"Faustina," he croaked. "Are you there? I don't feel so good."

He felt her kneel down beside him and take his hand. "What's wrong with you?" she asked.

"I dunno. Maybe Doc can help."

"Who's Doc?"

"Marion Morrison, the woman nursing my father," said John. "She's a djinn nurse."

Faustina helped him crawl into the kitchen where Doc was busy playing a harmonica, a sweet-sounding tune that seemed to soothe her and the cat, Monty. To John's surprise, there was someone else in the room. It was Finlay McCreeby. Neither he nor Doc saw the spirits of the two young djinn. But Monty did. He stood up, his back arching like a camel and all his gray-and-black fur standing on end, and hissed loudly at the invisible visitors. Doc put down her harmonica and looked around.

"What's the matter with that cat?" asked Finlay.

"I think we've got company," said Doc. She went over to the refrigerator and threw open the door so that a blast of cold air spilled onto the kitchen floor, slowly rendering the two young djinn half-visible.

"That's a cool trick," said Finlay.

John told Finlay that he didn't feel particularly cool crawling around the floor, but it was clear that the mundane boy couldn't hear him. Gradually, however, the cold air also seemed to amplify their voices; even made them a bit ghostly.

"'S'a matter with you guys?" asked Doc.

"Don't feel so good," croaked John. "Balance is gone."

"Sounds like a case of astral-sickness," said Doc. "It's when your supersensible body can't cope with being weightless any longer. If you've ever wondered why ghosts moan a lot, I guess now you know. I've heard it can be pretty unpleasant."

"I've been weightless for twelve years," said Faustina. "I never felt like that."

"Not everyone gets it," said Doc. "Twin djinn get it more often."

"Now she tells me," said John. "Is there a cure? I have to get to Italy."

"Your body is upstairs," said Doc. "You only have to get back inside it to feel better."

"I don't think I could make it up all those stairs," admitted John.

"Then the only thing you can do is to move your spirit self inside a human body for a spell." Doc looked pointedly at Finlay. "How about it, Finlay? Feel like doing a good deed today?"

"You mean you want me to share my body with him?"

"That's about the size of it," said Doc. "Unless you want to see your friend crawling around on his belly for the rest of however long it takes him to get his butt upstairs."

"All right," said Finlay.

Doc pointed at the floor. "You'd better lie down next to him," she said. "So that he can get under your skin without standing up."

Finlay sat down and then lay back.

"Couple of things you oughtta know about sharing a body," said Doc. "One is that good djinn are only supposed to do it for a short while in an emergency. Which I guess this is. Only evil djinn take over someone else's body, permanent-like. Another thing is that you, John, will have to respect that Finlay's in charge. It might feel like your body when you're in there, John. But it ain't. It's his, so you'll have to try to respect that. Let him take the decisions, like he normally does. Choose what he wants to eat, even if it's stuff you don't like. What TV programs he wants to watch. That kind of thing."

John crawled into his friend's body and instantly felt better. In the same moment he knew everything that Finlay did: that he had followed Dybbuk to New York, that Dybbuk had changed his name to Jonathan Tarot, and now had his own very successful TV show, and that he was living in the presidential suite at New York's Cimento dell' Armonia Hotel. No explanations were required. Nor was it necessary for John to see Dybbuk's TV show. Finlay had seen it and, therefore, John had access to Finlay's memory of having seen it.

Nor was it necessary to ask about Mr. Rakshasas. The old djinn's spirit had not reappeared to take possession of his own body again, and the body remained in John's bedroom, sitting in John's favorite chair, exactly where he had left it. Finlay knew about John's father, too. Mr. Gaunt was getting younger again. But, unfortunately, Mrs. Trump remained in a coma with no sign that she would ever get better.

"Well, that saves a lot of questions," John told Finlay, inside Finlay's head.

"Don't worry about things," Finlay told him. "Mr. Rakshasas and Mrs. Trump. I'm sure they'll be all right."

But, of course, John knew that Finlay was just saying that and didn't really think it at all.

Because John knew it, Finlay instantly knew all about Faustina and why she and John were going to Italy. He even knew that John had to leave his own body behind in New York and now wanted him to come along, so that he might avoid astral-sickness again. And John knew that this was cool with Finlay. But Finlay was hardly prepared for John's next idea. Indeed, John had only just thought of it himself.

"It might make traveling easier if we had Faustina join us in here with you, in your body," he told Finlay. "Just to make sure she doesn't get lost. Which is easy enough when you're invisible, let me tell you."

"I know."

"Plus, it'll save a lot of time trying to talk to her, and vice versa. It's not easy when you're out-of-body."

"I know."

"And I know you're not sure about it," said John. "On account of the fact that she's a girl."

"It's just that two's company, you know," Finlay told John. "And three's going to be a crowd in here. But I guess it'll be okay. Shall I tell her or will you?"

John glanced around and saw a thin bluish outline of a female human shape sitting on a chair in front of the open refrigerator door.

"There you are," he said. And told her his idea. To his surprise she agreed without hesitation.

"I was hoping you'd say that," she said. "Besides, if the three of us are all going to Italy it'll make communication a lot easier. There's just one thing I'm concerned about. How are we going to get there? Once we're all in Finlay's body, it's not like we'll be able to walk invisibly onto a flight. Who's going to pay for a plane ticket?"

John and Finlay looked at Doc. "Sorry to ask you, Doc," said John. "But could you fix us up with a ticket?"

"Sorry don't get it done," said Doc. She took out a big red handkerchief, looked at the knot tied in it, and then let out a big sigh. "Now what was it?"

"What was what?" John asked her.

"My focus word. Been so long since I used my focus word, I guess I must have forgotten it."

"I thought you came here on a whirlwind," said John.

"That's only what I told you. Fact is, I came here by airplane. I don't like people knowing I forgot my focus word. That's kind of embarrassing. Makes me look incompetent. And that's bad in a nurse."

"When did you forget it?" asked John.

"Six months ago. Maybe longer. When I was up the Amazon. There's a way of remembering a forgotten focus word. But I can't remember what that is." She shook her head. "Might take time to remember it. Lots of time. Might take weeks."

"We can't wait that long," said Faustina.

"If Mr. Rakshasas was here he could probably tell us how you could remember it," said John.

"Ifs don't pay for the steaks, kid," said Doc.

"Why don't you just use your old man's credit card and buy a ticket?" Finlay told John. "That's what I used to do when I wanted to get something he didn't want to give me."

"Good idea," said John.

"Not always," admitted Finlay.

"Are you ready to have me come on board?" Faustina asked Finlay.

"As ready as I'll ever be," said Finlay. "The things I do for this family."

Sharing one human body with two other people was, Faustina decided, like being in a cold bath with total strangers: uncomfortably close. Most of the time she didn't know where to put herself. The worst part of it was knowing what John and Finlay already knew. Not to mention them knowing what she already knew. Neither she nor John had bargained on the other discovering their true feelings for each other. This might not have seemed quite so embarrassing if Finlay had not been there, also.

"I never thought I'd feel unwelcome in my own body," Finlay said as he walked into the airport to catch a plane bound for London and then Venice.

"Who said you were unwelcome?" asked Faustina.

"Speaking of unwelcome," said John, "isn't that your father over there?"

"You know it is," said Finlay. "He must be on his way to London, too."

Virgil McCreeby wore a tweed suit and a chin beard that looked like a shoe brush, and did not look like a man who missed his only son.

"Do you think he saw you?" John asked Finlay.

"You know he hasn't," said Finlay. "The question is, what revenge am I going to take on my dad. I mean, I can't just let him get away with it. There has to be something unpleasant I can do. He had me turned into a bird, for Pete's sake."

"Only because you were irritating him," said John. "He lost his temper. That's what fathers do with sons."

"True, but if you remember, Nimrod told him to make a fourth wish, so that I could be turned back into a human being. And he didn't. He wanted to keep what he'd gotten from the first two wishes."

"Yes, that was bad," agreed John. "He shouldn't have done that."

"I read somewhere that they've got a no-fly list on the check-in screens," said Faustina. "To help identify suspicious-looking characters. I could slip out of your body and into the attendant and make her identify your dad as a suspicious character. And not let him on the flight. You don't need djinn power to do what comes naturally to any spirit."

"And then," said John, "when he complains, she can call a cop over. And I can possess the cop long enough to persuade him to make an arrest."

"He does look kind of suspicious," said Faustina. "Don't you think?"

"Oh, for sure," agreed Finlay. "He's a warlock, after all."
He nodded. "Go for it."

Finlay felt the two djinn slip noiselessly out of his body
and sat back to enjoy the show. It was true what some people
said, he thought: You don't always have to go to a theater to
see a good play.

CHAPTER 15

VENICE IN PERIL

Venice is Italy's most interesting city for the simple reason that the streets are made of water and the cars are boats. The Gravelli Palace was Venice's oldest and best hotel and looked out over the largest "street," which is the Grand Canal. Below Philippa's bedroom window, the bright morning sunlight danced on the waves like liquid music, and she thought she had never seen a more beautiful view. But Groanin was not impressed.

"It smells a bit, does Venice," he said, wrinkling his nose as they left the hotel to take a trip aboard a beautiful polished wooden motorboat through the limpid, bright green waters to the island of Torcello. "I say, it smells a bit, does Venice. Like it needs the services of a good plumber. I've been splashing my new aftershave on myself to cover the stink. Of course, I have a very sensitive sense of smell. Where are we going, anyway?"

"We're going to the Library of Attila the Hun," said Nimrod.

"What, him that sacked Rome?" said Groanin. "I wouldn't have picked him as much of a reader. I say, he's not a man I can easily picture reading the latest John Grisham."

"Books were a source of power and status in those days," explained Nimrod. "Regardless of whether you were a reader or not. Before he sacked Rome, Attila also sacked Constantinople, which was the capital of the eastern Roman Empire, and there he stole a library that the Byzantine emperor had stolen from the Persians, who, in turn, had stolen it from the Chinese."

"It's like I always say," said Groanin, "there's more theft in libraries than you'd ever credit." He nodded grimly. "I know. I used to work in a library. That's where —"

"I know," said Nimrod. "You lost your arm to a tiger in the British Library. You've told us many times."

"Pardon me for breathing," said Groanin, "I'm sure." He sniffed loudly and made another face as the smell of the canal prickled his sensitive nostrils.

"On his way back from Rome in A.D. 453, Attila left the library on Torcello," continued Nimrod. "And there it has remained ever since, in the care of the Knights of St. Mark. Today it's the best Oriental library in Europe."

"Well, speaking as an ex-librarian," Groanin said stiffly, "I've never heard of it."

"The Library of Attila is not open to the public," said Nimrod. "Only to the Knights of St. Mark, of whom I am a

Grand Commander." And so saying, Nimrod showed them both a gold medal he was wearing around his neck on a purple silk ribbon.

Now it was Groanin's turn to groan and roll his eyes at Philippa. "I might have known," he said. "It's like I always say, it's those who have a lot already who always get more."

Torcello was a small island full of rather simple, brightly painted houses, many of which looked like they were falling down. The entrance to the library was by boat, through a dank, dark water gate in an anonymous-looking area of wall that cleverly concealed its purpose; it was only after they had left the boat and mounted a series of slippery stone steps to open a heavy wooden door that Philippa was able to appreciate the building's true size and significance.

They were standing under a huge concrete dome, almost 150 feet tall, with a central opening or *oculus*, open to the sky.

"I never heard of a library with a hole in the roof," said Groanin. "Don't the books get wet when it rains? I say, don't the books get wet?"

"The books are housed in vaults around the circumference," said Nimrod. "They never get wet. When it rains, the librarians simply sweep the water down the steps."

He led them across the marble floor to where a librarian appeared to be waiting for them. But on closer inspection, it turned out to be two librarians. One was about seven feet tall, and he was carrying the other in his arms, who couldn't have been more than about four feet tall and who — despite his clothes — was of Asian origin. Both of them were wearing black silk stockings, silver buckled shoes, black brocade coats, periwigs, and white lace collars. Philippa thought they looked as if they had stepped straight out of the eighteenth century. The big one said nothing while the little one did all the talking.

"This is Peng Win," Nimrod told Philippa. "The master of the library. Peng Win, this is my young niece, Philippa, and my butler, Groanin."

"Welcome to the Universe," said Peng Win, "which others call the Library of Attila. Do you like books, Philippa?"

"Of course," said Philippa.

"And you, Mr. Groanin?"

"I can stand a bit of poetry. And I read the odd thriller now and again."

Seeing Philippa's uncertain smile, Peng Win said, "You are wondering why my friend, Mr. Borges, carries me around. It's because I don't have the use of my legs and there are many stairs in this library. Many more than you can see. Don't worry, my child. He is very strong and I am very light." He looked at Nimrod. "If it's an old book you're after, then you've come to the right place, my friend."

From a deep flap pocket in his elegant coat he took out a small pad of paper and an ancient-looking pen, so that he might write down the name of the book.

"I'm looking for a book on Chinese zombies," said Nimrod. "At least I think I am. There may be some confusion as to whether 'zombie' was the word that was actually used."

"The Chinese word for a revenant or reanimated corpse is *wui wan xi.*" Peng Win drew the Chinese characters that made up this word on his little pad of paper. "From *wui* — 'something that turns'; *wan* — 'soul or a spirit'; and *xi* or *shi* — meaning 'corpse or carcass.'" Peng Win shook his head, which was the largest part of his body. "But there is no exact word for 'zombie,' not even in ancient Chinese. Regretfully, *wui wan xi* is the closest you might come. And I'm certain there is no book on this subject. Even here. Where the library is complete."

Nimrod thought for a moment, which left a sufficient space in the cool air of the library for Philippa to admire Peng Win's pen.

"I'm glad you like it," he said. "All of the pens in this library were made from the Sword of Mars that belonged to Attila the Hun himself. It was done so that all men might know that the pen is indeed mightier than the sword."

"I wonder," said Nimrod. "If 'zombie' is the wrong word, then perhaps there is a Chinese word that sounds a bit like 'zombie.' After all, the word was heard in China. So that might make sense. Is there such a word, Peng Win?"

Peng Win thought for a moment. "Yes," he said. "There is one possibility that might fit what you're looking for. *Dong Xi.* For one thing it sounds a little like 'zombie.'" He shrugged. "A little. But it is perhaps closer to the true meaning of what you were asking about, Nimrod, old friend. *Dong Xi* means 'fool,' or 'thing,' something less than human, anyway. It also means 'creature.' It's some time since I read it, but I believe there may be a reference to *Dong Xi* in the *Jade Book* of the Emperor Chengzong of Yuan China."

"Did you say *Jade Book*?" asked Nimrod.

"Yes. Why do you ask?"

"Only that of late there have been many thefts of jade," said Nimrod. "You must take care of this book."

"Mr. Borges guards the books," said Peng Win. "I should hate to think what he might do to someone attempting to steal one."

As big as a telephone directory, the book was a series of thirty jade tablets strung together with yellow silk straps, with the Chinese text engraved in gold.

"Chengzong was the grandson of Kublai Khan," explained Peng Win. "His reign, from 1294 to 1307, was an unremarkable one. That is, apart from this magnificent book, written by the emperor himself, which is an account of ancient Chinese myths and legends, demons, fairies, and other subversive spirits. He was, by all accounts, a very superstitious man."

With Mr. Borges seated silently at a great oak table, and Peng Win seated upon his lap, the Chinese librarian put on a pair of half-moon glasses, opened the book, and began to turn the tablets carefully, with Nimrod, Groanin, and Philippa looking around their shoulders.

"What have we here? Ah, yes. Here it is. The *Dong Xi*." The librarian's face darkened a little as he read what was written in the fabulous book. "'Beware the shaped form that is the *Dong Xi* for he is neither dead nor alive. Beware his heated touch. Beware his invisibility. Beware the *Dong Xi*. Beware the warrior devil. His name is mud for this thing is a dirt shadow of that which is created by God. He is the raw material of evil and the word of destruction lies under his tongue. He is clumsy, he is slow, but he will not rest. Shun the warrior devil as you would shun the foulest demon, for he is also harbinger of death. Leave him buried and let him not see the light of day. Drive the warrior devil back into the pit where he belongs. Return him to the dust. Pray that he never escapes, but if he does, then seek the bones of the great one called Ma Ko. Only he will know how to help you. Beware the *Dong Xi*. Beware the warrior devils.'" Peng Win looked up and took off his glasses. "That is all there is," he said.

"Sounds like it's enough," said Groanin. "Whatever it is, I shouldn't like to meet one of them devil warriors on a dark night."

"Who was the great one called Ma Ko that the Emperor Chengzong was referring to?" asked Philippa.

"I'm afraid I don't know," confessed Peng Win. "Possibly some Confucian philosopher now forgotten."

"Pity," said Philippa. "He sounded like a pretty useful kind of guy to know."

"Thank you, Peng Win," said Nimrod, who was then silent until they were in the boat and on their way back to the hotel.

"Let's hope that the warrior devil wasn't what John was talking about," said Philippa.

"No, indeed," agreed Nimrod. "We shall have to question Faustina about it in more detail when, eventually, she and John arrive in Venice."

"That poor, poor girl," said Groanin. "I bet she's dying to get back inside her own body. I hope this idea of yours works, sir. It'd be a crying shame to drag that lass all this way and find that it didn't. Especially after building all her hopes up. I can't imagine what kind of a peculiar torture that would be, to see your body and not be able to climb back inside it. If it were me and it didn't work, I think I'd drown myself in that there Grand Canal."

"She can hardly drown herself if she hasn't got a body," said Nimrod.

Groanin shrugged. "Well then, I don't know what I'd do. I suppose that once you're a ghost, life's already done its worst. All that's happened, all that's ever going to happen, has happened."

"Faustina's not dead, Groanin," said Philippa. "That's the point of bringing her to Venice. She's not dead."

"Aye, miss, but if she can't get back into that body of hers, she might as well be. I say, she might as well be dead."

"As usual, Groanin," said Nimrod, "you have a point. A very sharp one. Just like that cologne you've taken to wearing."

*　　*　　*

Back at the hotel they were surprised to find Finlay McCreeby waiting for them in the lobby. He stood up and smiled at them sheepishly. And since it was Finlay's body, John and Faustina thought it best to let him explain that there were in fact three of them squeezed tight inside it, and that they were anxious to proceed with the transfer of Faustina's spirit back into her own physical form as quickly as possible.

"It's just that it's getting a little crowded inside my skin," said Finlay.

"Two's company and three's a crowd," said Groanin. "Right enough."

"Is Faustina's body here in Venice?" asked Finlay.

"She's upstairs in bed," said Nimrod, and led Finlay toward the elevator. "By the way, how's your father?"

"Him?" Finlay shook his head. "We haven't talked since he had me turned into a falcon. You remember that?"

"It doesn't do to bear a grudge about these things," said Nimrod.

"You're probably right," said Finlay. "Now that we're even." And, with great mirth, he described the events at JFK Airport in New York that had seen his father arrested as a suspected terrorist. "He was pretty mad about it. Especially when he saw me. I imagine he must have guessed what happened." Finlay chuckled. "Still, I expect they'll let him go. Eventually."

Nimrod had a suite of rooms on the top floor with its own private terrace, plunge pool, a living room, dining room, and several bedrooms. Finlay was impressed. "This place is like a palace," he said.

"That's because that's exactly what it was," said Nimrod. "A palace once owned by the Gravellis, one of the richest families of Venice. Which reminds me. The Sleeping Beauty is in here."

"The Sleeping Beauty?" Finlay sounded puzzled.

Nimrod opened a door on which was hanging a DO NOT DISTURB sign and showed Finlay into a darkened bedroom where they had left Faustina's body in a semblance of sleep.

"That's what they were calling her in the place where we found her," explained Nimrod.

As soon as Finlay saw her lying there, which was the first clear look he'd had at Faustina since meeting her spirit back in New York, Finlay understood why John liked her so much. Which was embarrassing for Faustina since she was able to read all of his thoughts. And for John, who didn't like to be reminded of just how quickly he had fallen for her. Or to think that he might now have a rival.

"It was in some catacombs at a place called Malpensa, in southern Italy," added Nimrod. "They stole her body from the storeroom at Madame Tussaud's and were passing her off as a mummified corpse."

Faustina could restrain herself no longer. "As a what?" she said. Her own voice sounded strange in Finlay's mouth, and it rather unnerved Groanin to hear it.

"The monks at Malpensa have been preserving the dead bodies of the local people for centuries," said Nimrod. "And then putting them on display." Nimrod smiled drily. "You were their main tourist attraction, my dear."

"You mean I was in some horrible crypt with dead bodies?" said Faustina.

"More than some," said Groanin. "There were about four or five hundred of them, to be precise. Many were little better than skeletons, with hands and jaws falling off. It were a regular chamber of horrors, and no mistake. Made that other one in Madame Tussaud's look like a Sunday school. Creepiest thing I've ever seen, I reckon. Proper horror film, so it was, miss. I don't doubt I shall have nightmares about the place for weeks to come."

Groanin bent down and switched on the bedside light, intending to be helpful, but it had the opposite effect.

Faustina screamed.

"My hair!" she yelled. "What happened to my hair?"

"We think some of the tourists must have been helping themselves to cuttings of it," said Philippa. "Don't worry. It'll grow back."

Faustina shook her head and bit her lip. "But I look so pale. And what about those shadows under my eyes? I look like a vampire."

"What do you expect?" said Philippa. "You haven't seen the light of day for twelve years. Anyone would look a bit Gothic after what you've been through."

"I suppose so," admitted Faustina.

Faustina used Finlay's hand to peek under the blankets of the bed in which her body was lying, and then screamed out loud, which was enough to make Groanin drop a glass of water that he'd just finished pouring to help him recover from his earlier shock.

"My clothes," she yelled. "What happened to my clothes? Don't tell me I was in that freak show — with no clothes on?"

"You had clothes on in the catacombs," said Nimrod. "But Philippa took them off and threw them away."

"Your clothes were in a shocking state," explained Philippa. "All dusty and moth-eaten. And smelly, too. We couldn't very well just leave you in them. Not in a hotel like this."

"What am I going to wear?"

"Nimrod and I got you some clothes from the shops here in Venice," said Philippa. "I think we got your size right. They're in the closet."

Finlay opened the closet and ran his fingers over a variety of expensive-looking designer clothes. "They look — very nice," said Faustina, getting a grip on herself again. "I'm sure they'll be fine. Thank you, Philippa."

"Look, if you don't mind," said John, who was still feeling Faustina's blushes himself. "Can we get on with this? I think the sooner there are just us two guys in Finlay's body, the better. It doesn't feel right, Faustina being in here as well. Poor Finlay hasn't had a shower in two days. He doesn't want to. Not in front of Faustina."

"Isn't that just ridiculous?" said Faustina. "As if I care."

"You seemed to care quite a lot when I saw your naked body just now," Finlay told Faustina.

"That was different," insisted Faustina.

"John's right," said Nimrod. "Maybe we'd better get on with it. And then you can tell me about Mr. Rakshasas. And this 'zombie' of yours."

"You make it sound like I made up the zombie," said Faustina.

"Since you mention 'sound,'" said Nimrod, "how certain are you about the word you heard? Try to remember. It could be important."

"It was in the cavern where they were working," said Faustina. "In China. There was a man there, different from the rest. I couldn't say who he was except that he was wearing green armor."

"Green armor," said Nimrod.

"And it was him who used the word 'zombie,'" said Faustina. "But the word seemed appropriate somehow, considering the way these guys were behaving. You know: dead, staring eyes and shuffling like they were in some kind of a trance."

"The Chinese word for 'zombie' is something very different," said Nimrod. "It's *wui wan xi.*"

Faustina thought for a moment and shook her head. "That wasn't it."

"It's just that it's not a word you would expect to hear in China," said Nimrod. "'Zombie' is a corruption of the word *nzambi*, meaning 'god,' and comes from the Bantu language in Africa."

"There was definitely an *om* or an *ong* sound in the word," insisted Faustina. "And an *ee* sound on the end. I'm sure of that much."

"Is it possible that the word that you thought you heard was actually *Dong Xi*?" asked Nimrod.

Faustina frowned. "*Dong Xi.*" She repeated the word several times. "Yes, I think it might have been."

Nimrod was quiet for a moment.

"Well," Philippa said brightly. "We solved that mystery, anyway. At least now we know what we're dealing with. Sort of."

"What's a *Dong Xi*?" asked Faustina.

"A warrior devil," said Groanin.

"Like a zombie," said Philippa, "only worse. Much worse."

She told Finlay and Faustina and John about what they'd discovered in the Library of Attila. "Now all we have to do is figure out the part about the bones of the great one called Ma Ko," she said.

"Is that all?" muttered Groanin. "I say, is that all?"

CHAPTER 16

SMARTER THAN THE AVERAGE BEARD

From his case, Nimrod produced a small syringe containing about a tablespoonful of blood. Finlay eyed the syringe uncomfortably.

"You're not going to give me a shot, I hope," said Faustina. "Because I hate shots."

"No, no," said Nimrod, showing Finlay the syringe. "Look, there's no needle. Besides, this is blood. Your mother's blood, to be specific. It will help to make up for the part of you that was lost when Dr. Thingummy took a sample of the prime minister's blood when you were in possession of his body. It will give you a bit of color, I hope." He glanced around. "Groanin, pull those curtains, would you? And open the windows. Let's get some sunlight in here."

"I still can't believe I did that," said Faustina. "I mean, that I took possession of the prime minister."

"Call it youthful high spirits, shall we?" said Nimrod.

He sat down on the bed beside Faustina's body.

"Anyway, there was no real harm done."

"You think?" said Faustina. "I've been locked out of my body for twelve years."

"I meant to the prime minister," said Nimrod. "He's been grateful to me ever since. Offered me a knighthood, which I turned down, of course."

Everyone had crowded into the bedroom to see what would happen. Nimrod squirted a little of Jenny Sachertorte's blood into Faustina's mouth, and smeared some more onto her lips and cheeks, like rouge.

"I wish Mr. Rakshasas was here," he said. "I've never actually done this before. I know what to do, but . . ." He smeared some blood onto her forehead and her earlobes. "You only need a very little, apparently." He squirted the rest onto the gorge of her throat, just above her collarbone. "Italy's a hot country of course, so that should make things easier."

When the last of the blood was used, he sat back and waited to see the effect that was supposed to take place, and gradually, he did. They all did. Faustina's skin reacted as if her mother's blood had been poured onto a piece of blotting paper. Miraculously, all of it was absorbed, with not a trace of it left anywhere on her skin, and immediately restoring Faustina's pallor to that of a living, normal person. Philippa gasped a little.

"Crikey," said Finlay. "Are you sure she's a djinn and not a vampire?"

"Shut up," said Faustina.

Nimrod nodded with satisfaction. "Well, that seemed to be quite effective, wouldn't you say?"

"What happens now?" asked Finlay.

"Now it's up to you, Faustina," said Nimrod. "If Mr. Rakshasas was right, you should be able to step back into your body without a hitch."

"Here goes," said Faustina. "Wish me luck."

John and Finlay felt her slip out of Finlay's body, each breathing a sigh of relief that there was now a lot more space. But the hotel room was warm and no one saw what happened next. Faustina lay down on the bed beside her body and rolled back into it. For a moment she just lay there, enjoying the sensation of being herself once again. Everything felt just the way she remembered it. Except for the fact that her scalp itched terribly. She needed to wash her hair. She tried to lift her hand to scratch her head. And nothing happened. She tried to speak. Silence. Panicking slightly, she tried to get out of her body and go back in again, but found that she could not move. In fact, she was stuck.

"Well?" said Groanin. "Shouldn't something have happened by now?"

"Yes," admitted Nimrod. He glanced around at Finlay. "You did feel her leaving your body, didn't you?"

"Of course."

"John," said Nimrod, "slip out of Finlay and take a quick look around the room, in case she's out here and we can't see her."

John was gone for a couple of minutes and when he went back into Finlay, he told Nimrod that there was no sign of her. "I called her name several times," he said. "If she was a spirit she would have heard me."

"Then she must be back inside her own body," said Nimrod. "There's nowhere else she could have gone." He grabbed the bedside light and, bringing it near to her eyes, saw her pupils narrow slightly. "As I thought. She's back in her body. Only she's paralyzed." He stood up. "Groanin, pick her up and carry her out onto the terrace. Put her on the sun lounger in direct sunlight. That might do the trick."

Groanin wrapped Faustina in a sheet and carried her outside onto the jasmine-scented terrace. In the distance, a heavy church bell was tolling dolefully, as if marking the failure of their venture.

Nimrod leaned forward and searched her eyes again. "I imagine she can hear every word we say," he said. "But after all these years she can't move a muscle. Hardly surprising when you think about it. Mr. Rakshasas warned me that something like this might happen."

"Now what?" John asked anxiously. "What are we going to do?"

"We need to administer an anaphylactic shock," said

Nimrod. "Something that will cause her body to undergo a massive allergic reaction to something relatively harmless."

"You mean like peanut butter?" said Philippa.

"In a way," said Nimrod.

"But how? She can't eat anything."

Nimrod took out his wallet and handed Groanin a business card and a fistful of money. "Groanin, I want you to go back to the place where we left the car and then drive to Padua. Go to the address on that card and speak to a local pig farmer called Cesare Medici. Give him the money and tell him there's more if he comes straight back here with you. Tell him we urgently require the assistance of his little friends. He'll know exactly what you mean. You'll easily recognize him. He often wears a very long beard. Which reminds me; don't be nervous when you see him. He's a little bit eccentric."

"Eccentric?" said Groanin, feeling nervous already. "Eccentric how? Your idea of eccentric is a little bit more eccentric than what most folk would think of as eccentric. Your idea of an eccentric is very likely what most folk would call 'monster raving loony.'"

"Perhaps I ought to keep Groanin company," suggested John. "I mean, Finlay and I."

"Thank you, Finlay," said Groanin. "I mean, John. Whoever you are."

"Oh, very well," said Nimrod. "Philippa and I will go and look at the sights while we're waiting for you to come back.

Padua's not very far. It shouldn't take you more than two or three hours. Oh, yes. And make sure you buy some of the special honey. Cesare Medici's special honey is the best in the world."

From the hotel, Groanin and Finlay took a boat back to the parking lot in the east of the city, and then drove south to Padua, which is the oldest medieval town in Italy, and the setting for one of Shakespeare's least funny comedies. As Nimrod had predicted, it took about an hour to drive there and to find Cesare Medici's pig farm.

As they drove up to the house, Groanin rolled down the window and sniffed the air suspiciously. "I must say, it doesn't smell much like a pig farm," he said, looking at a sign on the gate that read PROFUMO VIETATO/PERFUME FORBID-DEN. "Now why would someone want to forbid the use of perfume on a pig farm? Pigs smelling the way they do."

"Maybe perfume irritates the pigs," suggested John. "Maybe you should stay in the car when we get there."

"If I was wearing perfume, I might agree with you," said Groanin. "But I'm not. I'm wearing Viola del Pensiero. A very expensive men's aftershave. I got it at a duty-free shop in Venice."

"Aftershave's just perfume for men, isn't it?" said John.

"It is not," Groanin said stiffly. "What kind of man do you take me for?"

"Anyway, it's not the pigs that smell," said Finlay. "It's the food they eat. I read that somewhere."

"I can't smell anything except Groanin's aftershave," John complained.

"It is pretty powerful, isn't it?" agreed Finlay.

"Leave off talking about my aftershave," said Groanin. "I say, leave off talking about it, will you?"

Groanin stopped the car in the farmyard and looked around. A small girl about six years old came out of the farmhouse and looked at them inquisitively. Groanin tried a big toothy smile on her. "*Signor Medici, per favore?*" he said in an excruciating Manchester Italian accent.

The little girl came over and pointed at a peach orchard.

"*Grazie,*" said Groanin. He and Finlay started to walk in the direction indicated. "So far, so good," he said. "Nothing much eccentric about her. Or here. This is right nice, this is. Just smell that peach blossom."

Finlay and John agreed. It really did seem like an idyllic spot. Birds were singing, bees were buzzing, distant church bells were ringing. It was Italy at its nicest. At the far end of the orchard they saw a man with an enormous brown beard. They waved to him but he did not wave back. But very slowly and stiffly he started to walk toward them as if there might have been something wrong with his back.

"Nimrod was right, you know," said Groanin. "Talk about Rumpelstiltskin. Signor Medici does have the most enormous beard. You could hide a battalion in a beard like that."

"Maybe it's my imagination," said Finlay as they neared the man. "But his beard seems to be *growing*."

And even as Finlay spoke, Signor Medici's thick brown beard appeared to grow at least another two or three inches, from his chest down past his belly button.

"It's not growing," said John. "It's moving."

"And it's not a beard at all," said Finlay. "At least not a beard that's made of hair. Those are bees on his face and chest. Honeybees." Smiling nervously at the man now standing immediately in front of them, he said, "Good afternoon. Signor Medici?"

"Yes?" said Signor Medici, speaking English. "What can I do for you?" Apart from his bush hat and his bee beard he was a hard man to describe.

The air was noisy with the loud humming of bees now. Groanin turned to leave and saw that they were surrounded by beehives. The peach orchard was full of them.

"No, I wouldn't make any sudden moves, if I were you, Englishman," said Signor Medici. Even as he spoke, his beard was getting smaller and the bees were landing on Groanin's shoulders. "In fact, you would be well advised to keep quite still and not to panic. They won't harm you if you keep calm, okay?"

Groanin closed his eyes as a swarm of about fifty thousand bees settled on his double chin and his fat neck. "Blimey," he muttered, and blew one away from his mouth. "Help."

"I wouldn't speak, either," said Signor Medici. "In case they go in your mouth and you swallow one. Internal stings are always the worst. You must be wearing some kind of aftershave."

"And how," said Finlay. "He reeks of the stuff. Viola del Pensiero, I think he said it was, if that helps at all."

"That explains it," said Signor Medici. "Did you not see the sign on the gate? The one that says 'Perfume Forbidden.'"

"He thought that you meant women's perfume," said Finlay, trying to ignore the solitary bee that was crawling in his hair. He could only imagine what Groanin was feeling like, covered with bees. Groanin whimpered quietly as Signor Medici sniffed the air around him.

"Can you help him out here, Signor Medici?" asked Finlay.

"Your friend," said Signor Medici. "He smells just like the peach blossom." He chuckled. "That's what they like, my little friends. The smell of the peach blossom." The chuckle turned into a shrug. "He'll be all right, your friend, if he no make any sudden moves. Bees, they no like sudden moves. But I'll fix him, no problem."

Now that the bees had left Signor Medici's face, Finlay and John could see he was clean-shaven and completely unharmed by the bees. A small, blue-eyed man, with a round face that belonged in a Warner Brothers cartoon. He went to one of the many beehives and took out a frame containing a whole honeycomb. He put this in a large cardboard box and then laid it in front of Groanin. Then, using his hands,

Signor Medici started to gently brush the bees into the box and, gradually, Groanin lost his buzzing beard.

"Thank goodness for that," he said. "I thought I was toast. I say, I thought I was toast."

"That would be toast and honey, I imagine," said Finlay.

"You can laugh, young man," Groanin said angrily, "but it's not so comical when you're the one with a crowd of bees on your mug. I thought my time had come."

"My little friends, they like your perfume," said Signor Medici. "That's what the sign on the gate is for. Can't you read English?"

So those were the little friends that Nimrod had meant, thought John. *Bees. But what could bees do for Faustina? Unless he meant . . .*

"There's nothing wrong with my English," insisted Groanin. "For one thing, I'm as English as bread and butter. And for another, that's not perfume I'm wearing." Groanin mopped his large, heavily perspiring head with a handkerchief. "Not anymore. That's the sweat of sheer terror, Signor Medici."

"Why did you come here, anyway?" asked Signor Medici.

"We came on an errand of mercy," said Finlay. "Our friend in Venice has an urgent need of an anaphylactic shock. We were told your little friends might help."

"You mean it's some bees we're after?" Groanin asked Finlay.

"*Sì, sì,*" said Signor Medici. "As well as a beekeeper, I am a registered bee therapist. Bee venom is good for all kinds of ailments: poor circulation, arthritis, asthma, skin disorders, depression."

"Depression?" said Groanin. "How's that work then?"

"If you get stung a few times you don't think so much about your other problems," said Signor Medici. "Did you bring money?"

Groanin handed him a wad of cash. The Italian counted it and nodded.

"Okay. I find some of my little friends, put them in a box, and then we go."

"Can we get some special honey, too, please?" asked Finlay.

"Special honey? What do you know about my special honey?"

"Nothing," said Finlay. "Just that we were told to make sure we bought some."

Signor Medici counted the money again. "Okay. You give me enough. I will give you some special honey as well."

"What's so special about it?" Groanin asked.

Signor Medici laughed. "I will tell you in the car."

CHAPTER 17

FLOAT LIKE A BUTTERFLY...

While Groanin, Finlay, and John were traveling to and from Padua, Nimrod and Philippa went to the Piazza San Marco, which is the largest public space in Venice — a square with a famous church, a palace, a tall redbrick tower, lots of cafés, open-air orchestras, hundreds of well-fed pigeons, and thousands of tourists.

"Do you think Faustina will be all right where we left her?" Philippa asked Nimrod. "Lying on the terrace."

"If the maid comes, she'll just assume she's sunbathing," said Nimrod. "Besides, after twelve years inside, the hot sun will do her good. It's only mundanes who get sunstroke."

He bought a guidebook that he gave to Philippa. "Here," he said. "So you'll know what you're looking at when you go sightseeing."

"Aren't you coming, too?" she asked him.

"No," he said flatly. "For one thing, I've seen everything many times already. And for another, I want to do some serious thinking."

He sat down outside the Caffé Florian and ordered afternoon tea. Philippa didn't like tea very much. So, resisting the temptation to tell Nimrod he was being pompous, Philippa did as she was told, although it wasn't long before she almost wished she hadn't. Indeed, it wasn't very long before she almost wished she were somewhere else other than the Piazza San Marco. The heat didn't bother her. Extreme heat never bothers djinn very much. But the huge numbers of people did make her a little annoyed because it seemed that everyone was intent on seeing the same things she wanted to see. She had to wait in a long line to see the Doge's Palace, and another even longer line to go up the bell tower. She had never seen so many tourists, and from so many different countries. She began to understand why Nimrod didn't want to see anything, just to sit outside a café and drink tea and think. Even from the top of the 323-foot-tall tower, it was easy to see him in his red suit. He was, she realized with a smile, just about the easiest person to see in the whole of Venice.

The line for St. Mark's Church was especially long, and Philippa found herself in the middle of a large tour group of elderly Chinese tourists. All of them were friendly and polite and she was soon reproaching herself for originally wishing they would all disappear. Few of them spoke any English, however, and if she'd had any djinn power she might have wished she could speak Chinese so that she might say something nice to them as they shuffled along the front of the magnificent historic old church to the entrance door at the side.

After a while, her mind wandered a little and she found herself thinking about her mother and wondering how she was and hoping that Faustina might still recover in time for her to make it to Babylon and take over as the next Blue Djinn. Mrs. Trump was also in her thoughts; it was very worrying that she was still in a coma. Most worrying of all, perhaps, was the disappearance of Mr. Rakshasas. Was he dead, as John seemed to think? She hadn't dared to ask Nimrod what he thought. And she decided that maybe that was what he was thinking about: Mr. Rakshasas and the warrior devils. Quite probably he was trying to figure out the identity of the mysterious Ma Ko who had been mentioned in the emperor's *Jade Book*.

That was when she heard it.

Not once but several times. And snapping out of her hot afternoon reverie, she almost felt like pinching herself as she thought she heard one of the Chinese tourists use the words "Ma Ko." Instead, she tapped the shoulder of the Chinese man standing in front of her and smiled at him. He bowed politely back to her.

"Ma Ko?" she said, and shrugged, trying to indicate that she didn't know what it was.

"Ma Ko," he said, and grinned.

This time she threw up her hands. "Ma Ko? What is that?"

The Chinese man pointed to the church. "Ma Ko," he said.

"What is Ma Ko? A church?"

"Ma Ko." More pointing.

Philippa shook her head. The Chinese man's guidebook was the same as Philippa's, except that hers was in English. He took her book, turned to the relevant page detailing St. Mark's Church, and pointed to a mosaic picture of St. Mark.

"Ma Ko," he repeated.

"You mean Mark?" she said. "St. Mark?"

The Chinese man nodded. "Ma Ko," he said.

Another Chinese man was being pushed back along the line toward her. He was all teeth and glasses, his face one huge smile. It seemed he spoke some English. "Ma Ko?" he said. "That's how we say 'Mark' in Chinese. Ma Ko or sometimes Ma Ho, depending where you come from."

Philippa thanked him several times so that he wouldn't think that she was rude. Then she ran off to find Nimrod.

She found him where she'd left him, his eyes closed, his curious, intelligent face with its slightly crooked nose angled toward the sun like a satellite dish. On the table were the remains of a plate of sandwiches, scones, cakes, and several pots of tea. Pulling up a chair and flicking away a pigeon with Nimrod's napkin, she sat down, ate a little cake, and stared at him while trying to restrain the triumph she was feeling.

"How's the thinking coming along?" she said.

He opened his eyes slowly as if he had been asleep. "I was thinking about poor Mr. Rakshasas," he said. "To be absorbed, at his age. It's most worrying." He let out a sigh and drank some tea. "What's the matter with you? You look like you just found a pearl in an oyster."

"I did," she said. "In a manner of speaking. Ma Ko. I know who it is. You're looking at it."

Nimrod kept on thinking for a moment. Then he smacked his forehead hard with the flat of his hand. It sounded as loud as if someone had struck him in anger, and an amorous couple drinking champagne at the next table gave Philippa a funny look as if they suspected her of doing it.

"Of course," groaned Nimrod. "Saint Mark. How could I have been so stupid? And me a Grand Commander of the Order of St. Mark, too. Light my lamp, however did you guess?"

Philippa told him about all the Chinese people who were in the line to get into the church, and how she had overheard their conversations about Ma Ko.

He tutted loudly, exasperated with himself. "I'm afraid this business with Mr. Rakshasas has quite destroyed my powers of concentration," he said.

"According to my guidebook," said Philippa, "the church contains the bones of St. Mark."

"That's what they say," said Nimrod.

"Those must be the bones mentioned by the emperor in that *Jade Book*." She pointed to a picture in the book. "Look. That's the sarcophagus where he's buried."

Nimrod was looking doubtful.

"What?" she demanded. "Isn't the book right?"

"Oh, the book's right insofar as that is certainly what is claimed," said Nimrod. "But many people, myself included, think the body of the saint perished in the great fire of 976. It was certainly missing in 1094 when the Venetian authorities conducted a search for it. A few months later, there was a small earthquake and, it is believed, the saint's body was miraculously found again."

"Miraculously?"

"Not to say conveniently." Nimrod shrugged. "Wouldn't you agree?"

"So the bones aren't there at all? Is that what you're saying?"

"No, they might actually be there," said Nimrod. "Somewhere. Just not in that sarcophagus beneath the high altar. My own theory is that they are most likely lying rather more anonymously somewhere in the church reliquary. That's a place where all sorts of holy relics are kept. Bones, teeth, hair, bits of wood, blood, you name it. People used to claim all sorts of bits and pieces had come from one saint or another. Relics were big business back in the Middle Ages. The reliquary in St. Mark's is one of the biggest and oldest in the world. My guess is that if the bones are in there, that's where we'll find them. If the Emperor Chengzong and his

Jade Book is right, we're going to need them when we go to China."

"Are we going to China?" asked Philippa.

"Just as soon as we've helped Faustina," said Nimrod. "I don't doubt she's right, too — that something strange is happening in the world of spirit that we need to find out more about."

"The trick is letting the bee sting without killing the bee," said Signor Medici.

"Is that possible?" asked Nimrod.

"If you know what you are doing," he said.

"Sorry about this, Faustina," said Nimrod, "but it's for your own good, I think."

"I've never actually revived someone with the bee sting before," confessed Signor Medici. "This is a first for me. Where would you like the bee to sting her?" And holding one of his "little friends" with a pair of tweezers, Cesare Medici sat down on the sun lounger beside Faustina's immobile body. "On her back? On her shoulder? Please. You say where."

"On her earlobe," said Nimrod. "That's what Mr. Rakshasas told me, anyway."

"Oh, I say," said Groanin, covering his eyes, "I don't know where to look."

"On her earlobe?" repeated Signor Medici.

Nimrod nodded.

Signor Medici smiled and said something in Italian that Philippa took to be the Italian word for "earlobe." And still holding the bee by the head with the tweezers, he tapped it on the thorax a couple of times just to make it mad enough to sting. The bee did its job, stinging her almost immediately, and soon there was a livid red mark on Faustina's earlobe.

"Ouch," said Philippa, biting her lip.

Faustina twitched, quite noticeably, it seemed to Philippa, and then remained motionless.

"Two bees or not two bees," said Nimrod. "That is the question. Once more I think, Signor Medici. On the other earlobe this time."

The Italian nodded and extracted another bee from the little tackle box he had brought from Padua. Philippa had looked at it while he was going about his work with the tweezers; each bee lived in its own little glass-topped compartment with a few drops of honey to feed it. Like a little prisoner.

The second sting produced a much more violent twitch of Faustina's head, as if someone had passed a strong current of electricity through her. Like a frog in some school biology experiment. That was what Philippa thought. She'd always hated that part of doing biology.

"Ouch," said Philippa, more loudly this time

"I do bee-lieve we're almost there now," said Nimrod. "One more should do it. This time, on her bee-hind. No, perhaps not. On the inside of her wrist, I think, Signor Medici."

"I don't know how you can joke about this, Uncle Nimrod," said Philippa. "That looks painful."

"Okay," said Signor Medici. "Now I use my special bee. This bee, he's a very tough bee. Very angry. Got a real attitude problem. Not sweet and friendly like most of my bees. He doesn't even like honey. He doesn't like anything. It's why I keep him in a separate box. I call him Silvio."

From another box he took out a bee much larger than the other two, which had a buzz that sounded like a small chain saw.

Philippa looked at the bee and winced as Signor Medici held the bee on Faustina's wrist and then flicked it casually. The bee buzzed angrily, bent his abdomen down, braced himself against the flesh with his hind legs, and then stabbed his stinger into the girl's wrist with all his strength, delivering, for good measure, an extra amount of bee venom.

"Yarooo!"

Faustina let out a loud shriek, grabbed her wrist and then her earlobes with both hands, which knocked the tweezers out of Signor Medici's hands. Silvio, the bee, now free from his owner's control, settled on Faustina's forearm and then stung again. And then again.

"Yarooo!"

Faustina jumped up from the sun lounger, scrambled up onto the high balcony, and, seeing the bee come after her a fourth time, launched herself off the side of the hotel in an elegant swan dive straight down into the waters of the Grand Canal.

Nimrod and Philippa ran to the edge and looked over just in time to see Faustina rise to the surface and swim to the side of the canal. A small crowd gathered to watch. And quite quickly, it seemed to Philippa, it grew even larger. She grabbed a terry cloth robe and ran out of the door and downstairs, ready to save Faustina's blushes. Nimrod laughed loudly.

"A result, I think, Signor Medici," said Nimrod. "Mission accomplished. Well done, sir. Well done."

Signor Medici looked around and then shrugged. "I lost my best bee," he said unhappily.

Nimrod handed him another handful of banknotes. "Here," he said. "Get yourself a hiveful."

CHAPTER 18

STING LIKE A BEE

Faustina walked back into the hotel with Philippa. She hardly cared about the sensational effect her appearance in the water had worked on the gondoliers — Venice's famous boatmen — who were already calling her "*la sirena americana*," which is Italian for "American mermaid." All that mattered was that she was in her own skin again and that everything felt just great. She was deliriously happy. Even her dip in the Grand Canal had been enjoyable — especially as it had relieved the pain of five bee stings. What was even better was the realization that the djinn power was back in her body. Just feeling the hot Venetian sun on her face had told her that much.

They were walking toward the elevator when Faustina heard a voice she recognized.

"Faustina?"

"Mom?"

Jenny Sachertorte hugged the daughter she hadn't seen for twelve years and tried to control her tears. Faustina hugged her back, hardly caring if she got her mother wet or not. She was so happy to see her.

"Mom, what are you doing here?"

"Did you think I could stay away from my own daughter?"

"I was so mad at you," said Faustina. "I'm sorry."

"I know," said Jenny Sachertorte. "So am I."

"It wasn't your fault. What happened, with Dybbuk. I know that now. It wasn't your fault. I'm sorry I blamed you. I'm sorry I did what I did to the British prime minister."

"Let's talk about it later."

"But how did you know I was here?" asked Faustina.

"Nimrod, of course," said Dr. Sachertorte. "As soon as he heard your spirit had been found, he telephoned me. At first, I didn't dare come in case it didn't work. I mean, your getting back inside your own body. But then I realized I had to come, regardless of what happened."

"It very nearly didn't work," said Faustina, laughing. "When I got back in my body I sort of seized up. I couldn't move a muscle. I could hear and see everything around me, but I was paralyzed. But for the help of some bees I might still be that way."

"Bees?"

In the elevator, Faustina and Philippa explained about Signor Medici and his bee therapy.

"I never imagined I could be so happy to have my daughter stung by a bee," said Dr. Sachertorte.

"That's the way I feel about it, too." Faustina laughed out loud and hugged her mother again.

In Nimrod's suite of rooms, they found him drinking champagne in celebration of Faustina's restoration to good djinn health. Groanin was reading his newspaper and sipping a cup of tea. Finlay and John were watching television. The two boys greeted Faustina coolly because each was trying to pretend to the other that he didn't feel anything very much for her, but failing miserably because, of course, it's impossible to keep anything secret when two different people are sharing one physical body. And it goes without saying, Faustina knew that, too.

Nimrod stood up and embraced Dr. Sachertorte fondly. "It looks as if you have a daughter again," he said.

"Isn't it wonderful?" said Dr. Sachertorte.

"I thought you'd come a cropper, my lass, when you jumped off that balcony," said Groanin. "Must be thirty feet down to that canal. Water's absolutely filthy, of course. I mean, you do know that all the lavatories in Venice get emptied straight into it. That's why it smells the way it does. If I were you, miss, I'd have me stomach pumped immediately. Just in case you pick up some kind of tummy bug. Mind you, having said that, it's lucky you jumped off that side and landed in the canal. The other side, you'd have landed in the street. All that fuss over a few bee stings. I never saw the like."

"No harm done," said Nimrod. "That's the main thing."

"I was so sorry to hear about Mr. Rakshasas," Dr. Sachertorte told Nimrod. "Is there no hope?"

"I'm afraid we shan't know that," said Nimrod, "until we have discovered more about the being that absorbed him in the spirit world."

"Does that mean you're going back to New York?"

"Actually, no," said Nimrod. "I think we may have to stay here in Venice for a while. To do some further research."

"That's great," said Finlay. "I love Venice. I think Venice is cool."

"Do you?" murmured Groanin. His nose wrinkled with displeasure and, producing a small bottle from his jacket pocket, he dabbed some more aftershave behind his ears.

"How about it, Faustina?" asked Finlay. "Are you going to stay here in Venice with us for a while?"

"I'm afraid not," said Faustina. "I have other plans, as I think you already know."

"Oh, yeah," said Finlay. "Babylon. I forgot."

"Why don't you come and visit me when I'm the Blue Djinn?" she asked. "At my official residence in Berlin."

"Who, me?" said Finlay.

"Both of you."

"Is that allowed?" John asked. "I mean, I thought guys weren't allowed to visit with the Blue Djinn."

"That's only true in Babylon, John," said Faustina. "Besides, I intend to make some changes when I'm supreme djinn. Ayesha was in charge for so long that people have quite forgotten what it was like before her. You see, a lot of what we believe about being Blue Djinn came from her. And it doesn't have to be that way. Living beyond good and evil is one thing. Being that way is quite another. I did quite a bit of research on the subject."

"But I was there," said Philippa, "in Babylon. At one point, I thought I was going to be the Blue Djinn myself. I remember the effect the place had on me. I hardly recognized John when he showed up to rescue me."

"It's true," said John. "She was a real pig."

"I worked out a way for none of that to affect me."

"This should be interesting," said Nimrod, exchanging a glance with Dr. Sachertorte.

"I've learned a lot while I've been out of my body for twelve years. I spent two whole years studying the *Baghdad Rules*. Not the *Shorter Baghdad Rules*, compiled by Mr. Rakshasas, but the longer version. All two hundred volumes. If Ayesha had ever read them, she would have discovered that there's plenty in them about how a female djinn must spend thirty days in Iravotum if she is physically to become the Blue Djinn of Babylon. But there's nothing that says her spirit has to stay there, too. It's so obvious that I wonder why someone didn't think of it earlier."

"Are you suggesting that your spirit could be elsewhere?" said Nimrod. "That my mother could have been the Blue Djinn and still have managed to keep some warm feelings for my sister, Layla, and me?"

"I'm not suggesting it," said Faustina, "I'm stating it as a fact. As soon as I get there I'm going to leave my body and take my spirit somewhere else, for thirty days. I do believe I might go to Mount Olympus. I've heard it's very good for spirits there."

"So you're saying that while your body might be affected," said Nimrod, "your spirit can remain unchanged."

"That's exactly right. I can be the Blue Djinn without having to change very much at all. Isn't that marvelous?"

"But what about your ability to be impartial in the making of judgments between good and evil?" said Nimrod.

"Judges manage it all right," said Faustina. "They can seem totally inhuman in their administration of the law without actually being inhuman. They've been doing it for centuries."

"So you *can* have your cake and eat it, too," said Nimrod.

"Yes, isn't it wonderful?" Faustina smiled at Philippa and then at Finlay/John. "Which is why you guys can come and stay with me in Berlin."

"Great," said the three children.

"Well, I must say that's the best news I've heard all day," said Nimrod. He looked at Jenny Sachertorte. "Did you know any of this, Jenny?"

"No. It's the first time I heard of it." Dr. Sachertorte shook her head. "If only someone had discovered all of this sooner. You and Layla might have been spared the loss of your own mother."

"Yes," said Nimrod quietly.

"Which reminds me," said Faustina, "I had better leave right away if I'm going to stop Layla from becoming the Blue Djinn instead of me. You know, it's a pity Dybbuk's not here. I'd like to have seen him again before I left."

"You can see him now," said John, pointing with Finlay's hand at the TV. "There he is."

Everyone moved slowly toward the TV and watched as Jonathan Tarot, wearing a fabulous black, diamond-encrusted jumpsuit, performed a spectacular feat of close-up magic, making a mouse appear in a girl's hand. The studio audience applauded with huge enthusiasm.

"Except that he's not calling himself 'Dybbuk' these days," said John. "Now he's called Jonathan Tarot. And he's a huge star. You can hardly open a magazine or a newspaper without seeing his face."

Nimrod shook his head sadly. "Dybbuk, Dybbuk," he said with a sigh.

"I tried to talk him out of it," said Jenny Sachertorte. "But he wouldn't listen. I even tried to put a binding on him. But he's become too powerful for me to control, Nimrod."

"Djinn power was always strong in him," said Nimrod. "Stronger than his judgment."

"What did you expect?" said Dr. Sachertorte. "Look who his father is." She smiled apologetically at Faustina.

"He makes it look like it's a real illusion," said John. "If you know what I mean. Like it's just a trick. A good trick. But a trick nonetheless."

"If people ever thought it was real," said Philippa, "they'd probably start to question their whole world."

"Wise words, Philippa," said Nimrod. "That is the real danger of Dybbuk doing what he's doing. That he'll go too far and they'll find out that it's not an illusion at all."

As they watched, the TV cameraman cut away to a shot of the audience applauding a feat of magic that was remarkable to anyone but another djinn. In the audience was a fair-haired man with a chin beard who was wearing a curious white jacket. It was Adam Apollonius.

"He doesn't seem to realize the dangers of such profligate use of his djinn power," said Nimrod. "Using it all the time like that, on cheap conjuring tricks, will have serious consequences."

"Don't you think I told him that?" said Dr. Sachertorte. "He said he didn't care. And that it's his life, to do with as he wants." She sighed. "What's a mother to do? I sure don't know. It's not like I can threaten him with his father anymore. Especially now that he knows his father is not his father. He doesn't seem to care about what I say anymore. And after all I've done for him."

Everyone, apart from Groanin, continued to stare at the TV in silence.

"Hey," said Faustina. "That's the man from the cavern with the pyramid and the silver lake. The one I heard use the words *Dong Xi*." She waved her hand at the studio audience on the TV screen. "Him."

Faustina pointed to the man sitting next to Adam Apollonius. Almost immediately, the camera cut back to a smiling Dybbuk and only Philippa was quick enough to see the hard-looking young man to whom Faustina was pointing and to realize that she, too, had seen him before. At the Djinnversoctoannular Tournament in New York the previous Christmas. She most vividly remembered him for the amount of serious swearing he'd done after she'd defeated him in the first round. Her ears started to burn again as she recalled the many unpleasant things he had called her on his way out of the Algonquin Hotel.

Adam Apollonius had been sitting next to Rudyard Teer, one of the sons of Iblis the Ifrit, and half brother to Dybbuk. Not only that, but Philippa had half an idea that Teer had been sitting in front of another equally unpleasant Ifrit: Palis the Footlicker. She told all this to Nimrod and Dr. Sachertorte.

"Now I'm really worried," admitted Dr. Sachertorte.

"Calm yourself, dear lady," said Nimrod. "Calm yourself. Things may not be quite what they appear."

"Nimrod's quite right, Dr. Sachertorte," said Groanin. "I say, there's no point in getting upset by something that might turn out to be nothing at all. It's perfectly possible that these villains were there quite by chance. On the other hand, it may be that there is some evil design behind their being in that audience. That Dybbuk is in grave and mortal danger, right enough. But I wouldn't start worrying about that until you have to. I have found — yarooo!" A very red-faced Groanin leaped out of his armchair, threw down his newspaper, and, grimacing with pain, sprinted into the bathroom, slamming the door firmly shut behind him.

"Well, that's a relief, I must say," said Dr. Sachertorte.

"What did he say he'd found?" asked John.

"I think he just found Signor Medici's missing bee," said Philippa, trying not to laugh.

CHAPTER 19

THE TWO MARCOS

The Reliquary Room in St. Mark's Church was at the top of the building, in a dusty-looking room that was more like a prison cell in a castle tower. There was a high, barred window, and around the walls was a series of outsized wooden filing cabinets with deep drawers, in alphabetical order, according to the names of the saints whose relics were supposed to be kept in them.

The Keeper of the Relics was an elderly American nun by the name of Sister Cristina, who John thought looked like a bit of a relic herself. But he thought she must have been fitter than she looked: There were two hundred steps from the ground-floor entrance to the Reliquary Room, and Finlay's body was wheezing breathlessly by the time Nimrod and the children had climbed all the way up there.

Groanin had chosen to stay at the hotel, nursing a large bee sting on the top of his head that made it look like the red light on an ambulance. He was sulking because John and

Finlay thought it was very amusing to make noises like a siren every time he came into the room. Faustina had gone to Babylon by whirlwind. Her mother, Jenny Sachertorte, had taken a plane back to the United States after a very emotional good-bye scene with her daughter.

Sister Cristina was helpful and informative as was only to be expected given Nimrod's high status as a Knight Commander of the Order of St. Mark. But she was also quite honest about the dubious origins of many of the Reliquary's so-called relics.

"I don't know why we keep some of this junk," she confessed. "Really, I don't. Because that's what most of it is: junk. We've got everything from the toenails of St. Blaise to the earwax of St. Mungo. At my last count, we had thirty-three of the fingers of St. Anthony, fifteen toes belonging to St. Munditia, six thigh bones of St. Bartholomew, and three skulls of St. Barnabas. Teeth are in the greatest supply. We could probably replace half of the dentures in Italy with the teeth we have here. There are boxes full of them."

"What about St. Mark?" asked Nimrod. "Do you have any of his bits and pieces?"

Sister Cristina smiled. "You mean you don't believe that he's underneath our high altar?"

"I think, like a lot of people, I have my doubts," admitted Nimrod.

Sister Cristina shrugged and went over to a drawer with the word MARCO painted neatly on the outside. She opened the drawer and pointed at a jumble of bones, teeth, vials of blood, locks of hair, fingernails, toenails, arm and leg bones, and vertebrae. Wrapped in a piece of pearled velvet was a skull, complete with glass eyes and jeweled teeth. There was even a golden leg that allegedly contained Mark's femur.

"Quite a choice, isn't there?" said Sister Cristina. "We had most of these things carbon-dated a while back and none of it's older than a thousand years. In other words, most of this stuff is fake. But we keep it because it's a part of our history, from a time when relics mattered to people. When the faithful thought they had the power to heal them."

"Is there anything you keep here that you think really might have genuine power?" asked Philippa.

Sister Cristina thought for a moment.

"Yes, there is," she said. "Funnily enough, these are also supposed to be relics of St. Mark. And although they can't possibly be genuine, the box they're in, which is finely crafted and too big for the drawer, does emit a sort of power or energy, depending on what you want to call it. I find it most curious."

"Then why do you say these relics can't be genuine?" asked Philippa.

"Because we had them carbon-dated, as well. To find out how old they really are. From books, we know that St. Mark died in Alexandria during the eighth year of the Roman Emperor Nero, in about A.D. 63. But this particular skeleton has been dated to the early fourteenth century. About 1320. So you see, it can't possibly be that of St. Mark."

"Yes, I take your point," said Nimrod. "1320. I wonder."

"There's another thing," said Sister Cristina. "There are Chinese characters carved and inlaid with gold on every one of the two hundred and five bones."

"Did you say two hundred and five?"

"Exactly two hundred and five," repeated Sister Cristina.

"What kind of Chinese characters?" asked Nimrod.

"Numbers," said Sister Cristina. "Of course, there's no record of St. Mark ever having been to China. Egypt and Jerusalem are as far east as he ever traveled. So it simply can't be him, can it?"

"No. All the same, if you don't mind I would like to take a look at this particular skeleton," said Nimrod. "Just to satisfy my own curiosity."

Sister Cristina unlocked a large closet, moved a selection of bishop's miters, shepherd's staffs, crucifixion crossbeams, Roman pikes and spears, and longbows, and dragged out, along the floor, a dusty-looking wooden box that could have held a dozen rifles. Finlay, whose offer of help had been politely declined, was surprised at the strength of the old nun.

"It's kind of you to have offered, but this is my work, you see," she explained to Finlay.

She opened the box to reveal an ornate, polished brass chest that was inlaid with various Chinese numbers. "That's the name of St. Mark there, in Chinese," said Sister Cristina, pointing to an ivory plate mounted on the foot of the chest. "At least that's what the people who speak Chinese have told us it is." She laughed. "Although for all I know, it might say 'Made in Taiwan.'"

Nimrod ran his fingers across the ivory nameplate and the two Chinese characters that constituted "Mark."

Sister Cristina had been right, thought Nimrod. His fingertips detected that the box was charged with a sort of strange energy, but it was the design on the lid of the box that commanded his immediate attention.

"As you can see, it's a diagram of the human skeleton," said Sister Cristina. "Look at the way all of the bones are identified. Fascinating, isn't it?"

"Like something a medical student would use," agreed Philippa.

Then the telephone rang, and Sister Cristina went to answer it.

"It's a lot more than that, I think," Nimrod said quietly, so the old nun would not hear him. "Each bone seems to correspond with a number on this other design." He pointed to a square of thirty-six numbers that had been carved into the lid of the chest immediately above the head of the skeleton.

"What is that?" asked Philippa.

"If I'm not mistaken," said Nimrod, "that's a Chinese magic square. It's said the magic square was invented by a powerful djinn many centuries ago. And squares like this were often placed under the foundation stones of houses in

China to bring good luck. But they were also sometimes used to make a discrimens. You know, a wish that can exist independently of a djinn. Sometimes good and sometimes bad. And for an indefinite length of time. Only I've never ever heard of one lasting as long as this before."

"But what does it do?" asked Finlay.

"If only Mr. Rakshasas were here," said Nimrod. "He knows much more about these things than I do. I *think*, this is something called a *chuan dai zhe*. I'm not quite sure exactly what that means. Only that this box of bones has been designed to deliver some kind of message. I believe you have to draw a magic square on the floor, with all the numbers in the correct position, and then place each bone on the square indicated in the diagram. The message can then be delivered. *In person*."

"You mean the person whose bones these are?" said Philippa.

"Exactly so," said Nimrod.

"You're kidding," said Finlay. "A few lousy numbers can do all that?"

"On the contrary," said Nimrod. "Numbers are the basis of all matter. And therefore the basis of all mind over matter, too."

"It would certainly explain why the *Jade Book* mentioned Mark's bones specifically," said John.

"Indeed, it would," agreed Nimrod.

"But who is this Mark if it's not *St.* Mark?" asked Philippa.

"1320, Venice, China," said Nimrod. "Can't you guess? Goodness, what do they teach you in schools these days?"

Sister Cristina was winding up her telephone call.

"The question is," said Nimrod, "by what subterfuge are we to listen to the messenger without dear old Sister Cristina seeing him, too? It could prove to be a bit of a shock for her. She might even be frightened. It's not every day you get a message delivered by someone who's been dead for almost seven hundred years."

"Why not just zap her somewhere else?" said Finlay. "You're a djinn, after all."

"At her age?" said Nimrod. "I think not."

"How about one of us takes your cell phone outside," said John. "And then telephones her in here to say there's an urgent package for her at the front door. It takes fifteen minutes to get up here. There and back. She could be gone for as long as thirty minutes. More than enough time."

Nimrod bit his lip. "I dislike putting an old lady to the kind of effort you describe, John," he said. "However, I can see no practical alternative that does not involve the use of djinn power."

"She does seem to be very fit," added Philippa, by way of an excuse for what they were contemplating.

"I suppose it had better be me that makes the call," said Nimrod, "since I speak Italian."

Sister Cristina finished her call. "Now then," she said. "Where was I?"

Nimrod smiled at her politely. "Would you excuse me for one minute?"

He left the room and a minute later the telephone rang in the reliquary. Sister Cristina answered it, listened, made a loud tutting noise, spoke crossly in Italian, and then put the phone down. Nimrod came back into the room looking more than a little guilty, but Sister Cristina did not suspect that he was behind the telephone call; and, having excused herself "for as long as it takes me to go all the way down there and come back up again," she went out of the room, leaving Nimrod, Philippa, and Finlay/John alone with the brass chest of bones.

"Anyone got a stick of chalk?" asked Nimrod.

No one did, and so Nimrod used djinn power to make a piece appear in his hand. With this, he got down on his hands and knees and set about drawing the magic square of China on the stone floor of St. Mark's reliquary.

First, Nimrod drew a grid of thirty-six squares, which left Philippa feeling very impressed that her uncle was so good at drawing perfect straight lines. "Actually, it's a gift that all djinn are born with," murmured Nimrod. "The ability to draw perfectly straight lines and perfect circles. Much more difficult than you'd think. It's something humans can't do at all."

"Very useful, I imagine," said Finlay, and made a face.

"I suppose I had better make this quite a large square," said Nimrod, "given that each square is going to have five or six bones in it."

When the grid was completed, he started to fill in the numbers, from one to thirty-six, starting with twenty-seven in the bottom left-hand corner, and ending with ten in the top right-hand corner. "Of course, from a mathematical point of view, the interesting thing about the magic square," said Nimrod, "is that no matter what direction you go in — horizontal, vertical, diagonal — each line of numbers adds up to exactly one hundred and eleven." He stood up, wiped the chalk dust from his hands, and stood back to admire his handiwork. "There, I've finished."

"It doesn't look very magical to me," observed John.

"That's because you look but you don't you see," said Nimrod.

"I've noticed something," said Philippa. "With each line equalling exactly one hundred and eleven, that means all of the numbers in the square add up to six hundred and sixty-six."

"That's right," said Nimrod. "Well done, Philippa."

"Whoaa," said Finlay. "Isn't that the number of the beast? Something evil, anyway?"

"True, but there's nothing necessarily evil about a number, Finlay," said Nimrod. "Or good, for that matter. The Chinese consider the number six-six-six to be one of the luckiest of all numbers. It's how you use the number that matters. Six-six-six is what mathematicians call an abundant number. It's a triangular number. It's also a cardinal number. And an ordinal number. Six hundred and sixty-six is also the sum of the squares of the first seven prime numbers."

28	4	3	31	35	10
36	18	21	24	11	1
7	23	12	17	22	30
8	13	26	19	16	29
5	20	15	14	25	32
27	33	34	6	2	9

"Fascinating," said Finlay. He wasn't sure exactly what a prime number was, only that they had studied it at school.

"A prime number is a number that's only divisible by itself and one," John told him.

"I know what a prime number is," insisted Finlay.

"No, you didn't," said John. "Not until I told you just now."

"Listen," said Finlay, "if you're going to remain as a guest in my body, I think you ought to stop reading my mind, don't you?"

"I'd like to," said John. "Only it's not so easy, as you know only too well."

"Yeah, all right," admitted Finlay. "Sorry."

Nimrod was still talking about the number 666 and how if you wrote it out as the Roman numeral DCLXVI, it would use all of the Roman numeral symbols under one thousand and in reverse order of their respective values: D=500, C=100, L=50, X=10, V=5, and I=1.

"There's something else I've noticed," said Philippa. "There are exactly eighteen pairs of numbers that add up to the number thirty-seven."

"So what?" said John.

But Nimrod was nodding with enthusiasm. "Excellent, Philippa," he said. "And?"

She shrugged. "Well, it's obvious, isn't it?"

"Not to me," said Finlay.

"Me, neither," admitted John. "I'm still trying to remember who was alive in 1320."

"Eighteen times thirty-seven is six hundred and sixty-six," said Philippa. She grinned, pleased at her discovery. "Hey, no wonder they call this the magic square." Philippa picked up what looked like a leg bone — the femur — and handed it to Finlay. "There's a number from one to thirty-six on each one," she said. "This one is number twenty-seven."

Finlay laid the bone so that the end rested in the center of the bottom left-hand square.

About halfway through their placing the bones on the magic square, Nimrod said, "I hope this works. Sister Cristina said there are only two hundred and five bones in this box. But a complete human skeleton should have two hundred and six."

"I guess it all depends on which bone is missing," said John.

Philippa handed Nimrod the skull, which he placed carefully on box number one, next to a handful of vertebrae.

"This is like some weird kind of game show," said John. "We have to guess who it is before the skeleton reassembles."

"Even if it does reassemble," said Finlay, "I don't see how it's going to talk without muscles and a tongue and all the rest of it."

"Fortunately for us this is a magic square," said Nimrod, "and not the *Times* crossword puzzle."

Philippa emptied a little numbered silk bag of tiny bones, each of them smaller than her fingernail, into the palm of her hand. "Are these chips off one of the bigger ones?" she asked.

"Those will be the bones from the inner ear," said Nimrod. "There are three in each ear: the hammer, the anvil, and the stirrup." He laid them carefully in box number one, as directed by Philippa, who glanced inside the brass chest and declared that the box was now empty.

"That's the last of them," she declared. "Two hundred and five. Just as Sister Cristina said there were."

They stood up and stepped back from the magic square.

"Now what?" said Philippa.

"I don't know," said Nimrod. "We're missing something. Perhaps that missing bone."

"Like I said," said Finlay. "It doesn't look very magical."

"Actually, I think I said that," said John.

"Yes, you did," admitted Finlay. "But you were using my mouth."

"I'll be glad to get back into my own body," said John. "Right now I feel like a square peg in a round hole."

"What's that you said?" Nimrod asked John.

"I said I'm a square peg in a round hole."

"Yes, of course," said Nimrod. He knelt down by the brass box and, bringing a magnifying glass out of his pocket, examined the design on the lid more closely. A minute passed; he shook his head and sighed. "Nothing," he said. "I don't understand. I was sure that must be it."

"What?" said Philippa.

"Squaring the circle," said Nimrod. "A problem posed by ancient geometers."

"Here," said John. "Let me take a look."

He looked and, like Nimrod, saw nothing. But just then the Venetian sun appeared directly in front of the reliquary window, throwing a strong beam of light into the room, which reflected brightly on the brass box that had contained the bones. And, momentarily bored, John and Finlay amused themselves by focusing the sunbeam on the lid of the box using Nimrod's magnifying glass. Gradually, a smell of burning filled the air. A cloud of smoke appeared on top of the box and a thin rivulet of melted wax ran down the metal lid, and onto the floor.

"Hey, look at this," said John. "There's something else on the lid of this chest."

"Well done, John," said Nimrod, and wiped away the remains of the melted wax with his handkerchief. "Not all the wax was chased off when this was engraved," he said, and lifted the brass lid a little so that it caught more of the light. "Look. It's exactly as I thought. There's a circle all around the square except the four corners. Our design on the floor here is not yet complete."

He picked up his chalk and stood over the square. "The question is, how accurate does this circle have to be? Strictly speaking, the area of the circle that lies outside the square would have to be exactly equal to the area of the square that lies outside the circle. Normally, I wouldn't attempt this without a set of compasses and a pocket calculator." He started to draw. "However, time is of the essence."

Nimrod continued drawing his circle. "In this way people like Leonardo da Vinci attempted to depict two things: the material or worldly existence in the square, and the spiritual existence inside the circle." Closing the circle, he stood up. "There, that should do it. Better stand back, children."

Almost as soon as he had finished drawing the circle around the square, several remarkable things happened. First, the numbers all disappeared; then it was as if the squares retreated into the floor, one by one, as if pressed down like the keys on a typewriter by some unseen giant finger. The bones remained immobile for a moment and then began to smoke as if heated, until the smoke partially concealed the fact that the bones were reassembling themselves. But gradually, the smoke cleared to reveal a man lying on the floor, with his arms and legs outstretched in a spread-eagle position. Philippa remembered the famous Leonardo da Vinci drawing, which she supposed Nimrod had been talking about: It was the same drawing on the front of her school biology textbook. Except that this man was wearing the clothes of an early fourteenth-century Italian, and quite a rich one if his silks and the fur collar on his coat were anything to go by. He sat up and tried to get up off the floor but he was old and, seeing that he was having some difficulties in standing, John went to help him.

"No," said the man sharply. "Don't touch me. For I am not yet quite myself." Moderating his tone a little, and standing finally, he added with a groan, "It's best you don't touch me, my boy. My present condition might cause you some injury." He straightened, stretched a bit, let out a breath, and nodded with some satisfaction as he looked around the room. He was not a ghost, but a real, living man, although there was something in his face that could best be described as supernatural. Aged about seventy years old, he had a thick beard and a kind face. He smiled uncertainly at Finlay/John, and then at Nimrod and Philippa. Sniffing the air, he nodded again. "We are in Venice, yes?"

"Yes," said Nimrod.

"That smell," said the man. "It's quite unmistakable. There's nowhere quite like Venice."

"I quite agree," said Nimrod. "Permit me to introduce myself, esteemed sir. My name is Nimrod. This is my niece, Philippa, and her friend, Finlay. Finlay's body is also a temporary home to my nephew, John."

The man bowed gravely.

"Children, it's my honor and my pleasure to introduce you to the most famous explorer of all time," he continued. "Philippa, Finlay, John. This is the great Marco Polo."

CHAPTER 20

THE NUMBERS

"Have you seen these audience numbers?" Adam Apollonius was waving a sheet of paper as he walked into Jonathan Tarot's rooftop suite at the Cimento dell' Armonia Hotel in New York. "They're just amazing."

It was eleven o'clock in the morning but Jonathan was still in bed. The great thing about his new life was that no one ever told him to get up in the morning or to have a shower or to wear a clean T-shirt or how much he should eat at breakfast. He went to bed late, watched TV in his room, and ordered whatever he wanted from room service. He even had his own limousine and driver parked outside. Not that he really went anywhere these days. He was much too famous to walk around the streets of New York. For one thing, he was nearly always on TV. And for another, posters bearing his picture were everywhere. So instead he had a personal assistant named Julian whose job it was to go and buy whatever he wanted from a store: CDs, magazines, candy, DVDs, clothes, sneakers. Most of the stuff he got he wore just once and then threw away. His mother would have been appalled at the waste of it. Which was one of the reasons why he did it, of course.

"What's an audience number?" asked Jonathan.

"A rating," said Apollonius. "That's the number of people who watched your last TV show. There are about a hundred and ten million TV homes in the USA. You got a forty-one percent audience share. One hundred and forty-three million fans. It's incredible. Every kid in America must have watched that show. The advertisers are deliriously happy. You're the biggest thing since Elvis. They want another special, ASAP."

Jonathan yawned. When people started talking percentages, it reminded him of school and usually that made him want to reach for a bagel, pizza, or a muffin — something to throw at them, anyway. Sometimes he did throw things at people. Since becoming a big TV star, Jonathan had become much less tolerant of mundanes and their stupid, boring conversation. He threw a lot of pizza at the people who worked for him. But Adam Apollonius was different. Jonathan always treated him with courtesy and never threw pizza at him. Not even when he was being boring, like now. There was something about the man that commanded Jonathan's respect. Of course, he remained blissfully ignorant of his new friend and mentor's true identity; but, perhaps, there was some small subconscious part of Dybbuk that recognized his own kind, not to mention his natural father, Iblis.

"Now we can start making some serious money," said Apollonius. "And I mean serious. Like millions of dollars."

Money didn't interest Jonathan very much and he tried, unsuccessfully, to stifle another yawn. Money mattered a great deal to mundanes, of course, and so he was hardly surprised that Apollonius talked about it all the time. In this respect at least he seemed just the same as any other mundane.

"Like it or not, kid, money's what this racket is all about," said Apollonius. "Like the song says, it's what makes the world go around."

Of course, Iblis didn't believe that for a moment, and he wasn't interested in money any more than Jonathan/Dybbuk. But for the purposes of his plan, and the manipulation of Dybbuk that lay at the heart of this plan, it was still necessary to pretend that he was.

"Now then. For the next TV special, I was thinking maybe we could go for some kind of mass audience participation. Like everyone bending a spoon using mind over matter."

"Spoon bending?" Jonathan sneered. "Everyone's seen it before. And it sucks."

"Something else then," Apollonius said, cleverly letting Jonathan think he was going to have to come up with the idea.

"Like what?"

"I dunno. You're the genius here, not me. But it ought to be something that kids have to pay money for, of course."

"Like what?" asked Jonathan, mildly intrigued.

"I was thinking that, maybe, we could get them to buy a simple Chinese magic square," said Apollonius. "A simple sheet of plastic with some numbers on it. At a dollar a time, that would make maybe seventy or eighty million dollars. It would only cost us a few cents to manufacture. They lay it on the floor and then sit in one of the squares, inside number four — that's an important number — and then they all focus their minds to help you perform the most amazing feat of magic ever seen. How does that sound?"

"Better than bending a spoon," said Jonathan.

"I just said spoon bending as an example," said Apollonius. "But your idea is much better."

"My idea?"

"Mass mind over matter."

Jonathan nodded. "How about this? I could disappear," he said. "Live. On TV. Without any props." He snapped his fingers. "Just like that."

"Great. I love it. Could you do that?"

"Sure. No problemo."

"But let's try to do it with more drama than just . . ." Apollonius snapped his fingers. ". . . like that."

"Whatever," said Jonathan. He got up and wandered into the enormous marble bathroom, thought about taking a shower, and then thought better of it. He put on a thick terry cloth robe, and called room service on the bathroom telephone to order some breakfast. When the waiter asked what he'd like to eat he told the guy just to bring everything. Which seemed simpler than having to make a decision about something so ordinary. "And like, hurry it up, okay? I'm hungry."

He came out of the bathroom, switched on the TV, and threw himself down on the sofa.

"What do you mean that I should try to disappear with more drama?" he asked Apollonius.

"I mean, let's make your actual disappearance last longer than a few seconds."

"A disappearance is a disappearance," said Jonathan. "One minute you're there, and the next you're not. What else is there?"

"This isn't the hush-hush or the keep-it-a-secret business that we're in, kid," said Apollonius. "It's called show business, and for a good reason. No, if you are going to disappear just like that, we want to take our time to enjoy the moment. Maybe you could whirl around a bit first. Make a show."

Jonathan thought about that, figured he could whip up a whirlwind, stand on top of it, and then disappear in a puff of smoke.

"Sure," he said, flicking from one channel to another until he found one of his own TV shows. "I could do that. No problemo."

"Ever hear of the whirling dervishes?" Apollonius asked him.

"Sort of." Jonathan shrugged. "I think maybe I saw something in *National Geographic*. Maybe."

Apollonius grinned. He was sure of it. He'd left a copy of *National Geographic* with an article about the whirling dervishes of Mevlevi in Jonathan's bathroom for just that reason.

"Aren't they some Middle Eastern dudes who sort of dance around in a circle?" asked Jonathan.

"You make it sound like they bop around their handbags on a disco dance floor in Cocoa Beach. No, these guys really go for it. The dervishes are mystics who believe that the quicker they whirl around, the more hypnotic the effect of their dancing, and the more open to the next world they will be. 'Dervish' means 'doorway.' A doorway into the next world."

"Really?"

"Turning quickly becomes the empty place where the human and the divine can meet," said Apollonius. "When the gravitational pull of the dance gets stronger, the turn becomes molecular and galactic and a spiritual remembering of the power at the heart of the universe. Maybe even altering the power at the heart of the universe."

Jonathan yawned again. This time it had been the word "molecular" that did it. "Molecular" was a word that reminded him of chemistry, which, next to math, was his least favorite subject at school. All those stupid little symbols for what stuff meant. That was the worst thing about school, period. Having to learn lots of stupid little symbols for all kinds of stuff that was of no use to anyone. Least of all someone with djinn power.

Apollonius could see he'd gone too far with his explanation. It was best to keep it simple where Jonathan was concerned. It wasn't that the young djinn was stupid. Far from it. Merely that he was easily bored.

"You know, this is a brilliant idea of yours," he told Jonathan.

"You think?"

"Sure. Kids love to spin around in a circle. Didn't you do that when you were a kid? Spin around like a dervish until you were dizzy and fell over?"

"I guess so," said Jonathan, who was bored by all memories of when he was a child.

"Let me take this ingenious idea of yours one stage further," said Apollonius. "Do you mind?"

"Go right ahead."

"We combine the dervish angle with the magic square angle. They can get the instructions on how to dance like a real dervish when they buy the magic square. Let's make it two dollars a pop. Then, while the show is on, we get all the kids watching to sit in the number four square and concentrate the collective power of their minds to make you whirl faster and faster until you disappear."

Jonathan was nodding.

"Then, how about this? When they've seen you disappear after whirling around like a dervish, we get the kids to do the same." Apollonius chuckled. "Who knows? Maybe we can suggest that there's so much mathematical power in that simple magic square to multiply your magical power enough to make all those kids disappear as well. I mean, did you know that the numbers in each one of the columns in the magic square add up to one hundred and eleven? And that the columns add up to six-six-six? And that if you multiply six-six-six by the number of vertical, horizontal, and diagonal columns, you get one hundred and forty-four thousand, which is the number of the chosen few who are supposed to go to heaven?" He shrugged innocently. "Or something like that."

Jonathan winced at the mention of mathematics and felt his eyes glaze over at the long multiplication performed by Adam Apollonius. He wasn't sure if 666 times 6 times 6 times 6 did equal 144,000. But he was sure he didn't want to let down or disappoint his fans.

"What's the point of that?" asked Jonathan. "I mean, the kids won't actually disappear. So what's the point?"

"There is no point," said Apollonius. "No point at all. It's just a bit of fun. Call it hype. Call it good TV. Call it show business."

"Won't they be kind of disappointed when they don't actually disappear?"

"Naw," said Apollonius. "We'll just say on the Web site that they just didn't believe hard enough. Or that maybe they just didn't whirl around fast enough. Something like that." He shook his head. "Either way, they won't blame you, kid. They'll blame themselves. It'll be their fault. Not yours." He shrugged again. "Besides, who's going to complain after you disappear? I mean, they're going to see something they've never seen before, right? A disappearing trick that won't look like a trick. How about that?"

Jonathan nodded. "Right," he said, warming to his idea. "With no props. No capes to hide underneath. No trapdoors in the floor for someone to drop through. No trick photography. We can make a thing about me doing it on a hard concrete floor somewhere. We'll get some road worker to use a jackhammer to drill the floor just to underline that. With some guy from the FBI watching to make sure there are no trick cameras or mirrors."

"I love this idea of yours," said Apollonius. "It's so audacious. So without precedent. Houdini? Who's Houdini? Next to you, kid, he looks like an amateur."

There was a knock at the door of the suite. It was room service with several trolleys that were weighed down by Jonathan Tarot's breakfast.

"How do you do it, kid?"

Jonathan helped himself to a half dozen sausages, six strips of bacon, four buttermilk pancakes, some maple syrup, three fried eggs, and some orange juice, and grinned at Adam Apollonius.

"Practice," he said. "Just practice."

CHAPTER 21

MARCO POLO'S STORY

The tip of Marco Polo's little finger was missing. He noticed Philippa looking at it and lifted his hand self-consciously.

"I don't mean to be rude," explained Philippa. "We were wondering why you only had two hundred and five bones, instead of two hundred and six. And I guess now we know."

"*Questo?* This? I lost it at the Battle of Curzola in 1298," he explained. "When I was the gentleman commander of a Venetian naval ship. A Genoese cannonball exploded near my hand. This was after my first trip to China, you understand. In life, I had the honor and fortune to be an emissary of the great Chinese emperor, Kublai Khan. And in death also, I am his emissary, for he was very good to me always and I was much exalted by his grace and favor. Both during and after his reign, the great Khan sent out a number of emissaries in death like me. To the four corners of the known world.

So that men could be warned of the great danger that lay within his kingdom.

"This is why China closed itself to the world and to other foreign visitors for so long. To protect the world against the warrior devils. The *Dong Xi*. If this is indeed why I have been summoned from a sleep of almost two hundred years, then I am here to tell you a story and to offer you some help. If not, then please be kind enough to return my bones to the chest where you found them and disturb me no more."

"We do indeed seek your help against the warrior devils, sir," said Nimrod. "And we should be very honored to hear your story. Wouldn't we, children?"

"Yes," said Philippa. "But I'd like to know how it is that you speak such good English, sir."

"Death is the most important passport you can obtain," said Marco Polo. "When you die, all the mysteries are solved. Including that mystery that is how the English language works."

Marco Polo nodded at Sister Cristina's chair. "Would you mind if I sat down?" he asked. "It's a long story."

"Please," said Nimrod, pushing the chair, which was on wheels, toward the great explorer.

For a moment Marco inspected the chair and seemed fascinated by the wheels on the legs, then he sat down and started to tell his story.

"The first emperor of all China was the Emperor Qin Shihuang." Marco Polo pronounced the name of the emperor

"Chin Shir Hwong." "He lived many centuries before the Great Khan. Before him there was no China. Instead, there were seven separate kingdoms of which Qin was the largest and most warlike, and it was not long before the ambitious ruler of Qin had eaten up his neighbors like a silkworm devouring a mulberry leaf.

"You can tell what kind of a man he was by the name he gave himself: Qin Shihuang. It means 'the first emperor, God in heaven, and the most mighty in the Universe.' Despite this grandiose title, the Emperor Qin was scared of one thing: dying. He wanted to be like any other god and live forever and, to this end, he took many secret medicines to help prolong his life. None of them worked. But he had heard stories of an elixir of life that might enable him to achieve his wish. Therefore he summoned the wisest men in the kingdom to his palace — some four hundred and sixty of them — and ordered them to go and find it. He chose wisely because these men were scholars of the great philosopher Confucius, very practical, sensible men who tended not to believe in elixirs of life, nor indeed in life after death. They only believed in what could be proved to their own satisfaction. And being of a skeptical frame of mind they would not, the emperor reasoned, be easily tricked into believing something was an elixir of life when it was not.

"Now the emperor had banned all books in his kingdom to stop his people getting ideas above their station, as he saw it. Which meant that the scholars had little love for their emperor. But they had no choice but to do his

227

bidding, for all disobedience was met with immediate execution.

"One of these Confucian scholars was Yen Yu. He was very young but also very clever. Secretly, he had read many books about the great city of Baghdad, many hundreds of miles to the west of the Chinese empire. He had read stories of the magical things that had happened there. Yen Yu decided that if a magic elixir existed anywhere, it would be in Baghdad. So that was where he chose to go.

"When he got there, he was amazed at what he saw. The women were beautiful, the bookshops were full of interesting books, and the scholars he met were very enlightened. Most amazing to him was what he saw in the bazaar. Here there was a circus. Among the performers in the circus were fire-eaters, a beautiful lady sword-swallower, and a man who could throw his voice into a dog, a tree, or a bottle of wine. He was what you would call a ventriloquist. Thanks to the Emperor Qin, who hated the idea of his people amusing themselves with any idle luxuries, there existed nothing like this circus anywhere in China.

"Yen Yu was very impressed with these performers, even to the extent that he half believed they genuinely possessed supernatural powers; to him, it seemed only logical that they might also know about other things such as magic elixirs of life. The circus performers thought Yen Yu was stupid and laughed at him, and only the sword-swallower, who was herself Chinese, confessed that there was no great secret to what they did. Just practice. Now the ventriloquist, who loved the sword-swallower, was worried that Yen Yu might steal her affections away from him. And he told Yen Yu that a magic elixir was to be found in the desert outside Baghdad. In this way the ventriloquist hoped that Yen Yu would get lost in the desert and die.

"He very nearly did. When he traveled into the desert, to look for the elixir, Yen Yu ran out of water and quickly began to die of thirst. But crawling across the sand dunes, he came upon a long-necked bottle and, hoping that it was full of water, picked it up and shook it. The bottle was empty. As he tossed it away in despair, however, he heard a human voice coming from inside the bottle. The voice inside the bottle told Yen Yu that he was a djinn and begged Yen Yu to release him and promised him three wishes if he did.

"Desperate for water, Yen Yu, who suspected his mind was playing tricks on him, reasoned he had little choice but to agree and pulled out the cork. From the bottle came forth a large cloud of smoke that swiftly turned itself into a djinn, who thanked Yen Yu and said he would keep his word, and granted the young scholar three wishes.

"Yen Yu's first wish was for water, of course. But before making his second wish, he told the djinn about the Emperor Qin and how he wished to know the secret of eternal life. The djinn answered that it was impossible for anyone to live on Earth forever, but that anyone could live again in heaven if they wanted to, and that, most likely, his emperor wanted to know the secret of how to live well after he died or perhaps how to rule in the afterlife. For this he would need a quantity of djinn spit and the *Living Book of Life*, which was a most ancient and wise book. These two things would enable the emperor to achieve what he wanted. It goes without saying that Yen Yu's second wish was to have this book and some of the djinn's spit. The djinn was glad to spit a large quantity of his own spit into the bottle and to give it to Yen Yu, for he had no wish ever again to see a bottle in which he had been imprisoned for many long years.

"Almost as soon as his wish was granted and the *Living Book of Life* was in his hands, Yen Yu realized he was now in an awkward situation. For he had remembered that the emperor hated books. How was he going to present his emperor with a book without also forfeiting his life? Then he had an idea. Remembering the skill of the ventriloquist from the circus, Yen Yu decided that if he could throw his voice into a bottle, he might be able to command the emperor's attention. Better still, he might read whatever nonsense was in the book — for that was how Yen Yu regarded all such talk of an after-life — and use the voice in the bottle to retell its fantastic contents to the gullible emperor, and keep himself alive in the process. And this was his third wish: to have the skill of a great ventriloquist.

"So it was that armed with the book, his newfound voice-throwing skill, and the bottle containing the djinn's spit, Yen Yu, who loved his people and feared abandoning them to the cruelty of Qin, returned to China. He hoped that with his bottle of spit, the book, and his skill in throwing his voice, he might bring the emperor under the influence of Confucian thought, and make him a nicer person in the bargain. This was a not unreasonable ambition. And a very practical solution to his country's problems. But, as we shall see, it was also the scholar's mistake, for there are indeed more things in the world than in Confucian philosophy — certainly more than Yen Yu could ever have dreamed of.

"Arriving back in China, Yen Yu discovered that the other Confucian scholars that had returned before him, and with nothing to show for their extensive travels, had all been buried alive by the devil Emperor Qin. Yen Yu now took all of his courage in his hands and traveled to the palace, where he presented the bottle to the emperor. He told Qin that it contained the elixir of life, but that the elixir was not, as had been supposed by everyone, something to drink at all, but a wise oracle to whom all of the secrets of life were known. After which he threw his voice into the bottle that then announced that it would not speak to the emperor, but only to the man who had found him, namely Yen Yu.

"Momentarily, the emperor was furious and threatened to have Yen Yu buried alive, at least until the voice inside the bottle reminded the emperor that there was surely nothing to stop him listening to that which he could only tell Yen Yu: namely, the secret of how a man might rule forever in the afterlife. And seeing the sense of what the voice said, and persuaded that it would be better to rule the gods in heaven than a few stupid men on Earth, Qin spared Yen Yu's life.

Indeed, as his delight with the idea of ruling the gods grew and grew, the Emperor Qin even made Yen Yu his first minister.

"The *Living Book of Life*, which as you will remember was the book given to Yen Yu by the djinn, said that he who would rule the afterlife needed only to equip his tomb with models of soldiers to do his bidding. And thinking that he might divert his emperor with this apparently harmless activity, which would then leave the new first minister to govern the country properly, Yen Yu accordingly instructed Qin in the construction of the soldiers that would fight for him in the afterlife. These soldiers were to be made of terra-cotta (which is a kind of waterproof ceramic clay), the spit of the djinn, and then fired at great heat in enormous kilns. Certainly, it never occurred to Yen Yu that what was in the *Living Book of Life* was entirely feasible.

"Now Yen Yu had told the emperor that when the army was complete the voice inside the bottle would deliver the last part of the ritual that would bring Qin's army to everlasting and eternal life. But after a while, distracted by the business of trying to run the country justly and fairly, Yen Yu quite forgot the task he had effectively given his gullible emperor. He seemed harmlessly preoccupied with the nonsense from the book that Yen Yu's bottled voice told him about. The emperor, however, had never been a man to do things by halves and, over the years, Emperor Qin managed to assemble a terra-cotta army numbering some eighty thousand warriors. When he discovered this, Yen Yu was appalled for, quite unknown to him, a large number of poor peasants had been forced to work on the construction of Qin's underground tomb and terra-cotta army. But much worse was to follow.

"Prompted by his discovery of the true size of the terra-cotta army, Yen Yu sought to bring an immediate halt to Qin's lunacy and declared that the time had come when the voice inside the bottle would deliver the last part of the ritual. Now the plain fact of the matter was that Yen Yu, who believed only in what he could see, had never bothered to read to the end of the *Living Book of Life.* It is a failing in many scholars that they are easily distracted and not single-minded. If Yen Yu had read the end of the *Living Book of Life* (which perhaps might better have been called the *Deadly Book of Death*) he would surely never have started the business of the terra-cotta army. For the last page described how each terra-cotta warrior required to fight in the afterlife could only become the emperor's *Dong Xi*, or creature, if it was first animated by the souls of ten living children. Yen Yu was horrified, for while he thought there was no chance of the emperor's huge army of warrior devils ever being brought to spiritual life, it was horribly clear that if the emperor found this out he would certainly order the sacrifice of some eight hundred thousand children — which at that time was the number of all the children in China.

"But once again, Yen Yu's resourcefulness came to the fore. When the emperor ordered the bottle brought and commanded the voice to speak to Yen Yu — which was how it usually happened — the voice 'told' Yen Yu that with the army of *Dong Xi* now complete, it only remained for Qin to drink a large quantity of mercury and die so that he could live again more powerfully than before, and proceed with the conquest of heaven itself.

"Anyone other than Qin might have seen the obvious flaw in what the voice from the bottle had told Yen Yu must happen. But to Qin, this made perfect sense, and to everyone's relief he proceeded to do exactly what Yen Yu had suggested. He drank enough mercury to kill a horse and died. All the children in China were saved. Yen Yu then ordered that Qin be buried alongside his army of warrior devils in his tomb, with the important difference that the last part of the *Dong Xi* ritual was never completed. The burial mound containing the huge army of warrior devils was then very carefully covered over by several tons of earth, and all the exits sealed up so that no one would ever again find the emperor's terra-cotta army. And, in time, the Emperor Qin was forgotten."

"You know," said John, "I'll bet these are the same terra-cotta warriors that were found by some Chinese workmen in 1974. Some of which are on loan to museums all over the world."

"Including the Met," said Philippa.

"Of course," said John. "It was one of the terra-cotta warriors I saw. The one that absorbed Mr. Rakshasas. I don't know why I didn't realize this before."

"All of the trouble the museums have had," said Philippa, "the thefts of jade and the hauntings, they have followed the loan of the warriors."

"*Per favore*," said Marco Polo. "But my story is not yet over."

"My apologies to you, sir," said Nimrod. "Please finish your story."

"Yen Yu lived to a great age," said Marco. "But as he grew older, he became less certain of what he had once believed. This is common enough as people get older and death comes closer. The idea of an afterlife becomes more and more attractive. At the same time, Yen Yu began to worry that one day the warrior devil army might be discovered and used for evil and to conquer heaven, as the Emperor Qin had intended. So Yen Yu read the *Living Book of Life* again and, using the last of the djinn spit, made five golden tablets of command. With one of these tablets, a single good man might command unquestioning obedience from all men, as well as an army of warrior devils. Before he died, Yen Yu left these same five golden tablets to the succeeding emperors of China.

"This is what the great Kublai Khan told me," said Marco. "So that I might tell you what only the emperors of China once knew. To help protect the world, the great Khan also gave me one of these golden tablets of command. And I brought it back here to Venice."

It was at this point that Marco Polo let out a great heavy sigh. It was, Philippa reflected, a sigh that had been seven hundred years in the making. For the sigh was followed by a terrible admission and an abject apology.

"The golden tablet was to have been put in the brass chest with my bones so that I could deliver my message and hand it over to you now," said Marco Polo. "But unfortunately, I lost it. Somewhere here in Venice."

"You lost Kublai Khan's golden tablet of command?" Finlay was beside himself with outrage.

"You tell us a story like that," said John, "and then you tell us you've lost the one thing that could help us defeat these warrior devil things? How dumb is that?"

"You've no idea how sorry I am," confessed Marco, wringing his hands with remorse.

"*You're* sorry," said John, whose first thoughts were of Mr. Rakshasas. "One of these warrior devils just absorbed a good friend of mine. I don't see how we're ever going to bring him back unless we have that golden tablet."

Nimrod greeted the news with calm, as did Philippa. There seemed little point in getting angry with Marco Polo. For one thing, he was an old man. For another, it was plain that Marco Polo was still managing to be quite angry with himself, even after seven hundred years.

"Please ignore my young friends," said Nimrod. "They speak as young people often do, without the respect due to a man of your years and great reputation. If you could describe how you came to lose it, sir, we'd be grateful."

"I was in a gondola on my way to the house of Cuzzo in Cannaregio, here in Venice," said Marco. "To deposit the golden tablet of command in a bank vault there. The golden tablet was in a velvet bag. As I dismounted the gondola, there was a sudden swell of water and I lost my footing. The tablet slipped out of the bag and fell into the canal. The local boys dived in search of it for many days afterward, but it was never found. The water was too dirty and the mud much too deep. Without the golden tablet of command, the importance of my message is much reduced. But what am I to do? I fear it is lost forever."

"If it *is* lost forever," said Nimrod, "then so I fear are we."

CHAPTER 22

AN ERUPTION OF LOGIC

Iravotum is the secret world known only to the djinn, which lies deep underneath what was once Babylon, in modern-day Iraq. It is a strange and frightening place, as both John and Philippa could easily have testified. Both of them were still haunted by their memories of the place and the things they had seen there. And always would be.

When human beings wish for bad things or in anger, sometimes those wishes come true, and Iravotum is the place where all those inclement wishes go, in the hope of being corrected. They seldom are. But it's not just wayward wishes that end up in Iravotum. When old or very young djinn dream terrible dreams, sometimes those dreams become a ghastly reality, and these monsters from their sleeping minds must go to Iravotum, too.

Iravotum is also where a djinn — good or evil, but by ancient convention always a female — goes to become the most powerful djinn of all, the great Blue Djinn of Babylon;

it is her spiritual home and it is where, from time to time, she must return to renew herself. For here, there exists a Tree of Logic that is a near relation of those other two more famous trees: the Tree of Knowledge of Good and Evil, and the Tree of Life.

Everything in Iravotum is affected by the Tree of Logic. The air is full of the sweet scent of the tree's blossom, which, like its fruit, lasts all year long. Even the local water is affected by the roots of this unusual tree. Little is known about why the Tree of Logic affects the mind and heart of a djinn. But what is certain is that it takes only thirty days for a djinn to become the creature of Logic and wholly indifferent to things like right and wrong.

It was said by a famous philosopher that Logic needs only to look after itself, and that next to it everything seems mean- ingless. This is the djinn way of administering the Law. But life isn't always about doing what is logical. The freedom to do wrong is just as important as the freedom to do right. This is what makes life interesting. And it was generally agreed that becoming the Blue Djinn required a consider- able degree of sacrifice on the part of both good djinn and evil djinn. For it is no small thing to stop being what you are — be it benign Marid or despicably wicked Ifrit — and become something else. In effect, the process of becoming the Blue Djinn was almost to deny life itself.

Upon her arrival in Iravotum, almost the first thing Mrs. Gaunt did was to go into the garden and take a good look at the Tree of Logic, which, she knew, would work a powerful effect on her, and turn her from the nice, happy woman, who was the mother of two nice, happy children, into a being who was largely indifferent to anything but the administering of djinn justice.

It was a strange-looking tree, like nothing to be seen anywhere else on Earth. For one thing it was very old — much older than the oldest known giant sequoia — with gray-blue bark that was as hard as coral, and razor sharp-edged foliage that was a strange hue of blue-green. For another thing, one of the tree's enormous roots, some of which were growing above the ground, strongly resembled the head of a fierce lion, while another resembled the face of a very beautiful woman. In fact, the more Layla Gaunt looked at the tree root, the more she was certain that this was the face of Ishtar herself, the first Blue Djinn of Babylon, who was once worshipped as the queen of heaven, and whose symbols were the lion and the color blue.

The next thing Layla did was to sack Miss Glumjob, grant the woman three wishes — something Ayesha, Layla's predecessor, had neglected to do — and send her back to Greenville, North Carolina, which is where Miss Glumjob had come from. It only seemed fair after forty-five years of loyal service. Besides, Layla had brought her own future companion with her, a French Guianan peasant boy called Galibi who, because of a wicked diminuendo binding by Iblis, was currently imprisoned in a state of suspended animation as a kind of lifelike voodoo doll. As soon as she was the Blue Djinn and strong enough to overcome the power of Iblis, Layla was planning to take Galibi out of his cardboard box and turn him back into a living boy whom she might educate and eventually, after some years of service and companionship, send back into the world. At least that was her plan.

Layla tried not to think about what she had left behind her in New York, and she busied herself preparing for the elapse of thirty days and the precise moment at which she would become the Blue Djinn of Babylon. She made plans to change the famous hanging palace, so called because it used to hang on the edge of a precipice. Because Ayesha had never much cared for heights, she had used her powers to change it from the original palace built by King Nebuchadnezzar for Ishtar to an exact copy, in every detail, of Osborne House, which was the home of Queen Victoria for many years.

Osborne House was not to Layla Gaunt's taste. It was much too "old lady," with fussy curtains, tassels, gloomy oil paintings, and chintzy-looking furniture. And she decided that she would replace Osborne House with something else. Ishtar's original palace was still an option, of course. That was always there, and the matrix for any other palace created by the incumbent Blue Djinn. But all djinn carry a "dream house" in their heads, which is usually an image of how they tend to decorate the interior of their so-called magic lamps that are, of course, very much bigger on the inside than the outside. Nimrod's dream house was the famous pavilion on the English coast at Brighton; Mr. Rakshasas's dream house was a famous old library, in London's St. James's Square.

But Layla Gaunt's dream house was going to be something very different from these.

She had always loved a house called Fallingwater, built by the famous architect Frank Lloyd Wright in 1939. This house was built in a series of cantilevered concrete "trays" over a waterfall on Bear Run, a rushing mountain stream. Ever since she'd seen a picture of it as a child, Layla had wanted to live in that house. This was her chance, and it seemed a small compensation for what she had been obliged to give up.

Fortunately, Ayesha's library was a good one and there were several books about America's most famous architect, with many pictures of his best-known house. And Layla was able to study these carefully before destroying Osborne House and focusing all of her djinn power on the creation of its replacement. It was the work of several hours and left her feeling so exhausted that she had to delay the creation of the contents and furnishings until several days later. But after three weeks she felt quite at home, which, of course, was only the effect that Iravotum was having on her. The real Layla could never have felt at home without her husband and the children, not to mention Mrs. Trump, Monty the cat, and all her smart New York friends.

"I like your house," said a girl's voice. "It's very — organic. I approve. I'm not so sure I wouldn't choose to live in a house like this myself. Who knows? Maybe I will."

Layla, who was reading a newspaper in her magnificently appointed new living room, looked up from the photograph of Jonathan Tarot that was printed on the page, and fixed Faustina with a stare like a cat. "What on earth are you doing here?" she asked.

"Well, that's a fine way to greet someone you haven't seen for more than twelve years," said Faustina.

"Yes, I'd forgotten you'd only disappeared," admitted Layla.

"Most people had, I think," said Faustina. "Although not your brother, Nimrod, and your son and daughter. It was them who rescued me."

"Rescued?" Layla sounded surprised. "You mean you're not one of those indeterminate wish thingies that exist in the forest on the other side of the palace wall?"

"No. I'm the real thing." Faustina held out her hand. "See for yourself." Layla took her hand, and Faustina shivered. Layla's hand was hard and cold, and Faustina imagined her heart was already in the same state.

"So you are," said Layla. "How about that? So you managed to find your body again."

"Yes," said Faustina. "Or rather, they did."

"Well, good for you."

"Aren't you going to ask me how your family is?"

"How is my family?" Layla asked coolly

"Fine. They send you their love. And hope to see you very soon."

Layla said nothing.

"Like I said, Nimrod and Philippa found my body," Faustina continued. "It was in a catacomb somewhere in

Italy. And then John and Mr. Rakshasas came and brought my spirit back from my aunt's house, in Bannermann's Island. They've been wonderful. Especially John. He's very brave. Very good-looking, too. But I expect you're proud of them all."

"Seems like they went to a lot of trouble," said Layla, "to remedy something you brought on yourself, Faustina. Whatever possessed you to do such a stupid thing in the first place? To possess the prime minister?"

"Youthful high spirits?"

"You're just like your brother."

"Not quite."

"Well, I hope you've learned your lesson. You should count yourself lucky that they all bothered to find you again. Why did they?"

"They hoped to replace you with me," said Faustina. "As Blue Djinn of Babylon."

"And what makes them think I want to be replaced?" said Layla. "I like it here." She looked around, caught the sound of the waterfall in her ears, and nodded her approval. "It's rather nice, don't you think?"

"Perhaps you're forgetting something," said Faustina. "I was the anointed one. Not you."

"That was before you disappeared," said Layla. "Before you were presumed dead, Faustina."

"Well, clearly I'm not, Mrs. Gaunt."

"Layla. Just Layla will do fine. So where does all that leave us?"

"You tell me, *Layla*."

"I'd say you were too late," Layla said coldly. "The show's moved on. I am the Blue Djinn now. If I were you, I'd tell myself I'd had a lucky escape and go away from here and live my life."

"I don't agree."

Layla shrugged, indifferent to something as ordinary as Faustina's disagreement.

"Let's deal with this logically," said Faustina.

"By all means, let's."

"You promised Ayesha to take over when she died, right?"

"It was a solemn promise given in the last conversation she and I ever had."

"But I took an oath before you and was anointed by Ayesha herself. I don't remember it myself. But my mother always said I took an oath."

"How is your mother?"

"She worries. About my brother, Dybbuk."

"Good idea. To worry about him. That boy is trouble. The apple doesn't fall far from the tree."

"Meaning?"

"Like father, like son." Layla smiled thinly. "It will end in tears, you mark my words. He'll use up all his power, and then" — she snapped her fingers — "poof. Like that. The fire that burns inside him, it will go out. Have you ever seen a djinn who's lost all his power?"

"No."

"It's a sad sight. Like seeing a toothless lion. Quite pathetic."

Faustina sat down in a chair opposite Layla.

"We've strayed from the subject," she said. "We were talking about my anointment as Blue Djinn by your own mother. Which is why you were invited to that ceremony. Words were said. Important words. An oath was taken. By me. Not you. I take it you remember?"

"There's nothing wrong with my memory."

"And you've been here how long?"

"Twenty-six days."

"Therefore you're not what you claim to be. You're five days short of actually being the Blue Djinn. Can we agree on that also?"

"I can't fault your logic, child."

"Do you have a copy of the *Baghdad Rules* here?"

"Of course. What do you take me for? Some kind of amateur?"

"Merely a pretender."

"That remains to be seen, surely."

"I've had years to study the *Baghdad Rules*," said Faustina. "Twelve years to be exact. I think I can safely say I know the rules backward. Many of them would make more sense that way. If you will allow me to quote section four hundred fifty-nine, subsection eighteen, clause fourteen, paragraph twelve, line six: 'A solemn oath taken before two other witnessing djinn and under seal of anointment shall always take precedence over a solemn promise given to one witnessing djinn.' You can look it up yourself if you don't believe me."

"Oh, I believe you," said Layla. "The question is, who are your two witnessing djinn?"

"My mother. And you."

"I'm to be one of the witnesses against myself, is that it?"

"Do you deny that you were there?" asked Faustina.

"And if I did?"

"Where's the logic in lying? You were there when I took the anointed oath. Isn't that right?"

"Your logic is impeccable. I concede defeat. Your claim is better. Although one wonders why you want it. To be the Blue Djinn, I mean. I should think a girl of your age would have something better to do with her life. Such as, live it."

Faustina let that one go. This was her business.

"What will you do?" she asked Mrs. Gaunt.

"Make a whirlwind. Fly home."

"I think it's best that you leave as soon as possible, don't you?" said Faustina. "For obvious reasons."

"I agree." Mrs. Gaunt stood up. "There's a boy in a cupboard somewhere in here. He was the victim of a diminuendo inflicted by Iblis. You might care to restore him to normal life when you're powerful enough. He was to be my companion here."

"Sure. No problem." Faustina nodded. "Your daughter tells me that to counteract the effects of the Tree of Logic, you must wait until you are outside Iravotum, and then drink a large quantity of water."

"Thanks," said Mrs. Gaunt. "I'll try that."

She and Faustina shook hands. "Good luck," said Mrs. Gaunt, and then walked out of the house she had recently finished making.

Layla bought a box of tissues and a large bottle of mineral water at a small café in Baghdad's city center. She drank the whole bottle, and then threw up a poisonous-looking substance that had the color and consistency of oil. But the water worked a miraculous effect on her. With each eruption of logos — for that was what the substance was and the effect of the Tree of Logic — more of the old Layla was restored until she was able to recognize herself again. Immediately, she missed her husband, her children, and her home. Desperately. She waited until dark and then proceeded to a parking lot, where she started to create a powerful whirlwind. Minutes later, she was flying through the night sky, on her way back to New York.

Her aerial route took her east, across the Great Wall of China, Beijing, and Japan, and then the Pacific Ocean. Some of the time she was in tears of joy at the idea of going home. What mother doesn't look forward to being reunited with her family again? Her heart was full of hope and expectation. And Layla could hardly have expected that one of the three wishes her own daughter had granted to a humble New York policeman was about to radically affect her plans.

"You want to know my third wish?" the policeman had said to Philippa. "I wish no one in New York could eat pâté de foie gras. That's what I wish. That no one could eat pâté de foie gras."

That was what the policeman had wished, and that was what Philippa had made happen. She could hardly know that something as well-meant as this could have consequences. *Disastrous consequences.* For, as has often been said, there are times when granting wishes to a human has unseen, unpredictable results. Even a wish that's made with a good intent. As Mr. Rakshasas had been fond of saying, "Having a wish is like lighting a fire. It's reasonable to assume that the smoke might make someone cough."

And, in this particular case, there was no smoke without a great deal of fire.

Now, because Philippa had caused New York's entire supply of pâté de foie gras to disappear, the American importer requested another ton of pâté de foie gras to be delivered urgently from France.

Because of that, the French supplier in Périgord redirected the supply of pâté de foie gras from his poorer, more remote customers, in places like French Guiana, to New York.

Then, because Dr. Pierre Chartreuse in French Guiana did not receive the tin of pâté de foie gras he had ordered for his birthday, he took his gun and shot himself a pigeon for supper, which is another French delicacy.

Next, because that pigeon was shot, it did not eat the berries it had spied on the nearby branch of a tree.

Because these berries were not eaten by a pigeon, they

were eaten by a hungry mouse that otherwise would have starved to death.

And because this mouse stayed alive from eating those berries, it later chewed through a wire inside a French rocket that was scheduled to launch a satellite into space.

Now because the wire inside this rocket failed, there was a short circuit inside the rocket's guidance system.

Finally, because this French rocket malfunctioned, it jettisoned its launch stage prematurely and landed inside the Kilauea volcano in Hawaii, which is the world's biggest active volcano. The supercooled fuel chilled the magma inside the volcano, causing it to crust over and producing a pressure-cooker effect that would be relieved only when explosive pressures were reached. At the same time, a massive underwater land subsidence doubled the size of the magma chamber. And all of this created a major problem for Layla Gaunt because her whirlwind route home was carrying her directly over the crater of the Kilauea volcano at a height of five thousand feet. Just as it was getting ready to explode in the biggest eruption since the island of Krakatoa blew up way back in 1883.

Oops.

CHAPTER 23

THE GOLDEN TABLET OF COMMAND

Nimrod glanced awkwardly at Marco Polo and then at his wristwatch. He'd hoped to prompt the old Venetian explorer's disappearance by taking a cloth and rubbing out the Chinese magic square that had brought him into being, but Marco Polo showed no sign of taking this strong hint, and it was clear that Sister Cristina must return from her journey downstairs at any moment. Finlay was already standing anxiously in the doorway keeping a watchful eye on the long stairway that led up to the reliquary in St. Mark's.

As an English gentleman, Nimrod always recoiled from rudeness and bad manners, only he could see no way around it. He was going to have to come right out with it and baldly suggest that Marco Polo should leave — more or less.

"Um," he said rubbing his hands and, at the same time, meaningfully kicking the empty brass chest that had housed Marco Polo's bones. "Well, I'm sure we'd all like to thank the great Marco Polo for coming to speak with us today. Wouldn't we, children?"

Philippa fixed a rigid grin to her face. "Er, yes," she said.

"Thank you, sir," said John/Finlay. "Your story about Yen Yu and the *Dong Xi* was very interesting."

"Wasn't it?" agreed Nimrod. "But we mustn't keep him any longer, must we? I'm sure he has a thousand and one other things he ought to be doing right now." He smiled expectantly at Marco Polo. After a longish pause, he added, "So let's show him our appreciation and say good-bye in the usual way."

Nimrod started to clap, and without much enthusiasm, so did Philippa and Finlay/John.

There was another prolonged pause during which time Marco Polo remained firmly seated in Sister Cristina's office chair.

"Message delivered," Nimrod said with an air of finality he hoped would be infectious. "Completely. Absolutely. In full. More or less."

"Perhaps I didn't make myself quite clear," Marco said vaguely. "I'm a little more than a messenger. I'm supposed to help you destroy the warrior devils. I can't leave until they're gone. Not now."

Nimrod smiled awkwardly.

"Sister Cristina's on her way," said Finlay. "I can see her, coming upstairs. What are we going to tell her about him?"

"Um," said Nimrod.

"Use your powers," insisted Finlay. "And zap us out of there. Or turn the old bat into — I dunno, a bat, or something. But do something."

"What are you thinking?" Philippa asked her uncle.

By now they could hear her footsteps slowly ascending the stairs outside.

"I'm thinking Sister Cristina is about to discover that there's a little more to this world than she'd ever supposed," said Nimrod. "If she can manage those stairs, I think she can surely stand the shock of what we're going to tell her, don't you?"

Sister Cristina appeared, looking only a little breathless, in the doorway of the reliquary. To the surprise of Finlay/John and Philippa, she was holding a beautifully wrapped package in her hands. And Philippa guessed that Nimrod must have kindly arranged for a package addressed to Sister Cristina to appear downstairs, so that the old lady's journey would not seem like some cruel hoax.

"Look at this," she said happily.

"Wow," said Philippa. She caught her uncle's eye and he nodded his admission quietly back at her.

"I wonder what it can be," said Sister Cristina, not yet noticing the figure of Marco Polo in her chair. "I haven't had such a beautiful-looking package since I was a little girl."

She quickly unwrapped the package to reveal an expensive box of Venetian chocolates. And then she saw Marco Polo. "Oh, I'm sorry. I didn't know there was someone else with you."

Marco Polo stood up politely and bowed.

"Sister Cristina," said Nimrod coolly. "The box of bones turned out to be this man here. They sort of reassembled themselves when we laid them out in the floor." He said it as if it was the most natural thing in the world for a famous historical figure to come back from the dead.

"You don't mean to tell me he really is the blessed Saint Mark," said Sister Cristina.

"No, no. This is Marco Polo."

Marco Polo bowed again with great courtesy.

"You mean he's *the* Marco Polo? The one who went to China?"

Nimrod said he was.

"Oh, my. How wonderful. Would you like a chocolate, sir?"

"Yes, please," said Marco.

She opened the box and presented Marco with a series of little oblongs of milk chocolate wrapped in gold foil.

"I'm a great admirer of your book," she said. "And the movie they made of your life."

Marco smiled politely, although, of course, he had never seen a movie. He picked a chocolate, looked at it for a second, and held it up to show Nimrod and the children. "A golden tablet," he said. "*Madonna*, if only it was this one, eh?"

Then he unwrapped the chocolate and popped it into his mouth. "*Quando si viene al dunque* . . . things would be so much easier for us."

Sister Cristina offered her chocolates to all. Everyone took one. Finlay and John ate two chocolates, one after the other.

"I must say," said Sister Cristina, "this has been a most remarkable day. It's not every day one meets Marco Polo."

The children nodded. This seemed self-evident.

"For me, too," said Marco Polo. "It's not every day that one is raised from the dead."

"No, indeed," said Sister Cristina. "It's quite encouraging, really. For someone of my age. After all, if you're here now, there must be something more after this life. Another chocolate?"

"*Sì, per favore,*" said Marco. "These are very good. Not as good as ice cream, though. Have you ever tasted that? I brought the recipe back from China." He kissed his fingers. "Ice cream is *squisito* . . . delicious."

"Oh, yes," agreed Sister Cristina. "I like ice cream, too."

"There's something bothering me," admitted John. He looked at Nimrod. "I thought you said Marco had been dead for seven hundred years."

"That's right," said Nimrod. "He died in 1324. Is that not so, sir?"

"Yes. Why do you ask?"

Finlay/John was still looking bothered. "Well, it's something you said just now," said John. He was speaking to Marco

Polo now. "About this being a remarkable day. And something you said earlier. About how you'd been summoned from a sleep of two hundred years. Surely you meant to say you'd been asleep for seven hundred years."

"No, no," said Marco, helping himself to another chocolate. "I've been summoned back from the dead once before. In 1820, I think. And in this very room. I told my story to a young priest. But there was no threat from the warrior devils, so I stayed just long enough to tell my story and then returned to my box there."

"Including the part about the golden tablet of command?" asked Nimrod. "What it's for and how you dropped it in the canal and lost it forever?"

"Oh, yes."

"Just as a matter of interest," said Finlay, "when you say this golden tablet commands obedience from all, what kind of obedience are you talking about?"

"*Giuererei di averlo.*" He smacked his palm with the other hand, as if taking an oath. "Nobody could resist its power, not even if they wanted to. That kind of power. *Supernatural power.* A man who found it might do almost anything with the golden tablet. Advance himself in all kinds of ways, regardless of his merits."

"This priest," said Nimrod. "Do you remember his name?"

Marco Polo shook his head. "No. But he was a most charming fellow. We spoke for a long time."

"What did he look like?" asked Nimrod.

Marco made an Italian sort of face and shrugged as he tried to think of a description. "Like a priest," he said vaguely.

"Was this the man?" Sister Cristina was holding open a book she'd taken from the shelves. In the book was the picture of a priest.

Marco looked at the book and nodded. "I think so," he said.

Nimrod looked at the picture. "Cardinal Daniele Marrone," he said, reading the caption underneath the picture.

"But he wasn't a cardinal when I met him," said Marco.

"Then the old story might actually be true," said Sister Cristina.

"What old story?"

Sister Cristina hesitated. "I'm sorry, but no," she said, shaking her head. "It's not a long story but I can't tell it here. Not in St. Mark's. Somehow it wouldn't seem right telling you about Cardinal Marrone in this place." She thought for a moment and then spoke again: "Meet me in room 23 at the Accademia in one hour."

The Gallerie dell' Accademia, on the other side of the Grand Canal, has the largest collection of Venetian art in existence. And room 23 of the gallery contained an exhibition of paintings of whiskered people who had been important in Venetian history. There were portraits of several dull Venetian dukes who were called the "Doges," the astronomer

Galileo, the composers Vivaldi and Monteverdi, the notori-
ous diarist and libertine Casanova, the Emperor Napoleon,
the poet Lord Byron, and many others whom Philippa, John,
and Finlay had never heard of. Among these was a picture of
Cardinal Daniele Marrone, painted in 1820. And it was in
front of his picture that they found Sister Cristina waiting
for them.

She pointed at the man in the picture who was wearing the red robes of a cardinal in the Roman Catholic
Church. The man was standing in an oak-paneled library
and reading a large book from which was hanging a large blue
silk bookmark, and on the end of this bookmark was a gold
medal. The man was tall, fair-haired, but balding, with a large
dimple in his chin.

"This painting of Cardinal Marrone is by the great Italian
painter Niccolo Pollo," she said. "But before he became a
cardinal, Father Marrone, as he then was, had been one of
my predecessors as the Keeper of the Relics in St. Mark's. I
did not feel comfortable speaking frankly about him in a
place for which he did so much. And speaking frankly, I must
tell you that he wasn't much of a priest. He was too interested
in having a good time to be at all concerned with spiritual
matters.

"Father Marrone was a good friend of Lord Byron, a man
once described as 'mad, bad, and dangerous to know.' For a
priest, he was especially dangerous to know. The two men
would go drinking and afterward jump into the Grand Canal

to see which of them would be first to swim across. Like Lord Byron, Father Marrone was a tremendous swimmer. It's said he could hold his breath for four minutes and that he often liked to go swimming at night.

"It was clear to everyone Father Marrone's career in the church was going nowhere. And yet, in 1816, he took a trip to Rome and soon afterward was made a bishop. Nobody could say why. Nor did his advancement stop there. He was very quickly made an archbishop and then a cardinal. It's even said he could have been the Pope, but that he turned the job down because he was too lazy. He also became very rich. The church restoration of St. Mark's in 1820 was paid for by Cardinal Marrone. But again, no one could say from where his wealth had come, and to this day, it remains a great Venetian mystery.

"There are some who thought he discovered some hidden source of wealth in the reliquary," continued Sister Cristina. "But nothing was ever missed and nothing was ever proved." She looked at Marco Polo. "I was thinking that if it was Father Marrone to whom you told your story the first time, then maybe it was Father Marrone who found this golden tablet that you lost."

"Of course," said John. "That kind of thing would be a cinch for any man who could hold his breath for four minutes."

"Did you tell him whereabouts in the canal you dropped it?" asked Finlay.

"*Ma certo,*" said Marco. "Of course. He was a priest, after all. There are no secrets from a priest."

"Could the father's possession of the golden tablet of command explain his rapid advancement in the church?" asked Nimrod.

"It would," said Marco Polo. "There's no limit to the influence that the golden tablet might give a man. I myself could have been the Doge of Venice if I had wanted. I think that the five golden tablets are maybe one of the reasons the great Kublai Khan was the great Kublai Khan. His power always seemed a little unworldly."

"The question is," said Nimrod, "if he did have it, what did Father Marrone do with the golden tablet?"

"The answer to that question may be here," said Sister Cristina.

She led them to the next painting, which depicted the palace of the dukes of Venice. In front of the palace, which was the color of gold in the Venetian sunlight, were four peasants who appeared to be examining one of the foundation stones on which appeared an apparently nonsensical mathematical equation:

$$XI + I = X$$

"The painting is by Riccardo Furbogigione," said Sister Cristina. "And it's supposed to be the Doge's Palace here in Venice. The palace of gold, as it is called. It's said that it's not a particularly good painting. Some people have even called it boring. However, the picture was commissioned by Cardinal Marrone. And here in Venice it has always been said that it contains a great secret. Cardinal Marrone's secret. Certainly it's not very accurate. The artist has used the sunlight reflecting off the canal to make the palace seem to be a lot more gold than it actually is in real life. Also, the palace has no cornerstone like the one in the picture. Or anything like that inscription anywhere on the building."

"If those are supposed to be Roman numerals, then the equation doesn't make sense, either," observed Philippa. "Eleven plus one equals twelve, not ten."

"Precisely so," murmured Nimrod. "Fascinating."

"Clever clogs," whispered Finlay.

"The golden hue of the palace," said Nimrod, "would also seem to be telling us something."

"Gold," said Philippa. "Perhaps the golden tablet is hidden somewhere in there."

"There's also a series of almost illegible numbers that run along the bottom of the picture," said Sister Cristina. "But no one knows what they mean, either."

"Could it be a code?" said John.

"Most certainly that is what it is," said Sister Cristina. "Many scholars have tried to solve it. But none have succeeded. It would seem that Cardinal Marrone's secret died with him."

They stared some more at the picture. Nimrod walked back to the painting of Cardinal Marrone. The others followed.

"That bookmark in the cardinal's Bible," said Finlay. He stood as close to the painting as the museum's security devices permitted and scrutinized the bookmark more care-fully. "There's something written on it."

"Can you read what it says, boy?" asked Nimrod.

Finlay screwed up his eyes and poked his head even far-ther forward so that his nose was almost touching the canvas. "It says, 'Aurum — dii — tango.'"

"Aurumdii tango," said Nimrod. "It's Latin. It means 'I touch the gold of the gods.'"

"I guess that's the point of learning Latin," said Finlay.

John nodded. "I guess that clinches it. Old Dan Marrone had the golden tablet, all right. And he wanted someone to know that he had it."

Leaving Sister Cristina, they took a water taxi back to the hotel. Nimrod found another room for Marco Polo and then joined the children back in their top-floor suite, where they had just finished telling Groanin all that they had discovered.

"It's vitally important that we solve the mystery in that picture and find that golden tablet of command," said Nimrod. "Clearly, there's no time to delay. But it seems equally important that we get to China as quickly as possible and find this place that Faustina described."

"I don't get it," said Finlay. "Why is any of this important?"

"I agree with Finlay," said John. "All I want to do now is go back to New York and wait for Mom to turn up."

Nimrod told the boys about what he and Philippa had discovered in the *Book of Jade*, and how this tied in with what Marco Polo had told them. "Warnings from the past should never be ignored," he said. "There's something grave that's happening in the spirit world. These warrior devils are behind it, all right. We have to find out why."

"But if it's the spirit world, why is that important to us?" persisted Finlay. "I mean, spirits are dead, right? How much worse can it get for them than that?"

"A lot worse," said Nimrod. "And for us, too. The spirit world can affect the physical world in ways you can't possibly comprehend. It's not called the 'other side' for nothing. Think of it being like a coin. You can't have heads without also having tails. That's why we have to go to China."

"China?" Groanin did not sound pleased.

"China," repeated Nimrod. "But we shall have to divide our forces. Groanin, Finlay, John, and I will go to China. It's my belief that someone has unlocked the ancient secret of the terra-cotta warriors and is using them to his or her own advantage," said Nimrod.

"What about me?" asked Philippa.

"Philippa? I want you to stay here in Venice with Marco Polo and see if you can't solve the mystery in that painting. It's vital that you find that golden tablet of command. I had better provide Marco with a passport in case you have to travel anywhere to find it."

"Isn't that a little risky?" asked Philippa. "I mean, you going to China *without* the golden tablet of command."

"Perhaps," admitted Nimrod. "But necessary, I think. We shall scout it out, so to speak. Gather intelligence."

"I hate China," said Groanin darkly. "They eat dogs in China."

"Groanin," sighed Nimrod. "You've never even been to China."

Groanin looked imploringly at Nimrod. "Couldn't I stay here with Miss Philippa, sir?" he asked. "I don't think the *idea* of China agrees with my stomach. Bad enough that we're here in Italy. All that olive oil and garlic. They even put garlic on their bread and butter, for goodness sake. I could help Philippa solve the puzzle in the painting. I'm good at puzzles, I am. You know I am. Nobody does the *Daily Telegraph* crossword puzzle quicker than me, and that's a fact."

"I'm sorry, Groanin, but no," said Nimrod. "After your wrestling bout with that angel, it's clear you'll be more useful to us as a bodyguard. We may have need of the strength in that special arm of yours if it comes to a fight with these warrior devils."

Groanin groaned loudly. "I were afraid of that. We won't be there five minutes before there's mutt on the menu. I can see it coming. You mark my words."

"Oh, Mr. Groanin, they don't eat dogs in China," said Philippa. "That's just an old wives' tale."

"They don't?" said Groanin. "It is?" He was silent for a moment and then nodded. "Well, then I suppose it'll be all right. Only I'm fond of dogs. I had a dog. When I were a lad."

"Small world," said John.

CHAPTER 24

THE BEE AND THE ALBATROSS

As soon as Layla Gaunt had left Fallingwater in Iravotum, Faustina set about preparing for her own departure. She didn't want her spirit to spend one minute more in that weird place than was absolutely necessary for fear of something unpleasant happening to her, as had clearly already happened to Layla.

Faustina's plan was to find a nice comfortable bed, lie down on it, and then leave her body to absorb the atmosphere of Iravotum that was necessary to becoming the Blue Djinn while taking her spirit off somewhere else for thirty days. But where was she to go? There was no question that she would have to occupy another living creature for that length of time, otherwise she might never be able to pull herself together again. And what shape was she to adopt?

Experience had taught Faustina to be wary about

borrowing human bodies. Being inside the British prime minister had had catastrophic results she never wanted to see repeated. But if not a human being, then what kind of creature's shape was she to take? Since arriving in Iraq she'd seen evidence that the country appeared to be hazardous to all forms of life, not just human beings. Just about the only animals Faustina had seen that seemed to be thriving were scorpions, but Faustina had an instinctive loathing of these creatures, which are more poisonous to djinn than they are to humans. So that was out as, for the same reason, were all spiders. She didn't like snakes. Which left what? It was all very worrying and she decided that it was probably best if she let serendipity make the choice for her. This is just another way of saying that she would let fortune decide, which was, of course, a very djinnlike choice.

She lay down on Layla's big bed and closed her eyes. After a minute or two of concentration, she lifted her spirit clear of her body and rose high into the air through the concrete roof of Fallingwater until she reached the near invisible ceiling of the huge underground world that is Iravotum. Then straight up for thousands of feet through dense rock strata and shifting layers of hot shale and sand, until she found herself floating free again in the cool early morning light of Babylon.

For a while, Faustina floated around, enjoying the breezy liberty of the air after the darkly claustrophobic grip of the ground. But all the time she was searching for a suitable living host. In quick succession she rejected a kitten, a goat, a reed warbler, and a man with a black turban. Finally, she elected to become a honeybee. Bees were hardworking, inoffensive creatures. Besides, Faustina was very fond of honey. But it was a choice that would have an unforeseen and longlasting effect that was the result of her taking a bee's shape while a residual amount of bee venom still remained in Faustina's earlobes.

Forever after, Faustina would buzz when she was happy.

Around this time, Layla Gaunt was looking forward to seeing her family and enjoying her whirlwind flight home. As usual, she had furnished her breezy conveyance atmospherically, which is to say the interior of the whirlwind had all the leather-lined comforts and fitted-carpet elegance of a small and extremely expensive private jet. But as she was a powerful, experienced djinn, there was little need for her to pay more than a minimal amount of attention to the actual flying of the whirlwind. The idea of an autopilot in which a computer flies a conventional aircraft is also known to the djinn, except that they call such a device an *"idée fixe,"* from the French. Inside the mind of a djinn piloting a whirlwind, this *"idée fixe"* exists as an independent thought or "fixed idea," and its operation is more easily explained when it is understood that because of the way a djinn's brain is constructed, a mature djinn can think of at least two things at the same time. When weather conditions are favorable, a djinn can simultaneously fly a whirlwind and watch an in-flight movie, read a newspaper, or even sleep.

Before leaving Baghdad, Layla had taken the trouble to check the weather and found that flying conditions over the Pacific Ocean were near perfect. Cloud cover was minimal, winds were light, and, even at lower altitudes, visibility was excellent. Cocooned in the comfort of her own private whirlwind, Layla sped through the sky like some modern-day Nut, who, as anyone knows, was the ancient Egyptian goddess of the sky and the heavens. (She is also the improbable but true origin of the old djinn motto about not flying a whirlwind in bad weather, which says that "you'd have to be Nut to fly in this.")

Layla had one eye on the in-flight movie, one eye on her glossy magazine, and an "*idée fixe*" somewhere at the back of her mind. It wouldn't have occurred to her, or anyone else for that matter, to have avoided the air space around the island of Kilauea. There had been no reports of any recent volcanic activity, which meant that the vulcanologists working on the lip of the crater of the world's largest volcano were about to receive the surprise of their lives.

Indeed, it would prove to be the last surprise of their lives.

Inside the huge Kilauea crater, the pressure-cooker effect relieved itself. Which is to say that explosive pressures were reached, and then breached with spectacular effect. The first explosion fired about one whole cubic mile of ash and rock thousands of feet into the air, followed by a burning cloud of superheated gas that vulcanologists know as the pyroclastic flow.

Now djinn are made of fire and super-resistant to heat. But there is heat and then there is the heat from a pyroclastic flow, which can exceed eight hundred degrees Celsius. What is more, words like "cloud" and "flow" hardly describe the speed with which the hot gas of a pyroclastic flow travels. A speed of more than 150 miles per hour is not uncommon. It was this pyroclastic flow that incinerated Layla Gaunt's body. Burnt it to a crisp. Or a potato chip. Completely.

Anyone but a djinn would have been killed. Like those poor vulcanologists. And in a way Layla Gaunt *was* killed, for the body her children and husband were used to was now completely gone, reduced to an airborne cinder in less than a second. But somehow her spirit survived. The second that the volcano erupted, Layla's "*idée fixe*" took control like the ejector seat in a military jet, firing her spirit high into the comparative safety of the stratosphere. A moment later and her spirit would have been atomized, just like her body. A pyroclastic flow will do that.

It was several minutes before the disembodied Layla figured out what had happened and gathered herself — what was left of herself — together in a sort of ghostly mist. At that kind of altitude, Layla might have drifted off into space and been lost forever — quite quickly. And it was fortunate that less than an hour after the eruption, a bird flew into the small cloud that was Layla, enabling her to take possession of its twenty-six-pound body — for this was no ordinary bird, it was an albatross and, among birds, the albatross — a bird for whom the breeze seemed to have been created — is considered to be a bit of a star.

Layla counted her blessings and tried to look on the positive side of things. Returning to New York to see her family in the shape of an albatross wasn't exactly what she had had in mind, but at least she wasn't dead. She still had a living spirit and, while the *Baghdad Rules* are strict about occupying the bodies of humans without their permission, taking on the shape of a cat or a dog back in New York remained a strong possibility. All she had to do was get there. Which made it all the more fortunate that she was in the body of an albatross. These are the greatest long-distance travelers on the planet. If albatrosses had a frequent flier plan, they'd bankrupt an airline.

Nothing could have been easier for an albatross than a flight across half of the Pacific Ocean and the whole North American continent. Layla climbed higher and, using a combination of gravity and solar power, she calculated her position.

Her latitude was 21.18 degrees north; her longitude was 157.51 degrees west. She set a course for New York: latitude 40.45 degrees north and longitude 73.59 degrees west. Instinctively, she calculated the distance she would have to fly as 4,956.41857 miles. Her ground speed was just over seventy miles an hour. She would be home in just 2.9502 days.

The albatross is nothing if not a bird that is very precise in its navigation.

CHAPTER 25

THE PITS

Some 7,777 miles to the west of the sky above Hawaii, which contained the albatross that was now Mrs. Gaunt, her brother, Nimrod, was flying out of Venice cocooned in a whirlwind with John/Finlay and Groanin.

Over Eastern Europe the sky was warm and clear of anything but the color blue. And they made good progress for several hours until, a few miles short of the Chinese border, they saw something on the crimsoning horizon that looked like the black mushroom cloud of a nuclear explosion, with one major difference: This cloud appeared to be moving not vertically but horizontally.

"What is that?" said Finlay.

"If I were Moses," said Mr. Groanin, "I might say it were a pillar of cloud to lead us along the right way. But I'm not. And it isn't."

"Relax," said Nimrod. "It's only a typhoon. A tropical cyclone. It won't bother us."

"I thought you said the weather ahead of us was all clear," remarked Groanin. "I say, I thought you said weather was grand for flying these whirlwind thingies."

"I did," said Nimrod. "And it was. But typhoons can blow up out of nowhere at this time of year. Especially in this part of the world. Northeast of the Ganges basin has always been a major area for tropical cyclones. We'll just have to fly around it, that's all."

Nimrod adjusted their course accordingly; he was surprised when, a few minutes later, it was pointed out to him by the keen-eyed Finlay/John that the typhoon still appeared to be coming their way.

"That's odd," said Nimrod. "Typhoons generally don't change course as abruptly as that. They're cyclonic, which is to say that the winds rotate around an area of low atmospheric pressure."

"Er, what would happen if it managed to intercept us?" asked Finlay.

"Tish, tosh," said Nimrod, and chuckled loudly at the obvious discomfort of his two/three traveling companions. "It won't intercept us. That would imply that it's being controlled by some kind of intelligence. There's nothing to worry about, I tell you."

At the same time, however, he took the precaution of steering the whirlwind they were flying into a higher altitude, so that they could not only go around the typhoon but climb over it, too. But the typhoon was bigger than he had thought. Much bigger. And it was quickly clear they would not be able to fly over it. Nor around it. Nimrod's face started to take on an expression of quiet concern.

"How high can we go?" asked John.

"It would seem, not as high as the typhoon," said Nimrod. "Perhaps we had better turn back. Just for the moment. Just to be on the safe side. I confess, I really can't understand it. In all my years of piloting whirlwinds, this has never happened to me before." He bit his lip uncertainly as the enormous column of cloud appeared to thicken and then darken, until it looked like a huge black cobra. "Normally, typhoons are quite predictable. I mean, after all, it is just a lot of hot air rotating in a circle."

"Don't tell me," said Groanin. "Tell the typhoon."

"Mr. Groanin's right," said John. "It appears to be pursuing us now."

"I wish I'd taken a plane," said Groanin. "I hate these things. Unnatural, so it is. If man had been meant to fly in a whirlwind, God would have made us prophets like Elijah, or gods like Apollo, and then he'd have been out of a job."

By now, the typhoon appeared to be a mile or two away, which would have been a lot if it hadn't also been three or four miles tall. And Nimrod was forced to admit that John was right: The typhoon appeared to be chasing them. Except that he knew typhoons just didn't behave like that. Not unless . . .

"There is another possibility," he yelled, increasing speed of the whirlwind to the maximum in an effort to outrun the malevolent black column. And he was shouting because the typhoon was now closing in fast, so close that they could hear the sound of the five-hundred-mile-an-hour winds that were being generated by the typhoon. "There remains a distinct possibility that someone is flying that thing. Someone who doesn't want us to get to China."

"You mean another djinn?" shouted Finlay.

"Well, it's not Charles Lindbergh," Groanin bellowed crossly. "I say, it's not Charles Lindbergh. Of course, he means another djinn." He looked at Nimrod. "Can't you make this thing go any faster?"

"I'm going as fast as I can," yelled Nimrod. "There's not enough air in here to go any faster." Sweat was pouring off his forehead as he concentrated every fiber of his djinn being into flying the whirlwind, zigzagging one way and then the other in the hope that he could bring about their escape.

John looked around and found Finlay's heart was in his mouth. By now, the typhoon was almost close enough to touch. He felt it sucking at the edge of the whirlwind like a giant vacuum cleaner. They were inches away from being vacuumed up. And was he mistaken, or did he see the vaguely sinister shape of someone sitting inside the dark depths of the cloud?

"Do something, Nimrod!" he yelled. "It'll overtake us in a minute."

Nimrod didn't answer. Just the thought-power needed to answer his nephew would have required that he direct a crucial amount of energy away from flying the whirlwind.

"Next time I go to China — if there is a next time," shouted Groanin, staring back into the column, "I'm going to make sure I do like the song says and take a slow boat to China."

"Groanin," said Nimrod. "You're a genius. Why didn't I think of that? Of course! That's how we can generate more hot air inside this whirlwind and go faster. *We can sing.*"

"Me? Sing?" yelled an incredulous Groanin. "I can't sing. I say, I can't sing. Sing what exactly?"

"It doesn't matter," shouted Nimrod. "Sing anything. But sing as if your life depended on it. Which it rather does, I'm afraid."

He himself started to sing the British national anthem as loud as he could and, uncertain of what to sing himself, Groanin started to sing that, too.

John would have sung the American national anthem but, of course, it was not his physical body and so he felt obliged to leave the choice of national anthem to Finlay, who was, of course, British. Generating as much hot air as possible seemed to demand some consistency in their singing and so, putting aside his political feelings about kings and queens, Finlay thought it best to join in with Nimrod and Mr. Groanin.

"God save our gracious Queen,
Long live our noble Queen,
God save the Queen.
Send her victorious,
Happy and glorious,

Long to reign over us,
God save the Queen!"

Soon all three of them were bellowing "God Save the Queen" at the top of their voices and with such enthusiasm that it left poor John feeling quite left out of things.

"Light my lamp, I can feel it working," cried Nimrod. "Keep singing."

Twenty minutes passed. Then half an hour. And maintaining a distance of just a few feet in front of the huge typhoon that threatened to annihilate them, they still continued to sing the British national anthem. All *six* verses. Again and again and again.

Hot air swelled the whirlwind, slowly adding to its power. Half an hour became an hour. Which turned into ninety minutes. The typhoon made a last deafening, terrifying attempt to suck them into its cold, black maw, before the whirlwind gradually began to inch away. Inches became feet. Feet turned into yards. Yards added up to furlongs. Until, certain that the malevolent typhoon was far behind them, Nimrod said they could stop singing at last.

For several minutes, no one said anything. They just caught their breath and rested their vocal cords and wiped the sweat from their brows. It was Finlay who spoke first. "If I ever hear that song again," he said, "I think I'll kill someone. Myself probably."

"Me, too," puffed Groanin.

"Talking of killing someone," said John. "Back there just now, someone was trying to kill *us*. I'm pretty sure I saw a human shape inside that typhoon."

"Someone who doesn't want us to get to China, perhaps," said Finlay.

"It would certainly appear that way," observed Nimrod.

"But who?" asked John.

"I don't know," said Nimrod. "But they've certainly wasted their time." He pointed down. "Look."

Several hundred feet below them was what looked like the exposed bony spine of some elongated green dragon.

"Wow!" said John. "It's the Great Wall of China."

"Now that's what I call a wall," said Finlay.

"If you ask me, there are too many walls in this world," said Groanin. "Keeping this lot of people in and that lot of people out. I don't care how old it is. Best thing you can do with a wall like that is what they did with the one in Berlin. Knock it down."

"You surprise me, Groanin," said Nimrod. "I never guessed you had such an appetite for democracy."

"I don't know about an appetite for democracy," observed Groanin. "But I do have an appetite. All that singing has made me so ravenously hungry I could eat a horse. I say, I could eat a horse."

"I thought you didn't like foreign food, Mr. Groanin," said Finlay, helping himself to another bowl of steaming-hot boiled rice.

They were having dinner at the Shikua Urchi Restaurant in Snack Street, in Xian, the capital city of ancient China. The picturesque street was well-named, as there were almost a hundred eating establishments from one end to the other, all of them full of Chinese people stuffing themselves with a wide variety of exotic dishes. The restaurant was just around the corner from the Most Wonderful Hotel in Xian, which was the name of the hotel where they were staying.

"Ordinarily that's very true," said Groanin, tucking into a bowl of what looked like fried chicken legs. "But these are extenuating circumstances. First, I don't happen to have brought my own supply of baby food. Second, the guidebook says this is the best restaurant in this part of China. And third, after what happened to us this afternoon, I could eat a horse. I say, I could eat a horse."

"You've been saying that since we landed," said Finlay.

"For once, the guidebook is right," said Nimrod. "Xian is the capital of Chinese delicacies such as the chow chow you're eating now, Groanin. Not to mention popular Szechuan cuisine like the hot pot Finlay ordered. And without question this is the best restaurant in Xian."

"So there," Groanin told Finlay, with an air of triumph.

"Xian is also where Faustina found herself when there was that disturbance in the world of spirit," continued Nimrod. "And the home of the famous terra-cotta warriors. Which is why we're here. As soon as we've finished dinner, we shall go and take a look at them. They've been on show in the local exhibition hall since they were unearthed by accident in 1974 by some peasant farmers. Eighty thousand Chinese soldiers, chariots, and their horses."

"What, no China dogs?" said Groanin. He chuckled. "You'd think they'd have included a couple of China dogs, wouldn't you? My auntie Florence used to have a pair of ornamental China dogs on her mantelpiece. Everyone did where I come from."

"Those dogs were not made in China, Groanin," said Nimrod. "But in Staffordshire, England. For the dog-loving English market. The Chinese themselves look on dogs as something wholly unfavorable. Which is why you won't see many pet dogs in China. Mostly they're just kept for meat."

"Meat?" Groanin stopped eating for a moment. "Did you say that dogs are kept for meat?"

"That's right."

"But Miss Philippa said that was just an old wives' tale."

"What on earth does she know about it?" demanded Nimrod. "I don't think she's ever been to China. Has she, John?"

"She doesn't even like Chinese food," said John.

Groanin looked unhappily at the plate of chicken legs he had been eating. Except that they weren't chicken legs. If they had been, those chickens would have been several feet tall. With tails. And personalities. And collars. "You don't mean — ?"

Nimrod nodded.

Groanin spat a large piece of meat out of his mouth, which flew across the restaurant and stuck to a glass tank full of nervous-looking goldfish. He swallowed biliously. "But you said this was chow chow."

"*Chow chow* is Chinese for 'dog,'" said Nimrod. "Look here, Groanin, I'm really sorry but I thought you wouldn't mind. In India, you ate all kinds of things you don't normally eat."

"Yes, but I were an Indian back then," said Groanin. "With an Indian stomach. I'm back to being English now."

"Besides, you said you were so hungry you could eat a horse," said Nimrod. "You've already eaten horse. You ordered it as a starter. I therefore assumed you would have no ethical objection to eating dog."

"That were a figure of speech," said Groanin, putting his hand to his mouth and looking generally nauseous. "I say, that were a figure of speech. Besides, there's a heck of a difference between eating a horse and eating a dog."

"Nonsense," said Nimrod. "Basically if it moves, it's on the menu here at Shikua Urchi's. That's what 'Shikua Urchi' means. Four legs, two wings. Dog, horse, cow, sheep, and pigs. People come from hundreds of miles around to eat here. We're very lucky to get a table at all. Snakes, rabbits, pigeons, foxes, cats. And rats, of course."

"But rats are filthy animals," objected Groanin.

"So's a pig," said Nimrod. "But I notice it doesn't stop you cooking yourself bacon and eggs in the morning when we're back in London. In China, a pound of rat meat costs twice as much as pork or chicken. Which might indicate how prized a delicacy the meat is."

"A pig's different," said Groanin, who was looking very pale.

"The rat here is excellent. Better than any pig."

Suddenly, Groanin sprang up from the table and, holding his hand to his mouth, ran out of the restaurant.

John/Finlay had stopped eating, too. "Tell me you're kidding," said Finlay.

"Not at all," said Nimrod. "That spicy bean hot pot you're eating is called *ping shu guo*, and its principal ingredient is a fat juicy rat. They burn the hair off them with a blowtorch, wash them, chop 'em up, season them, and then fry 'em up. Delicious."

John, who had once eaten locusts, didn't really mind that he had just eaten a rat. It tasted delicious, after all, if not quite as good as locust. And it wasn't like rats were an endangered species or anything. Even so, it was immediately clear to John, who was inside Finlay's body of course, that Finlay's stomach didn't agree at all with the very idea of eating a rat. John did his best to talk Finlay around and to overcome his evident disgust, but it was no good and a minute or two later he found himself outside in Snack Street, alongside Groanin, throwing up into the gutter, much to the amusement of several Chinese people who had seen them running out of the restaurant.

A minute or two later, Nimrod came outside and eyed his companions sadly. "Well, I've heard it said that if you eat too much rat you get a nosebleed, but this is ridiculous. I shall never be able to show my face here again." He sighed and pointed up the neon-lit street. "Come on. We'd better be getting along to the exhibition hall. It ought to be closed by now."

There were, in fact, three exhibition halls, each of them covering an enormous burial pit where hundreds or thousands of terra-cotta warriors had been found. The exhibition hall covering the main pit was a modern-looking building that was the size and shape of an aircraft hangar. The hall was closed for the night and, once again, Nimrod used the little skeleton key to make an unauthorized entry. Finlay/John helped themselves to a guidebook in English as they made their way past the gift shop and into the main body of the hall.

Finlay/John pointed one of the flashlights, which they had bought from a late-night hardware store, into the echoing depths of the building and gradually began to appreciate the enormity of what had been discovered here. The hall was vast — about twice the size of a football field — so vast that the beams of their flashlights couldn't reach the ceiling or any of the four walls.

In the pit immediately below them stood a vanguard of 204 warriors and behind them an army that numbered about six thousand figures that were slightly larger than life-size. A few were missing heads and hands but all of them stood facing east, in neat ranks, as if at any minute they might start marching somewhere on the orders of the devil Emperor

Qin. Everything — figures and pit — was the same dusty shade of gray, like the color of death itself.

"Why do we always have to visit these places at night?" complained Groanin. He shuddered as the damp smell of an ancient grave pricked his nostrils and he caught his first sight of the crowded ranks of terra-cotta warriors. "Freaks me out, creeping around in the dark like this. And them all staring at us blankly like that. I say, it freaks me out, so it does. Feels like we've intruded on something private."

Groanin did not exaggerate. The place was undeniably creepy. But then, it's an unusual mass grave that doesn't give you a little pause for thought. Nimrod climbed over the barrier. "Stay here while I take a closer look."

"At what, exactly?" said Groanin.

"I don't know," said Nimrod. "I won't until I see it, probably."

Nimrod jumped down into the actual pit so that he stood shoulder-to-shoulder with the terra-cotta warriors.

"Be careful, Uncle Nimrod," said John. "I wouldn't want you to get absorbed, like poor Mr. Rakshasas."

"May I remind you that we don't have that golden tablet of command?" said Groanin. "Look here, sir, John's right. If one of them comes to life now, you'll be stuffed, and no mistake."

"We're not leaving yet," said Nimrod. He ran the beam of his flashlight up and down the torso of the nearest warrior. It might have been more than two thousand years old, but the figure was fantastically well-preserved. He touched it carefully and then tapped at the torso with his flashlight. The warrior sounded hard and hollow, like a heavy china vase. "This chap is a little bit like Groanin," he said. "I don't think it will absorb anything very much. These fellows down here are solid terra-cotta."

"Very amusing," said Groanin.

"All the same, that's what happened," said John. "Mr. Rakshasas went inside the body of the warrior devil of Dendur, and never came out again."

"Oh, I'm sure you're right," said Nimrod. "But this one seems quite harmless."

They all glanced overhead as something flew above their heads and, a little surprised by the sudden movement, Nimrod dropped his flashlight.

"What was that?" said Groanin, flicking the beam of his flashlight at the distant ceiling.

"Probably just a bat," said Nimrod, bending down to retrieve his flashlight from the brick-paved floor.

"It had better be careful," muttered Groanin. "I expect the Chinese eat those, too."

"Wait a minute," said Nimrod. Something had caught his eye as he picked up the flashlight. He steered the powerful beam along the floor of the pit. "Look, here. Shine your flashlights onto where mine is, would you?"

Groanin and Finlay/John concentrated their flashlights on a gap in the ranks of the warriors, illuminating several sets of footprints in a thick layer of dust that lay on the floor, as if six or seven of the terra-cotta warriors had simply stepped off their little plinths and walked to the back of the pit.

"That's odd," said Nimrod.

"It's a little more than that," said Groanin, glancing nervously over his shoulder. "I say, it's a little more than odd when statues go walkabout."

Still standing on the viewing gangway while keeping their lights trained on Nimrod, Finlay/John and Groanin made their way to the back of the exhibition hall as the English djinn trailed the footprints along the pit.

"Strange," he said. "The footprints end abruptly in front of this brick wall. Almost as if they went straight through it."

Shining his flashlight up the side of the pit wall, Nimrod ran his hand across the dusty surface, and then uttered a noise that seemed to indicate he'd found something.

"What is it?" asked Finlay.

"Some writing," said Nimrod, rubbing away some of the dust with the flat of his hand. And then: "I don't believe it."

"What does it say?" asked John.

"It's a sort of command," said Nimrod. "Only it's in Chinese. Which is rather odd because I always thought this kind of kabbalistic command was only seen in tombs of the Middle East. Never in China."

"Cannibalistic?" said Groanin. "Is there anything these people won't eat?"

"Not *cannibalistic*," said Nimrod. "*Kabbalistic*. It means 'mystic' or 'occult.' You have food on the brain, my dear fellow."

"Is it any wonder since there's none in my stomach?" complained the butler. "Not since dinner, anyway."

But Nimrod wasn't listening. "These words. They amount to the same command used by Ali Baba to open the door of the robbers' den in the story of 'Ali Baba and the Forty Thieves.' It seems out of place here in China."

"You mean the story in the *Thousand and One Nights*?" said John.

"Yes. Literally translated, these Chinese words mean 'open sesame.'"

"Please don't say them," said Groanin.

But even as the butler spoke, Nimrod had pronounced the words in such a way as befits a magical word of command. "*Kai Shen*," he said loudly.

Immediately, a hidden door in the brick wall rumbled open to reveal a long dark passageway. "The footprints go in here," he announced, shining his flashlight inside. "And seem to lead in a westerly direction for quite a distance."

"I'll bet the tunnel goes all the way to the Emperor Qin's burial mound," said John, looking at the map in his guidebook. "It's about half a mile to the west of where we are now, on the other side of the River Wei."

Finlay read a little more. "For some reason, the burial mound remains unexcavated," he said. "There's also another exhibition hall over pit number four that's unfinished. I wonder why it's unfinished."

"With eight thousand warriors already dotted about the place, they probably figured they had enough," said Groanin.

"Yes, I wonder why, too," admitted Nimrod, ignoring Groanin's explanation. "Interesting, isn't it?"

"Something scared them off, perhaps," suggested Finlay.

"I can't imagine what on earth could scare people who are prepared to eat dogs and rats," observed Groanin.

"Perhaps something not *on* earth," remarked Finlay. "But underneath it."

"We certainly won't find out by staying here," said Nimrod.

"Surely you're not going in there on your own?" said Groanin.

"Of course not, Groanin," said Nimrod. "You're coming with me."

"It could be a trap."

"True. And so, John and Finlay, you had better wait for us back at the Most Wonderful Hotel in Xian. Just in case something happens." He tossed the little box holding the skeleton key up to Finlay, who caught it and slipped it into his pocket. "You might need the key to get back in here."

"Do I have to?" protested Finlay/John. "Wait out here, I mean."

"Not that anything will happen, of course," Nimrod

added quickly, for Groanin's benefit. "It would be a foolish creature that ever imagined it could best a djinn in a fight."

"Then why do you want me along, sir?" said Groanin.

"You're my butler, man," said Nimrod. "An English gentleman doesn't like to go anywhere without a butler."

"If you say so, sir."

"Stop moaning, Groanin, and get down here," insisted Nimrod.

"Very well, sir. If you insist." Groanin climbed over the barrier and slithered down the side of the pit. Covered in dust, he arrived on the floor still on his backside, but stood up without another complaint and tried to brush himself off. "Shall I lead the way, sir?" he said, glancing into the passage.

"No, Groanin, I'd better go first," said Nimrod. "Just in case."

Finlay/John watched the two men enter the passage until the stone door rumbled shut behind them. They remained there for several minutes.

"Do you really want to go back to the hotel?" Finlay asked John.

"Nope," he said. "I think we should wait a couple more minutes and then follow. Just to keep an eye on them. Make sure they don't get into any trouble."

Finlay/John climbed over the barrier and down into the damp-smelling pit, keeping a close eye on the warriors in case one of them came alive and started behaving aggressively, like the warrior devil back at the Temple of Dendur in the Metropolitan Museum in New York.

"Groanin's right," said Finlay. "This place is the pits."

John wasn't listening because, of course, being inside Finlay's body, he knew what Finlay was going to say before Finlay actually said it.

You're right, thought Finlay. *From now on we should just exchange thoughts.*

Did you hear something? thought John.

You know I did, thought Finlay, switching off the flashlight. *Someone's coming.*

Finlay/John crouched down behind one of the figures as the lights in the hall came on and an American's footsteps echoed on the gantry above them. They knew he was an American because the author of the footsteps was also making a call on his cell phone.

"Dad, it's me, Rudyard," said a loud but youthful voice. "You know how Nimrod and those other dumb clowns got away from my typhoon? Well, they're here at the exhibition hall in Xian. And guess what? All of them just walked straight into the trap we set for them. That's right. They went inside the 'open sesame' tunnel. Just like you said they would. Yeah." He laughed an unpleasant sort of laugh. "Like rats in a trap. Boy, are they in for some surprises when they get to the silver lake. I am so looking forward to seeing their faces when they realize how this place works."

John peeped out from behind a terra-cotta warrior and caught a glimpse of a pale-faced, red-haired boy about fifteen years old, wearing a dark, Chinese-style suit and dark glasses. He'd only seen the youth once before, at the Djinnversoctoannular Tournament, the previous December in New York's Algonquin Hotel. But it was hardly a face he would have forgotten. The young man on the cell phone was a djinn, an Ifrit, and a thoroughly nasty piece of work. Philippa had easily bested him in her first game and, predictably, he had been a sore and foulmouthed loser. It was Rudyard Teer, one of the many sons of Iblis.

"So how's Operation Magic Square coming along, Dad? . . . It is? . . . Cool. That Dybbuk kid is so dumb . . . I know he's your son, too, Dad. But you have to admit, he's a schmuck. . . . All right, all right, if you say so. He's my half brother, okay. More like half-witted, if you ask me. Listen, Dad, forget that. I've got the latest Keyfitz numbers for you."

What's a Keyfitz number? thought Finlay.

I have no idea, admitted John silently.

"We're up to ninety billion souls accounted for and dealt with," said Rudyard Teer. "That's right. Ninety billion absorbed by your warrior devils. Isn't it incredible? We're only six billion short of completely clearing out the whole lousy spirit world ahead of the operation. . . . Dad? Dad, your signal's breaking up. Did I hear you right? You don't want me to bother with those other six billion souls? . . . Okay, Dad. Whatever you say. And you're right. Six billion is just too few to get in the way of what we're planning. Okay, Dad. Call you tomorrow. Bye."

Still laughing, Rudyard Teer walked back along the

gangway. Seconds later, the lights in the exhibition hall went out, and the terra-cotta warriors and the boy hiding behind one of these were plunged back into darkness.

What was all that about? thought Finlay.

I'm still thinking about it, replied John.

We have to warn Nimrod, said Finlay.

If we follow him through that door, won't we just be walking into the same trap? asked John.

Good point.

Look, Nimrod is a very powerful djinn, said John. *And Groanin has an extra-powerful arm. We have to assume that they can look after themselves, but if they can't, we're not likely to be able to help him. I mean, I have no djinn power. And you're just a normal mundane kid.*

Can't argue with any of that, admitted Finlay.

If Rudyard Teer thinks we're in the same boat as Nimrod and Groanin, and we're not, that gives us a possible advantage, said John. *Which we might just throw away by going through the open sesame door like they did. I think our best bet is to go back to the hotel and wait there and hope that Philippa is able to solve Cardinal Marrone's mystery in the painting back in Venice, and that she's able to find that golden tablet of command. The way I see it, if we're to go after Nimrod and Groanin, we ought to have something in our arsenal that can dig them out of any spot they might get themselves into. Marco Polo's golden tablet is the one thing that can do that.*

What if she doesn't? asked Finlay. *What if Philippa can't solve the mystery in that painting?*

If anyone can solve that puzzle, it's her, said John. *My twin sister has a brain in her head the size of a basketball. Especially since she spent that time* being groomed as the next Blue Djinn. But I dunno what happens next if she doesn't crack it. I really don't. From the sound of what that jerk Rudyard Teer was saying just now, I guess Philippa's solving the mystery in that painting might just be a matter of life and death. In fact, it could be more important than that.

CHAPTER 26

A WILD-GOOSE CHASE

At the Gallerie dell' Accademia in Venice, Philippa sat alone in front of the painting of the Doge's golden palace. The four peasants who were examining the foundation stone of the palace on which appeared the apparently nonsensical Roman numeral equation looked every bit as puzzled as Philippa felt herself to be. She bent her brain one way and then the other, certain that the answer to the problem lay in solving the insoluble $XI + I = X$. Which being insoluble, wasn't going to be easy. How could eleven plus one ever equal ten? It didn't make sense. Of course, that was the whole point. If it had made sense, it wouldn't have been a mystery. She spent a whole day just looking at the picture and thinking about it.

Philippa was alone in the Gallerie because she had told Marco Polo to stay at the hotel to stop him from distracting her. Having tasted Italian ice cream — the recipe for which he claimed to have brought from China at the end of the thirteenth century — Marco had kept on telling her just how much better it was than Chinese ice cream. Frankly, Philippa wasn't in the least surprised by that news. She was quite fond of Italian ice cream herself. Marco was also enthusiastic about pasta, coffee, Bellini cocktails, and, of course, the women of Venice, who are among the most beautiful in all of Italy. He did not, however, think very much of television. "It would be better," he had declared, "if it wasn't always the same thing on TV. This boy wizard, Jonathan Tarot, really irritates me."

Philippa wasn't inclined to disagree with him there, either.

A couple of times Sister Cristina turned up at the Gallerie and asked how Philippa was getting on. She even brought Philippa a book about the Cardinal Marrone mystery written by a man called Michel Bustinadité, and this was an easy way for her to make a note of the numbers that were painted along the bottom of the picture:

3376 619 77345 35007 32135 3704 0705 3751 1704 539076 535509 335 06 07734

Philippa wondered if these might be a code, like the dancing snakes she and John and Dybbuk had encountered in the picture that had taken them on their adventure to Kathmandu and Lucknow; as a result, she spent several hours trying to find the most common letters that might break the rest of the code. Using this method, she ended up with a message that started with "ee," and since the only word she could think of beginning with two e's was "eel," she hardly thought that this method of unlocking what the numbers meant promised to be very enlightening. There are no eels in Venice.

Weary from her extended brain work, Philippa lay down on the bench, which, being long and upholstered with leather, was very comfortable — more like a bed, in fact; after a while, she went to sleep.

She woke up with a pain in her neck. Her head had slipped off the bench while she was asleep and when she opened her eyes everything was upside down. Somehow the picture made better sense that way, which made her think she must still be half asleep and, shaking her head clear of sleep, Philippa sat up. It was a minute or two before it dawned on her that looking at the painting upside down was just about the only way she hadn't looked at it.

Whipping off her jacket, Philippa made a sort of cushion out of it, and laid it on the floor, next to the wall. With her back to the picture, she knelt down, placed the crown of her head on the makeshift cushion, and then kicked her legs high into the air, into a headstand. Philippa hoped she might avoid the scrutiny of one of the museum attendants long enough to make the upside-down discovery she now felt was imminent.

"Eureka!" she whispered as her head filled with blood and a sudden understanding of the Roman numeral equation. "I've found it." And she *had* found it, too. Upside down, the equation XI + I = X looked like X = I + IX. This, of course, made perfect sense since ten does equal one plus nine. This meant that the picture was only supposed to make sense as a message when it was upside down. This surely meant the numbers along the bottom of the picture were also supposed to be read upside down.

Excited, she dropped to the floor, found the sheet of paper upon which she had carefully copied out these numbers from the painting, and turned it around so that the bottom was now at the top. And, after a moment or two, she saw that what the artist had done was basically just the same stupid, infantile trick that John had once shown her using a pocket calculator: how when you keyed the number 07734 and then turned it upside down, you got the word "hello."

Cardinal Marrone's hidden message was longer and less obviously meaningful.

The message read as follows:

HELLO. GO SEE BOSSES GLOBES. HOLI ISLE. SOLO HOLE. SEIZE LOOSE SHELL. BIG GLEE.

Of course, reading the message was one thing. Understanding what it meant was quite another. These words were clearly directions of some kind. And very likely something involving the Duke's palace. But it was clear to Philippa that she was going to need an older brain than hers to work out some of the references. She decided to return to St. Mark's and enlist the help of Sister Cristina.

Scattering a flock of pigeons in her haste to be across St. Mark's Square, Philippa saw that the line outside the palace was the biggest she had seen and seemed to stretch right down to the Grand Canal. She patted herself on the back that she'd had the good sense to see the palace already. Which was when it started to dawn on her that maybe some of the message wasn't so hard to understand after all. What else were the Doges or dukes of Venice than the *bosses* of Venice? And didn't the palace have two of the largest *globes* Philippa had ever seen?

Hello, the cardinal seemed to be saying, *this is the place to start.* Where better to begin a search for a magical treasure than in an ancient map room?

Changing course halfway across the square, Philippa made for the line outside the palace; an hour later, she found herself running up the stairs and through the palace to the map room where she remembered the two globes being on display.

These were considerably larger than any globes she had ever seen before. Each of them was as tall as an upright piano, about as wide as a car, and the color of old leather. Possibly they were very valuable. Certainly they were very old.

Philippa walked around the globes like a sculptor surveying his subject, and wondering why even in a palace anyone had ever needed two enormous globes. Made in the eighteenth century, the two globes, which stood next to each other on a marble floor, were protected by a small metal fence that was supposed to stop people from touching them. This was exactly what Philippa wanted to do. How else was she to find the Holi Isle? There was another problem, too. Being not much taller than the equator on the globes, how was she ever going to search the two northern hemispheres?

For the moment, she confined her search to the two southern hemispheres. Getting as close to the globes as she dared, she crept around them looking for — she didn't know what exactly. Yet, at the same time, she presumed Cardinal Marrone would have left some indication on one of the globes as to where the holy isle was to be found.

When her search of the southern hemispheres was complete, she considered returning to the hotel and getting Marco Polo so that she might sit upon his shoulders, and then rejected the idea. Marco was much too old to manage something like that. Besides, the palace would be closing soon. There was no time to go back to the hotel and then have to wait in line again. What she needed was a set of steps . . .

Even as this last thought entered Philippa's head, a man who was at least as tall as a set of steps entered the map room. He was black and good-looking and wore a New York Giants T-shirt that made her think he might be some kind of football player, and an American, to boot. She followed him around the room for a moment, noted that his guidebook to the palace was in English, and then made her move.

"Hi," she said brightly. "You from the States?"

"New York," said the man. "Just like it says on the shirt." He smiled. "Where are you from, honey?"

"New York. I was wondering if you could do me a small favor."

"Anything for a fellow New Yorker."

"I need to see on top of those globes," she said. "Only I'm too short. Could you maybe lift me up? On your shoulders?"

The man grinned. "Sure," he said. "Why not?" He dropped down to his knees. "Climb aboard. By the way, the name's John Nevada."

Even Philippa had heard of John Nevada.

"The football player?"

"Yes."

"Pleased to meet you, John. My name is Philippa Gaunt."

Philippa clambered onto Nevada's shoulders and then uttered a quiet squeal as he stood up again, carrying her to a height of more than seven feet from which it was easy to see the tops of the two globes.

"I'm not too heavy for you, I hope."

"Heck, no." Nevada walked slowly around the globes. "What are you looking for, anyway?"

"I don't know exactly," she admitted. "But I'll know it when I see it."

"This isn't a trick, I hope," said Nevada.

"No, no. I'm perfectly serious. I have to write about these globes, you see. For a school paper. But it's a little hard to study them when you can only see half of them." She added plausibly, "I just wanted to see how accurate eighteenth-century mapmaking actually was."

"Fair enough," he said. "How accurate is it?"

"Europe looks pretty much the same."

"That's what I've been thinking ever since I got here."

"Wait," said Philippa. "Stop a second."

She leaned forward to take a closer look. Something gold on top of one of the globes was glinting in the sunlight streaming through the palace window. It was a little gold cross painted on the globe. Just off the west coast of Scotland.

That had to be it. How else would a cardinal mark a holy isle than with a cross? And with a gold cross for a golden tablet. That made perfect sense, too. When she got back to the hotel, she would look up this holy isle on the Internet and see what other clues she might discover to shed further light on the remainder of Marrone's message.

"I think I've seen enough now," she said.

Nevada knelt down and allowed her to dismount from his broad shoulders.

"Thank you," said Philippa. "That was very enlightening."

"No problem," said Nevada, standing up once more. "Bringing enlightenment to the world. That's my thing, you know?"

Feeling justly proud of herself and excited by this latest discovery, Philippa returned quickly to the hotel and went straight into the business center, where she logged on to a computer and began an Internet search for information on the holy isle.

There were two holy isles: one off the coast of northwest England, and the other — the one she was looking for — in the Firth of Clyde, off the west coast of central Scotland, inside Lamlash Bay on the larger Isle of Arran. The island had a long history as a sacred site, with a spring said to have healing properties. It was also the site of the hermit cave of a sixth-century monk called St. Laserian.

A hermit cave?

Philippa looked again at the message revealed in the upside-down numbers. If a hermit was a person who lived a solitary life, sometimes in a cave, for the sake of his religion, might that explain the part of the secret message that used the words "solo hole"?

It had to be, although at the same time it did seem to Philippa that a remote Scottish island was a very long way to travel from Venice to hide the golden tablet of command. Fortunately, Michel Bustinadité's book about Cardinal Marrone mentioned that toward the end of his life, the cardinal had taken a holiday on the Isle of Arran; this helped to persuade Philippa that it really might be worth the effort for her and Marco to fly all the way to Scotland and look for the golden tablet there.

Philippa booked the plane tickets. Two hours later, she and Marco Polo were on their way to the Venice airport. Marco was very impressed by the discovery that the Venice airport was named after himself. And even more so by the discovery that they would be traveling to Scotland aboard a plane.

"How long would it take to fly to China in one of these planes?" he asked Philippa.

"Maybe ten or twelve hours," she said.

"And to think it took me ten months to get there," he said, shaking his head. "Which is fortunate for me, I suppose. I don't imagine anyone would have been interested in my book of travels if it had taken me just ten hours to get to China."

"I think that's what's wrong with the world today," said Philippa. "It seems too small, I guess."

Before they boarded the plane, Philippa called Nimrod on his cell phone to tell him the good news and was disappointed to discover that she couldn't get through. So she called home instead, hoping for some good news about her mother; while there was no news of her, either, she did at least get to speak to her father, who was sufficiently recovered from the Methusaleh binding to hold a meaningful conversation.

Thinking that it would be a nice surprise for him, she didn't tell him that Layla was on her way back home — which was probably just as well, given what had happened. And she confined her conversation to a few general remarks about Venice and Scotland and China. Her father told Philippa he missed her and John a lot and urged her to hurry home. This was enough to bring a tear to her eye, as she missed home and her parents and her twin brother. She also was badly missing having her djinn power, not because she wanted to do anything particular with it but because having it gave her a tremendous sense of well-being and confidence, neither of which she had felt in a long while.

To Philippa's great surprise, Marco did not display any nervousness during his first flight. Despite this — not to mention his own reputation as a great explorer — Marco quickly revealed himself as a difficult person to travel with. He complained about almost everything: There were too many people on the airport bus; the seat in the plane was much too small; the in-flight meal was tasteless; the wine tasted like vinegar; air travel was very boring since there was nothing to see except air. During the flight, Philippa thought that she would go crazy, he complained so much.

But it was only when they arrived in Scotland, at the not so imaginatively named Glasgow City Airport, that Marco Polo really got going with the complaints: Scotland was too wet and too cold; the people looked mean and smelled strange; nobody was wearing tartan, as he had expected them to do; Glasgow was grim and dirty and there was not enough sunlight; the food — especially the ice cream — was cheap and nasty; the air smelled strongly of beer; the taxi stank of air freshener and cigarettes — which, admittedly, is an unpleasant combination of smells; he couldn't understand a word of the English that was spoken in Scotland.

Philippa could hardly fault Marco for this last complaint. Even she had to admit that it was hard to understand the mangled type of English spoken by Scots. The taxi driver they hired to drive them southwest to Ardrossan — from where they planned to take a ferry to the island — seemed especially hard to understand. Friendly, but quite impossible to hold any kind of conversation with. He seemed to have no trouble understanding what Philippa said. It was just that she couldn't comprehend anything at all of what he was saying back to them.

Arriving in the little town of Ardrossan about an hour later, following a journey made exhausting by misunderstanding, Philippa and Marco caught the ferry to Arran and, following a one-hour sea voyage, they reached the island just before dark, and spent the night at the Broons Hotel in Brodick, which is the main port.

Like the hotel, the next morning was cold and inhospitable. The sun shone on the sandstone-colored buildings with a hard uncompromising light that was very different from the light in Venice. And yet, somehow, it was beautiful, too. They hired a small boat with an outboard motor, and sailed off across a freezing, glassy sea to the holy island. Philippa felt they were traveling to the rim of the world, which was hardly made any easier by Marco's insistence that the Earth was flat and that they would surely sail off the edge of the sea to their doom. But, after a while, the island hove into view, much to Marco's relief.

The holy island is owned by Tibetan lamas, and there is a large Buddhist monastery on the island, which struck Philippa as a bit strange — following her experiences at the Jayaar Sho Ashram in India — even a little suspicious. Like the disciples of Guru Masamjhasara, the monks at the Peace Center on the holy isle wore orange robes and did lots of yoga. But there the similarities ended, for these were kind, hospitable people and their spiritual leader, Dr. Yes, who was Chinese, seemed especially pleased to be spoken to in his own language by Marco, although for obvious reasons, Philippa thought it best that Marco should not tell the doctor his real name.

She and Marco told the doctor only that they had come to visit the hermit cave of St. Laserian of Leighlin, and the doctor lent them the services of a monk to guide them to the other side of the island, where the cave was to be found.

"I've never seen the point of being a hermit," Philippa told Marco as they walked up one steep hill and down another. "I mean, what exactly do hermits do that makes them so holy?"

"I think the whole point is not to do very much at all," said Marco. "Just stop yourself from having a good time."

"I guess that's easy enough if you live in a cave on a remote Scottish island," said Philippa.

"I think hermits are just people who are very bad at resisting temptation," said Marco. "This is probably why they come to places like this in the first place."

"Good point."

Close by the seashore they found the cave, which was not much to look at, and it was hard to imagine anyone living there, let alone a cardinal choosing to hide something valuable in the cave. It was covered over with moss and grass and a large, round, flat rock that looked like it had been a popular nesting site for geese since time immemorial. Going too near the nests was guaranteed to make the geese honk and hiss at them aggressively.

Marco dropped to his knees and clasped his hands and, after a minute or two, the monk politely went away. Minutes passed and then Marco spoke. "Well?" he said. "We're here. What's the next part of the message? Come on."

"I'm sorry," said Philippa. "After your performance in the boat — all that flat Earth stuff — I thought you were praying."

"No," said Marco. "I just did that to get rid of our Buddhist guide. People always leave you alone when you look like you're praying."

"Good thinking."

Philippa hardly needed to consult the sheet of paper bearing the cryptic message from the cardinal's painting.

"Seize loose shell," she said. "Big glee."

"Do you see a shell in there?" asked Marco, looking around.

"No," said Philippa.

The cave was small, to say the least, and Marco had to stoop to go inside. "St. Laserian must have been quite a short man," he observed, glancing around.

"But a tough one, I suspect," said Philippa. "Do you suppose he ever had a door or a wall on the entrance? To keep out the wind and the rain and the sea spray."

"I think not," said Marco. "When I was alive toward the end of the thirteenth century, Europe was full of hermits. There were some who used to stand in the open air. Others who used to sit on top of a pillar. And a few who used to shut themselves up in a cell. Quite mad, mostly. I think they all welcomed a bit of wind and rain. To test themselves."

A gust of wind peppered their faces with icy rain, as if the spirit of St. Laserian had been trying to remind them of his sufferings. The wild geese nesting on top of the cave honked noisily like New York taxis, warning the pair to keep their distance.

Philippa touched some ancient writing on the wall of the cave. "I wonder what language this is written in," she said.

"I don't know," said Marco. "But I'd say this writing was probably here on the wall of the cave long before St. Laserian took up residence in it." He paused. "*Bene*. What do you think we should do now?"

"Dig," said Philippa, and produced a trowel from the sleeve of her jacket.

"Where did you get that?" asked Marco.

"I borrowed it from the monks' garden," confessed Philippa, and, kneeling down, she began to dig.

Half an hour passed. And then an hour. Philippa found an old coin, a button, and a piece of rusting iron that looked like a piece of old fence post. But of a shell or a golden tablet of command there was no sign. Angry and frustrated, Philippa went out of the cave and threw the old fence post into the sea.

"I don't get it," she said. "We know Cardinal Marrone came here on vacation. There's a golden cross marking the holy isle on the globe in the Doge's Palace. And there is only one hermit cave on this holy isle. This just has to be the right place. But there is no loose shell to seize."

"Perhaps someone else stumbled upon it," suggested Marco, "by accident."

"Cardinal Marrone was too clever for that," said Philippa. "He meant for that tablet to be found. But only by someone who solved his clues."

"Then maybe you made a mistake," said Marco. "In which case we've endured a miserable journey and come all the way to this godforsaken country for no reason at all. We'll never find the golden tablet." He sighed. "This has been a complete wild-goose chase."

"What did you say?"

"I said we seem to have come here for no reason at all."

"No, no, you said something else." There was something nagging at the back of Philippa's mind. But what was it? "Something relevant."

Marco shrugged silently.

"Look, I didn't make a mistake," said Philippa. "I couldn't have. But it's just possible that someone else did. The man who wrote that book about Cardinal Marrone. Michel Bustinadité. I used his book as the source for the numbers on the bottom of the painting — the ones that give us the message when they're turned upside down — because unlike him, I wasn't able to touch the painting myself." She was searching her bag for the book. "But if he made a mistake copying them down, then it's just possible we're looking for the wrong thing."

She found the book that Sister Cristina had given her back in Venice, studied a close-up photograph of the numbers on the painting for a while, and then let out a hoot.

"What is it?" asked Marco.

"This number 35007," she said. "It's very faint. But that's not a seven at all. It's a six! It's 35006. Look."

"Yes, you're right," admitted Marco. "But where does that get us?"

"Everywhere," insisted Philippa. She wrote the number out and then turned it upside down. "It's not a 'loose' shell we should be looking for. It's 'goose' shell. Well, don't you see? The tablet's not in the cave. It's on top of it!"

They eyed the geese nesting on top of the cave uncertainly. One that was the size of a German shepherd dog — or possibly a German shepherd — occupied a nest bigger than the rest on a sort of small rocky plateau. And sensing some danger, it hissed loudly and flapped its wings in a warning display. The wings sounded like someone shaking heavy beach towels in the wind.

Philippa and Marco kept on looking. And the more she looked, the more Philippa thought this seemed a perfect spot to hide something precious. Especially as the goose is a bird known for its aggression when guarding its nest.

"That big bird's nest is the one we need to look under," said Philippa.

Marco nodded in agreement. "Nasty temperament, the goose," he said. "But good eating all the same."

The goose fixed them both with a beady and distrustful eye. Philippa didn't doubt for a moment that the goose would give them a sharp peck if they got too close. A peck or something worse. A sharp blow from a flapping goose wing can break a human arm.

"How are we going to move that goose long enough for us to take a closer look at what's underneath?" asked Philippa. She was a clever girl, but not a cruel one, especially where animals were concerned.

Marco Polo, who came from a different time, knew no such restraint. "Easy," he said, and began to pelt the goose with stones.

The goose stood up, honked loudly, took a stone in the chest, flapped its wings, received another well-thrown stone to the head, and, before Philippa could protest at Marco's cruelty, it flew away, apparently none the worse for wear.

"Come on," said Marco. "Let's see what's there. Before it comes back again."

They did their best to move the nest and the eggs it contained with care, so that the mother goose might come back to them later on. Their efforts were complicated by the amount of goose dirt that lay on the little plateau; and soon it was unpleasantly clear to them both that geese had been nesting on that particular spot for a very long time indeed. Holding her nose, Philippa began to scrape at the site with the trowel.

"It's lucky I brought this," said Philippa. "I'd hate to be doing this with my bare hands."

The rock under the nest was hollowed into a saucer shape and, eventually, they scraped enough dirt away to reveal a square stone, like a plug in a basin, which looked as if it had been placed there deliberately, to hide something.

Marco took the trowel, pried the stone loose, and then levered it up. Underneath the stone was a deep hole. Philippa disliked the idea of putting her hand in the hole, but she took a deep breath, reached inside, felt around for a moment, and then withdrew a rectangular object wrapped in oil-skin and leather. It was a heavy object and it looked as if it had been there for at least a hundred years.

"Yes!" she yelled with enormous satisfaction. "Yes, yes, yes! We've found it, I'm sure."

"It's certainly the right size, all right," admitted Marco.

They retreated to the shelter of the cave and then unwrapped the package to reveal an object the size of a large bar of chocolate, covered with Chinese writing. Shining brightly in the cold, harsh Scottish morning sunlight, it looked like something fallen from heaven. It was the golden tablet of command.

"After all these centuries," Marco gasped. "I thought I'd never set eyes on this again," he said with real tears in his eyes. "And thanks to you, I have." But he did not touch it.

"Go ahead," said Philippa, wiping her hands. "Pick it up."

"I'm afraid it always made me rather nervous," confessed Marco. "I think that's one of the reasons I managed to lose it in the first place. The responsibility of such power was too great for me. No, you take it."

Philippa, who was used to the responsibility of power, hefted the object in her hand. The golden tablet was heavy. And not just with weight. There was something about it — a feeling of electricity — that gave her the sense of having a supernatural power back at her command. Like djinn power.

"Just how powerful is this thing?" she asked Marco Polo.

"It's irresistible," said Marco. "Whatever you order. It will be done. Those to whom you issue commands, they will have no choice but to obey. That is how it is with the golden tablet. That is how it has always been."

"Well, now that we've found it," she said, "we'd better think of how we're going to get ourselves all the way to China."

"It's a journey I've taken before," said Marco. "But now that you have the golden tablet of command it will be easy enough."

Marco sighed and wandered down to the shore where he took a deep breath and looked out to sea. Philippa thought the expression on the old man's face was a sad one.

"*Va bene,*" he said. "It's been good to be back in the living world after all these years. I've enjoyed it. But my work here is now complete. The message is delivered and the golden tablet of command is in your possession. It's time for me to leave."

Marco Polo might have been a terrible traveling companion but suddenly the prospect of going to China by herself seemed infinitely worse to Philippa. "Don't go," she said.

"Not now. I'd have thought a trip to China would have appealed to you."

"Once that was true," said Marco. "But not anymore. Besides, I don't think I could face a ten-hour flight to China. I don't know how anyone could. Anyway, I've done what I promised the great Khan I would do. Now I just want to rest. I hope you enjoy China as much as I did." He bent down and kissed Philippa on both cheeks, in the Latin way. *"Arrivederci, cara mia."*

"But what will I tell Dr. Yes and those monks?" she asked. "They'll wonder what's happened to you."

"No," he said. "Not if you don't want them to. You'll find that people do exactly what you want, Philippa. So long as you are holding the golden tablet of command. Good luck, my child. You're a remarkable little girl. Good luck and God-speed."

"But what's going to happen to you?" she asked anxiously.

"What can happen to me that hasn't happened already?" said Marco calmly. He sat down on the beach and then lay down and stared up at the sun as if it had been a hot summer's day and he was a man without a care in the world.

"You can't stay there," said Philippa.

"I won't be here for long," said Marco. "I'm a Venetian, after all. The sea will come and get me."

Philippa glanced around hardly knowing what to expect. And then she saw it. Out at sea. It was a large wave, perhaps five or six feet tall, rolling steadily toward the beach they were on, moving like a herd of drowning horses, as if it had some sort of titanic purpose.

"There's a big wave coming this way," she told him. "You're going to get very wet if you don't move."

"*Bene,*" he sighed, and closed his eyes.

Instinctively, Philippa withdrew to the safety of the rock on top of the hermit's cave and waited. For a moment it crossed her mind to use the golden tablet of command to make Marco leave the beach and accompany her to China. But somehow that hardly seemed fair. Besides, it was clear that he welcomed what was about to happen.

Seconds later, the big wave hit the beach with an enormous whiplashing roar, engulfing Marco and all the rocks and pools that surrounded him. And when the turbulent, leaden wave ebbed quietly away, the old explorer was gone without a trace. Philippa stood there for a long time looking out to sea, searching the undulating waves and the misty horizon for some last sign of him. But there was none and it was as if he had never been there, as if the sea had reclaimed him.

Philippa stood there for a long time, her face wet with sea spray and salty tears, unable to tell the taste of one from the other. Then she wiped her face and, with the golden tablet of command safely in her bag, she set off back across the island to the monastery.

If the golden tablet worked in the way Marco said it would, she thought she might be in China in less than twenty-four hours.

CHAPTER 27

THE MAGIC SQUARE

The Jonathan Tarot Magic Square (with simple, easy-to-learn instructions on how to whirl like a dervish) sold over one hundred million units in stores all over the world. It was the biggest-selling "toy" of all time. People not able to get to a store were able to download, from the Jonathan Tarot Web site, a design that they could draw on a floor. Anyone measuring the download design or the sheet of plastic (that was backed with adhesive so that it could stick to the floor) would have observed that the magic square was exactly III inches by III. Few people, if any, guessed the true cosmic significance of these dimensions. And children everywhere — to say nothing of quite a few adults — made careful preparations to use the collective power of their own minds to "assist" Jonathan Tarot's disappearance from the concrete roof of a New York parking lot, live on television.

Of course, the true purpose of the exercise was much more sinister. But this was only to be expected of someone like Iblis who was currently possessing the human body of Adam Apollonius. Sinister and a bit complicated.

As students of the djinn know well, there exists in the universe a balance of power between good luck and bad luck. This is called the Homeostasis. Sometimes there is more good luck and sometimes there is more bad luck, but mostly the Homeostasis prevails. Now the djinn have a natural ability to control luck. They can make it bad or they can make it good, depending on their natural inclination to grant wishes. But they are few in number — too few to radically affect the Homeostasis one way or the other.

The same is not true, however, of human beings. People have a much greater capacity to affect the Homeostasis than the djinn. This is because there are many more of them. Which is why human will — especially the will of children in whom the life force is very strong — is the most powerful force in the universe. Of course, in practice, this force never amounts to very much because, in the normal state of affairs, human beings think in very different ways and according to their individual interests, not as one unified will. At least, they had seldom acted as one unified will until Iblis hatched his horrible plot to bring about the opposite of the normal, chaotic state of human affairs and create the largest pattern of single will in the universe since the dawn of man. He even had a word for this: He called it the "Negentropy." Television was ideal for his purpose, especially if there was just one TV show that everyone could focus on. Television is the one thing on planet Earth that has the potential to deliver a hundred million minds all thinking exactly the same thought at exactly the same time. Such a television show had never existed. *Until now.* Jonathan Tarot was Iblis's master stroke, for his was the television show that it seemed everyone was going to watch at the same time, thanks to the miracle of satellites. It was the one television show that was going to make everyone think the one same thought at exactly the same moment.

And having done all that, what then?

To say that the Homeostasis would be affected radically by Negentropy and that bad luck would dominate the universe hardly begins to describe the terrible result Iblis had planned. The true horror of what would follow was a word that is only ever whispered by good djinn. It was a sort of curse that exploits the natural tendency among humankind to wish for good things to happen, and then creates its exact opposite. Thus, a man wishing for black would end up with white; wishing for light would bring only dark. This was what Iblis planned. Of course, the djinn had a word for this, too. The djinn have a word for everything. They call this state of affairs, in which the natural order of the universe would be turned upside down, a state of "Enantodromia."

Big words. With even bigger consequences. For everyone in the world.

All of this was going to be brought about through the mathematical power of the magic square and the dance of the whirling dervishes. And, of course, Jonathan Tarot.

*   *   *

On the night that Jonathan Tarot's live TV special entitled "The Disappearing Dervish" was to be screened, people left school or work early, to make sure they were home in time to see the show. They drew or unfolded their Jonathan Tarot Magic Squares in front of their television sets, and sat on the number four, which, of course, is also the Chinese word for "death," and waited.

In the hour of the broadcast, cinemas, theaters, and restaurants in cities all over the world remained empty as people stayed at home to watch their TVs and to participate in what was billed as "the largest feat of mind over matter of all time." Television audiences were projected to be bigger than the audiences for the Olympic Games, the Superbowl, and the F.A. Cup Final, *put together*.

Most adults remained skeptical and thought that the whole thing was a trick. No one could just disappear into thin air. It was an illusion. A feat of prestidigitation. It would probably be a good one, it had to be admitted, if Jonathan Tarot's previous feats were anything to go by. But just a trick, nonetheless. That was what adults said.

It goes without saying, of course, that becoming a grown-up is largely about losing the capacity to believe in anything very much. Only children had the capacity to really believe in the possibility of what was going to happen, in the same way that they believe in the Tooth Fairy and Santa Claus. Only children believed that it might actually be possible to focus their thoughts simultaneously on just one thing and thereby help Jonathan disappear from a Manhattan rooftop.

Children all over the world believed in Jonathan Tarot. That was what Iblis was counting on.

As the show went on air, the atmosphere was electric. At seven o'clock, Jonathan Tarot went on a Manhattan rooftop and stood inside a giant magic square, just like Adam Apollonius had told him to do. Several helicopters circled overhead to film the event but also to prove there was going to be no trickery from above. A construction worker drilled at the number four on which Jonathan was planning to stand in order to prove that the roof was solid. An invited audience of movie stars and celebrities sat in a circle around the square to make sure there were no props to assist Jonathan's disappearance.

Just about the only celebrity who was not there was Adam Apollonius. Unknown to Jonathan, Apollonius was already on his way to Xian in China, so that he could mastermind the next stage of the Ifrits' evil plan.

Then, at precisely eight P.M. Eastern time, Jonathan, wearing his lightest, shiniest Elvis outfit, addressed a camera that was beaming his handsome, glamorous image to millions of kids.

"Hi, everyone, and welcome to my TV special," said Jonathan. "And what a special it's going to be. Someone once said that with enough faith you can move mountains. Let's hope so. Because tonight I'm going to show the world something never before seen on live television. I'm going to show that with enough faith — your faith in me — something can disappear into thin air.

"This is not a trick. This is not an illusion. There are no boxes or silk bags for me to hide in. There are no trapdoors. As you've seen, this rooftop is solid concrete. There are no mirrors to deceive the eye. No giant turntables to move things around. There are no aerial wires to lift me up. In fact, there are no props at all. Instead, there are powerful floodlights so that you can see everything in the sharpest detail. Everything you see and then don't see will be the real thing. Not an illusion in the normal sense of that word. The only thing I have to help me tonight is this Chinese magic square and the collective power of your own minds to harness its mathematical power and provide me with the energy needed to perform this disappearance. That's all. And to everyone who says it can't be done, I say, watch this space. This space, right here."

Jonathan grinned and pointed at the magic square under his feet.

"The ancient dervishes believed that turning the body quickly in a circle was the way to achieve enlightenment. That it would open the door to enable the body to receive a certain kind of energy. The word 'dervish' actually means 'doorway.' With your help, boys and girls, it's a doorway that I intend to open tonight. The energy of your thoughts will enable me to spin faster. The power of your thoughts will enter my upward extended right hand and then leave my lower left hand to enter this rooftop. And while I am spinning, I will disappear through that doorway into another world."

As far as Jonathan Tarot was concerned, all of this was complete nonsense. As he was a djinn, his disappearance was guaranteed. He tried to keep the sneer out of his voice and to conceal the contempt he felt for his young audience. But he considered nearly all of what he was saying to be laughable and nothing more than hype thought up by Adam Apollonius to help generate the largest television audience ever and to make lots of money for Adam Apollonius and to make him, Jonathan Tarot, the most famous man in the world. Bigger than John Lennon and Elvis and Houdini and all the rest of them put together. At least that's what he thought.

"However, it's also possible," continued Jonathan Tarot, "that tonight we may go even further than just my own disappearance. If, as I expect, I do step through that doorway into another world, I want you all to follow my example and try it for yourself. Using the power of the magic square, I want you all to spin like a dervish on the number four. Perhaps you, too, will disappear just like me. Let's hope so. Right now, however, all I want you to do is to sit there and watch me spinning and, using the power of your collective thoughts, *will* me into a state of nothingness."

Jonathan clapped his heavily ringed hands and stepped onto the number four. "All right. Let's do it."

He waved at the band — a Turkish band — that played a subtle, hypnotic, gyrating music that was designed to help build an atmosphere. That had been Adam Apollonius's idea, too. Hypnosis was an important part of his plan for the mass television audience. Naturally, Jonathan didn't need it. He didn't need anything except djinn power.

Jonathan walked a turn to his right several times, with arms raised and arms down, the way he had seen the dervishes do it in the film Apollonius had shown him. They always began with a turn to the right. Adam Apollonius had been quite insistent about that. Then he dropped his head onto his chest, looked at the floor, then at the sky. And only after seven complete turns did he switch arm positions and begin turning to the left, counterclockwise. Counterclockwise is always the direction evil travels in most comfortably.

As Jonathan Tarot turned and whirled, millions of children concentrated on making him disappear with all the life force at their command. Gradually, he started to turn faster in time to the music, and the invited celebrity audience clapped or rattled their expensive jewelry. Two minutes passed. Then three. There was no doubting Jonathan Tarot's showmanship. Or his speed in the turns. He was like a spinning top. This was quite a show. Even the skeptics held their breath.

After a while, to everyone who was watching on the roof or on television, it seemed that Jonathan's body began to blur and then to leave a slight trail of smoke, as if the speed of his turns was generating heat. Heat was part of it, certainly. Djinn are made of fire, after all, and when a transubstantiation takes place, it's fire that turns a body into smoke.

The rooftop audience gasped. Some of them stood up so that they could see better. Others, distrusting the evidence of their own eyes, took out glasses and put them on. The blur became less humanly shaped, more like a cloud. Some began to shout their amazement and approval in that whoop-whooping way Americans have when they express loud enthusiasm for something. One or two whistled. Others began to applaud vigorously. And quite a few cheered. For it was plain to see — or not to see, depending on how you looked at it — that Jonathan Tarot had indeed disappeared in a puff of moving and then rapidly dispersing smoke.

Millions watching at home felt their jaws drop and their eyes pop out of their heads. The same series of thoughts dominated young minds everywhere. *He's gone. He's disappeared. We did that. We made someone disappear into thin air.*

And, *If he did it, then, perhaps, we can disappear, too.*

So they stood up. Millions of children. All over the world. They stood up and danced a solitary dervish dance in an ever decreasing circle. Spinning until they became dizzy, and yet dancing on and on. And because they were all doing it at the same time with the same half-baked thought in their dizzy, half-conscious minds, the gravitational pull of the dance became stronger, the turn became molecular and galactic and a spiritual remembering of the power at the heart of the universe, and the effect Iblis had predicted, happened.

They disappeared.

But it was not their bodies that disappeared. Iblis had no use for those. There's no power at all to be gained from the puny body of a child. But the strong spirit of a child was a different story. These were what the Ifrit was after. And it was these, the spirits of children — millions of them — that slipped and fell unseen, through the dervish doorway made possible by Dybbuk's whirling example and the mathematics that are contained in the Chinese magic square, into the world that lies alongside the physical world: the spirit world.

Now normally, as you might expect, the spirit world is a very crowded place. Naturally, it is full of ghosts. It has been estimated by a scientist and mathematician called Keyfitz that the number of people who have ever lived upon the Earth is ninety-six billion. And, but for the actions of the warrior devils, this is the number of ghosts that would usually have been abroad in the spirit world. They would certainly have impeded the progress of the spirit children to the place Iblis had prepared for them. This was why he had done what he had done. For he had no use, either, for those in whom the life force had already been extinguished.

"Genocide" is a word that only relates to the extermination of living peoples. And there is no actual word for the extermination of dead ones. If it is not a contradiction in words, Iblis and his sons had made an industrially efficient job of exterminating billions of ghosts and spirits. Using the warrior devils and the tiny amount of djinn spit contained in the terra-cotta that made them, Iblis had managed to send thousands of them into the spirit world where some ninety billion human souls had been absorbed. This left only six billion souls left in the world of spirit and therefore plenty of room to move the souls of millions of children efficiently and unimpeded through the spirit world to Xian.

The same swift, irresistible, and magnetic-like force that Faustina had experienced in the spirit world some months before and that dragged her all the way to Xian in China now did exactly the same thing to the spirits of millions of living children. Swept along by an invisible tsunami, the terror of the children cannot be underestimated and did not stop until they reached the source of the force, which was a huge pyramid that lay at the heart of the devil emperor Qin's hidden mausoleum. For it was there that Iblis planned to store their spirits and the energy they contained for the next stage in his plan.

Meanwhile, back in the physical world, quite a few parents thought their children had merely fainted, what with all the excitement of watching someone disappear for real. For there could be no doubting that this had indeed happened. *Jonathan Tarot had disappeared.* Others became angry as they accused their children of pretending to be in a trance or hypnotized. Most people didn't know the difference. Some picked up their children and tried to shake them awake.

As the evening wore on, panic and pandemonium ensued. All around the world, mothers and fathers slowly began to grasp the reality of what had happened and that their children were not dead but unconscious, catatonic, comatose. Hospitals and clinics quickly filled with anxious parents and their own Sleeping Beauties. Psychiatrists, mediums, priests, rabbis, and imams were consulted. Presidents and prime ministers summoned their cabinets. A medical emergency was declared on a worldwide scale.

Doctors conducted examinations and agreed upon a single conclusion. A case of mass hysteria or hypnosis was diagnosed. Senior members of the medical profession went on television and assured mothers and fathers everywhere that in time the effects would wear off. That the children would awaken. Calm was urged upon those who were near hysterical with worry. Patience was prescribed.

The world held its breath and prayed.

Meanwhile, Jonathan Tarot was held partly responsible for what had happened, arrested, and taken into protective custody by New York City police. Naturally, he had viewed the arrival in his suite at the Cimento dell' Armonia Hotel of New York's Finest with a certain amount of amusement and disdain and had thought to use djinn power to escape but, to his horror, found that he could not. At first, he assumed it was because he was tired. Or even sick. And it would be several days before the true character of his terrible fate dawned on him.

CHAPTER 28

INTELLIGENCE GATHERING

Nimrod and Groanin should have been back by now, observed Finlay.

I quite agree, thought John. *Something must have happened to them.*

That guy we heard using his cell phone, thought Finlay. *The Ifrit. Rudyard Teer.*

Right. We were supposed to fall into his trap, too. Suppose he comes looking for us.

He doesn't know you, Finlay. He's never seen you before. It's me he might recognize. Me, and my sister.

If she ever gets here.

Finlay had telephoned the Gravelli Hotel in Venice and they knew only that she and Marco Polo had checked out. But Philippa had not thought to leave a message as to where she was going. Or what she was doing.

She wouldn't have checked out unless she'd solved the mystery in the painting, thought John.

So why isn't she here?

My guess is that when she figured out the message, she and Marco had to go somewhere else to get their hands on the golden tablet. Probably the place where that stupid cardinal hid it.

If she does show up with the golden tablet —

She will, thought John. *I'm certain of it. If this was my body I was in now, I bet I could feel it in my bones.*

All right, when *she does show up with it,* thought Finlay, *it might be nice if we already knew how we're going to handle it. What to expect. That kind of thing.*

Intelligence gathering.

Precisely, thought Finlay. *That's why we came here ahead of her in the first place, remember? And who could be better at gathering intelligence than an invisible spy?*

You're right. I could slip out of your body, go back into the exhibition hall in spirit form, and along that open sesame passageway. By the time I come back, maybe Philippa will have shown up here with the golden tablet of command.

By when, you'll know just how to handle it, thought Finlay, pleased that John had agreed with his plan.

Makes a lot of sense, thought John. *More sense than us both sitting around and waiting for her to show up.*

Right, agreed Finlay. *You don't think you'll get another attack of, what do you call it? Astral-sickness.*

I'm not going to be gone for very long, thought John. *I think it only comes on after you've been out of body for quite a while. Besides, I think we could both use a break from each other, don't you?*

I'm glad you think that, because I do, too. I'm beginning to feel like a whatsit? When someone has got two personalities.

A psycho?

Precisely.

Okay. Ready when you are, thought John.

Go for it.

I'll be able to see and hear you, but you won't be able to hear me, or see me, of course, thought John. *Not until I'm back. And I hope you won't mind if I step straight into your body. Just to save time.*

Be my guest, thought Finlay. *And John. Be careful.*

Sure.

At last, John felt able to step out of Finlay's body, experiencing a tremendous sense of liberation as he did so. It was like taking off a tuxedo or unbuttoning a very tight shirt collar. He felt as if he could breathe again and, if he had possessed any physical lungs, he might have let out a euphoric sort of sigh.

Finlay felt his djinn friend go and feeling a little faint, he was obliged to sit down on a chair to stop himself from falling over. It made him realize just how much he'd been leaning on John's spirit to help him carry out his normal physical functions such as walking and picking things up.

After a while, he lay down and, unable to think of anything else to do, and quite at peace with himself — for a change — went to sleep.

John floated down the stairs, through the front door of the hotel — without opening it, of course — and headed back across Xian in the direction of the exhibition hall.

It being daytime now, the hall was full of tourists, many of them Americans, all loudly agog at the sheer number of clay figures that filled pit number one. John passed silently over their heads, floated across the barrier, and down through the silent ranks of terra-cotta warriors at the back of the pit. There he paused a little, watched the terra-cotta warrior nearest him for some sign that it might move off its plinth and try to absorb him, and then turned to face that part of the wall Nimrod had identified as a secret door.

He realized it was just as well that he could walk through walls and solid doors, as he could not remember the Chinese words Nimrod had uttered to make the entrance "open sesame" like in the Ali Baba story. It was careless of him, he told himself, not to have remembered something that could have been vital.

John went through the hidden door and into the passageway, which stretched ahead of him for several hundred yards, perhaps more. Being a spirit meant he had no need of a flashlight: All ghosts and spirits can see in the dark. Cautious now that he had actually entered the Ifrit trap — he might have been invisible to a human eye but he could hardly depend on that being enough to protect him from the Ifrit — he floated slowly along the passageway hoping against hope that he might find Nimrod and Groanin coming in the opposite direction. The passageway seemed to be empty, however. At least it was empty of anything that could be seen.

But it was not empty of sound. Far from it.

At first, John thought he was hearing the high-pitched, resonant sound of thousands, perhaps millions of birds in a big cavern ahead of him. But as he got nearer and the racket grew louder, it seemed that what he heard was more human. Like the sound of an enormous herd of children in a school playground at break time or recess, or whatever Chinese kids called it when they weren't having lessons. Except that there was nothing carefree or happy about this clamorous noise. Nothing at all. This was the sound of despair.

John felt as if his hair should have been standing on end and probably it would have been if he'd had any. Certain he was approaching a terrible place where millions of lost souls were in torment, he slowed his progress. By now the sound was almost deafening and all of his instincts told him to go back. But John's spirit was, as always, full of courage. Onward he floated, although he dreaded what he might see at the end of the passageway: people being pushed into bottomless pits with long sharp sticks; others with hugely long trumpets blown into their faces; rampaging demons and bird-headed monsters. Hieronymus Bosch. Hell.

So it was all the more surprising when, reaching the end of the passageway, he looked down into an enormous cavern and saw nobody at all. At least, not the millions of tormented souls he had expected to see. Nor any fiery pits. Just an enormous green pyramid surrounded by a silver lake and patrolled by several hundred of the warrior devils — the same as the living terra-cotta warrior he had seen back at the Temple of Dendur in New York.

Trying to block out the terrible noise in his ears, John floated out of the passage and across the unnatural-looking silver lake. This did not seem to be made of water for there was no depth to it and but for the odd tremor and ripple he saw on the surface he might even have said it was glass.

The pyramid at the center of the lake was easily as big as the Great Pyramid of Khufu in Egypt. But this one was in much better repair and made of a curious-looking greenish stone. But what was most curious about the pyramid was the realization that it was the source of the deafening noise that filled the cavern. Inside the pyramid were what sounded like millions of children, stuffed one on top of the other like a factory full of sardines. Once again, he felt a real sense of horror as, quite definitely, he heard one muffled voice from just inside the pyramid, one that was not speaking Chinese.

"Help me," said the voice, which seemed to be that of an American girl. "Help me. I want to go home. Please let me go. Please, I don't want to be in here. Something happened to me when I was watching TV! Help me!"

Try as he might, John could not pass through the super-smooth wall of the pyramid and do as the voice had asked. Whatever the pyramid was made of, it was quite impervious to spirit. He floated to the top of the pyramid and saw that the apex appeared to be made of diamond or something similar, and only just touching the rocky roof of the cavern. Curious, he inspected the points of contact more closely and saw that in fact there was a hair's breadth gap between the two.

Experimentally, he thinned his spirit finger and slid it into the gap. This was not a good idea. A giant electrical spark escaped from the diamond apex, stunning John and blowing him into the air like a swatted fly down onto the surface of the silver lake. It was several minutes before he was able to collect himself. At first, he thought the electric shock he had received had muddled his senses. For what he saw was Groanin, standing a few yards away from him, surrounded by a circle of the warrior devils. These were quite motionless, dormant even, like the ones in the pit. But it was quite plain that any attempt to escape from their midst would have brought them to life again.

Groanin did not say anything. He did not move. His eyes were open, but they did not seem to see anything. Of Nimrod there was no sign. For a while, John wondered what, if anything, had happened to Groanin; it finally dawned on him that the best way of finding out what had happened was simply to enter the butler's body and read his mind in the same way he had been reading Finlay's mind.

Carefully, John slipped between the legs of one of the warrior devils and into Groanin's mind and body.

Thank goodness for that, the cavalry's here, thought Groanin. *I've been stood here like this for I don't know how long. Every time I try to move I get a smack from one of these stupid mud men. Did you bring that golden thingy of command to get us all out of this dreadful place?*

Philippa hasn't shown up with it yet, admitted John.

Marvelous, moaned Groanin. *Some cavalry you are. I say, some cavalry you are, sunshine.*

Despite Groanin's continuing complaints, John was able to search the butler's memories and understand just what had happened to him and to Nimrod after going through the open sesame in the burial pit, and, as a result, exactly why Groanin's mind appeared to be in such a mess. This is what he found out:

Groanin followed Nimrod to the end of the passageway. "What's a pyramid doing down here?" he muttered. "We're a long way from Egypt. I say, we're a long way from Egypt."

"The use of burial pyramids has been important to many different civilizations," said Nimrod. "Not just the Egyptians. The Mayans, the Aztecs, and the Cambodians all used pyramid designs for their important tombs and holy places. I imagine this pyramid is the tomb of the Emperor Qin. The one Marco Polo told us about in the story of Yen Yu. The emperor believed that he and his terra-cotta army would pass out through the apex of the pyramid and into the land of the immortals." He shook his head with wonder. "Although I must say I've never seen a pyramid that's made of jade before. It must be priceless. Curious stuff, jade. Djinn power can't go through it, you know."

They approached the edge of the lake surrounding the pyramid. Nimrod bent down and touched the surface with his finger.

"That's awkward," he said.

"What is?" asked Groanin.

"Groanin, I think it might be best if you were to return to the hotel," he said.

"Why?" Groanin put the toe of his boot into the liquid and found that it remained quite dry. "This lake is not at all deep. And not at all wet, by the look of it. I'm in no danger of drowning, that's for sure. What is this stuff, anyway? It's certainly not water."

"It's mercury, Groanin. Sometimes called quicksilver. It's excellent for conducting djinn power and is one of the reasons why medieval alchemists were so fascinated with the stuff. But it also gives off fumes that are slowly poisonous to humans. If you stay down here long enough, you'll go mad. Or worse. This is why you ought to go back."

"What about you?"

"Oh, I'll be quite all right, I can assure you."

"If it's all the same, I'll stay with you, sir," said Groanin, who wasn't nearly as cowardly as he sometimes liked to pretend he was. "Hopefully, we won't be down here for very long. And in my experience a little bit of madness never hurt anyone."

"Stout fellow," said Nimrod.

They walked carefully across the silver lake.

"I suppose mercury is another thing that's harmless to you lot," said Groanin. "First prize in the lottery of life. That's what being a djinn is, if you ask me. Once upon a time it was quite enough just to be English."

"Yes," admitted Nimrod. "Mercury's quite harmless to a djinn like me."

"I wouldn't say harmless," said a voice. "Not exactly. No, not by a long chalk."

Nimrod and Groanin turned around to find themselves faced by a young man wearing a strange suit of armor that matched the jade pyramid. It was Rudyard Teer and he was accompanied by a dozen or two of the warrior devils. These looked similar to the inanimate warriors Nimrod and Groanin had seen in the burial pit, but different: Their bodies moved in a robotic, mechanical way and they were full of menace, although their faces remained quite expressionless.

"QWERTYUIOP!" Nimrod hardly hesitated, uttering his focus word loudly, and clearly he had intended to work some immediate and devastating effect on a young man who, as the son of Iblis, he knew to be his mortal enemy. But nothing happened. And seeing Nimrod's surprise, Rudyard Teer laughed loudly.

"I'm immune to your power, Nimrod," he said.

Seeing the warrior devils grab Groanin by his arms, Nimrod tried to direct another bolt of pure djinn power at them; but again, nothing happened. And the next second, they had grabbed him, too.

"So are my *Dong Xi* warriors," added the son of Iblis.

Groanin tried to put his extra-strong arm into action against the warrior devils, but there were too many of them, and both Nimrod and Groanin were quickly held prisoner.

"Actually, that's not exactly true," said Teer, smirking. "The fact is that you have no djinn power at all while you and these *Dong Xi* warriors are standing on this lake of mercury. Like all of my terra-cotta warriors, this lake contains a tiny amount of djinn spit. My dad put a special djinn binding on the mercury. An *adligare*. It works like a djinncantation."

"I know what an *adligare* is, thank you," Nimrod said crisply.

"It makes you subject to my will and command. Just the same as one of these warrior devils."

Rudyard Teer pointed his arm at Nimrod and, for a minute or two, had him running up and down on the spot, just to prove his point.

"See what I mean? I can make you do anything at all."

He pointed again and this time Nimrod put his hands around Groanin's throat and started to throttle him.

"I can make you strangle him if I want." Rudyard Teer laughed his insane, childish laugh.

Groanin's face started to turn red and then purple.

"And there's nothing you can do about it."

"All right, Rudyard," said Nimrod, panting from the exertion of trying to squeeze the air out of his own butler's windpipe. "You've made your point."

Rudyard Teer dropped his arm and, suddenly, Nimrod was able to let go of his butler's neck. Groanin leaned over to catch his breath and to cough.

"I'm sorry about that, Groanin," he said.

"That's quite all right, sir."

"And how is it that your djinn power remains active?" Nimrod asked Rudyard Teer. "The jade suit of armor, I suppose."

"Right," said Rudyard Teer. "We had them made up especially by a specialist tailor in Hong Kong. To the same pattern as the ones once worn by the emperors of China. Do you know, there are two thousand one hundred fifty-six pieces of jade in this suit? Dad is quite a historian, you know. He has a theory that the emperors of China may have made these jade suits to make themselves immune to djinn power."

"I suppose that would explain why so much jade has been stolen from museums all over the world," said Nimrod. "I was wondering about that. I ought to have suspected the Ifrit was behind it."

"That's right," Rudyard Teer said proudly. "You should have."

"Let me see," said Nimrod, thinking aloud. "First of all, you sent warrior devils into the spirit world to purge it, to absorb billions of poor defenseless ghosts to give you enough elbow room in the spirit world to carry out your plan. Then you loaned some of these terra-cotta warriors to museums all over the world. So that they could release some of the spirits they'd absorbed to scare people out of museums long enough to give you and your people enough time to steal precious jade artifacts. You needed a lot of jade to make that preposterous suit. And make yourself immune to the power of another djinn, like me." Nimrod shook his head. "I suppose one shouldn't expect anything else of a tribe who continue to dedicate themselves to all that's horrible in the world. But really. Stealing jade. Destroying ghosts. Your father should be ashamed of himself."

"They're dead already, aren't they? So who cares? What's a few billion ghosts beside my dad's plan for the universe?"

"'The *universe.*" Nimrod smiled. "Iblis *is* getting more ambitious."

"You'd better believe it, Nimrod."

"I imagine that pyramid is central to whatever your ultimate plan might be."

"You're not nearly as dumb as you look, Nimrod. Dad always said you were the cleverest djinn around."

"I'm flattered," said Nimrod.

"So what does that make me?" said Rudyard Teer. "The djinn who caught you."

"Lucky?" said Nimrod.

Rudyard Teer lifted his arm and seemed about to inflict some further humiliation on his djinn captive when a loud bray of a huge invisible trumpet distracted him. This was, perhaps, fortunate for Nimrod. "You know what, clever guy? That trumpet means you're just in time to see what this is all about. You two have got front seats at perhaps the greatest crime ever committed."

"Is that all?" said Nimrod. "A crime. What is so interesting about crime to you people? I can't understand it. Your thinking is so very grubby. So utterly small."

"I don't mean a crime that's committed against any stupid human laws," said Rudyard Teer. "I mean a crime against some universal ones. My dad is going to change the character of the universe forever. You're going to see that pyramid fill with power. And then we're going to turn it upside down."

Nimrod frowned. "An Enantodromia. You can't be serious."

"Never more so."

"But to do that you would need the most powerful source of energy in the universe," said Nimrod. "More powerful than the force of the atom. The force of life itself, and on a massive, unprecedented scale. Impossible."

"You got it, big nose." Rudyard Teer grinned horribly and then pointed at the pyramid. "Watch this space."

It were horrible, Groanin explained to John, when the boy djinn's spirit had finished searching his short-term memory. *You think it's noisy now? You should have heard it back then. It were total pandemonium, it were. Like a storm of childish panic had hit this place. All you could hear were the screams and cries of frightened children as the apex of that pyramid opened up and started to fill up with their little spirits. Like a fuel tank, so it was. Gurgle, gurgle as they all went in, one on top of the other. Hours it lasted. From where they came, I don't know. From the sheer number of them, it must have been all over the world. That's all I know. I don't know very much, I'm afraid. My mind is not as clear as it was. Sorry, John. I feel confused, really. There's quite a lot I can't remember now I come to think about it. And a lot more I've forgotten, besides. I feel like an idiot.*

That must be the effect of the mercury fumes, thought John. *No wonder your mind looks like a mess. You can't help feeling like an idiot, Mr. Groanin. We've got to get you out of here. And soon.*

Forget about me. You've got to stop them. They're planning to turn one of the fundamental laws of the universe upside down, thought Groanin. *To take the natural tendency among humankind to wish for good things and then bring about its exact opposite. None of us will know where we are. None of us will know which side to wish on.*

Where's Nimrod now?

They took him somewhere.

John followed Groanin's eyes to a doorway in the jade pyramid.

In there? asked John.

I think so. Groanin tried to clear his thoughts of the mercury fumes and remember more, but it was no use. His mind remained thoroughly befuddled. *Iblis said something about having his revenge on him.*

Iblis is here? You've seen him?

Yes. No. I'm not sure. It didn't look like Iblis. Frankly, it looked like that magician bloke off the telly. Adam Apollonius. But Rudyard Teer kept on calling him "Dad."

That would explain a lot, thought John. *Iblis must have taken over the guy's body to gain some influence over poor Dybbuk. He always did like that stupid cabaret magician.*

Anyway, whoever it was arrived about halfway through the filling up of the pyramid. Look here, you don't really think Iblis will kill him, do you, Johnnie? I don't know what I'd do without Nimrod to look after.

No one's going to kill anyone, Groanin. John placed this thought at the front of his mind so that it might be the last thing Groanin remembered him thinking about. But at the back of his mind he was thinking how it was a matter of life and death that Philippa reach the emperor's mausoleum with the golden tablet of command as soon as possible. And thinking about it again, John thought it was probably even more important than that. *I'd better go. Find Philippa. Bring her back here.*

"Let's hope that golden tablet of command really works."

The butler was not used to having conversations with a stranger inside his own skull. Few sane people are. It was especially difficult for Groanin because of the mercury fumes which, while being entirely odorless, are, as Nimrod had said, quite powerful and confusing to the human mind. So it was that these last words of Groanin were *spoken out loud.*

Suddenly, the warrior devils seemed to come to life again. Each of them took one step forward. One of the warriors took Groanin by the arm and this might have been painful if it hadn't been his extra-strong arm that was held. A second turned on his heel and made a guttural sort of noise, like a largish and brutal ape, as if trying to summon assistance from the jade pyramid.

"Oh — oh — oh!" it shouted. "Oh — oh — oh!"

For a moment, John thought they might be onto him. Then it dawned on him that it had been Groanin's mention of the golden tablet that seemed to have worked a galvanic effect on the warrior holding him. He decided to sit tight in the hope of gathering yet more intelligence.

Rudyard Teer came out of the pyramid. He was followed by Adam Apollonius, also wearing a jade suit of armor. The warriors stood back as Iblis and his son came near to Groanin.

"You mentioned the magic words, I believe," said Iblis.

"What magic words?" asked Groanin. "I say, what magic words are you on about?"

"These *Dong Xi* warrior devils of mine," said Iblis. "They only understand Chinese, you know. But I've programmed them to wake up at the mention of certain English keywords and phrases I've given them. Even in a foreign language. One of these key phrases is the 'golden tablet of command.' The question is what do you know about the golden tablet? And why you should have mentioned it just now."

"That's two questions," said Groanin.

"Don't get funny with me, Jeeves, or whatever your name is," said Iblis. "This mundane body I'm using belongs to a big, big star in Las Vegas. Do you know what that means? It means it doesn't have a sense of humor. Do you know what a quaesitor is?"

Groanin sighed wearily. "I have no idea what it is," he said. "But I feel sure you're going to tell me."

"That's a smart mouth you've got there, fat man." Iblis smiled and shook his head. "Some of the things that come out of it. I bet they even surprise you sometimes, eh?"

John knew what a quaesitor was. Once, he'd been subjected to a quaesitor himself. But even as he silently explained to Mr. Groanin that it was a djinn binding designed to find out all of the things he found unpleasant and then make them appear in his mouth, he felt something wriggle and crawl up the butler's throat.

Groanin spat and pushed something out from under his tongue. The thing clung to his chin for a moment and then dropped onto the floor. Groanin glanced down just in time to see a fat cockroach scurrying away even as something else crawled into his mouth. Groanin coughed and retched, and then spat a small rat onto the floor. This was soon followed by a rather wet-looking, bird-eating spider that scrambled up Groanin's face and sat on top of his head. Groanin screamed.

"I think you'd better tell me everything, don't you?" said Iblis, and flicked the spider into the middle distance. "Before the creatures start getting bigger."

John knew there was no way that Groanin could withstand a torture like this. And thinking that his own capture might stop Groanin from telling Iblis anything about Philippa and the golden tablet of command, he prepared to reveal himself. Even as the thought occurred to him, the next object that came up Groanin's throat was a piece of broccoli. For vegetables were what John really detested.

"All right, all right, you've got me," said John. "The fact is there are two of us in this body. There's Groanin, Nimrod's butler. And there's me. John Gaunt. Nimrod's nephew."

"A twofer," crowed Rudyard, and punched the air.

"A what?" said Groanin.

"He means two for one," said Iblis, waving his hand and muttering what John presumed must be his focus word, and the air around Groanin's body suddenly became very cold. A frost appeared on the bodies of the warriors, and Groanin's breath billowed in front of his face.

John guessed Iblis had reduced the temperature so that he might easily be seen if he tried exiting the butler's body.

"Ever since our last meeting," said Iblis, "I've looked forward to our next. Very much. And now here you are. I ought to have known the quaesitor had found two of you in there when I saw that piece of broccoli coming out the butler's mouth. It's rare people hate such very different things like a rat and a piece of broccoli."

"I dunno," said John. "You're very different from a piece of broccoli, aren't you?"

Iblis smiled a snakelike smile and then nodded at the warrior devils. "Bring him," he said. "Bring him into the pyramid. We shall soon learn exactly what he knows about the golden tablet of command."

CHAPTER 29

SHE WHO MUST BE OBEYED

As Marco Polo had predicted, the golden tablet of command made Philippa's journey to China easy. Or at least it ought to have been. The trouble was, ordering people around did not come naturally to Philippa. If not exactly meek, she was naturally democratic and respectful, and it took a while for her to grasp the true power of the ancient Chinese artifact now at her disposal, and to put it to good use. It was simply a question of telling people what to do. The biggest problem with telling people what to do, however, was that they did it, immediately — the tablet never failed in that respect — and she soon discovered that there were as many pitfalls in issuing commands as there were in making wishes. It was quickly apparent to her just why it was that Marco Polo had been nervous of the enormous power that was contained in the golden tablet. Using it required the bearer to think very carefully about the full consequences of giving an order. And an insight into the loneliness and responsibility of government and leadership — of being president or prime minister — was soon apparent to Philippa.

For example, in a rare moment of extreme irritation, she told a creepy man, who was following her at Heathrow Airport in London, to get lost and was astonished when he walked into a broom closet and closed the door behind him. She was equally surprised when upon her telling the attendant at check-in to "have a nice day" the woman took off her shoes, put her feet up on the desk, and started to read a magazine.

There were benefits to be had from her possession of the golden tablet, of course: Despite her not even having had a ticket, Philippa was allocated the best seat in first class on a plane to Beijing (there was, it seemed, no direct flight from London to Xian). Then she was allowed into the first class departure lounge, and, a few minutes before takeoff, Philippa went into the cockpit and proceeded to tell the captain, the first officer, and the navigator that there would be a change in their final destination. She didn't like doing this, knowing that it would greatly inconvenience her fellow passengers, but she thought it was a price worth paying if the world really was at risk from the warrior devils.

A minute or two later the plane took off, carrying them high over London and, soon after that, the English Channel. It was a perfect, clear blue sky and far below she watched a flock of seabirds wheeling over the White Cliffs of Dover. Suddenly, she was aware of the strangest feeling in her bones:

that her mother had arrived back in the United States and was on her way home. And, for a moment, she tried to picture Mrs. Gaunt, landing on the ground in New York, looking glamorous as always.

Half of this was true, at any rate. Philippa's feeling, although uncanny, was more or less accurate. Following her long haul flight from halfway around the globe, Mrs. Gaunt had, indeed, at just that moment arrived in New York's Central Park. But Philippa could hardly have guessed that her mother was looking a lot less glamorous than she had ever looked in her entire life. Indeed, Philippa would never have recognized her. Not in a million years.

Mrs. Gaunt made an ungainly landing, typical of the albatross, which is a bird suited to flight, not dry land. But, in spite of her undignified arrival back in New York, Mrs. Gaunt had navigated well to just south of Transverse Road, and she was almost exactly parallel to the spot where 77th Street joins Fifth Avenue, which marks the eastern border of Central Park.

Albatrosses are a rare sight in New York. And a couple of ornithological-minded people pointed out the "gooney bird" to their uncaring children. Not that Mrs. Gaunt paid them much heed; as soon as she was recovered from her landing, she lifted her spirit out of the albatross, returning the body of the bird to its own control, and floated straight home. Along the street she knew so well. Crossing Madison

Avenue. Past the famous Carlyle Hotel. Of course, if she'd been an Ifrit, she might have stolen a suitable mundane body somewhere along the way. But the Marid is a tribe of djinn that has always obeyed the *Baghdad Rules* on human body snatching. As a result it was pure spirit that came through the big black door of number 7 East 77th Street.

Much of what had happened in New York during her time in Iravotum had been made clear to her by Faustina Sachertorte. As a result she already knew the disastrous effect her Methusaleh binding had had upon her husband, how he was being nursed by Marion Morrison, and how her children were in Italy or, quite possibly, China, with Nimrod and Groanin.

She found Mr. Gaunt looking older than she remembered, of course, but not nearly as old and decrepit as the children had found him upon their own return from India. Apart from some gray hairs and liver spots on his hands, she guessed it would not be long before he was entirely back to normal.

A great deal more of what had already happened became apparent when she slipped into her husband's sleeping body and, without waking him — for she had no wish to damage his recovery by revealing that much of the wife he had loved was gone forever — searched his short-term memory to fill in some of the blanks of what she knew.

She was delighted to discover that her son's body was at home awaiting the return of his spirit, but she was horrified to learn the fate that had befallen Mr. Rakshasas. And sleep-walking Mr. Gaunt upstairs and into John's room, she found the two of them still there, John lying on his bed, and Mr. Rakshasas seated in John's favorite armchair.

John was warm to the touch and gave the appearance of one who was merely asleep, but it was a different story with Mr. Rakshasas. The old djinn's skin was cold and rigid like stone, and it was clear to Mrs. Gaunt that something grave had happened to his spirit and that he was most probably dead.

Mrs. Gaunt let out a sigh and sat her husband down, feeling very sad that she would never again see Mr. Rakshasas and knowing how upset John and Philippa would be when they found out. Supposing that they didn't know about it already. Perhaps they were in some danger themselves. Mrs. Gaunt decided she would try to find her children as soon as she had addressed the problem of what to do about her lack of a mundane body — she hardly fancied becoming a dog or a cat, or any other animal so soon after being an albatross. That experience had left her feeling sick, with a bad taste in her husband's mouth. It was a strong taste of salt (gooney birds drink salt water) and rotten fish heads discarded from an ocean-going oil tanker — she'd been obliged to eat these and regurgitate them several times, in order to keep herself going on the long flight over the continental United States. Mrs. Gaunt got a glass of water from the faucet in the bedroom and drank it quickly.

"What are you doing out of bed?"

Mrs. Gaunt turned her husband's head toward the door. It was Marion Morrison, his djinn nurse.

"We haven't met," said Mrs. Gaunt, using her own voice and holding out her hand. "I'm Layla Gaunt. I'm just using my husband's body for a while until I can figure out what to do about my own. Or rather my lack of one. You see, I had a bit of an accident on my way back from Iraq. My old body has been destroyed. Which is a great shame, as I was rather fond of it."

"Too bad," said Marion, shaking Mr. Gaunt by the hand. "Couldn't you borrow your son's while he's not using it?"

"No, I don't think that would be appropriate," said Mrs. Gaunt. "A boy should be allowed to keep some secrets from his mother, don't you think?"

"I guess you're right." She nodded at Mr. Rakshasas. "I'd suggest maybe taking the old fellow's. But it seems to me that he's dead."

"That was also my impression," said Mrs. Gaunt.

"Death can be hard to pin down when it involves a djinn who's undergoing an out-of-body experience," said Marion. "But Mr. Rakshasas has been getting colder for days. I've had the heating turned up all the way to no effect. I think rigor has set in. He's as stiff as a board, which ain't normal."

"Dear old Rakshasas," said Mrs. Gaunt. "We were very fond of him." She let out another sigh and wiped a tear from her husband's rheumy eye. "I'm afraid it's all been a bit of a disaster, really. My leaving home."

"And how." Marion told Mrs. Gaunt about what had happened to Mrs. Trump. "I didn't think it was the right time to tell your husband about her accident," she added by way of explanation. "I wanted him to make a full recovery first. That's why he doesn't know about it."

"Poor Mrs. Trump," said Mrs. Gaunt. "A coma. None of this would ever have happened if I'd stayed here in New York."

"That's how it is," said Marion, and placed a large caring hand on Mr. Gaunt's shoulder. "Safest place to stay is bed, I guess. But it sure ain't the most interesting. A person needs to see more than just pillows and sheets if they're ever to make the best of life."

"True," admitted Mrs. Gaunt. "What am I going to do?"

"Fate's a funny thing," said Marion. "Sometimes it deals you a hole card you don't know you need until you need it. Reckon, maybe that's what happened here."

"I'm not sure I follow," said Mrs. Gaunt.

"Mrs. Trump," said Marion. "I think you should go and take a look at her. Might be she's just the answer you're looking for, pilgrim."

Still a little uncertain as to what Marion meant, Mrs. Gaunt decided to go and visit her, anyway. And, having returned her husband to bed, Mrs. Gaunt left his body and floated out of the house. Invisibly, she drifted across the backyard, through the wall of the hospital on 78th Street, and in and out of the various rooms until she found the one with her comatose housekeeper.

Mrs. Trump looked very well for a seriously injured person. She was unconscious, but her skin was clear and her hair was lustrous and shiny. She had lost quite a bit of weight and, for the first time, Mrs. Gaunt saw something of the former beauty queen in her silent, closed-eyed housekeeper.

The door opened and a posse of doctors came into the room led by Saul Hudson, Mrs. Trump's neurologist. He grabbed the notes on the bottom of Mrs. Trump's bed, glanced over them, and shook his head. None of them could see Mrs. Gaunt, of course.

"I think it's time we considered moving this woman to a long-term vegetable facility," he said unkindly. "After more than thirty days showing no vital signs, it seems highly unlikely that she will ever recover from her fall. I'm afraid we have to face the fact that this woman is now broccoli."

It angered Mrs. Gaunt to hear Mrs. Trump spoken of in this disrespectful way, and by a member of a so-called caring profession.

She's not a vegetable, thought Mrs. Gaunt. *Is she?*

Mrs. Gaunt slipped into the housekeeper's body and started to acquaint herself with all of Mrs. Trump's physical functions. Everything seemed to be in perfect working order. Everything except her brain. But even that was undamaged. It was as if some of the spirit had been knocked out of her during the fall.

"Dear Mrs. Trump," said Layla. "How are you?"

"Mrs. Gaunt," she whispered. "How nice to see you again. I had an accident. I can't seem to wake up."

"Perhaps I can help you," said Layla. It was already clear to her that Mrs. Trump would never be quite herself again. Not without the assistance of Layla herself. "Perhaps we can help each other."

Mrs. Gaunt took a deep breath and opened Mrs. Trump's eyes.

Dr. Hudson was still telling his medical students how Mrs. Trump's brain injury was quite typical of someone who had received a severe blow on the back of the head, and that she might live for ten or twenty years, but that barring some kind of a miracle, she would be like this for the rest of her life. Given the shortage of neurological resources that had been caused by the recent epidemic of brain seizures among children, the doctor told his students, it might be best if her life support was just switched off.

"I don't believe in miracles," he said. "They just don't occur. We've tried everything with this patient. But the golden rule in modern neurology is recognizing when you're just beating your head against a wall." He smiled apologetically. "If you'll pardon the expression. That there comes a time when you admit that you've failed and that you have a hopeless patient. So, you wash your hands and then move on to the next patient. Of which, thanks to Jonathan Tarot, we have a great many."

"Sir," said one of the students, "the patient appears to be awake."

"What?"

"The patient, sir. She's conscious."

Dr. Hudson spun around on his heel and saw his "hopeless" patient smiling back at him. Mrs. Gaunt took a certain pleasure in watching the man's jaw hit the floor.

"You're awake," said an astonished Dr. Hudson.

Layla made Mrs. Trump swallow — with some difficulty because her throat was so dry. Then, taking control of Mrs. Trump's vocal cords, she whispered, "Give me some water. I'm feeling rather thirsty."

"You're conscious," he said, handing her some water and spilling half of it on himself with shock. "But that's impossible."

"That's what you think," said Layla. She drank the water. "Now hand me my robe. I'm getting up."

"But you can't," spluttered the doctor. "You have to stay in bed. We have to run some tests. Your muscles will be weakened. You mustn't try to stand."

"Fiddlesticks," said Layla, and stood up.

"You're still a patient," protested Dr. Hudson. "Er, that means that you have to be patient."

"I am extraordinarily patient." One of the junior doctors handed her a robe. "Provided I get my own way in the end."

And, of course, she did.

Landing in Xian some ten hours later, Philippa encountered a problem with using the golden tablet of command that, as an intelligent person, she felt she ought to have anticipated. She realized that it is one thing issuing a command, but it's quite another making the command understood. The fact of the matter was this: She didn't speak Chinese, and as she did not speak Chinese, her commands, which were spoken in English, were not understood, and therefore could not be obeyed. The taxi driver at the airport had no idea what she was talking about and even when she held the tablet right under his nose and told him to take her to the Most Wonderful Hotel in Xian, he continued to shake his head and look blankly at her. And it was only when she showed him the address of the hotel, printed in Chinese script, that he was able to take her to her destination.

It was just as well, she reflected, that she would be handing the golden tablet to Nimrod, who spoke a little Chinese and could easily have used djinn power to brush it up a bit.

But when she reached the Most Wonderful Hotel in Xian and was told by Finlay that Nimrod and Groanin had disappeared in pit number one, Philippa despaired. Doubly so when Finlay confessed that John had gone to look for them, in spirit form, and had failed to return.

"Now what are we going to do?" she asked. "What's the use of having a golden tablet of command if no one understands a single word you say?"

"We could always try to learn some Chinese," suggested Finlay.

"A language course?" said Philippa. "Why don't we take a test while we're at it? This is no time to be going to school, Finlay. Nimrod and John and Groanin are in grave danger."

"What about a phrase book?" asked Finlay.

"A phrase book?" Philippa sounded doubtful. "This is the golden tablet of command. Not a weekend in Paris."

"Do you have a better idea?"

"Well," Philippa said thoughtfully. "We *could* find someone who speaks English and give them a list of possible commands for them to translate into Chinese."

"I've been here for two days," said Finlay. "None of the locals speak English. The menus in the restaurants are all in Chinese. I have no idea what I'm eating even while I'm eating it. After you've been in China for a while, England begins to seem as far away and as alien as Mars. That's how they think of us, you know. As aliens. Worse. As foreign devils. Nimrod says that's what they call us. Nobody here speaks English, Philippa. And why would they bother to learn it when the two billion other people who live in this country don't speak it, either?"

"Maybe there's an American embassy or consulate in Xian," said Philippa. "Someone there could help us."

"What makes you think they'll just drop everything to help us?" asked Finlay.

"This," she said, and showed Finlay the golden tablet of command.

Philippa telephoned the U.S. Embassy in Beijing and discovered that the American vice consul came to Xian just once a week on a Tuesday, which meant they would have to wait almost a week for his return. But the embassy official told them that there was a British vice consul who lived in Xian from Monday to Friday. As soon as Philippa and Finlay had the British vice consul's address, they left the hotel and found a taxi driver who understood just enough English to take them there.

The office of the British vice consul was in Xiao Zhai, in the southern part of the city. It was a busy commercial area, and Mr. Blunt, the vice consul, worked in a few dull rooms above the Pu Yi laundry. On the wall behind his desk was a portrait of the Queen by Rolf Harris, and a map of the world with all the former British colonies crossed out. Mr. Blunt was a small man with curly gray hair, small hands, a fluting sort of voice — more like a little old lady than a man — and he regarded the arrival of two children in his office with a conspicuous lack of enthusiasm.

"Yes?" he said. "What is it?"

"Are you Mr. Blunt?"

"That's what it says on my membership card from the Keep Kids out of the Office Society."

In the face of such astonishing rudeness, Philippa hesitated.

"Well?" he snapped.

"We need your help," said Philippa. "With some translations into Chinese. We'd like you to look at a list of phrases we've prepared, in English, and translate them into Chinese. You do speak Chinese, don't you?"

"I am fluent in six dialects of Chinese, including Mandarin, Wu, Cantonese, Min, Xiang, and Hakka," he said stiffly. "Look here, I'm the British vice consul, not some ragamuffin businessman from the Purley Chamber of Commerce.

But neither am I here to help juvenile Americans mangle the language of Confucius and Lao-tzu. I look at your bubble-gum pink faces and I weep for the future. Good day to you both."

"I'm not American," said Finlay. "I'm English."

"Consider yourself ennobled. But since you are English, it is my diplomatic duty to offer you the following consular advice. Buy yourself a phrase book from the nearest *syu guk*. That's Chinese for 'bookshop.' Once again, good day to you both."

Philippa sighed and delved into her bag to look for the golden tablet of command. "I don't know why we even bothered trying to be polite about this."

"Is your understanding of English equal to your ignorance of Chinese?" demanded Mr. Blunt. "I said good day to you both." He made a rude, brushing gesture with the back of his hand. "Now, shoo. *Go.* I have work to do."

Philippa held up the golden tablet in front of her. It glistened under the bright lights of the office, and she felt the power of it in her fingertips as if she had been holding the two terminals of a car battery.

"You will help us," she said firmly.

Mr. Blunt straightened in his chair and then stood up, as if the Queen had come into the room.

"I will help you," repeated Mr. Blunt dumbly.

"Impressive," murmured Finlay.

"You will write out these translations. Just like we asked you to."

"I will write out the translations. Just like you asked me to."

"*Very* impressive."

Philippa handed over two sheets of notepaper on which she and Finlay had written almost every command in English they could think of that might come in handy with the warrior devils. Mr. Blunt put on some glasses, picked up his pen, and quickly wrote out the translations. It took him less than ten minutes, after which time he handed them over.

"Was there anything else?" he asked crisply.

Philippa cast her eye over his work and let out a small scream of frustration. "But this is written in Chinese!" she cried.

"Which language did you expect Chinese translations to be written in?" asked Mr. Blunt. "Eskimo, perhaps? Flemish? Klingon? Of course it's written in Chinese, you nincompoop."

"Couldn't you write the phrases out in English, showing the way we might pronounce them?" asked Finlay. "The phone-something spellings."

"Phonetic," said Philippa.

"All varieties of spoken Chinese use tones," said Mr. Blunt. "Mandarin has five. High level, high rising, low falling-rising, high falling, and neutral. Not to mention a great variety of sounds that are seldom used in the English language. For that reason, the way *you* might pronounce these phrases would almost certainly sound quite incomprehensible to a Chinese. Like a dog trying to speak to an archbishop."

Mr. Blunt picked up a carafe and was about to pour himself a glass of water. But Philippa had had enough of the Englishman's conceit and decided to teach him a lesson.

"Pour it on your stupid limey head, you horrible little man," she said.

Mr. Blunt did as he was told, of course, and poured the water onto his head. When he'd finished, he wiped his face and said, "I don't know why I did that."

"No offense," Philippa told Finlay. "About limeys, I mean."

"None taken." He shrugged.

"What are we going to do?"

"We'll have to take him with us," said Finlay.

"Him? But he's a pain in the neck."

"Maybe so, but he speaks six dialects of Chinese. We have no idea which dialect of Chinese gets spoken in these parts. Least of all by the warrior devils."

"Good point."

"Besides," added Finlay, "I just remembered. We'll need someone who reads Chinese to speak the Chinese equivalent of 'open sesame.'"

"Very well. You will come with us, please," Philippa told Mr. Blunt.

The vice consul did not hesitate. He got his jacket off the back of his chair, his hat off the hat stand, his umbrella from the umbrella stand, and followed the two children through the steamy glass door.

"Where are we going?" he asked.

"Do you have a car?" asked Finlay.

"Yes."

"Take us to the terra-cotta warriors," said Finlay. "Exhibition hall, number one."

"Why should I?"

Philippa shook her head at Finlay. "You're not holding the golden tablet," she explained, and repeated the order.

Mr. Blunt glanced at his watch. "But the exhibition will be closed now," he said.

"All the better," said Finlay.

"But how will we get in?" asked Philippa.

Finlay showed her the little box with the skeleton key Nimrod had given him for safekeeping. "With this," he said. "Don't leave home without one."

CHAPTER 30

THE DAY OF THE DJINN WARRIORS

I don't like this at all," said Mr. Blunt as they entered the huge, dark exhibition hall and climbed down into pit one. "I really don't like this. These warriors are priceless artifacts. If the Chinese caught us in here they'd probably assume we were trying to steal them. The penalty for this kind of theft in China is almost certainly death."

"That's enough," said Philippa, brandishing the golden tablet of command. "It sounds horrible and I don't want to hear any more about it, Mr. Blunt. Please speak the words written in Chinese on the wall in front of us and then be silent until I specifically tell you that you may start speaking again."

"You mean these words?" asked Mr. Blunt. *"Kai Shen?"*

As soon as he spoke, the hidden door in the wall of the pit slid open to reveal the secret passageway.

"That's right," added Philippa. "Not another word unless I say so."

They walked into the passageway and the door slid silently shut behind them. After a while, Finlay said, "What's that noise?"

"It sounds like birds," said Philippa. "Millions of birds."

Inside the jade pyramid everything was very modern and high-tech. A thin layer of mercury covered the floor, reflecting people and objects like a giant mirror: some complicated electrical machinery, Iblis and his son Rudyard operating it, several dozen warrior devils who lined the walls like suits of armor in a medieval castle, and, chained to a wall, Groanin/ John and Nimrod. Opposite them was a thick, triangular glass wall, like a giant fish tank. Instead of fish, this particular tank, which took up most of the space in the pyramid, contained the spirits of millions of children compressed, one on top of the other, like so many sardines. Moving like a fluid, and giving off a silvery-bluish light, they looked visibly electric, like a sky that was chock-full of lightning. From time to time, small, ghostly human faces would appear next to the glass, mouthing some silent entreaty — for the room was soundproofed — and this was as amusing to Iblis and his son Rudyard as it was alarming to Groanin/John and Nimrod.

Iblis was in his element and took great pleasure in describing all of the details of his operation and the workings of his infernal machinery to his two/three prisoners. He did this because he knew how much distress it caused them, and his appetite for torture was undiminished despite having already tortured Groanin/John with another quaesitor. Groanin/John had little choice but to tell him everything he/they knew about Philippa and the golden tablet of command.

As a result, Iblis was also feeling quite relaxed. He felt certain that Philippa would never solve the mystery in the painting. He himself had no clue how XI + I could ever have equaled X and, in his arrogance, Iblis did not think a mere child could have solved something he could not solve himself. He was satisfied Philippa would never find the golden tablet of command in time to stop him from carrying out his plan.

While Iblis preened himself in front of his prisoners, Rudyard Teer kept an eye on the instrumentation panel in front of him. Both men continued to wear their jade suits of armor that rendered them immune to Nimrod's djinn power.

"Critical mass in eight minutes," Rudyard told his father.

"Capital," said Iblis. "In less than eight minutes," Iblis told Nimrod, "the energy in that tank will cause the pyramid to invert. And, all over the world, fate and luck will also turn upside down. I can hardly wait to see the results. Whatever that's wished for will achieve its opposite result." Iblis chuckled his insane laugh. "For the rest of time, humankind will look like the face of some pathetic kid on Christmas morning when you've handed him a nicely wrapped package that turns out to be empty."

This was an image that seemed to delight Rudyard, who laughed like a drain. He and Iblis then executed a high five, which wasn't easy because of the heavy jade suits they were wearing.

"Does it really give you pleasure, Iblis?" asked Nimrod. "To do evil for the sake of doing evil?"

Iblis looked surprised at the question. "Yes," he said. "Of course."

"Seven minutes and counting," said Rudyard Teer.

"Just in case you were thinking of how you might turn things around, so to speak," said Iblis. "How you might turn the pyramid the right way up again. You can't. What I'm doing here is quite irreversible. For one thing, humans like your butler, Mr. Groanin, would have to start wishing the very opposite of what they really wanted. Which, I'm sure you'll agree, is quite impossible. After all, it's hard enough to get humans to know what they really want, let alone the very opposite.

"And, for another thing, you'd never be able to harness as much life-force energy as I have done with the spirits of all these kids. No, Nimrod, once this pyramid is inverted, that's it for the world." He laughed. "I mean, forget breaking a mirror and seven years of bad luck. This is like seven billion years of bad luck ahead of us. Marvelous!"

"Wonderful," said Rudyard.

"Very clever," said Nimrod. "I have to admit, yours was a complex but ingenious plan. Loaning terra-cotta warriors you had commandeered for your own purposes to the world's major museums. Tell me, Iblis, the devil warrior at the Metropolitan Museum in New York. Is it still there?"

"Why do you ask?"

"Because it absorbed my friend Mr. Rakshasas."

"That is good news," said Iblis. "Sadly, however, I won't be able to find him and torture him myself. That would take too long. The warrior sent to the Metropolitan Museum in New York is now back here in Xian. One of eighty thousand at my command. It would take forever to find him now, mixed up with all the rest." He chuckled cruelly. "I mean, have you ever tried counting to ninety billion?"

"Stealing jade, flushing out the spirit world, using poor Dybbuk to focus all of human attention on one event to create a Negentropy," said Nimrod. "Ingenious and quite the most obscene thing I've ever heard of."

"Thank you, Nimrod. I take that as a great compliment from someone like you."

"But your own son," said Nimrod. "Your own son." He nodded at Rudyard. "Oh, I don't mean this booby here. I mean Dybbuk. Don't you feel the least bit of regret for having used your own flesh and blood so ruthlessly?"

"Six minutes and counting," said Rudyard, ignoring Nimrod's insult. "The spirit level has reached maximum power, Dad. Final countdown sequence initiated."

"A little, yes," admitted Iblis. "The boy was not without talent. But then again he was not without a conscience, either, and no Ifrit that's worthy of the name could ever have much use for one of those."

"The boy *was* not without talent," repeated John. "You used the past tense, Iblis. Is Dybbuk all right?"

"He'll live," said Iblis. "If you can call it living."

"What did you do to him?"

"Nothing," said Iblis. "I didn't have to. He did it to himself. Through his profligate overuse of djinn power in the performance of cheap tricks, sleight of hand, and cabaret-style illusions, the power has deserted the boy *forever*. Quite simply, he exhausted all of his power trying to be the great magician. As if that was a proper ambition for a djinn of his talents. I'm afraid now he's no better than some miserable mundane."

"Five minutes and counting."

"You mean that he won't be able to grant three wishes, transubstantiate, or make something disappear ever again?" asked John.

Iblis shrugged carelessly and then nodded.

"What a terrible thing to do to your own son," said Nimrod. "Your *youngest* son. To lose his power. It is the greatest tragedy that can affect any djinn, but especially tragic when it affects a young one."

"Do stop going on about him being my own son," said Iblis. "You're being a bore, Nimrod."

"Is there something else we can call him?" asked Nimrod.

"Does it matter?"

"I think it might matter to you," observed Nimrod. "Sons are important to us djinn. Even, dare I say, to the Ifrit."

"All right, all right," snarled Iblis. "I'm sorry for what happened to the boy. Are you satisfied? It wasn't something I expected to happen. He must have been using a lot more power to do those tricks than I imagined. But it can't be helped."

"And what about his career as an entertainer?" asked Groanin. "As Jonathan Tarot?"

"You're joking, aren't you?" said Iblis. "After what happened to all those stupid kids, he's finished as an entertainer. In the ears of half the people in the world, the name of Jonathan Tarot is now mud. You should see what the newspapers have been writing about him."

"Poor Dybbuk," whispered John.

"To use your own son like that, Iblis," said Nimrod. "What a crime that was."

"He's still alive, isn't he?" snarled Iblis.

"Three minutes and counting."

"Perhaps that's the greatest of your crimes," said Nimrod, who was trying to needle Iblis into making some kind of mistake. A mistake he might yet take advantage of. "To use your own son like that."

"You think that's a crime?" yelled Iblis. "Believe me, Marid, you ain't seen nothing yet." Iblis took hold of a lever.

"In less than three minutes, when I throw this lever, every one of those little life-force energies I've got stored up in here will be used up forever. And won't their mommies and daddies be sad? Millions of them. Now that's a crime, mate!"

"Two minutes and counting."

"Think about what you're doing, Iblis," said Nimrod. "If everything is about to start going your way, *forever*, where will be the pleasure in defeating me? There won't be any. Even if their wishes remain unfulfilled, people still need to be able to wish for good things to happen to them in the future, *just to make life interesting.* And it's the same for you. Don't you understand, Iblis? It's the hope of things, good or evil, that makes life interesting. That makes it worth living."

"What are you talking about?" asked Iblis scornfully.

But Nimrod could see he had the evil djinn's attention now. "All these years you've been a djinn, Iblis, and still you don't understand. It's like my friend Mr. Rakshasas used to say: 'A wish is a dish that's a lot like a fish — once you've eaten it, you can hardly throw it back.' Sometimes it's not good to get exactly what you want. Sometimes the hope or expectation of something is better than the reality. Be careful what you wish for. That's true for evil as much as it's true for good."

"One minute and counting," said Rudyard. "Don't listen to him, Dad. He sounds like some awful self-help book."

"I'm not listening," insisted Iblis. "Your philosophy, Nimrod, is not without merit, I'll grant you. But it does not command my respect. It's too woolly. Too vague. Too wishy-washy. Only pure evil commands my respect."

"Then perhaps this will command your respect," said a voice. "But if not your respect, then perhaps your obedience."

"Thank goodness for that," said Groanin. "I say, thank goodness for that. The cavalry's here at last."

In the doorway of the operations room in the jade pyramid stood Philippa, and in her hands was the golden tablet of command. Beside her stood Finlay McCreeby and Mr. Blunt, the British vice consul.

"You think you can thwart my plans with that bauble?" sneered Iblis. "Well, your golden tablet won't work on us. That's why we're wearing these jade suits of armor." He turned to the warrior devils and shouted several commands in Chinese which set them in motion again.

"*Saat taa mun!*" he shouted. "*Caan can taa mun! Wai taa mun!*"

The warriors advanced on the newly arrived trio with menacing intent.

"Listen to me, Philippa," shouted Nimrod. "Forget Iblis and Rudyard. Because of their jade suits, they can't harm you. Djinn power won't travel through jade. Nor will the power of the golden tablet. It will only work on the warrior devils. The Chinese words to turn the *Dong Xi* against their Ifrit masters are —"

"Silence him!" shouted Iblis, and straightaway one of the warrior devils put a big terra-cotta hand over Nimrod's mouth.

Coolly, Philippa took hold of Mr. Blunt's hand, so that the power of the golden tablet would enter his body, too.

"Tell the warriors to stop," she told the vice consul. "Tell them to obey me. Tell them in Chinese, or we'll all be killed."

But to her surprise and alarm Mr. Blunt remained silent.

"Thirty seconds and counting," shouted Rudyard.

Philippa repeated the command but still, Mr. Blunt looked blankly at her and said nothing.

"Why doesn't he obey me?"

The warrior devils moved slowly toward Philippa and Mr. Blunt like zombies, but by now they were only a few feet away.

"Your last command to Mr. Blunt," said Finlay. "That must be interfering with your new command. It's the only possible explanation."

Philippa racked her brains. "I said not another word unless I say SO!" Philippa shouted the last word in triumph as she guessed that until she uttered it, Mr. Blunt would continue to remain silent.

Mr. Blunt blinked several times, as if waking up. "What's that?" he said.

A second before Philippa found herself grabbed painfully by two of the terra-cotta warriors, she shouted a series of commands for Mr. Blunt to translate into Chinese. "Tell the *Dong Xi* to obey!"

"*Dong Xi! Teng ting ting,*" said Mr. Blunt in faultless Chinese.

"Tell them to stop!"

"Zj," shouted Mr. Blunt. "Zj!"

"Twenty seconds and counting," said Rudyard Teer.

The warrior devils stopped in their tracks.

From inside Mr. Groanin, John shouted out to his twin sister. "Philippa, you have to stop Iblis from pulling that lever. Millions of children's lives are depending on it."

"Ten seconds and counting!"

"Mr. Blunt," yelled Philippa, "tell the warrior devils to arrest those two men in the jade suits of armor. At all costs, they must be stopped, do you hear? Don't let him pull that lever!"

Mr. Blunt was simultaneously translating what Philippa was saying. His Chinese was as fluent and fluting and elegant as his English. And as soon as the first words were out of his fastidious little mouth, the warrior devils released him and Philippa and turned slowly, on their former masters.

"Five seconds and counting." Through his jade helmet they could see Rudyard Teer grinning wildly. But Iblis was looking altogether more determined and perhaps only he could see how much danger they both were in now from the warrior devils.

"Four!"

One of the warriors took hold of Rudyard. There were dozens of them now. Hundreds. They seemed to be streaming into the pyramid from some underground source.

"Three!" yelled Rudyard.

Another warrior laid both hands on Iblis, who tried to shrug him off and failed.

"Two!" yelled Rudyard, and the next second found himself thrown violently to the ground.

Iblis started to pull on the lever that would turn the jade pyramid upside down. The next second he was felled by a blow from two of the warriors.

"Turn off the machinery!" said John. "It's the big jade switch."

Finlay sprinted to throw the switch that would halt and then reverse the flow of life-force energy in the jade pyramid.

Struggling to pick himself up off the floor, inside the weight of his armor, Iblis stuck out a foot and tripped Finlay, who collapsed on top of him. Iblis pushed Finlay's winded body to one side and slowly got to his feet only to find himself hit again by a huge terra-cotta forearm.

This time he fell and stayed still.

Letting go of Mr. Blunt's hand, Philippa ran to the other side of the operations room and threw the switch to reverse the flow of life energy. The machinery that had been humming loudly now stopped.

"You did it, Phil!" yelled John. "You did it!"

"I did, didn't I?" said Philippa.

"Next to the big lever that Iblis was holding," said John, "there's another switch that opens the apex of the pyramid. It will release the millions of children whose spirits were kidnapped by Iblis."

Hardly hesitating, Philippa threw the switch. For a moment nothing happened. Then there was a juddering sound as the diamond apex opened up. A second later it was ás if the very gates of the largest school in the universe had opened and the spirits of millions of children went rushing home. Of course, the noise was deafening. What large number of children ever travels in silence? It was the sound of several million poltergeists. But it was also the sound of happiness and relief and hope — the loud and boisterous sound of life itself. So loud that it sent a powerful vibration that was like an earth tremor through the entire pyramid, and causing everyone who wasn't chained to a wall to fall onto the floor.

Philippa picked herself up and looked around for the golden tablet of command that she had dropped during the commotion of spirits that her throwing the switch had caused. But it wasn't on the jade floor anymore. Someone had picked it up.

Iblis was holding it.

CHAPTER 31

THE GREAT KHAN

T hat's torn it," said Groanin. "I said, that's torn it, you handless young pup."

"Torn?" said Iblis. "Torn to pieces. I like the sound of that, Jeevesey old bean. Excellent idea. Yes, I really think that's what I'm going to do. I'm going to have the *Dong Xi* tear you all into little pieces. It'll be a variation on what the Chinese call *lingchi*. Death by a thousand cuts. Only this will be death by a thousand tears. My warrior devils will tear off ten fingernails, followed by ten toenails, ten fingers, and then toes. Ears, eyelids, hanks of hair. You're really going to regret messing up my plans, you bunch of meddling slugs."

"I'm regretting it already," groaned Groanin.

"Well done, Mr. Groanin." Finlay's voice was heavy with sarcasm. "Well done for giving him the idea."

Someone cleared his throat politely. It was Mr. Blunt.

"Sorry to interrupt," he said. "Look here, if you don't mind, I'll be leaving now. This was nothing to do with me. I was acting under coercion as I'm sure you understand, given the nature of this golden tablet thingy. As a member of Her Majesty's Diplomatic Corps, it's not my job ever to interfere in the affairs of another sovereign power. So I'll bid you good day and —"

"Stay where you are," said Iblis. And of course, because Iblis was holding the golden tablet of command, that's exactly what Mr. Blunt was obliged to do.

Iblis turned to Nimrod. "What's the matter, Nimrod? Cat got your tongue?" He laughed. "It'll have it soon, I can assure you of that."

But Nimrod wasn't saying anything because one of the warrior devils still had a terra-cotta hand over his mouth.

"Let him go," said Iblis. "I want to hear you beg for your life, Nimrod. And put your back into it. Beg me like you really mean it."

"What a tiresome fellow you are," said Nimrod.

"Didn't you hear my dad?" Rudyard came up to Nimrod and twisted his nose. "Beg him."

"You're even more of a booby than he is," said Nimrod. "Can't you see it's over? Quit while you still have your lives. And don't issue any more orders. If you two don't change direction you may end up where you are heading. That's my advice."

"End up where we're heading?" sneered Rudyard. "What does that mean?"

"You're in no position to offer me advice, Nimrod," said Iblis. He waved one of the warrior devils toward him and then pointed to Nimrod. "Tear this one to pieces, first."

When nothing happened, Iblis looked puzzled. Then he glanced at the golden tablet of command he was holding in his hands and, seeing that it had started to glow like an ember from a very hot fire, he dropped it instinctively. "What on earth?" he said. "What's wrong with it? That shouldn't be happening. Should it?"

"I think we're about to find out," said Nimrod.

Black smoke began to billow off the glowing golden tablet. But it was not the smoke of combustion or from a chemical reaction. To everyone except Mr. Blunt, who had never before seen one, this looked more like the smoke from a djinn transubstantiation.

After a few more seconds had elapsed, there could be no doubt about it: A djinn was taking on a human shape inside the operations room of the jade pyramid. And gradually, as the smoke cleared, they saw it was the figure of a hugely tall, bearded, slightly fat Chinese man, wearing white silken robes and a black cap that covered his massive neck. His sandals were little wooden platforms about six inches off the mercury. Which might have explained how his djinn power remained unaffected. But what was strangest of all about him were his fingernails, which were at least six or seven inches long. One of these was now pointed at Iblis.

"Who is it that dares to use one of my golden tablets of command for evil?" said the figure. He was speaking Chinese and, being a good and conscientious diplomat, Mr. Blunt felt obliged to offer a simultaneous translation for all those who spoke only English.

"Iblis, of the Ifrit," said Iblis bravely. "And who are you when you're at home, chubby?"

"I *am* at home," said the Chinese djinn. "I am Borjigin of the Borjigi. Also called Khiyad. Also called Setsen Khan. But better known by my given name, which is Kublai Khan, Khan of the Mongols, Emperor of Yuan China and grandson of the great Lord Temudjinn, Genghis Khan."

"*Temudjinn*?" said Iblis.

"That's right. *Temud Djinn.*"

"Genghis Khan was a djinn?" Iblis sounded surprised.

"Of course," said Kublai Khan. "How else do you think he conquered such a large empire?"

"Which means . . ."

"That I am, too. You're not as dumb as you look."

Kublai Khan smiled. But it was not a smile that filled the heart of Iblis with gladness. Far from it.

"Yes, I'm a djinn," said the great Khan. "How else could I have ruled such a large empire? How else could I have known that, in the wrong hands, the djinn power that is in the *Dong Xi* could be so destructive? Why else did I leave five golden tablets of command, to bind them to the will of someone with a good heart?"

Iblis swallowed loudly.

The long fingernail pointed to Philippa. "She has a good, brave heart," said Kublai Khan. "But you do not. Which is why I am here, to punish you."

"And how is it that you think you can punish me?" demanded Iblis. "What gives you the right?"

"This right, as you call it, was given to me by none other than the Blue Djinn of Babylon herself, in the year 1290," said the great Khan. "My transubstantiation is occult. Which means that it is her power that brings me here to you now. Not mine."

Iblis laughed. "Well then, Khan, you've had a bit of a wasted journey. My son and I are invulnerable to djinn power in these jade suits of armor of ours. You can't touch us. Come, Rudyard. Let's leave these djinn fools to play with their pet mundanes."

Kublai Khan waved the warrior devils forward to block the exit of the two Ifrit.

"It's true," said the Khan, "that those jade suits protect you from my power. So it is fitting that they should also protect the world of men from the likes of you, Iblis. They shall be your prisons. And, in time, they shall also be your sepulchers."

"What are you talking about?" said Iblis.

"Hold them," said the Khan in a voice that was used to issuing commands.

The warriors took hold of Iblis and Rudyard and held them tightly by the arms.

"Lay them down upon the ground," said the Khan.

"What are you going to do to us?" demanded Iblis. "Help, Nimrod. Say something in my defense, please, old friend, before this overweight lunatic does something drastic."

"I wouldn't know what to say, Iblis," Nimrod said sadly. "What can be said in defense of one who would have gladly sacrificed the lives of millions of children? Whatever the great Khan has in mind as punishment for you is very probably less than what you deserve."

"It was all a joke," said Rudyard. "A joke that got out of hand, that's all."

"Nobody's laughing," said Groanin. "I say, nobody's laughing."

The great Khan collected the golden tablet in his bare hand. It looked much too hot to touch, not that this seemed to bother him much. He held it over the jade suit worn by Rudyard Teer and some of the gold began to melt, running into the crevices between the various pieces of jade, all 2,156 of them, so that, gradually, the suit of mobile armor became a solid sarcophagus.

"I can't move," shouted Rudyard. And then gradually, as the reality of what the great Khan was doing dawned on him, he started to curse and then to plead for mercy. But the great Khan was deaf to the young Ifrit's many loud and wailing appeals for mercy; within just a few minutes, he had sealed every piece of jade, including the mask, with molten gold.

With Rudyard Teer silenced inside a living tomb, the great Khan advanced on Iblis, who lay beside his son on the triangular floor.

"You can't seal me up in my own suit like this," protested Iblis. "It's burial alive, that's what it is. Tell him, Nimrod. This is inhuman."

"When have you ever cared for humanity?" demanded the great Khan.

"Tell him, Nimrod," begged Iblis as the great Khan bent over him to seal up his suit with gold. "Tell him this punishment is cruel and unusual and quite unconstitutional. No court in the world would allow such a thing."

"You were going to have the warriors tear us apart," said John. "You said so yourself."

"A misunderstanding," insisted Iblis.

"You were looking forward to it," said Finlay.

"Look, I know I've been bad and that I deserve to be punished," said Iblis. "But not like this."

"Sealed up," said the great Khan, and continued to drip molten gold into the crevices of the jade suit. "In your own priceless armor. Forever. With gold and djinn power and the jade you stole from museums. The most powerful binding there is. Impossible for djinn power to get into or out of. A living statue to be left gathering dust in the quietest corner of this museum. That's the fate that awaits you, Iblis."

"It's not fair," said Iblis. "I shall write to my congressman. My senator. I shall appeal to the Blue Djinn of Babylon herself."

"You mean Dybbuk's sister?" said Nimrod. "I wouldn't recommend it, Iblis."

"Stop it!"

"Horrible," whispered Philippa, and looked away. Even Iblis did not merit such a terrible fate as this, she felt. "Horrible." But there were no words she could find to plead for mercy. They stuck in her throat when she recalled what had happened to Mr. Rakshasas. And before him, the French Guianan boy, Galibi. And of course, poor, poor Dybbuk. Nimrod had been right. This seemed the worst of all.

"He's got it coming, in spades," said John, who was made of harder stuff than his sister.

"Stop," screamed Iblis as slowly the great Khan slid down the jade visor over Iblis's face and began to weld that tightly shut, too. "Stop," came a muffled cry. "Stop. I beg you."

But when the last drop of molten gold had filled the final fissure between the 2,155th piece and the 2,156th piece of the suit, all was silence.

The great Khan stood up and surveyed his ruthless handiwork. Two solid jade suits lay on the floor like stone knights lying in some medieval crypt. Impenetrable. Impervious to djinn power. No one ever would have guessed that inside the two suits were the bodies of two living djinn. "It is finished," he said. "These two won't trouble mankind ever again. Take them away."

Eight of the warrior devils carried the figures out of the pyramid.

"Talk about the 'Man in the Iron Mask,'" said Finlay. "Wow."

"Awesome," added John. "Really awesome."

The great Khan waved some warriors toward the prisoners chained to the wall. "Release them," he said.

Nimrod caught Philippa's eye, saw the tear that was there, and nodded silently at her, acknowledging her pity for

Iblis and his son and, to some degree, understanding it, too. He winced as, once his arms were released from their shackles, the blood rushed back into his shoulders; he flexed his arms a little before folding them around his niece. "It's all right, Philippa," he said. "It's all over."

"It is for Iblis and that mongrel son of his," said Groanin. "At least I hope it is."

"If you don't mind," Mr. Blunt said nervously, addressing Philippa and Finlay, "I'd better be getting back to the consulate. It's been most interesting, I don't mind telling you. Most, most interesting. But I don't suppose anyone would ever believe me if I told them, so I won't. You may rest assured of that. It would probably cost me my career if I mentioned any of this. Her Majesty's government takes a very dim view on the reporting of tall tales and far-fetched stories." He raised his hat politely. "Good day to you." And then he left. Quickly. Before anything else that was far-fetched and therefore unreportable could happen to him.

"Thank goodness he's gone," said Finlay. "He's the kind of stiff-necked Englishman who gives the rest of us a bad name."

"I thought he was quite sweet, really," said Philippa.

"You see the good in everyone," scoffed Groanin. "I say, you see the good in everyone." He shook his head. "I suppose that's why we're so fond of you, Miss Philippa. Come here and give us a hug."

Philippa embraced him warmly.

"Thank you for rescuing us," said Nimrod, and bowed politely for, after all, Kublai Khan had been one of the greatest emperors that ever existed. "We're very grateful to you. Aren't we?"

"Yes," said everyone.

"The spirits of the children who were imprisoned here?" asked Nimrod. "What's happened to them?"

"On their way home to their families," said the great Khan. "Some will take longer than others, I expect. But rest assured they'll all get there in the end."

"If you don't mind my asking," said Nimrod, "how is it that your being could be summoned back here after so many years and from an artifact that you yourself gave Marco Polo? You mentioned occult transubstantiation. I've heard of it, of course. But how does it work?"

"Concerned about the possible risk that the *Dong Xi* might pose to future generations, I asked the great Blue Djinn to come and visit me in China," explained the great Khan. "It was her idea to make five golden tablets of command. We made them together using my own fingernails in the smelting of the gold. So that my spirit could be summoned again by her powerful binding."

"But you told Marco Polo that Yen Yu had made the golden tablets," said Nimrod. "In order to protect your own great secret. That you yourself were a powerful djinn. Isn't that right?"

"Marco was a good friend," said Kublai Khan. "But he would not have understood the true nature of our power. He was a man of his time and might have assumed that I was some kind of witch or warlock or perhaps something worse.

The devil himself, perhaps. People were very superstitious back in fourteenth-century Europe."

"And the warrior devils?" asked Nimrod. "The *Dong Xi*? What is to become of them? Not to mention all those ghosts and spirits who were absorbed. The warriors are still full of those spirits, aren't they? Don't they still pose a threat to mankind?"

"Yes, they do," the Khan said bluntly. "It will be my job over the coming months to conduct many exorcisms and empty the spirits from them. Of necessity, it will be a brutal, destructive process. And it is to be regretted that few, if any, spirits will survive. Most of them will find themselves freed from the Earth, forever."

"A good friend of ours was a djinn who was in spirit form and found himself absorbed by one of the warriors," said John. "His name is Mr. Rakshasas. Is it possible he might survive the process of exorcism?"

"I doubt it," said the Khan. "With more than eighty thousand warriors to exorcise here in Xian, I have my work cut out for me, I'm afraid. I think it will be impossible to find one among so many and take a great deal of extra care with his exorcism. Which is what it would require."

"Poor Mr. Rakshasas." John bit his lip. "He was trying to distract the devil warrior in the Temple of Dendur away from me and Faustina," he said. "So that we could make our own getaway." John swallowed loudly. "I'm going to miss him a lot."

"We'll all miss him," said Nimrod. "He was a great soul."

"Life and death are one thread, the same line viewed from different ends," said the great Khan. "Try to remember this: That clay is molded to form a cup. But it is on its nonbeing that the utility of the cup depends. Doors and windows are cut out to make a room, but it is on its nonbeing that the utility of the room depends. Therefore, turn being into advantage and turn nonbeing into utility. Nonbeing is the greatest joy."

"I don't understand," confessed Philippa.

The great Khan laid his hand upon her head. "Words of truth are always confusing," he said. "But know this for certain, child. Great acts are made up of small deeds such as yours."

"Hear, hear," said Groanin. And John, who was, of course, still inside the English butler's body, agreed.

"You have been a great soul, too. And in reward I give you these strawberry slippers."

The great Khan pointed a fingernail at Philippa's feet and a pair of beautiful shoes appeared on them.

"Thank you very much, Your Imperial Majesty," she said. "But they're gold, aren't they?"

"Yes, but they smell of strawberries," said the great Khan.

"How lovely."

"I have a small favor to ask of you, sir," said John. "If I may."

The great Khan nodded.

"When you're doing your exorcisms in those museums, like you said you would, I wondered if you might like to exorcise the Temple of Dendur in the Metropolitan Museum in New York. There's a friend of mine who's trapped there. His name is Leo Politi and he's been the Ka servant at the temple for more than two hundred years. If it's possible, he'd like to be released from his duties. If you don't mind, sir."

"It will be my pleasure," said the great Khan.

"Thanks," said John. "I appreciate it."

"Come on, it's time we were going home," said Nimrod.

"With any luck, Mom will be there already," said Philippa. "I can't wait to see her again. Or to recover my power. I feel kind of naked without it."

"*You* feel naked." John's voice sounded unsympathetic in Groanin's mouth. "What about me? I don't even have my body. Stuck in here with Groanin. It's like having to share a small tent with an elephant."

"I'll thank you to keep your personal observations to yourself, young fellow me lad," said Groanin. "It's not exactly been a picnic for me having to share my most intimate secrets with you, you know?"

"Do tell," said Finlay.

A whirlwind carried them all across the Pacific Ocean and the continental United States. They landed in Central Park, at night, and said their good-byes in the dark.

"Don't you want to come back to the house and say hello to Mom?" Philippa asked Nimrod.

"Not this time," said Nimrod. "Your father should have recovered by now. And I expect all of you will have a lot to tell each other. So it's best we leave you alone for a while. To enjoy being a family again."

"What about Mr. Rakshasas?" she asked. "His body was in John's room when we left. What happens when a djinn dies? Is there a funeral?"

"Since it happened in her house, it's your mother's right to make the arrangements," said Nimrod. "Tell her I'll call when I get back to London. And that I'll be back for the OE. Obsequies and exequies. That's what a djinn funeral is called."

After Philippa had embraced Groanin and her uncle Nimrod, Groanin allowed John, who was still inside his body, to take over long enough to thank Finlay for all that he had done.

"It's been interesting," said Finlay with considerable understatement.

"What happens to you now?"

"I'll go and see my dad," said Finlay. "Nimrod's right. I ought to see if I can make it up with him. After that, I'll go to boarding school." They shook hands.

Then John transferred his spirit into his sister's body. A minute or two later, Philippa stepped off the whirlwind and waved it off as Nimrod, Groanin, and Finlay flew on to London.

Sharing one body for the short time it took John and Philippa to walk along East 77th Street did not cause either of them any real problems. They were twins, after all, and twins rarely have any secrets from each other. Besides, there was, they decided, a lot to be said for reading each other's thoughts, and they welcomed the chance to catch up with all the details of what each had done during the other's absence without actually having to take the trouble of explaining anything.

"You know something?" said John. "Adventure is not all it's cracked up to be. Frankly, I'm kinda tired of adventure. I just want to go home and get my body back and see Mom and Dad. I want to eat the food *I* like, not the stuff Groanin or Finlay eats. Make my own choices, you know? Be myself again. Be a family again. Go back to school. Ordinary stuff like that."

"Me, too," admitted Philippa. "I'm just going to fix myself something to eat and talk to Mom and Dad and watch TV, and then, later on, go and see Mrs. Trump."

Philippa stopped in front of a newsstand long enough for the two of them to read the story on the front page of the *New York Post*. Millions of children all over the world were now "recovered" from the "mass hypnosis" inflicted upon them by "disgraced magician Jonathan Tarot." Which was a great relief to these two children of the lamp. As well as a source of considerable sadness, too.

"Poor Dybbuk," said Philippa.

"It's Buck, remember?" said John. "He hates that name."

"I wonder what will become of him."

"Says there he's disappeared." John shrugged. "Whatever that means."

"I know. I can read. I just wondered what was going to become of him. It's been difficult enough not having any power for four weeks. I can't imagine what it might feel like to lose djinn power for the rest of your life."

"I know. I feel like I've been missing an arm."

"I suppose you'd get used to that feeling," observed Philippa. "Eventually. Groanin did."

Arriving home, they were disappointed to find that their mother had not yet arrived back from Iravotum, although there was a letter in her familiar, copperplate handwriting, explaining that she would be with them again very soon. John noticed that the letter was on her personal stationery, the ludicrously expensive stuff she had made especially with her name and address on top in gold lettering, and which she kept in the French bureau in her study. It struck him as a little strange, perhaps, that she could have been using this to write on, at least until he reminded himself that his mother was a powerful djinn and could do more or less whatever she liked.

The disappointing news that she had not yet arrived home was, to some extent, lessened by the discovery that Mrs. Trump was there to greet them warmly, having made a spectacular recovery from her head trauma. If anything, she looked better than they remembered her ever looking before, even, it has to be said, more than a little glamorous. She was wearing some very expensive clothes and a new set of pearls, and her hair had been done in a way that reminded the twins of their mother's hairstyle. Somehow Mrs. Trump seemed more graceful, too, and hardly like a housekeeper at all.

Their father was much recovered, too. His hair was gray rather than white. And he was able to stand rather than sit in a wheelchair. He was even a little taller than they remembered. His hands had stopped shaking and the pungent, musty old-people smell that had once hung about his person was now gone. So near back to normal was he that Marion Morrison had now left New York to go and look after another victim of a malicious djinn binding. Mr. Gaunt's voice had recovered most of its strength, too. Not to mention its authority.

"John," said Mr. Gaunt. "Why don't you go upstairs and reclaim your body? And Philippa, why don't you go and recover your djinn power. When you are both quite yourselves again, I want you to meet me in the library. I think we should have a little talk. It's been so long since we had a proper conversation as a family, and so much has happened that we need to sit down and catch up with all that's taken place. You, me, and Mrs. Trump."

Intrigued, Philippa ran quickly upstairs. John thanked her politely for the ride and then stepped out of his sister and back into his own body.

"Oh man, that feels good," he said. "I am myself again."

"Before you get too comfortable," said Philippa, "you still have to blow in my ear."

"What?"

"So I can get my power back," she said. "If you don't mind."

"All right," John said grimly. "Let's get it over with."

When it was done, John spat on the floor, several times.

"You don't have to make such a song and dance about it," said Philippa, wiping her ear daintily.

"Don't I?" muttered John.

But Philippa hardly cared. She had djinn power back in her body. Not having djinn power was exactly like having just one arm. John had been right about that. She felt great. She took off the golden slippers the great Khan had presented to her and sniffed them. It was true, they smelled of fresh strawberries.

"Did you notice?" said John. "That's the first time Dad ever mentioned djinn power in front of Mrs. Trump."

"You're right, he did, didn't he? And Mrs. Trump. She seems different, too. Don't you think? As if a blow on the head did her a lot of good. I never saw her looking so good. I wonder what Dad wants to tell us."

"When a parent summons you to a meeting like that," said John, "it's never good news. Perhaps Mom isn't coming back after all."

"What about the letter? It said she was coming back very soon, didn't it? I'd recognize her handwriting anywhere." Philippa shook her head. "I wonder what Dad wants to tell us," she said again.

"Perhaps it's about Mr. Rakshasas," said John. "Did you notice? His body is gone."

"Of course I noticed," said Philippa. "But I can't imagine Dad wants to talk about that, can you? After all, he's not a djinn. He leaves all that kind of stuff to Mom. Always has. It makes him feel uncomfortable."

"Well, whatever it is he wants to talk about, you can bet it's going to be something weird," said John. "There's nothing normal about this family."

A minute or two later, he and Philippa were sitting in the library facing an awkward-looking Mr. Gaunt and a strangely serene-looking Mrs. Trump. Monty the cat had even turned up to witness the scene.

"Is something wrong, Dad?" asked Philippa.

"Is it about Mr. Rakshasas?" asked John.

"Where's Mom?" they said in unison.

Mr. Gaunt looked at Mrs. Trump and nodded. "Under the circumstances, Mrs. er . . ." he said. "Perhaps this had better come from you."

Mrs. Trump smiled kindly. "Nothing's wrong," she said. "Not from where I'm sitting, anyway. But yes, something has happened. No doubt about that. Something important. Something peculiar. Something that might take quite a bit of getting used to. Yes, indeed. You see, children, the thing is, you're going to have to get used to a few changes around here. We all are. From now on, things are going to be a little different. Let me explain how."

ABOUT THE AUTHOR

P. B. Kerr was born in Edinburgh, Scotland, where he developed a lifelong love of reading. Although the Children of the Lamp books are P. B. Kerr's first for children, he is well known as the thriller writer Philip Kerr, author of the Berlin Noir series, including most recently *The One from the Other*, *A Philosophical Investigation*, *Gridiron*, *The Shot*, and many other acclaimed novels. Mr. Kerr lives in London with his family. You can visit him on his Web site at www.pbkerr.com.

100

DAILY DEVOTIONS
FOR PEOPLE
WHO SERVE
ON THE
FRONT LINE

*The quoted ideas expressed in this book (but not Scripture verses) are not, in all cases, exact
quotations, as some have been edited for clarity and brevity. In all cases, the author has attempted
to maintain the speaker's original intent. In some cases, quoted material for this book was obtained
from secondary sources, primarily print media. While every effort was made to ensure the accuracy
of these sources, the accuracy cannot be guaranteed. For additions, deletions, corrections, or
clarifications in future editions of this text, please write Freeman-Smith, LLC.*

..ver Design by Kim Russell / Wahoo Designs
.. Layout by Bart Dawson

I..
..8-1-60587-165-3

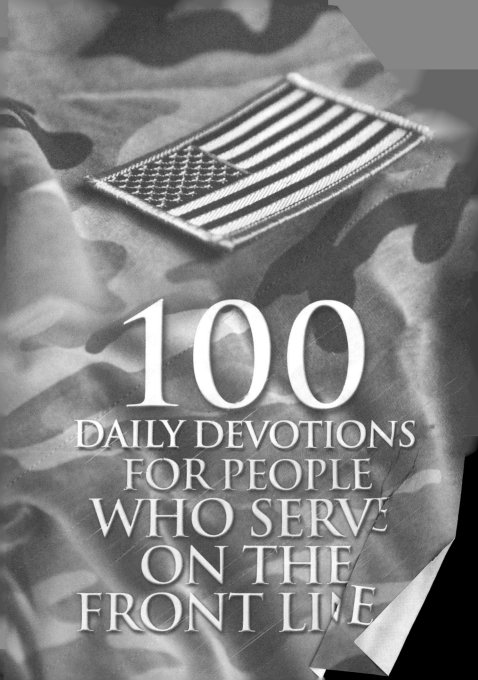

100

DAILY DEVOTIONS
FOR PEOPLE
WHO SERVE
ON THE
FRONT LINE

"Follow Me"

— God

INTRODUCTION

Life on the front line is intense. And the emotions of the battlefield don't magically disappear when the fighting stops. So how can you find peace on the front lines of life? And how can you find the genuine peace that Jesus describes in John 16:33? By making God a full partner in every aspect of your life, that's how.

On the pages that follow, you'll be asked to spend a few minutes each day thinking about ways that you and God, working together, can overcome your challenges, organize your life, prioritize your duties, redirect your thoughts, and follow the path that your Heavenly Father intends for you to take. When you do these things, you'll receive the peace and the spiritual abundance that can, and should, be yours. So, for the next 100 days, please try this experiment: Read a chapter a day and internalize the ideas that you find here.

This text contains Biblically based prescriptions for the inevitable challenges of tough times. As you consider your own circumstances, remember this: whatever the size of your problems, God is bigger. Much bigger. He will instruct you, protect you, energize you, and heal you if you let Him. So let Him. Pray fervently, listen carefully, work diligently, and treat every single day as an exercise in spiritual growth because that's precisely what every day can be—and will be—if you learn how to let God help you rise above the challenges of life on the front line.

I have told you these things
so that in Me you may have peace.
In the world you have suffering.
But take courage!
I have conquered the world.

—

John 16:33 Holman CSB

HE OFFERS PEACE

Peace I leave with you. My peace I give to you. I do not give to you as the world gives. Your heart must not be troubled or fearful.

John 14:27 Holman CSB

These are turbulent times, difficult days when life on the front line can be painful and exhausting. Worries are easy to identify and peace may be a scarce commodity. But no times are too turbulent for God. And if you sincerely desire the peace that passes all understanding, you'll find it in Him.

The familiar words of John 14:27 remind us that Jesus offers us peace, not as the world gives, but as He alone gives. Have you found the genuine peace that can be yours through Jesus Christ? Or are you still rushing after the illusion of "peace and happiness" that the world promises but cannot deliver?

When you welcome God's love into your heart, your life will be transformed as the Father's peace will become yours.

This day, complete with its assortment of ups and downs, is a gift from the Creator. This day will contain many blessings and many opportunities to serve. This day will provide quiet moments for prayer and praise. And, this day offers yet another opportunity to welcome the Father into your heart and to share His good news with the world. So honor Him and thank Him: It's the right thing to do—in good times and in hard times—and it's the best way to find peace on the front lines of life.

Sometimes we get tired of the burdens of life,
but we know that Jesus Christ
will meet us at the end of life's journey.
And, that makes all the difference.

—

Billy Graham

Christ alone can bring lasting peace—peace with God—peace among men and nations—and peace within our hearts.

Billy Graham

God cannot give us happiness and peace apart from Himself, because it is not there. There is no such thing.

C. S. Lewis

"My peace I give unto you"; it is a peace all over from the crown of the head to the sole of the feet, an irrepressible confidence.

Oswald Chambers

A TIMELY TIP

Even on the front lines of life, God offers peace that passes human understanding . . . and He wants you to make His peace your peace.

HE IS SUFFICIENT

The Lord is my rock, my fortress, and my deliverer.

Psalm 18:2 Holman CSB

I t is easy to become overwhelmed by the demands of life on the front line, but if you're a faithful follower of the One from Galilee, you need never be overwhelmed. Why? Because God's love is sufficient to meet your needs. Whatever dangers you may face, whatever heartbreaks you must endure, God is with you, and He stands ready to comfort you and to heal you.

The Psalmist writes, "Weeping may endure for a night, but joy comes in the morning" (Psalm 30:5 NKJV). But when we are suffering, the morning may seem very far away. It is not. God promises that He is "near to those who have a broken heart" (Psalm 34:18 NKJV).

If you are experiencing the intense pain of a recent loss, or if you are still mourning a loss from long ago, perhaps you are now ready to begin the next stage of your journey with God. If so, be mindful of this fact: the loving heart of God is sufficient to meet any challenge, including yours.

God is always sufficient in perfect proportion to our need.

Beth Moore

God is, must be, our answer to every question and every cry of need.

Hannah Whitall Smith

God will call you to obey Him and do whatever he asks of you. However, you do not need to be doing something to feel fulfilled. You are fulfilled completely in a relationship with God. When you are filled with Him, what else do you need?

Henry Blackaby and Claude King

I grew up learning to be self-reliant, but now, to grow up in Christ, I must unlearn self-reliance and learn self-distrust in light of his all-sufficiency.

Mary Morrison Suggs

A TIMELY TIP

Whatever you need, God can provide. He is always sufficient to meet your needs.

TRUSTING GOD'S PLAN

"For I know the plans I have for you"—[this is] the Lord's declaration—"plans for [your] welfare, not for disaster, to give you a future and a hope."

Jeremiah 29:11 Holman CSB

It's an age-old riddle: Why does God allow us to endure times of uncertainty and pain? After all, since we trust that God is all-powerful, and since we trust that His hand shapes our lives, why doesn't He simply rescue us—and our loved ones—from all hardship and pain?

God's Word teaches us again and again that He loves us and wants the best for us. And the Bible also teaches us that God is ever-present and always watchful. So why, we wonder, if God is really so concerned with every detail of our lives, does He permit us to endure emotions like grief, sadness, pain, or fear? And why does He allow tragic circumstances to invade the lives of good people? These questions perplex us, especially on the front lines of life.

On occasion, all of us face adversity, and throughout life, we all must endure life-changing personal losses that leave us breathless. When we pass through the dark valleys of life, we often ask, "Why me?" Sometimes, of course, the answer is obvious—sometimes we make mistakes, and we must pay for them. But on other occasions, when we have done nothing wrong, we wonder why God allows us to suffer.

Even when we cannot understand God's plans, we must trust them. And even when we are impatient for our situations to improve, we must trust God's timing. If we seek to live in accordance with His plan for our lives, we must continue to study His Word (in good times and bad), and we must be watchful for His signs, knowing that in time, He will lead us through the valleys, onward to the mountaintop.

So if you're enduring tough times, don't give up and don't give in. God still has glorious plans for you. So keep your eyes and ears open . . . as well as your heart.

When terrible things happen, there are two choices, and only two: We can trust God, or we can defy Him. We believe that God is God, He's still got the whole world in His hands and knows exactly what He's doing, or we must believe that He is not God and that we are at the awful mercy of mere chance.

Elisabeth Elliot

Every misfortune, every failure, every loss may be transformed. God has the power to transform all misfortunes into "God-sends."

Mrs. Charles E. Cowman

Don't let circumstances distress you. Rather, look for the will of God for your life to be revealed in and through those circumstances.

Billy Graham

This battle is not yours—it's the Lord's!

Anonymous

A TIMELY TIP

Even when you cannot understand why things happen, you must continue to trust your Heavenly Father. Ruth Bell Graham once said, "When I am dealing with an all-powerful, all-knowing God, I, as a mere mortal, must offer my petitions not only with persistence, but also with patience. Someday I'll know why." So even when you can't understand why God allows certain things to happen, you must trust Him and never lose faith!

IN TURBULENT TIMES, GOD PROTECTS

For whatever is born of God overcomes the world. And this is the victory that has overcome the world—our faith.

1 John 5:4 NKJV

If you're serving our nation at home or abroad, you are certainly no stranger to adversity. Thankfully, God's promises offer assurance and hope whether you're at home or abroad.

When we face the inevitable difficulties of life on the battlefield, God stands ready to protect us. Our responsibility, of course, is to ask Him for protection. When we call upon Him in heartfelt prayer, He will answer—in His own time and in accordance with His own perfect plan.

Are these the toughest of times for you? If so, you must trust in God's power, His mercy, and His grace. For it is only when we place our lives in God's hands that we are truly secure.

Troubles we bear trustfully can bring us a fresh vision of God and a new outlook on life, an outlook of peace and hope.

Billy Graham

A faith that hasn't been tested can't be trusted.

Adrian Rogers

If things are tough, remember that every flower that ever bloomed had to go through a whole lot of dirt to get there.

Barbara Johnson

The sermon of your life in tough times ministers to people more powerfully than the most eloquent speaker.

Bill Bright

A TIMELY TIP

When you find yourself on the front lines of life, work as if everything depended on you and pray as if everything depended on God.

FAITH MOVES MOUNTAINS

For I assure you: If you have faith the size of a mustard seed, you will tell this mountain, "Move from here to there," and it will move. Nothing will be impossible for you.

Matthew 17:20 Holman CSB

Because we live in a demanding world, all of us have mountains to climb and mountains to move. Moving those mountains requires faith. And the experience of trying, with God's help, to move mountains builds character.

Faith, like a tender seedling, can be nurtured or neglected. When we nurture our faith through prayer, meditation, and worship, God blesses our lives and lifts our spirits. But when we neglect to commune with the Father, we do ourselves and our loved ones a profound disservice.

Are you a mountain-moving person whose faith is evident for all to see? Or, are you a spiritual underachiever? As you think about the answer to that question, consider this: God needs more people who are willing to move mountains for His glory and for His kingdom.

Every life—including yours—is a series of victories and defeats. Every step of the way, through every triumph and tragedy, God walks with you, ready and willing to strengthen you. So the next time you find your character being tested, remember to take your fears to God. If you call upon Him, you will be comforted. Whatever your challenge, whatever your trouble, God can handle it.

When you place your faith, your trust, indeed your life in the hands of your Heavenly Father, you'll receive a lesson in character-building from the ultimate Teacher. So strengthen your faith through praise, through worship, through Bible study, and through prayer. And trust God's plans. With Him, all things are possible, and He stands ready to open a world of possibilities to you . . . if you have faith.

Trials are not enemies of faith
but opportunities to reveal God's faithfulness.

—

Barbara Johnson

Despair is always the gateway of faith.

Oswald Chambers

Shout the shout of faith. Nothing can withstand the triumphant faith that links itself to omnipotence. For "this is the victory that overcometh the world." The secret of all successful living lies in this shout of faith.

Hannah Whitall Smith

It may be the most difficult time of your life. You may be enduring your own whirlwind. But the whirlwind is a temporary experience. Your faithful, caring Lord will see you through.

Charles Swindoll

A TIMELY TIP

If your faith is strong enough, you and God—working together—can move mountains.

MAKE PEACE WITH THE PAST

Peace I leave with you, my peace I give unto you: not as the world giveth, give I unto you. Let not your heart be troubled, neither let it be afraid.

John 14:27 KJV

Some of life's greatest roadblocks are not the ones we see through the windshield; they are, instead, the roadblocks that seem to fill the rearview mirror. Because we are imperfect human beings who lack perfect control over our thoughts, we may allow ourselves to become "stuck" in the past—even though we know better. Instead of focusing our thoughts and energies on the opportunities of today, we may allow painful memories to fill our minds and sap our strength. We simply can't seem to let go of our pain, so we relive it again and again . . . with predictably unfortunate consequences. Thankfully, God has other plans.

Philippians 3:13-14 instructs us to focus on the future, not the past: "One thing I do, forgetting those things which are behind and reaching forward to those things which are ahead, I press toward the goal for the prize of the upward call of God in Christ Jesus" (NKJV). Yet for many of us, focusing on the future is difficult indeed. Why?

Part of the problem has to do with forgiveness. When we find ourselves focusing too intently on the past, it's a sure sign that we need to focus, instead, on a more urgent need: the need to forgive.

Focusing too intently on the past is, almost without exception, futile. No amount of anger or bitterness can change what happened yesterday. Tears can't change the past; regrets can't change it. Our worries won't change the past, and neither will our complaints. Simply put, the past is, and always will be, the past. Forever.

Can you summon both the courage and the wisdom to accept your past and move on with your life? Can you accept the reality that yesterday—and all the yesterdays before it—are gone? And, can you entrust all those yesterdays to God? Hopefully you can.

So if you've endured a difficult past, learn from it, but don't live in it. Instead, build your future on a firm foundation of trust and forgiveness: trust in your Heavenly Father, and forgiveness for all His children, including yourself.

If you are God's child, you are no longer bound to your past or to what you were. You are a brand new creature in Christ Jesus.

Kay Arthur

Our yesterdays present irreparable things to us; it is true that we have lost opportunities which will never return, but God can transform this destructive anxiety into a constructive thoughtfulness for the future. Let the past sleep, but let it sleep on the bosom of Christ. Leave the Irreparable Past in His hands, and step out into the Irresistible Future with Him.

Oswald Chambers

God forgets the past. Imitate him.

Max Lucado

Shake the dust from your past, and move forward in His promises.

Kay Arthur

A TIMELY TIP

The past is past, so don't invest all your energy there. If you're focused on the past, change your focus. If you're living in the past, it's time to stop living there.

IN TURBULENT TIMES, GOD TEACHES AND LEADS

Leave inexperience behind, and you will live; pursue the way of understanding.

Proverbs 9:6 Holman CSB

Complete spiritual maturity is never achieved in a day, or in a year, or even in a lifetime. The journey toward spiritual maturity is an ongoing process that continues, day by day, throughout every stage of life. Every stage of life has its opportunities and its challenges, and if we're wise, we continue to seek God's guidance as each new chapter of life unfolds.

From time to time, all of us encounter circumstances that test our faith. When we encounter life's inevitable tragedies, trials, uncertainties, and disappointments, we may be tempted to blame God or to rebel against Him. But the Bible reminds us that the trials of life should be viewed as opportunities for growth: "Consider it a great joy, my brothers, whenever you experience various trials, knowing that the testing of your faith produces endurance. But endurance must do its complete work, so that you may be mature and complete, lacking nothing" (James 1:2-4 Holman CSB).

Have you recently encountered one of life's inevitable tests? If so, remember that God still has lessons that He intends to teach you. So ask yourself this: what lesson is God trying to teach me today?

Your greatest ministry will likely come out of your greatest hurt.

—

Rick Warren

Adversity is not simply a tool. It is God's most effective tool for the advancement of our spiritual lives. The circumstances and events that we see as setbacks are oftentimes the very things that launch us into periods of intense spiritual growth. Once we begin to understand this, and accept it as a spiritual fact of life, adversity becomes easier to bear.

Charles Stanley

It is a fact of Christian experience that life is a series of troughs and peaks. In his efforts to get permanent possession of a soul, God relies on the troughs more than the peaks. And, some of his special favorites have gone through longer and deeper troughs than anyone else.

Peter Marshall

A TIMELY TIP

The times that test our souls can also be times of intense personal growth. Elisabeth Elliot observed, "I am not a theologian or a scholar, but I am very aware of the fact that pain is necessary to all of us. In my own life, I think I can honestly say that out of the deepest pain has come the strongest conviction of the presence of God and the love of God."

SERVE HIM

The greatest among you will be your servant. Whoever exalts himself will be humbled, and whoever humbles himself will be exalted.

Matthew 23:11-12 Holman CSB

We live in a world that glorifies power, prestige, fame, and money. But the words of Jesus teach us that the most esteemed men and women in this world are not the self-congratulatory leaders of society but are instead the humblest of servants.

Are you willing to become a humble servant for Christ? Are you willing to pitch in and make the world a better place, or are you determined to keep all your blessings to yourself? The answers to these questions will determine the quality and the direction of your day and your life.

Today, you may feel the temptation to take more than you give. You may be tempted to withhold your generosity. Or you may be tempted to build yourself up in the eyes of your friends. Resist those temptations. Instead, serve your friends quietly and without fanfare. Find a need and fill it . . . humbly. Lend a helping hand . . . anonymously. Share a word of kindness . . . with quiet sincerity. As you go about your daily activities, remember that the Savior of all humanity made Himself a servant, and we, as His followers, must do no less.

In the very place where God has put us,
whatever its limitations,
whatever kind of work it may be,
we may indeed serve the Lord Christ.

—

Elisabeth Elliot

God wants us to serve Him with a willing spirit, one that would choose no other way.

Beth Moore

Through our service to others, God wants to influence our world for Him.

Vonette Bright

So many times we say that we can't serve God because we aren't whatever is needed. We're not talented enough or smart enough or whatever. But if you are in covenant with Jesus Christ, He is responsible for covering your weaknesses, for being your strength. He will give you His abilities for your disabilities!

Kay Arthur

A TIMELY TIP

Wherever you happen to be—whatever your age, whatever your loss—you can find people to help and ways to serve. And the time to begin serving is now.

NO PROBLEMS ARE
TOO BIG FOR GOD

Is anything too hard for the LORD?

Genesis 18:14 KJV

Here's a riddle: What is it that is too unimportant to pray about yet too big for God to handle? The answer, of course, is: "nothing." Yet sometimes, when the challenges of life on the front line seems overwhelming, we may spend more time worrying about our troubles than praying about them. And, we may spend more time fretting about our problems than solving them. A far better strategy, of course, is to pray as if everything depended entirely upon God and to work as if everything depended entirely upon us.

Life is an exercise in problem-solving. The question is not whether we will encounter problems; the real question is how we will choose to address them. When it comes to solving the problems of everyday living, we often know precisely what needs to be done, but we may be slow in doing it—especially if what needs to be done is difficult or uncomfortable for us. So we put off till tomorrow what should be done today.

The words of Psalm 34 remind us that the Lord solves problems for "people who do what is right." And usually, "doing what is right" means doing the uncomfortable work of confronting our problems sooner rather than later. So with no further ado, let the problem-solving begin . . . now!

The grace of God is sufficient for all our needs,
for every problem and for every difficulty,
for every broken heart,
and for every human sorrow.

—

Peter Marshall

Trial and triumph are what God uses to scribble all over the pages of our lives. They are signs that He is using us, loving us, shaping us to His image, enjoying our companionship, delivering us from evil, and writing eternity into our hearts.

Barbara Johnson

No matter how heavy the burden, daily strength is given, so I expect we need not give ourselves any concern as to what the outcome will be. We must simply go forward.

Annie Armstrong

Measure the size of the obstacles against the size of God.

Beth Moore

A TIMELY TIP

Everyone has problems, but not everyone deals with their problems in the same way. The way you address your problems—whether you choose to avoid them or address them—determines how successfully—and how quickly—you overcome them.

BEYOND ANXIETY

Be anxious for nothing, but in everything by prayer and supplication, with thanksgiving, let your requests be made known to God.

Philippians 4:6 NKJV

If you risk life and limb in service of our country—or if your loved one has chosen to serve and protect America—it is inevitable: You worry. From time to time, you worry about safety, health, finances, family, and countless other concerns, some great and some small.

What should you do when the uncertainties of tomorrow trouble your soul and drain your strength? Take your troubles to God. Take your fears to Him; take your doubts to Him; take your weaknesses to Him; take your sorrows to Him . . . and leave them all there. Seek protection from the One who offers you eternal salvation; build your spiritual house upon the Rock that cannot be moved.

Anxiety does not empty tomorrow of its sorrows, but it empties today of its strength.

C. H. Spurgeon

So often we pray and then fret anxiously, waiting for God to hurry up and do something. All the while God is waiting for us to calm down, so He can do something through us.

Corrie ten Boom

Worry and anxiety are sand in the machinery of life; faith is the oil.

E. Stanley Jones

We must lay our questions, frustrations, anxieties, and impotence at the feet of God and wait for His answer. And then receiving it, we must live by faith.

Kay Arthur

The fierce grip of panic need not immobilize you. God knows no limitation when it comes to deliverance. Admit your fear. Commit it to Him. Dump the pressure on Him. He can handle it.

Charles Swindoll

A TIMELY TIP

Remembering God's faithfulness in the past can give you peace for today and hope for tomorrow.

ASK HIM

The intense prayer of the righteous is very powerful.

James 5:16 Holman CSB

How often do you ask God for His help and His wisdom? Occasionally? Intermittently? Whenever you experience a crisis? Hopefully not. Hopefully, you've acquired the habit of asking for God's assistance early and often. And hopefully, you have learned to seek His guidance in every aspect of your life.

Jesus made it clear to His disciples: they should petition God to meet their needs. So should you. Genuine, heartfelt prayer produces powerful changes in you and in your world. When you lift your heart to God, you open yourself to a never-ending source of divine wisdom and infinite love.

James 5:16 makes a promise that God intends to keep: when you pray earnestly, fervently, and often, great things will happen. Too many people, however, are too timid or too pessimistic to ask God to do big things. Please don't count yourself among their number.

God can do great things through you if you have the courage to ask Him (and the determination to keep asking Him). But don't expect Him to do all the work. When you do your part, He will do His part—and when He does, you can expect miracles to happen.

God stands at the door and waits. When you knock, He opens. When you ask, He answers. Your task, of course, is to make God a full partner in every aspect of your life—in good times and in hard times—and to seek His guidance prayerfully, confidently, and often.

☆ ☆ ☆ ☆

God will help us become the people
we are meant to be,
if only we will ask Him.

—

Hannah Whitall Smith

We sometimes fear to bring our troubles to God, because they must seem so small to him who sitteth on the circle of the earth. But, if they are large enough to vex and endanger our welfare, they are large enough to touch his heart of love.

R. A. Torrey

Don't be afraid to ask your Heavenly Father for anything you need. Indeed, nothing is too small for God's attention or too great for his power.

Dennis Swanberg

The God of the galaxies is the God who knows when your heart is broken—and He can heal it!

Warren Wiersbe

A TIMELY TIP

If you want more from life, ask more from God. If you're searching for peace and abundance, ask for God's help—and keep asking—until He answers your prayers. If you sincerely want to rise above the stresses of life on the front line, ask for God's help many times each day.

IN TIMES OF UNCERTAINTY, TRUST GOD'S TIMING

I waited patiently for the LORD; and He inclined to me, and heard my cry.

Psalm 40:1 NKJV

The Bible teaches us to trust God's timing in all matters, but we are sorely tempted to do otherwise, especially when times are tough. When we find ourselves squarely on the front lines of life, we are understandably anxious for a quick conclusion to our hardships. We know that our problems will end some day, and we want them to end NOW. God, however, works on His own timetable, and His schedule does not always coincide with ours.

God's plans are perfect; ours most certainly are not. So we must learn to trust the Father in good times and hard times. No exceptions.

Elisabeth Elliot advised, "We must learn to move according to the timetable of the Timeless One, and to be at peace." And Billy Graham observed, "As we wait on God, He helps us use the winds of adversity to soar above our problems."

So today, as you face the uncertainties of everyday life, do your best to turn everything over to God. Whatever "it" is, He can handle it. And you can be sure that He will handle it when the time is right.

Will not the Lord's time
be better than your time?

—

C. H. Spurgeon

By his wisdom, he orders his delays so that they prove to be far better than our hurries.

C. H. Spurgeon

Waiting on God brings us to the journey's end quicker than our feet.

Mrs. Charles E. Cowman

God is in no hurry. Compared to the works of mankind, He is extremely deliberate. God is not a slave to the human clock.

Charles Swindoll

A TIMELY TIP

You don't know precisely what you need—or when you need it—but God does. So trust His timing.

TURBULENT TIMES BUILD CHARACTER

The one who lives with integrity lives securely, but whoever perverts his ways will be found out.

Proverbs 10:9 Holman CSB

Charles Swindoll correctly observed, "Nothing speaks louder or more powerfully than a life of integrity." Righteous men and women agree.

Character is built slowly over a lifetime. It is the sum of every right decision, every honest word, every noble thought, and every heartfelt prayer. It is forged on the anvil of honorable work and polished by the twin virtues of generosity and humility. Character is a precious thing—difficult to build but easy to tear down. As believers in Christ, we must seek to live each day with discipline, honesty, and faith. When we do, integrity becomes a habit.

Psalm 145 promises, "The Lord is near to all who call on him, to all who call on him in truth. He fulfills the desires of those who fear him; he hears their cry and saves them" (vv. 18-20 NIV). And the words of Jesus offer us comfort: "These things I have spoken to you, that in Me you may have peace. In the world you will have tribula-

tion; but be of good cheer, I have overcome the world"
(John 16:33 NKJV).

The times that try your soul are also the times that
build your character. During the darker days of life, you
can learn lessons that are impossible to learn during sun-
ny, happier days. Times of adversity can—and should—be
times of intense spiritual and personal growth. But God
will not force you to learn the lessons of adversity. You
must learn them for yourself.

Character is both developed and revealed
by tests, and all of life is a test.

—

Rick Warren

Every time you refuse to face up to life and its problems, you weaken your character.

E. Stanley Jones

Jesus—the standard of measurement, the scale of weights, the test of character for the whole moral universe.

R. G. Lee

Character cannot be developed in ease and quiet. Only through experience of trial and suffering can the soul be strengthened, vision cleared, ambition inspired, and success achieved.

Helen Keller

A TIMELY TIP

On the front line, character is always more important than popularity.

IN TURBULENT TIMES, KEEP PRAYING

Is anyone among you suffering? He should pray. Is anyone cheerful? He should sing praises.

James 5:13 Holman CSB

God is trying to get His message through . . . to you! Are you listening?

Perhaps, if you're experiencing tough times or uncertain times, you may find yourself overwhelmed by the press of everyday life. Perhaps you forget to slow yourself down long enough to talk with God. Instead of turning your thoughts and prayers to Him, you may rely upon our own resources. Instead of asking God for guidance, you may depend only upon your own limited wisdom. A far better course of action is this: simply stop what you're doing long enough to open your heart to God; then listen carefully for His directions.

Do you spend time each day with God? You should. Are you in need? Ask God to sustain you. Are you troubled? Take your worries to Him in prayer. Are you weary? Seek God's strength. In all things great and small, seek God's wisdom and His grace. He hears your prayers, and He will answer. All you must do is ask.

I have found the perfect antidote for fear. Whenever it sticks up its ugly face, I clobber it with prayer.

Dale Evans Rogers

God always answers the prayers of His children—but His answer isn't always "Yes."

Billy Graham

Prayer accomplishes more than anything else.

Bill Bright

I have witnessed many attitudes make a positive turn-around through prayer.

John Maxwell

A TIMELY TIP

There's no corner of your life that's too unimportant to pray about, so pray about everything.

YOU'RE NEVER ALONE

The Lord is the One who will go before you. He will be with you; He will not leave you or forsake you. Do not be afraid or discouraged.

Deuteronomy 31:8 Holman CSB

I f God is everywhere, why does He sometimes seem so far away? The answer to that question, of course, has nothing to do with God and everything to do with us.

When we begin each day on our knees, in praise and worship to Him, God often seems very near indeed. But, if we ignore God's presence or—worse yet—rebel against it altogether, the world in which we live becomes a spiritual wasteland.

Are you tired, discouraged, or fearful? Be comforted because God is with you. Are you confused? Listen to the quiet voice of your Heavenly Father. Are you bitter? Talk with God and seek His guidance. Are you celebrating a great victory? Thank God and praise Him. He is the Giver of all things good.

In whatever condition you find yourself, wherever you are, whether you are happy or sad, victorious or vanquished, troubled or triumphant, celebrate God's presence. And be comforted. God is not just near. He is here.

God is not hurried along in the Time-stream of this universe any more than an author is hurried along in the imaginary time of his own novel. He has infinite attention to spare for each one of us. He does not have to deal with us in the mass. You are as much alone with Him as if you were the only being He had ever created. When Christ died, He died for you individually just as much as if you have been the only man in the world.

C. S. Lewis

The real test of being in the presence of God is that you either forget about yourself altogether or see yourself as a very small object. It is better to forget about yourself altogether.

C. S. Lewis

God's silence is in no way indicative of His activity or involvement in our lives. He may be silent, but He is not still.

Charles Swindoll

A TIMELY TIP

When you're on the front line, God is right there with you. And He's willing to talk with you any time, any place.

ACCEPTING ADVICE

A wise man will hear and increase learning, and a man of understanding will attain wise counsel.

Proverbs 1:5 NKJV

If you find yourself caught up in the inevitable challenges of life on the front lines, it's probably the right time to start searching for friends and mentors who can give you solid advice. Why do you need help evaluating the person in the mirror? Because you're simply too close to that person, that's why. Sometimes, you'll be tempted to give yourself straight A's when you deserve considerably lower grades. On other occasions, you'll become your own worst critic, giving yourself a string of failing marks when you deserve better. The truth, of course, is often somewhere in the middle.

Finding a wise mentor is only half the battle. It takes just as much wisdom—and sometimes more—to act upon good advice as it does to give it. So find people you can trust, listen to them carefully, and act accordingly.

It takes a wise person to give good advice, but an even wiser person to take it.

Marie T. Freeman

God guides through the counsel of good people.

E. Stanley Jones

Yes, the Spirit was sent to be our Counselor. Yes, Jesus speaks to us personally. But often he works through another human being.

John Eldredge

A single word, if spoken in a friendly spirit, may be sufficient to turn one from dangerous error.

Fanny Crosby

A TIMELY TIP

If you can't seem to listen to constructive criticism with an open mind, perhaps you've got a severe case of old-fashioned stubbornness. If so, ask God to soften your heart, open your ears, and enlighten your mind.

SELF-ESTEEM ACCORDING TO GOD

For you made us only a little lower than God, and you crowned us with glory and honor.

Psalm 8:5 NLT

What are you telling yourself about yourself? When you look in the mirror, are you staring back at your biggest booster or your harshest critic? If you can learn to give yourself the benefit of the doubt—if you can learn how to have constructive conversations with the person you see in the mirror—then your self-respect will tend to take care of itself. But, if you're constantly berating yourself—if you're constantly telling yourself that you can't measure up—then you'll find that self-respect is always in short supply.

So the next time you find yourself being critical of the person you see in the mirror, ask yourself if the criticism is really valid. If it is valid, make changes . . . if not, lighten up.

Being loved by Him whose opinion matters most gives us the security to risk loving, too—even loving ourselves.

Gloria Gaither

As you and I lay up for ourselves living, lasting treasures in Heaven, we come to the awesome conclusion that we ourselves are His treasure!

Anne Graham Lotz

Your self worth is more important than your net worth.

Anonymous

The Creator has made us each one of a kind. There is nobody else exactly like us, and there never will be. Each of us is his special creation and is alive for a distinctive purpose.

Luci Swindoll

A TIMELY TIP

Don't make the mistake of selling yourself short. No matter the size of your challenges, you can be sure that you and God, working together, can handle them.

ON THE FRONT LINE, GUARD YOUR THOUGHTS

Finally brothers, whatever is true, whatever is honorable, whatever is just, whatever is pure, whatever is lovely, whatever is commendable—if there is any moral excellence and if there is any praise—dwell on these things.

Philippians 4:8 Holman CSB

Do you pay careful attention to the quality of your thoughts? And are you careful to direct those thoughts toward topics that are uplifting, enlightening, and pleasing to God? If so, congratulations. But if you find that your thoughts are hijacked from time to time by the negativity that seems to have invaded our troubled world, you are not alone. Ours is a society that focuses on—and often glamorizes—the negative aspects of life, and that's unfortunate.

God intends that you experience joy and abundance. So, today and every day hereafter, celebrate the life that God has given you by focusing your thoughts upon those things that are worthy of praise. And while you're at it, count your blessings instead of your hardships. When you do, you'll undoubtedly offer words of thanks to your Heavenly Father for gifts that are simply too numerous to count.

Your thoughts are the determining factor as to whose mold you are conformed to. Control your thoughts and you control the direction of your life.

Charles Stanley

The things we think are the things that feed our souls. If we think on pure and lovely things, we shall grow pure and lovely like them; and the converse is equally true.

Hannah Whitall Smith

Attitude is the mind's paintbrush; it can color any situation.

Barbara Johnson

Every major spiritual battle is in the mind.

Charles Stanley

A TIMELY TIP

Either you can control your thoughts, or they most certainly will control you.

ON THE FRONT LINE, STUDY GOD'S WORD

All Scripture is inspired by God and is profitable for teaching, for rebuking, for correcting, for training in righteousness, so that the man of God may be complete, equipped for every good work.

2 Timothy 3:16-17 Holman CSB

The words of Matthew 4:4 remind us that, "Man shall not live by bread alone but by every word that proceedeth out of the mouth of God" (KJV). As believers, we must study the Bible and meditate upon its meaning for our lives. Otherwise, we deprive ourselves of a priceless gift from our Creator.

God's Word is unlike any other book. The Bible is a roadmap for life here on earth and for life eternal. As Christians, we are called upon to study God's Holy Word, to follow its commandments, and to share its Good News with the world.

Jonathan Edwards advised, "Be assiduous in reading the Holy Scriptures. This is the fountain whence all knowledge in divinity must be derived. Therefore let not this treasure lie by you neglected." God's Holy Word is, indeed, a priceless, one-of-a-kind treasure, and a passing acquaintance with the Good Book is insufficient for Christians who seek to obey God's Word and to understand His will. After all, man does not live by bread alone . . .

The strength that we claim from
God's Word does not depend on circumstances.
Circumstances will be difficult,
but our strength will be sufficient.

—

Corrie ten Boom

God has given us all sorts of counsel and direction in his written Word; thank God, we have it written down in black and white.

John Eldredge

If you want to know whether you're thinking correctly, check it out in the Word.

Charles Stanley

Weave the fabric of God's word through your heart and mind. It will hold strong, even if the rest of life unravels.

Gigi Graham Tchividjian

A TIMELY TIP

God intends for you to use His Word as your guidebook for life on the front line . . . your intentions should be the same.

IN TURBULENT TIMES, DON'T GIVE UP!

For a righteous man may fall seven times and rise again.

Proverbs 24:16 NKJV

As Americans living in a difficult and dangerous world, we know that the key to success, both as individuals and as a nation, is often nothing more than a willingness to persevere. Sometimes, however, when the storm clouds form overhead and we find ourselves in the dark valley of despair, our faith is stretched to the breaking point. But, as believers, we can be comforted: Wherever we find ourselves, whether at the top of the mountain or the depths of the valley, God is there, and because He cares for us, we can live courageously.

The next time you find your courage tested to the limit, remember that God is as near as your next breath, and remember that He offers strength and comfort to His children. He is your shield and your strength; He is your protector and your deliverer. Call upon Him in your hour of need and then be comforted. Whatever your challenge, whatever your trouble, God can help you persevere. And will.

We don't give up. We look up. We trust. We believe. And our optimism is not hollow. Christ has proven worthy. He has shown that he never fails. That's what makes God, God.

Max Lucado

Stand still and refuse to retreat. Look at it as God looks at it and draw upon his power to hold up under the blast.

Charles Swindoll

Just remember, every flower that ever bloomed had to go through a whole lot of dirt to get there!

Barbara Johnson

Failure is one of life's most powerful teachers. How we handle our failures determines whether we're going to simply "get by" in life or "press on."

Beth Moore

A TIMELY TIP

Are you being tested? Call upon God. God can give you the strength to persevere, and that's exactly what you should ask Him to do.

LIVE COURAGEOUSLY

He will not fear bad news; his heart is confident, trusting in the Lord. His heart is assured; he will not fear.

Psalm 112:7-8 Holman CSB

Every person's life is a tapestry of events: some wonderful, some not-so-wonderful, and some downright disastrous. When we visit the mountaintops of life, praising God isn't hard—in fact, it's easy. In our moments of triumph, we can bow our heads and thank God for our victories. But when we fail to reach the mountaintops, when we endure the inevitable losses that are a part of every person's life, we find it much tougher to give God the praise He deserves. Yet wherever we find ourselves, whether on the mountaintops of life or in life's darkest valleys, we must still offer thanks to God, giving thanks in all circumstances.

The next time you find yourself worried about the dangers of today or the uncertainties of tomorrow, ask yourself this question: are you really ready to place your concerns and your life in God's all-powerful, all-knowing, all-loving hands? If the answer to that question is yes—as it should be—then you can draw courage today from the source of strength that never fails: your Father in heaven.

God is with you always, listening to your thoughts and prayers, watching over your every move. If the demands of everyday life weigh down upon you, you may be tempted to ignore God's presence or—worse yet—to lose faith in His promises. But, when you quiet yourself and acknowledge His presence, God will touch your heart and restore your courage.

At this very moment—as you're fulfilling your obligations and overcoming tough times—God is seeking to work in you and through you. He's asking you to live abundantly and courageously . . . and He's ready to help. So why not let Him do it . . . starting now?

Faith not only can help you through a crisis, it can help you to approach life after the hard times with a whole new perspective. It can help you adopt an outlook of hope and courage through faith to face reality.

John Maxwell

Courage is fear
holding on a minute longer.

—

George S. Patton

A TIMELY TIP

Today, think about the rewards of living courageously.
And remember: The best way to overcome stress is by taking your concerns to God . . . and leaving them there.

GOD'S PROTECTION

Though I sit in darkness, the Lord will be my light.

Micah 7:8 Holman CSB

Have you ever faced challenges that seemed too big to handle? Have you ever faced big problems that, despite your best efforts, simply could not be solved? If so, you know how uncomfortable it is to feel helpless in the face of difficult circumstances. Thankfully, even when there's nowhere else to turn, you can turn your thoughts and prayers to God, and He will respond.

God's hand uplifts those who turn their hearts and prayers to Him. Count yourself among that number. When you do, you can live courageously and joyfully, knowing that "this too will pass"—but that God's love for you will not. And you can draw strength from the knowledge that you are a marvelous creation, loved, protected, and up-lifted by the ever-present hand of God.

Whatever hallway you're in—no matter how long, how dark, or how scary—God is right there with you.

Bill Hybels

God helps those who help themselves, but there are times when we are quite incapable of helping ourselves. That's when God stoops down and gathers us in His arms like a mother lifts a sick child, and does for us what we cannot do for ourselves.

Ruth Bell Graham

Life is literally filled with God-appointed storms. These squalls surge across everyone's horizon. We all need them.

Charles Swindoll

God will not permit any troubles to come upon us unless He has a specific plan by which great blessing can come out of the difficulty.

Peter Marshall

A TIMELY TIP

You are protected by God . . . now and always. The only security that lasts is the security that flows from the loving heart of God.

THANK HIM EVERY DAY

God is Spirit, and those who worship Him must worship in spirit and truth.

John 4:24 Holman CSB

God's Word makes it clear: a wise heart is a thankful heart. Period. We are to worship God, in part, by the genuine gratitude we feel in our hearts for the marvelous blessings that our Creator has bestowed upon us. Yet even the most saintly among us must endure periods of bitterness, fear, doubt, and regret. Why? Because we are imperfect human beings who are incapable of perfect gratitude. Still, even on life's darker days, even when we're struggling on the front lines of life, we must strive to cleanse our hearts of negative emotions and fill them, instead, with praise, with love, with hope, and with thanksgiving. To do otherwise is to be unfair to ourselves, to our loved ones, and to our God.

When your grief presses you to the very dust, worship there.

C. H. Spurgeon

I am of the opinion that we should not be concerned about working for God until we have learned the meaning and delight of worshipping Him.

A. W. Tozer

Worship is a daunting task. Each worships differently. But each should worship.

Max Lucado

To worship Him in truth means to worship Him honestly, without hypocrisy, standing open and transparent before Him.

Anne Graham Lotz

A TIMELY TIP

When you worship God with a sincere heart, He will guide your steps and bless your life.

THE NEED TO FORGIVE

*All bitterness, anger and wrath, insult and slander must be
removed from you, along with all wickedness. And be kind and
compassionate to one another, forgiving one another, just as
God also forgave you in Christ.*

Ephesians 4:31-32 Holman CSB

It has been said that life is an exercise in forgiveness.
And it should be added that forgiveness is an essential
step in overcoming tough times.

Christ understood the importance of forgiveness when
he commanded, "Love your enemies and pray for those
who persecute you" (Matthew 5:43-44 NIV). But sometimes, forgiveness is difficult indeed.

When we have been injured or insulted, we feel the
urge to strike back and to hurt the ones who have hurt us.
But Christ instructs us to do otherwise. Christ teaches us
that forgiveness is God's way and that mercy is an inte-
gral part of God's plan for our lives. In short, we are commanded to weave the thread of forgiveness into the very
fabric of our lives.

Do you invest more time than you should reliving
the past? Are you troubled by feelings of anger, bitterness,
envy, or regret? Do you harbor ill will against someone

whom you simply can't seem to forgive? If so, it's time to finally get serious about forgiveness.

When someone hurts you, the act of forgiveness is difficult, but necessary. Until you forgive, you are trapped in a prison of your own creation. But what if you have tried to forgive and simply can't seem to do so? The solution to your dilemma is this: you simply must make forgiveness a higher priority in your life.

Have you sincerely asked God to forgive you for your inability to forgive others? Have you genuinely prayed that those feelings of anger might be swept from your heart? If so, congratulations. If not, perhaps it's time to move past your own particular tough times by freeing yourself from the chains of bitterness and regret.

To be a Christian means to forgive
the inexcusable, because God has forgiven
the inexcusable in you.

—

C. S. Lewis

God expects us to forgive others as He has forgiven us; we are to follow His example by having a forgiving heart.

Vonette Bright

Sometimes, we need a housecleaning of the heart.

Catherine Marshall

To hold on to hate and resentments is to throw a monkey wrench into the machinery of life.

E. Stanley Jones

How often should you forgive the other person? Only as many times as you want God to forgive you!

Marie T. Freeman

A TIMELY TIP

Forgiveness is its own reward. Bitterness is its own punishment. Guard your words and your thoughts accordingly.

FINDING STRENGTH ON THE FRONT LINE

I can do all things through Christ who strengthens me.

Philippians 4:13 NKJV

God's love and support never changes. From the cradle to the grave, God has promised to give you the strength to meet any challenge. God has promised to lift you up and guide your steps if you let Him. God has promised that when you entrust your life to Him completely and without reservation, He will give you the courage to face any trial and the wisdom to live in His righteousness.

God's hand uplifts those who turn their hearts and prayers to Him. Will you count yourself among that number? Will you accept God's peace and wear God's armor against the temptations and distractions of our dangerous world? If you do, you can live courageously and optimistically, serving on the front lines of life, knowing that you have been forever touched by the loving, unfailing, uplifting hand of God.

When trials come your way—as inevitably they will—do not run away. Run to your God and Father.

Kay Arthur

The same God who empowered Samson, Gideon, and Paul seeks to empower my life and your life, because God hasn't changed.

Bill Hybels

A divine strength is given to those who yield themselves to the Father and obey what He tells them to do.

Warren Wiersbe

One with God is a majority.

Billy Graham

A TIMELY TIP

Need strength? Slow down, get more rest, engage in sensible exercise, and—most importantly—turn your troubles over to God.

TODAY IS A NEW BEGINNING

You are being renewed in the spirit of your minds; you put on the new man, the one created according to God's likeness in righteousness and purity of the truth.

Ephesians 4:23-24 Holman CSB

Each new day offers countless opportunities to serve God, to seek His will, and to obey His teachings. But each day also offers countless opportunities to stray from God's commandments and to wander far from His path.

Sometimes, we wander aimlessly in a wilderness of our own making, but God has better plans of us. And, whenever we ask Him to renew our strength and guide our steps, He does so.

Consider this day a new beginning. Consider it a fresh start, a renewed opportunity to serve your Creator with willing hands and a loving heart. Ask God to renew your sense of purpose as He guides your steps. Today is a glorious opportunity to serve God. Seize that opportunity while you can; tomorrow may indeed be too late.

No matter how badly we have failed, we can always get up and begin again. Our God is the God of new beginnings.

Warren Wiersbe

No man need stay the way he is.

Harry Emerson Fosdick

More often than not, when something looks like it's the absolute end, it is really the beginning.

Charles Swindoll

When you're through changing, you're through!

John Maxwell

A TIMELY TIP

If you're traveling to a new front line, make God your partner. If you do, He'll guide your steps, He'll help carry your burdens, and He'll help you focus on the things that really matter.

WHEN THE TRAUMA JUST WON'T GO AWAY

An anxious heart weighs a man down....

Proverbs 12:25 NIV

Traumatic events often leave lasting emotional scars. And if you're suffering from the aftermath of trauma, it may seem as though you'll never feel normal again. But with God, all things are possible.

Post-traumatic stress disorder is both dangerous and treatable—dangerous if you ignore it and treatable if you don't. So if you're having flashbacks, depression, numbness, guilt, or any other PTSD symptom, it's time to seek treatment. Today.

God wants you to experience His abundance and His peace. And He wants you to focus on His promises for your future, not on the tragedies of your past. So when it comes to your mental health, don't ignore troublesome symptoms, and don't hold everything inside. Help is available—so ask for it. Today.

God often keeps us on the path by guiding us through the counsel of friends and trusted spiritual advisors.

Bill Hybels

God knows what each of us is dealing with. He knows our pressures. He knows our conflicts. And, He has made a provision for each and every one of them. That provision is Himself in the person of the Holy Spirit, dwelling in us and empowering us to respond rightly.

Kay Arthur

When you and I hurt deeply, what we really need is not an explanation from God but a revelation of God. We need to see how great God is; we need to recover our lost perspective on life. Things get out of proportion when we are suffering, and it takes a vision of something bigger than ourselves to get life's dimensions adjusted again.

Warren Wiersbe

A TIMELY TIP

Some events are so traumatic that you'll never forget them, but you can move past them. And the sooner you can move on with your life, the better.

CONSIDER THE POSSIBILITIES

For nothing will be impossible with God.

Luke 1:37 Holman CSB

Are you afraid to ask God to do big things—or to make big changes—in your life? Is your faith threadbare and worn? If so, it's time to abandon your doubts and reclaim your faith in God's promises.

Ours is a God of infinite possibilities. But sometimes, because of limited faith and limited understanding, we wrongly assume that God cannot or will not intervene in the affairs of mankind. Such assumptions are simply wrong.

God's Holy Word makes it clear: absolutely nothing is impossible for the Lord. And since the Bible means what it says, you can be comforted in the knowledge that the Creator of the universe can do miraculous things in your own life and in the lives of your loved ones. Your challenge, as a believer, is to take God at His word, and to expect the miraculous.

Man's adversity is God's opportunity.

Matthew Henry

God specializes in things thought impossible.

Catherine Marshall

If all things are possible with God, then all things are possible to him who believes in him.

Corrie ten Boom

Do we not continually pass by blessings innumerable without notice, and instead fix our eyes on what we feel to be our trials and our losses? And, do we not think and talk about our trials until our whole horizon is filled with them, and we almost begin to think we have no blessings at all?

Hannah Whitall Smith

A TIMELY TIP

Focus on possibilities, not roadblocks: The road of life contains a number of potholes and stumbling blocks. Of course you will encounter them from time to time, and so will your family members. But, don't invest large quantities of your life focusing on past misfortunes. On the road of life, regret is a dead end.

THE ART OF ACCEPTANCE

Come to terms with God and be at peace; in this way good will come to you.

Job 22:21 Holman CSB

Sometimes, we must accept life on its terms, not our own. Life has a way of unfolding, not as we will, but as it will. And sometimes, there is precious little we can do to change things.

When events transpire that are beyond our control, we have a choice: we can either learn the art of acceptance, or we can make ourselves miserable as we struggle to change the unchangeable.

We must entrust the things we cannot change to God. Once we have done so, we can prayerfully and faithfully tackle the important work that He has placed before us: doing something about the things we can change . . . and doing it sooner rather than later.

Can you summon the courage and the wisdom to accept life on its own terms? If so, you'll most certainly be rewarded for your good judgment.

Surrender to the Lord is not a tremendous sacrifice, not an agonizing performance. It is the most sensible thing you can do.

Corrie ten Boom

He does not need to transplant us into a different field. He transforms the very things that were before our greatest hindrances, into the chief and most blessed means of our growth. No difficulties in your case can baffle Him. Put yourself absolutely into His hands, and let Him have His own way with you.

Elisabeth Elliot

How changed our lives would be if we could only fly through the days on wings of surrender and trust!

Hannah Whitall Smith

Ultimately things work out best for those who make the best of the way things work out.

Barbara Johnson

A TIMELY TIP

When you encounter situations on the front line that you cannot change, you must learn the wisdom of acceptance . . . and you must learn to trust God.

TRUSTING GOD'S PROMISES

Cast your burden on the Lord, and He will support you; He will never allow the righteous to be shaken.

Psalm 55:22 Holman CSB

These are times of great uncertainty. As we have become accustomed to, and at times almost numbed by, a steady stream of unsettling news, we are reminded that our world is in a state of constant change. But God is not. So when the world seems to be trembling beneath our feet, we can be comforted in the knowledge that our Heavenly Father is the rock that cannot be shaken.

Every day that we live, we mortals encounter a multitude of changes—some good, some not so good. And on occasion, all of us must endure life-changing personal losses that leave us heartbroken. When we do, our Heavenly Father stands ready to comfort us, to guide us, and—in time—to heal us.

Is the world spinning a little too fast for your liking? Are you facing troubling uncertainties, difficult circumstances, or unwelcome changes? If so, please remember that God is far bigger than any problem you may face. So, instead of worrying about life's inevitable challenges, put your faith in the Father and His only begotten Son. After all, "Jesus Christ is the same yesterday, today, and forever" (Hebrews 13:8 NKJV). And it is precisely because your Savior does not change that you can face your challenges with courage for today and hope for tomorrow.

Are you anxious about situations that you cannot control? Take your anxieties to God. Are you troubled? Take your troubles to Him. Does your little corner of the universe seem to be a frightening place? Seek protection from the One who cannot be moved. The same God who created the universe will protect you if you ask Him . . . so ask Him . . . and then serve Him with willing hands and a trusting heart.

Never be afraid to trust an unknown future
to a known God.

—

Corrie ten Boom

When I am secure in Christ, I can afford to take a risk in my life. Only the insecure cannot afford to risk failure. The secure can be honest about themselves; they can admit failure; they are able to seek help and try again. They can change.

John Maxwell

No matter what trials we face, Christ never leaves us.

Billy Graham

Sometimes your medicine bottle says, "Shake well before using." That is what God has to do with some of his people. He has to shake them well before they are usable.

Vance Havner

A TIMELY TIP

Change is inevitable; growth is not. God will come to your doorstep on countless occasions with opportunities to learn and to grow. And He will knock. Your challenge, of course, is to open the door.

A RENEWED SENSE OF PURPOSE

You will show me the path of life; in Your presence is fullness of joy; at Your right hand are pleasures forevermore.

Psalm 16:11 NKJV

If you're experiencing tough times on the front line, you may be asking yourself, "What does God want me to do next?" Perhaps you're pondering your future, uncertain of your plans, unsure of your next step. But even if you don't have a clear plan for the next step of your life's journey, you may rest assured that God does.

God has a plan for the universe, and He has a plan for you. He understands that plan as thoroughly and completely as He knows you. If you seek God's will earnestly and prayerfully, He will make His plans known to you in His own time and in His own way.

Perhaps your vision of God's purpose for your life has been clouded by a wish list that you have expected God to dutifully fulfill. Perhaps, you have fervently hoped that God would create a world that unfolds according to your wishes, not His. If so, you have probably experienced more disappointment than satisfaction and more frustration than peace. A better strategy is to conform your will to

God's (and not to struggle vainly in an attempt to conform His will to yours).

Sometimes, God's plans and purposes may seem unmistakably clear to you. If so, push ahead. But other times, He may lead you through the wilderness before He directs you to the Promised Land. So be patient and keep seeking His will for your life. When you do, you'll be amazed at the marvelous things that an all-powerful, all-knowing God can do.

God will make obstacles serve His purpose.

—

Mrs. Charles E. Cowman

Whatever clouds you face today, ask Jesus, the light of the world, to help you look behind the cloud to see His glory and His plans for you.

Billy Graham

Underneath each trouble there is a faithful purpose.

C. H. Spurgeon

God never calls without enabling us. In other words, if he calls you to do something, he makes it possible for you to do it.

Luci Swindoll

God does not discipline us to subdue us, but to condition us for a life of usefulness and blessedness.

Billy Graham

A TIMELY TIP

God has a plan for your life, a definite purpose that you can fulfill . . . or not. Your challenge is to pray for God's guidance and to follow wherever He leads.

GETTING ENOUGH REST?

Come to Me, all you who are weary and burdened, and I will give you rest. Take My yoke upon you and learn from Me, because I am gentle and humble in heart, and you will find rest for your souls. For My yoke is easy and My burden is light.

Matthew 11:28-30 Holman CSB

Physical exhaustion is God's way of telling us to slow down. God expects us to work hard, of course, but He also intends for us to rest. When we fail to take the rest that we need, we do a disservice to ourselves and to our families.

We live in a world that tempts us to stay up late—very late. But too much late-night TV, combined with too little sleep, is a prescription for exhaustion.

Jesus promises us that when we come to Him, He will give us rest—but we, too, must do our part. We must take the necessary steps to insure that we have sufficient rest and that we take care of our bodies in other ways, too.

As adults, each of us bears a personal responsibility for the general state of our own physical health. Certainly, various aspects of life on the front line are beyond our control. But for most of us, physical health is a choice: it is the result of hundreds of small decisions that we make every day of our lives. If we make decisions that promote good health, our bodies respond. But if we fall into bad habits and undisciplined lifestyles, we suffer tragic consequences.

Are your physical or spiritual batteries running low? Is your energy on the wane? Are your emotions frayed? If so, it's time to turn your thoughts and your prayers to God's Son. And when you're finished, it's probably time to lay down your head, close your eyes, and get some sleep.

Taking care of yourself physically really helps emotionally. People who get a lot of sleep, and who do the things that relieve stress, can withstand more stress.

—

Laura Bush

Satan does some of his worst work on exhausted Christians when nerves are frayed and their minds are faint.

Vance Havner

Sleep is the golden chain that ties health and our bodies together.

Thomas Dekker

Notice what Jesus had to say concerning those who have wearied themselves by trying to do things in their own strength: "Come to me, all you who labor and are heavy laden, and I will give you rest."

Henry Blackaby and Claude King

A TIMELY TIP

God wants you to get enough rest. The world wants you to burn the candle at both ends. Trust God.

BEATING STRESS ONE DAY AT A TIME

This is the day the LORD has made; we will rejoice and be glad in it.

Psalm 118:24 NKJV

Face facts: just getting by in these turbulent times can be stressful . . . very stressful. You live in a world that is brimming with demands, distractions, and deadlines (not to mention temptations, timetables, requirements, and responsibilities). Whew! No wonder you may be stressed.

What can you do in response to the stressors of everyday life? A wonderful place to start is by turning things over to God.

Psalm 118:24 reminds us that this day, like every other, is a glorious gift from the Father. How will you use that gift? Will you celebrate it and use it for His purposes? If so, you'll discover that when you turn things over to Him—when you allow God to rule over every corner of your life—He will calm your fears and guide your steps.

So today, make sure that you focus on God and upon His will for your life. Then, ask for His help. And remember: No challenge is too great for Him. Not even yours.

There are very few certainties that touch us all in this mortal experience, but one of the absolutes is that we will experience hardship and stress at some point.

James Dobson

Life is strenuous. See that your clock does not run down.

Mrs. Charles E. Cowman

If you're willing to repair your life, God is willing to help. If you're not willing to repair your life, God is willing to wait.

Marie T. Freeman

Prescription for a happier and healthier life: resolve to slow down your pace; learn to say no gracefully; resist the temptation to chase after more pleasure, more hobbies, and more social entanglements.

James Dobson

A TIMELY TIP

If you become your own worst critic, you're creating needless stress for yourself and your loved ones.

THE MORNING WATCH

Every morning he wakes me. He teaches me to listen like a student. The Lord God helps me learn...

Isaiah 50:4-5 NCV

Each new day is a gift from God, and if you are wise, you will spend a few quiet moments each morning thanking the Giver. When you do, you'll discover that time spent with God can lift your spirits and relieve your stress.

Warren Wiersbe writes, "Surrender your mind to the Lord at the beginning of each day." And that's sound advice. When you begin each day with your head bowed and your heart lifted, you are reminded of God's love, His protection, and His commandments. Then, you can align your priorities for the coming day with the teachings and commandments that God has placed upon your heart.

So, if you've acquired the unfortunate habit of trying to "squeeze" God into the corners of your life, it's time to reshuffle the items on your to-do list by placing God first. And if you haven't already done so, form the habit of spending quality time with your Father in heaven. He deserves it . . . and so do you.

How motivating it has been for me to view my early morning devotions as time of retreat alone with Jesus, Who desires that I "come with Him by myself to a quiet place" in order to pray, read His Word, listen for His voice, and be renewed in my spirit.

Anne Graham Lotz

How paltry must be the devotions of those who are always in a hurry.

William Law

I suggest you discipline yourself to spend time daily in a systematic reading of God's Word. Make this "quiet time" a priority that nobody can change.

Warren Wiersbe

Every day has its own particular brand of holiness to discover and worship appropriately.

Annie Dillard

A TIMELY TIP

God is available to you every morning . . . and you should make yourself available to Him.

THE RIGHT PRIORITIES

We can't afford to waste a minute, must not squander these precious daylight hours in frivolity and indulgence, in sleeping around and dissipation, in bickering and grabbing everything in sight. Get out of bed and get dressed! Don't loiter and linger, waiting until the very last minute. Dress yourselves in Christ, and be up and about!

Romans 13:13-14 MSG

Have you fervently asked God to help prioritize your life? Have you asked Him for guidance and for the courage to do the things that you know need to be done? If so, then you're continually inviting your Creator to reveal Himself in a variety of ways. As a follower of Christ, you must do no less.

When you make God's priorities your priorities, you will receive God's abundance and His peace. When you make God a full partner in every aspect of your life, He will lead you along the proper path: His path. When you allow God to reign over your heart, He will honor you with spiritual blessings that are simply too numerous to count. So, as you plan for the day ahead, make God's will your ultimate priority. When you do, every other priority will have a tendency to fall neatly into place.

There were endless demands on Jesus' time. Still he was able to make that amazing claim of "completing the work you gave me to do." (John 17:4 NIV)

Elisabeth Elliot

Getting things accomplished isn't nearly as important as taking time for love.

Janette Oke

Have you prayed about your resources lately? Find out how God wants you to use your time and your money. No matter what it costs, forsake all that is not of God.

Kay Arthur

Forgetting your mission leads, inevitably, to getting tangled up in details—details that can take you completely off your path.

Laurie Beth Jones

A TIMELY TIP

Your Heavenly Father wants you to prioritize your day and your life. And the best place to start is by putting God first.

CONTROLLING YOUR EMOTIONS

Don't abandon wisdom, and she will watch over you; love her, and she will guard you.

Proverbs 4:6 Holman CSB

Who is in charge of your emotions? Is it you, or have you formed the unfortunate habit of letting other people—or stressful situations—determine the quality of your thoughts and the direction of your day? If you're wise—and if you'd like to build a better life for yourself and your loved ones—you'll learn to control your emotions before your emotions control you.

Human emotions are highly variable, decidedly unpredictable, and often unreliable. Our emotions are like the weather, only far more fickle. So we must learn to live by faith, not by the ups and downs of our own emotional roller coasters.

Sometime during this day, you will probably be gripped by a strong negative feeling. Distrust it. Reign it in. Test it. And turn it over to God. Your emotions will inevitably change; God will not. So trust Him completely as you watch those negative feelings slowly evaporate into thin air—which, of course, they will.

Wisdom always waits for the right time to act, while emotion always pushes for action right now.

Joyce Meyer

I may no longer depend on pleasant impulses to bring me before the Lord. I must rather respond to principles I know to be right, whether I feel them to be enjoyable or not.

Jim Elliot

If you are going to be a person who is committed to the Word of God, you will have to learn to be led by the Spirit and not by your emotions.

Joyce Meyer

Our feelings do not affect God's facts. They may blow up, like clouds, and cover the eternal things that we do most truly believe. We may not see the shining of the promises—but they still shine! His strength is not for one moment less because of our human weakness.

Amy Carmichael

A TIMELY TIP

Here are the facts: God's love is real; His peace is real; His support is real. Don't ever let your emotions obscure these facts.

PERSPECTIVE FOR TODAY

Don't turn your back on wisdom, for she will protect you. Love her, and she will guard you.

Proverbs 4:6 NLT

Sometimes, amid the demands of daily life, we lose perspective. Life seems out of balance, and the pressures of everyday living seem overwhelming. What's needed is a fresh perspective, a restored sense of balance...and God.

If a temporary loss of perspective has left you worried, exhausted, or both, it's time to readjust your thought patterns. Negative thoughts are habit-forming; thankfully, so are positive ones. With practice, you can form the habit of focusing on God's priorities and your possibilities. When you do, you'll soon discover that you will spend less time fretting about your challenges and more time praising God for His gifts.

When you call upon the Lord and prayerfully seek His will, He will give you wisdom and perspective. When you make God's priorities your priorities, He will direct your steps and calm your fears. So today and every day hereafter, pray for a sense of balance and perspective. And remember: your thoughts are intensely powerful things, so handle them with care.

When we look at the individual
parts of our lives, some things appear unfair
and unpleasant. When we take them
out of the context of the big picture,
we easily drift into the attitude that
we deserve better, and the tumble down
into the pit of pride begins.

—

Susan Hunt

Like a shadow declining swiftly . . . away . . . like the dew of the morning gone with the heat of the day; like the wind in the treetops, like a wave of the sea, so are our lives on earth when seen in light of eternity.

Ruth Bell Graham

Earthly fears are no fears at all. Answer the big questions of eternity, and the little questions of life fall into perspective.

Max Lucado

Gratitude unlocks the fullness of life. It turns what we have into enough, and more. It turns denial into acceptance, chaos to order, confusion to clarity. It can turn a meal into a feast, a house into a home, a stranger into a friend. Gratitude makes sense of our past, brings peace for today, and creates a vision for tomorrow.

Melody Beattie

A TIMELY TIP

When you focus on the world, you lose perspective. When you focus on God's promises, you gain clearer perspective.

ASKING FOR HELP

Iron sharpeneth iron; so a man sharpeneth the countenance of his friend.

Proverbs 27:17 KJV

As you meet the demands of life on the front line, you will find it helpful to utilize all the resources that are available to you. God intends that you have a meaningful, abundant life, but He expects you to do your part in claiming His blessings. Thus, it is your responsibility to seek out help when you need it.

So if you're stressed to the breaking point, don't endure it alone. If you're grieving, don't grieve alone. If you're fearful, or tired, or discouraged, or bitter, don't suffer in silence. And whatever you do, don't convince yourself that your situation is helpless. In truth, help is always near. Your job is to ask for help when you need it.

Let us not be content to wait and see what will happen, but give us the determination to make the right things happen.

Peter Marshall

Bitterness only makes suffering worse and closes the spiritual channels through which God can pour His grace.

Warren Wiersbe

Perseverance is more than endurance. It is endurance combined with absolute assurance and certainty that what we are looking for is going to happen.

Oswald Chambers

Battles are won in the trenches, in the grit and grime of courageous determination; they are won day by day in the arena of life.

Charles Swindoll

A TIMELY TIP

When you're facing life's toughest battles, it's tempting to hold everything inside—tempting, but wrong. So instead of holding everything inside, find someone to talk to, and express your emotions as honestly as you can.

SAYING YES TO GOD

Cast your burden on the Lord, and He will support you; He will never allow the righteous to be shaken.

Psalm 55:22 Holman CSB

Your decision to seek a deeper relationship with God will not remove all problems from your life; to the contrary, it will bring about a series of personal crises as you constantly seek to say "yes" to God although the world encourages you to do otherwise. You live in a world that seeks to snare your attention and lead you away from God. Each time you are tempted to distance yourself from the Creator, you will face a spiritual crisis. A few of these crises may be monumental in scope, but most will be the small, everyday decisions of life. In fact, life here on earth can be seen as one test after another—and with each crisis comes yet another opportunity to grow closer to God . . . or to distance yourself from His plan for your life.

Today, as you serve on the front lines of life, you will face many opportunities to say "yes" to your Creator—and you will also encounter many opportunities to say "no" to Him. Your answers will determine the quality of your day and the direction of your life, so answer carefully . . . very carefully.

We all go through pain and sorrow, but the presence of God, like a warm, comforting blanket, can shield us and protect us, and allow the deep inner joy to surface, even in the most devastating circumstances.

Barbara Johnson

The only way to learn a strong faith is to endure great trials. I have learned my faith by standing firm amid the most severe of tests.

George Mueller

Recently I've been learning that life comes down to this: God is in everything. Regardless of what difficulties I am experiencing at the moment, or what things aren't as would like them to be, I look at the circumstances and say, "Lord, what are you trying to teach me?"

Catherine Marshall

A TIMELY TIP

If you're facing a crisis, don't face it alone. Enlist God's help. And then, when you've finished praying about your problem, don't be afraid to seek help from family, from friends, or from your chaplain.

IN HIS HANDS

Don't brashly announce what you're going to do tomorrow; you don't know the first thing about tomorrow.

Proverbs 27:1 MSG

Because we are saved by a risen Christ, we can have hope for the future, no matter how troublesome our present circumstances may seem. After all, God has promised that we are His throughout eternity. And, He has told us that we must place our hopes in Him.

Of course, we will face disappointments and failures while we are here on earth, but these are only temporary defeats. Of course, this world can be a place of stresses, trials, and tribulations, but when we place our trust in the Giver of all things good, we are secure. God has promised us peace, joy, and eternal life. And God keeps His promises today, tomorrow, and forever.

Are you willing to place your future in the hands of a loving and all-knowing God? Do you trust in the ultimate goodness of His plan for your life? Will you face today's challenges with optimism and hope? You should. After all, God created you for a very important purpose: His purpose. And you still have important work to do: His work.

Today, as you live in the present and look to the future, remember that God has a plan for you. Act—and believe—accordingly.

That we may not complain of what is, let us see God's hand in all events; and, that we may not be afraid of what shall be, let us see all events in God's hand.

Matthew Henry

Hoping for a good future without investing in today is like a farmer waiting for a crop without ever planting any seed.

John Maxwell

Tomorrow's history has already been written—at the name of Jesus every knee must bow.

Paul E. Kauffman

A TIMELY TIP

Even when the world seems dark, the future is bright for those who look to the Son.

THE BATTLE HAS BEEN WON

Cast your burden on the Lord, and He will support you; He will never allow the righteous to be shaken.

Psalm 55:22 Holman CSB

C hristians have every reason to live courageously. After all, the ultimate battle has already been won on the cross at Calvary. But even dedicated followers of Christ may find their courage tested by the inevitable disappointments and fears that visit the lives of believers and non-believers alike.

When you find yourself worried about the challenges of today or the uncertainties of tomorrow, you must ask yourself whether or not you are ready to place your concerns and your life in God's all-powerful, all-knowing, all-loving hands. If the answer to that question is yes—as it should be—then you can draw courage today from the source of strength that never fails: your Heavenly Father.

What counts is not the size of the dog in the fight, but the size of the fight in the dog.

Dwight D. Eisenhower

Like dynamite, God's power is only latent power until it is released. You can release God's dynamite power into people's lives and into the world through faith, through words, and through prayer.

Bill Bright

The Lord is glad to open the gate to every knocking soul. It opens very freely; its hinges are not rusted, no bolts secure it. Have faith and enter at this moment through holy courage. If you knock with a heavy heart, you shall yet sing with joy of spirit. Never be discouraged!

C. H. Spurgeon

Down through the centuries, in times of trouble and trial, God has brought courage to the hearts of those who love Him. The Bible is filled with assurances of God's help and comfort in every kind of trouble.

Billy Graham

A TIMELY TIP

If you trust God completely and without reservation, you have every reason on earth—and in heaven—to live courageously. And that's precisely what you should do.

UNDERSTAND DEPRESSION

Why am I so depressed? Why this turmoil within me? Put your hope in God, for I will still praise Him, my Savior and my God.

Psalm 42:11 Holman CSB

The sadness that accompanies any significant loss is an inevitable fact of life. In time, sadness runs its course and gradually abates. Depression, on the other hand, is a physical and emotional condition that is, in almost all cases, treatable with medication and counseling. Depression is not a disease to be taken lightly. Left untreated, it presents real dangers to patients' physical health and to their emotional well-being.

If you find yourself feeling "blue," perhaps it's a logical reaction to the ups and downs of daily life. But if your feelings of sadness have gone on longer than you think they should—or if someone close to you fears that your sadness may have evolved into clinical depression—it's time to seek professional help.

Some days are light and happy, and some days are not. When we face the inevitable dark days of life, we must choose how we will respond. Will we allow ourselves to sink even more deeply into our own sadness, or will we do the difficult work of pulling ourselves out? We bring light to the dark days of life by turning first to God, and then to trusted family members, friends, and medical professionals. When we do, the clouds will eventually part, and the sun will shine once more upon our souls.

Emotions we have not poured out
in the safe hands of God
can turn into feelings of
hopelessness and depression.
God is safe.

—

Beth Moore

Self blame over the past leads to depression in the present and poor decisions for the future.

Barbara Johnson

Feelings of uselessness and hopelessness are not from God, but from the evil one, the devil, who wants to discourage you and thwart your effectiveness for the Lord.

Bill Bright

Don't let aridity distress you: perfection has nothing to do with such things—only with virtues. Your devotion will come back when you are least expecting it.

St. Teresa of Avila

A TIMELY TIP

If you or someone you know seems to be dangerously sad, don't sit around and wait for things to get better. Get help ASAP.

PROTECTING THE AMERICAN DREAM

The Lord bless you and protect you; the Lord make His face shine on you, and be gracious to you.

Numbers 6:24-25 Holman CSB

"The American Dream": this phrase is unique to the nation we call home. Nowhere do we hear the phrase the "Russian Dream," even though Russia is a nation struggling to become a working democracy. We don't talk about the "Chinese Dream," the "Mexican Dream," the "Indian Dream," or the "French Dream." In many places around the globe, democracies rule, but no place on earth is like America. No nation offers more opportunities and more personal freedoms, no nation offers more possibilities and more fresh starts than the good old USA. America is a land tailor-made for dreamers, especially those willing to work for their dreams.

Americans of this generation have a grand opportunity: we can leave an enduring legacy to our children. That legacy, of course, is a nation strong and free, and we, as protectors of liberty's flame, must do our utmost to leave to the next generation a better nation than the one we received from the last. May our legacy be worthy of those

who sacrificed so much to ensure that the Dream will never die. And may God bless America forever.

We, here in America,
hold in our hands
the hope of the world.

—

Theodore Roosevelt

America was not built on fear. America was built on courage, on imagination, and on an unbeatable determination to do the job at hand.

Harry S Truman

Throughout its history, America has given hope, comfort, and inspiration to freedom's cause in all lands.

Adlai E. Stevenson

America is a passionate belief in freedom and in the worth and dignity of the human personality. We must not let the song die on our lips.

Harry Emerson Fosdick

A TIMELY TIP

Freedom isn't free. As Franklin Roosevelt observed, "In the truest sense, freedom cannot be bestowed; it must be achieved."

LIFE ETERNAL

I assure you: Anyone who hears My word and believes Him who sent Me has eternal life and will not come under judgment, but has passed from death to life.

John 5:24 Holman CSB

Your life here on earth is merely a preparation for a far different life to come: the eternal life that God promises to those who welcome His Son into their hearts.

As a mere mortal, your vision for the future is finite. God's vision is not burdened by such limitations: His plans extend throughout all eternity. Thus, God's plans for you are not limited to the ups and downs of everyday life. Your Heavenly Father has bigger things in mind . . . much bigger things.

How marvelous it is that God became a man and walked among us. Had He not chosen to do so, we might feel removed from a distant Creator. But ours is not a distant God. Ours is a God who understands—far better than we ever could—the essence of what it means to be human.

God understands our hopes, our fears, and our temptations. He understands what it means to be angry and what it costs to forgive. He knows the heart, the conscience, and the soul of every person who has ever lived, including you.

As you struggle with the inevitable hardships and tragedies of life on the front line, remember that God has invited you to accept His abundance not only for today but also for all eternity. So keep things in perspective. Although you will inevitably encounter occasional defeats in this world, you'll have all eternity to celebrate the ultimate victory in the next.

Salvation is God's sudden, calming presence
during the stormy seas of our lives.

—

Max Lucado

Suffering will be either your master or your servant, depending on how you handle the crises of life.

Warren Wiersbe

Let us see the victorious Jesus, the conqueror of the tomb, the one who defied death. And let us be reminded that we, too, will be granted the same victory.

Max Lucado

So I say to you, seek God, and discover Him and make Him a power in your life. With Him we are able to rise from the midnight of desperation to the daybreak of joy.

Martin Luther King, Jr.

A TIMELY TIP

God offers you life abundant and life eternal. If you have not accepted His gift, the appropriate moment to do so is now.

WHEN TIMES ARE TOUGH, GET BUSY

And whatever you do, do it heartily, as to the Lord and not to men.

Colossians 3:23 NKJV

I t isn't easy to overcome tough times—it takes hard work and lots of it. So if you're facing adversity of any kind, you can be sure that God has important work for you to do . . . but He won't make you do it. Since the days of Adam and Eve, God has allowed His children to make choices for themselves, and so it is with you. You can either dig in and work hard, or you can retreat from the battlefield and hope that things get better on their own.

The Bible instructs us that we can learn an important lesson of a surprising source: ants. Ants are among nature's most industrious creatures. They do their work without supervision, rumination, or hesitation. We should do likewise. When times are tough, we must summon the courage and determination to work ourselves out of trouble.

God has created a world in which diligence is rewarded and sloth is not. So whatever you choose to do, do it with commitment, excitement, and vigor. God didn't create you for a life of mediocrity or pain; He created you for far greater things. Reaching for greater things—and defeating tough times—usually requires work and lots of it, which is perfectly fine with God. After all, He knows that you're up to the task, and He still has big plans for you. Very big plans . . .

Let us not be content to wait and see
what will happen, but give us
the determination to make
the right things happen.

—

Peter Marshall

All work, if offered to Him, is transformed. It is not secular but sacred, sanctified in the glad offering.

Elisabeth Elliot

Pray as if it's all up to God, and work as if it's all up to you.

Anonymous

God has lots of folks who intend to go to work for him "some day." What He needs is more people who are willing to work for Him this day.

Marie T. Freeman

A TIMELY TIP

Today, pick out one important obligation that you've been putting off. Then, take at least one specific step toward the completion of the task you've been avoiding. Even if you don't finish the job, you'll discover that it's easier to finish a job that you've already begun than to finish a job that you've never started.

BE OPTIMISTIC

My cup runs over. Surely goodness and mercy shall follow me all the days of my life; and I will dwell in the house of the Lord Forever.

Psalm 23:5-6 NKJV

Are you an optimistic, hopeful, enthusiastic Christian? You should be. After all, as a believer, you have every reason to be optimistic about life here on earth and life eternal. As C. H. Spurgeon observed, "Our hope in Christ for the future is the mainstream of our joy." But sometimes, you may find yourself pulled down by the inevitable demands and worries of life here on earth. If you find yourself discouraged, stressed, or both, then it's time to take your concerns to God. When you do, He will lift your spirits and renew your strength.

Today, make this promise to yourself and keep it: vow to be a hope-filled Christian. Think optimistically about your life, your profession, your family, and your future. Trust your hopes, not your fears. Take time to celebrate God's glorious creation. And then, when you've filled your heart with hope and gladness, share your optimism with others. They'll be better for it, and so will you.

The popular idea of faith is of a certain obstinate optimism: the hope, tenaciously held in the face of trouble, that the universe is fundamentally friendly and things may get better.

J. I. Packer

The people whom I have seen succeed best in life have always been cheerful and hopeful people who went about their business with a smile on their faces.

Charles Kingsley

Go forward confidently, energetically attacking problems, expecting favorable outcomes.

Norman Vincent Peale

A TIMELY TIP

Be a realistic optimist. You should strive to think realistically about the future, but you should never confuse realism with pessimism. Your attitude toward the future will help create your future, so you might as well put the self-fulfilling prophecy to work for you by being both a realist and an optimist. And remember that life is far too short to be a pessimist.

LOOK UP AND MOVE ON

All bitterness, anger and wrath, insult and slander must be removed from you, along with all wickedness. And be kind and compassionate to one another, forgiving one another, just as God also forgave you in Christ.

Ephesians 4:31-32 Holman CSB

The world holds few if any rewards for those who remain angrily focused upon the past. Still, the act of forgiveness is difficult for all but the most saintly men and women. Are you mired in the quicksand of bitterness or regret? If so, you are not only disobeying God's Word, you are also wasting your time.

Being frail, fallible, imperfect human beings, most of us are quick to anger, quick to blame, slow to forgive, and even slower to forget. Yet as Christians, we are commanded to forgive others, just as we, too, have been forgiven.

If there exists even one person—alive or dead—against whom you hold bitter feelings, it's time to forgive. Or, if you are embittered against yourself for some past mistake or shortcoming, it's finally time to forgive yourself and move on. Hatred, bitterness, and regret are not part of God's plan for your life. Forgiveness is.

Be so preoccupied with good will that you haven't room for ill will.

E. Stanley Jones

Acrid bitterness inevitably seeps into the lives of people who harbor grudges and suppress anger, and bitterness is always a poison.

Lee Strobel

Anger breeds remorse in the heart, discord in the home, bitterness in the community, and confusion in the state.

Billy Graham

Bitterness is the trap that snares the hunter.

Max Lucado

A TIMELY TIP

You can never fully engage in the present if you're bitterly reliving yesterday's battles. So, instead of living in the past, make peace with it . . . and move on.

FINDING PEACE

These things I have spoken to you, that in Me you may have peace. In the world you will have tribulation; but be of good cheer, I have overcome the world.

John 16:33 NKJV

Oftentimes, our outer struggles are simply manifestations of the inner conflict that we feel when we stray from God's path. Jesus offers us peace, not as the world gives, but as He alone gives. Our challenge is to accept Christ's peace into our hearts and then, as best we can, to share His peace with our neighbors. When we accept Jesus as our personal Savior, we are transformed by His grace. We are then free to accept the spiritual abundance and peace that can be ours through the power of the risen Christ.

Have you found the genuine peace that can be yours through Jesus Christ? Or are you still rushing after the illusion of "peace and happiness" that the world promises but cannot deliver? Today, as a gift to yourself, to your family, and to your friends, claim the inner peace that is your spiritual birthright: the peace of Jesus Christ. It is offered freely; it has been paid for in full; it is yours for the asking. So ask. And then share.

Prayer guards hearts and minds and causes God to bring peace out of chaos.

Beth Moore

Before God changes our circumstances, He wants to change our hearts.

Warren Wiersbe

When we do what is right, we have contentment, peace, and happiness.

Beverly LaHaye

To know God as He really is—in His essential nature and character—is to arrive at a citadel of peace that circumstances may storm, but can never capture.

Catherine Marshall

A TIMELY TIP

God's peace surpasses human understanding. When you accept His peace, it will revolutionize your life.

THE GRIEVING PROCESS

The Lord is near to those who have a broken heart.

Psalm 34:18 NKJV

Grief is a uniquely personal experience. But grief is also a universal experience, a journey that has been clearly mapped by those who have documented the common elements of human suffering.

Grief usually begins with shock and then gives way to intense pain. Over time, as the mourner regains his or her emotional balance, the pain begins to fade. Gradually—sometimes almost imperceptibly—a new life is raised from the ashes of the old. And even though the mourner may never "get over" his losses, he can, in time, reorganize his life and move beyond the intensity of the initial pain. Some losses are, of course, so profound and so painful that a mourner is forever changed. But for Christians who place their faith completely in their Creator—and in His only begotten Son—the experience of grief is different in one very important respect: Christians face grief armed with God's promises.

Through the Holy Bible, God promises to comfort and heal those who call upon Him. And He promises that the grave is not a final resting place; it is, instead, merely a place of transition—a way station on the path to eternal life—for those who give their hearts to God's Son.

As you ponder the ideas contained in this book, think carefully about your own situation: your emotions, your thoughts, your experiences, and your pain. And as you do, think carefully about the ways that you're responding to your own particular loses. The more you understand about the grieving process—and the more you understand about your own grieving process—the better you can cope with its many twists and turns. But whatever the nature of your loss, always remember this overriding truth: God is with you, God is good, and you are protected.

☆　☆　☆　☆

When the full impact of our loss hit home,
it seemed that everything
moved in slow motion.

Zig Ziglar

Sorrow is a fruit; God does not make it grow on limbs too weak to bear it.

Victor Hugo

In grief nothing "stays put." One keeps on emerging from a phase, but it always recurs. Round and round. Everything repeats. Am I going in circles, or dare I hope I am on a spiral?

C. S. Lewis

Tears have a language all their own, a tongue that needs no interpreter.

Charles Swindoll

Grief is the aftermath of any deeply significant loss.

Wayne Oates

A TIMELY TIP

The grieving process takes time. God does not promise instantaneous healing, but He does promise healing: "I have heard your prayer, I have seen your tears; surely I will heal you" (2 Kings 20:5 NKJV).

A PROMISE TO COUNT ON

Blessed is a man who endures trials, because when he passes the test he will receive the crown of life that He has promised to those who love Him.

James 1:12 Holman CSB

Throughout the seasons of life, we must all endure life-altering personal losses that leave us breathless. When we do, we may be overwhelmed by fear, by doubt, or by both. Thankfully, God has promised that He will never desert us. And God keeps His promises.

Life on the front line is always challenging, but as Christians, we must trust the promises of our Heavenly Father. God loves us, and He will protect us. In times of hardship, He will comfort us; in times of sorrow, He will dry our tears. When we are troubled, or weak, or sorrowful, God is with us. His love endures, not only for today, but also for all of eternity.

God whispers to us in our pleasures, speaks in our conscience, but shouts in our pain.

C. S. Lewis

The closer we are to God, the more confidence we place in him when we are under fire.

C. H. Spurgeon

The roots grow deep when the winds are strong.

Charles Swindoll

A promise has credibility only in the capacity of the person to guarantee it. God's character is perfect, and he has the complete capacity to guarantee any promise that He makes.

Franklin Graham

Success is how high you bounce when you hit bottom.

George S. Patton

A TIMELY TIP

When times are tough, you should guard your heart by turning it over to God.

HOPE FOR TODAY

You have already heard about this hope in the message of truth, the gospel that has come to you. It is bearing fruit and growing all over the world, just as it has among you since the day you heard it and recognized God's grace in the truth.

Colossians 1:5-6 Holman CSB

Despite God's promises, despite Christ's love, and despite our countless blessings, we frail human beings can still lose hope from time to time. When we do, we need the encouragement of Christian friends, the life-changing power of prayer, and the healing truth of God's Holy Word. If we find ourselves falling into the spiritual traps of worry and discouragement, we should seek the healing touch of Jesus and the encouraging words of fellow Christians. Even though this world can be a place of trials and struggles, God has promised us peace, joy, and eternal life if we give ourselves to Him. And, of course, God keeps His promises today, tomorrow, and forever.

Hope is faith holding out its hand in the dark.

Barbara Johnson

131

Hope is the power of being cheerful in circumstances which we know to be desperate.

G. K. Chesterton

Down through the centuries in times of trouble and trial, God has brought courage to the hearts of those who love Him. The Bible is filled with assurances of God's help and comfort in every kind of trouble which might cause fears to arise in the human heart. You can look ahead with promise, hope, and joy.

Billy Graham

When you accept the fact that sometimes seasons are dry and times are hard and that God is in control of both, you will discover a sense of divine refuge because the hope then is in God and not in yourself.

Charles Swindoll

A TIMELY TIP

If you're experiencing hard times, you'll be wise to start spending more time with God. And if you do your part, God will do His part. So never be afraid to hope—or to ask—for a miracle.

FACING FEARS

Don't be afraid, for I am with you. Do not be dismayed for I am your God. I will strengthen you. I will help you. I will uphold you with my victorious right hand.

Isaiah 41:10 NLT

We live in a world that is, at times, a frightening place. We live in a world that is, at times, a discouraging place. We live in a world where life-changing losses can be so painful and so profound that it seems we will never recover. But, with God's help, and with the help of encouraging family members and friends, we can recover.

During the darker days of life, we are wise to remember the words of Jesus, who reassured His disciples, saying, "Take courage! It is I. Don't be afraid" (Matthew 14:27 NIV). Then, with God's comfort and His love in our hearts, we can offer encouragement to others. And by helping them face their fears, we can, in turn, tackle our own problems with courage, determination, and faith.

God knows that the strength that comes from wrestling with our fear will give us wings to fly.

Paula Rinehart

His hand on me is a father's hand, gently guiding and encouraging. His hand lets me know he is with me, so I am not afraid.

Mary Morrison Suggs

Adversity is always unexpected and unwelcomed. It is an intruder and a thief, and yet in the hands of God, adversity becomes the means through which His supernatural power is demonstrated.

Charles Stanley

Facing our deepest fears means making peace with our seen self and with our unseen self.

Sheila Walsh

A TIMELY TIP

Are you feeling anxious or fearful? If so, trust God to handle those problems that are simply too big for you to solve. Entrust the future—your future—to God. Then, spend a few minutes thinking about specific steps you can take to confront—and conquer—your fears.

INFINITE POSSIBILITIES

Is anything too hard for the LORD?

Genesis 18:14 KJV

Are you afraid to ask God to do big things in your life? Is your faith threadbare and worn? If so, it's time to abandon your doubts and reclaim your faith in God's promises.

Ours is a God of infinite possibilities. But sometimes, because of limited faith and limited understanding, we wrongly assume that God cannot or will not intervene in the affairs of mankind. Such assumptions are simply wrong.

God's Holy Word makes it clear: absolutely nothing is impossible for the Lord. And since the Bible means what it says, you can be comforted in the knowledge that the Creator of the universe can do miraculous things in your own life and in the lives of your loved ones. Your challenge, as a believer, is to take God at His word, and to expect the miraculous.

If we take God's program, we can have God's power—not otherwise.

E. Stanley Jones

You can believe in the Holy Spirit not because you see Him, but because you see what He does in people's lives when they are surrendered to Christ and possess His power.

Billy Graham

The task ahead of us is never as great as the Power behind us.

Anonymous

God is the silent partner in all great enterprises.

Abraham Lincoln

A TIMELY TIP

God is in control of His world and your world. Rely upon Him. Vance Havner writes, "When we get to a place where it can't be done unless God does it, God will do it!"

CONTAGIOUS FAITH

Set your minds on what is above, not on what is on the earth.

Colossians 3:2 Holman CSB

The stronger your faith, the better you can rise above the inevitable stresses of life on the front line. And the more enthused you are about your faith, the better you can share it.

Are you genuinely excited about your faith? And do you make your enthusiasm known to those around you? Or are you a "silent ambassador" for Christ? God's preference is clear: He intends that you stand before others and proclaim your faith.

Genuine, heartfelt Christianity is contagious. If you enjoy a life-altering relationship with God, that relationship will have an impact on others—perhaps a profound impact.

Does Christ reign over your life? Then share your testimony and your excitement. The world needs both.

Faith is caught, not taught.

Anonymous

We act as though comfort and luxury were the chief requirements of life, when all we need to make us really happy is something to be enthusiastic about.

Charles Kingsley

Your enthusiasm will be infectious, stimulating, and attractive to others. They will love you for it. They will go for you and with you.

Norman Vincent Peale

When we wholeheartedly commit ourselves to God, there is nothing mediocre or run-of-the-mill about us. To live for Christ is to be passionate about our Lord and about our lives.

Jim Gallery

Don't take hold of a thing unless you want that thing to take hold of you.

E. Stanley Jones

A TIMELY TIP

When you become genuinely enthused about your mission and your faith, you'll guard your heart and improve your life.

EXPRESSING YOUR EMOTIONS

Blessed are those who mourn, for they shall be comforted.

Matthew 5:4 NKJV

In the Old Testament, Job's example teaches us that it's okay to express grief. Job cried bitter tears; he cursed the day he was born (Job 3:1-3); he expressed questions that he could not answer; and he gave voice to his suffering. But he never grieved alone. When everyone else failed him, including friends and family, Job knew that God still ruled over the entire world and over Job's own corner of the world. Job trusted that God was always present . . . and so should you.

God gave you emotions, and He intends for you to use them. When you express your emotions sincerely, you will begin the process of healing. But if you suppress your emotions or if you ignore your feelings altogether, you may needlessly prolong your pain.

So, if you have experienced a significant loss at the front line or a profound disappointment back home, don't bottle up everything inside. Express your feelings; talk openly to loved ones; allow tears to flow. Even if you'd rather ignore your pain, don't do it. Instead, reach out to the people you love and trust.

By honestly expressing your grief, you will take an active role in God's plan for your recovery. And in time, you'll experience the comfort and the joy that can—and should—be yours.

There is no way around suffering.
We have to go through it
to get to the other side.

—

Barbara Johnson

If we are not willing to feel negative emotions, then we shall not experience the richness of our positive emotions.

C. S. Lewis

Christians are told not to stifle their grief or to behave unscripturally stoic.

Charles Stanley

When we cry, we allow our bodies to function according to God's design—and we embrace one of the "perks" he offers to relieve our stress.

Barbara Johnson

A TIMELY TIP

Think about the last time you found yourself in a seriously down mood. And think about what may have caused your moodiness. Were you exhausted? Overcommitted? Stressed? Disappointed with yourself? Had you skipped your daily devotional? Make notes about the things that can predictably put you in an emotional tailspin, and while you're at it, think about ways to express your feelings productively, not destructively.

CHRIST'S ABUNDANCE

I have come that they may have life, and that they may have it more abundantly.

John 10:10 NKJV

The familiar words of John 10:10 convey this promise: Jesus came to this earth so that you might have a life of abundance. But what, precisely, did Christ mean when He talked of the abundant life? Was He promising His followers an abundance of fame and fortune? Hardly. The Prince of Peace came to this world not to give it prosperity, but to give it salvation. Thankfully for Christians, our Savior's abundance is both spiritual and eternal; it never falters—even if we do—and it never dies. We need only to open our hearts to Him, and His grace becomes ours.

The spiritual abundance that Jesus promises is, indeed, available to you. Your task, as a follower of the One from Galilee, is to accept Christ's abundance and to claim His gifts. The fullness of life in Christ can—and should—be yours, but no one can claim those riches on your behalf . . . you must claim them for yourself.

Do you sincerely seek the riches that our Savior offers to those who give themselves to Him? Then follow Him completely and obey Him without reservation. Follow Him today, tomorrow, and every day that you live. When you do, you will receive the love and the abundance that He has promised.

Seek first the personal transformation that is available through a genuine relationship with Christ, and then claim the joy, the peace, and the spiritual abundance that the Shepherd offers His sheep.

The only way you can experience
abundant life is to
surrender your plans to Him.

—

Charles Stanley

Jesus wants Life for us, Life with a capital L.

John Eldredge

The man who lives without Jesus is the poorest of the poor, whereas no one is so rich as the man who lives in His grace.

Thomas à Kempis

We honor God by asking for great things when they are a part of His promise. We dishonor Him and cheat ourselves when we ask for molehills where He has promised mountains.

Vance Havner

A TIMELY TIP

Abundance and obedience go hand-in-hand. Obey God first and expect to receive His abundance second, not vice versa.

ACCEPTING GOD'S GUIDANCE

The steps of the Godly are directed by God. He delights in every detail of their lives.

Psalm 37:22 NLT

As life unfolds along the front lines, we are constantly confronted with opportunities to learn, to explore, and to mature, and that's as it should be. The journey toward spiritual maturity is never a single destination; it is, instead, an ongoing process that continues moment by moment and day by day throughout every stage of life.

Every chapter of life has its own possibilities and its own challenges. If we're wise, we continue to seek God's guidance as each new stage unfolds. When we do so, we allow the Creator who made us to keep remaking us.

Today, focus your thoughts—and attune your heart— to the Father. He will teach you, He will shape you, and He will lead you along a path of His choosing. And if you're not sure of your next step, keep watching, keep listening, and keep praying. The answers will come.

Are you serious about wanting God's guidance to become a personal reality in your life? The first step is to tell God that you know you can't manage your own life; that you need his help.

Catherine Marshall

I believe that the Creator of this universe takes delight in turning the terrors and tragedies that come with living in this old, fallen domain of the devil and transforming them into something that strengthens our hope, tests our faith, and shows forth His glory.

Al Green

God will prove to you how good and acceptable and perfect His will is when He's got His hands on the steering wheel of your life.

Stuart & Jill Briscoe

A TIMELY TIP

If you're wise, you'll allow God to guide your steps along the front lines of life. When you pray for guidance, God will give it.

CONFIDENCE RESTORED

I've told you all this so that trusting me, you will be unshakable and assured, deeply at peace. In this godless world you will continue to experience difficulties. But take heart! I've conquered the world.

John 16:33 MSG

Are you a confident, faithful believer, or do you live under a cloud of uncertainty and doubt? As a Christian, you have many reasons to be confident. After all, God is in His heaven; Christ has risen; and you are the recipient of God's grace. Despite these blessings, you may, from time to time, find yourself being tormented by stressful, destructive emotions—and you are certainly not alone.

During turbulent times like these, even the most faithful Christians are overcome by occasional bouts of fear and doubt. And you are no different. But even when you feel very distant from God, remember that God is never distant from you. When you sincerely seek His presence, He will touch your heart, calm your fears, and restore your confidence.

Feelings of confidence depend upon the type of thoughts you habitually occupy. Think defeat, and you are bound to be defeated.

Norman Vincent Peale

Jesus gives us the ultimate rest, the confidence we need, to escape the frustration and chaos of the world around us.

Billy Graham

Believe and do what God says. The life-changing consequences will be limitless, and the results will be confidence and peace of mind.

Franklin Graham

Bible hope is confidence in the future.

Warren Wiersbe

A TIMELY TIP

Do you lack confidence? If so, pay careful attention to the direction of your thoughts. And while you're at it, pay careful attention to the promises contained in God's Holy Word. Remember: the more you trust God, the more confident you will become.

A WORTHY DISCIPLE

He has told you men what is good and what it is the Lord requires of you: Only to act justly, to love faithfulness, and to walk humbly with your God.

Micah 6:8 Holman CSB

When Jesus addressed His disciples, He warned that each one must, "take up his cross and follow Me." The disciples must have known exactly what the Master meant. In Jesus' day, prisoners were forced to carry their own crosses to the location where they would be put to death. Thus, Christ's message was clear: in order to follow Him, Christ's disciples must deny themselves and, instead, trust Him completely. Nothing has changed since then.

If we are to be disciples of Christ, we must trust Him and place Him at the very center of our beings. Jesus never comes "next." He is always first.

Do you seek to be a worthy disciple of Christ? Then pick up His cross today and every day that you live. When you do, He will bless you now and forever.

Discipleship is a daily discipline: we follow Jesus a step at a time, a day at a time.

Warren Wiersbe

Discipleship means personal, passionate devotion to a Person, our Lord Jesus Christ.

Oswald Chambers

Discipleship is a decision to live by what I know about God, not by what I feel about him or myself or my neighbors.

Eugene Peterson

Discipleship means allegiance to the suffering Christ, and it is therefore not at all surprising that Christians should be called upon to suffer.

Dietrich Bonhoeffer

A TIMELY TIP

Jesus invites you to become His disciple . . . and the rest is up to you.

HE OVERCOMES

These things I have spoken to you, that in Me you may have peace. In the world you will have tribulation; but be of good cheer, I have overcome the world.

John 16:33 NKJV

The hope that the world offers is fleeting and imperfect. The hope that God offers is unchanging, unshakable, and unending. It is no wonder, then, that when we seek security from worldly sources, our hopes are often dashed and our stresses are often increased. Thankfully, God has no such record of failure.

Where will you place your hopes today? Will you entrust your future to man or to God? Will you seek solace exclusively from fallible human beings, or will you place your hopes, first and foremost, in the trusting hands of your Creator? The decision is yours, and you must live with the results of the choice you make.

For thoughtful believers, hope begins with God. Period. So today, as you embark upon the next stage of your life's journey, consider the words of the Psalmist: "You are my hope; O Lord GOD, You are my confidence" (71:5 NASB). Then, place your trust in the One who cannot be shaken.

When you say a situation or a person is hopeless, you are slamming the door in the face of God.

Charles Allen

Without the certainty of His resurrection, we would come to the end of this life without hope, with nothing to anticipate except despair and doubt. But because He lives, we rejoice, knowing soon we will meet our Savior face to face, and the troubles and trials of this world will be behind us.

Bill Bright

Oh, remember this: There is never a time when we may not hope in God. Whatever our necessities, however great our difficulties, and though to all appearance help is impossible, yet our business is to hope in God, and it will be found that it is not in vain.

George Mueller

A TIMELY TIP

Never give up hope. Other people have experienced the same kind of hard times you may be experiencing now. They made it, and so can you.

TRUST GOD'S PROMISES

As for God, his way is perfect. All the LORD's promises prove true. He is a shield for all who look to him for protection.

Psalm 18:30 NLT

What do you expect from the day ahead? Are you willing to trust God completely, or are you living beneath a cloud of doubt and fear? God's Word makes it clear: you should trust Him and His promises, and when you do, you can live courageously.

For thoughtful Christians, every day begins and ends with God's Son and God's promises. When we accept Christ into our hearts, God promises us the opportunity for earthly peace and spiritual abundance. But more importantly, God promises us the priceless gift of eternal life.

Sometimes, especially when we find ourselves caught in the inevitable dangers of life on the front line, we fail to trust God completely.

Are you tired? Discouraged? Fearful? Be comforted and trust the promises that God has made to you. Are you worried or stressed? Be confident in God's power. Do you see a difficult future ahead? Be courageous and call upon God. He will protect you and then use you according to His purposes. Are you confused? Listen to the quiet voice of your

Heavenly Father. He is not a God of confusion. Talk with Him; listen to Him; trust Him, and trust His promises. He is steadfast, and He is your Protector . . . forever.

Joy is not mere happiness.
Nor does joy spring from a life of ease, comfort,
or peaceful circumstances.
Joy is the soul's buoyant response
to a God of promise, presence, and power.
—

Susan Lenzkes

The meaning of hope isn't just some flimsy wishing. It's a firm confidence in God's promises—that he will ultimately set things right.

Sheila Walsh

In Biblical worship you do not find the repetition of a phrase; instead, you find the worshipers rehearsing the character of God and His ways, reminding Him of His faithfulness and His wonderful promises.

Kay Arthur

Gather the riches of God's promises which can strengthen you in the time when there will be no freedom.

Corrie ten Boom

A TIMELY TIP

God's Word can guide your steps and guard your heart. Let your Bible be your guide.

WORRIED?

Give your worries to the Lord, and he will take care of you. He will never let good people down.

Psalm 55:22 NCV

Because life on the front line is difficult, and because you have understandable fears about the uncertainty of the future, you worry. At times, you may find yourself fretting over the countless details of life. You may worry about your safety, your relationships, your finances, your health, or any number of potential problems, some large and some small.

If you're a "worrier" by nature, it may be time to rethink the way that you think! Perhaps you've formed the unfortunate habit of focusing too intently on negative aspects of life while spending too little time counting your blessings. If so, take your worries to God . . . and leave them there. When you do, you'll learn to worry a little less and to trust God a little more—and that's as it should be because God is trustworthy, you are protected, and your future can be intensely bright.

Worry is the senseless process of cluttering up tomorrow's opportunities with leftover problems from today.

Barbara Johnson

Things can be very difficult for us, but nothing is too hard for Him.

Charles Stanley

Today is mine. Tomorrow is none of my business. If I peer anxiously into the fog of the future, I will strain my spiritual eyes so that I will not see clearly what is required of me now.

Elisabeth Elliott

We are given one life, and the decision is whether to wait for circumstances to make up our mind, or whether to act, and in acting, to live.

Omar Bradley

A TIMELY TIP

You have worries, but God has solutions. Your challenge is to trust Him to solve the problems that you can't.

THE RIGHT KIND OF FEAR

The fear of the Lord is the beginning of knowledge.

Proverbs 1:7 Holman CSB

Do you have a healthy, fearful respect for God's power? If so, you are both wise and obedient. And, because you are a thoughtful believer, you also understand that genuine wisdom begins with a profound appreciation for God's limitless power.

God praises humility and punishes pride. That's why God's greatest servants will always be those humble men and women who care less for their own glory and more for God's glory. In God's kingdom, the only way to achieve greatness is to shun it. And the only way to be wise is to understand these facts: God is great; He is all-knowing; and He is all-powerful. We must respect Him, and we must humbly obey His commandments, or we must accept the consequences of our misplaced pride.

A healthy fear of God will do much to deter us from sin.

Charles Swindoll

It is an act of the will to allow God to be our refuge. Otherwise, we live outside of his love and protection, wondering why we feel alone and afraid.

Mary Morrison Suggs

The remarkable thing about fearing God is that when you fear God, you fear nothing else, whereas if you do not fear God, you fear everything else.

Oswald Chambers

It is not possible that mortal men should be thoroughly conscious of the divine presence without being filled with awe.

C. H. Spurgeon

A TIMELY TIP

If you have a healthy fear of God, you're wise—if you don't, you're not.

BEYOND FAILURE

For a righteous man may fall seven times and rise again.

Proverbs 24:16 NKJV

The occasional disappointments and failures of life are inevitable. Such setbacks are simply the price that we must occasionally pay for our willingness to take on the risks and responsibilities of service. But even when we encounter bitter disappointments, we must never lose faith. What's required is perseverance, not perfection.

When we encounter the inevitable difficulties and stresses of life on the front line, God stands ready to protect us. Our responsibility, of course, is to ask Him for protection. When we call upon Him in heartfelt prayer, He will answer—in His own time and according to His own plan—and He will heal us. And, while we are waiting for God's plans to unfold and for His healing touch to restore us, we can be comforted in the knowledge that our Creator can overcome any obstacle, even if we cannot.

The almighty Father will use life's reverses to move you forward.

Barbara Johnson

So you have failed? You have not failed; you have gained experience. Go forward!

Josemaria Escriva

One of the ways God refills us after failure is through the blessing of Christian fellowship. Just experiencing the joy of simple activities shared with other children of God can have a healing effect on us.

Anne Graham Lotz

Do not be one of those who, rather than risk failure, never attempt anything.

Thomas Merton

A TIMELY TIP

Time and again, the Bible preaches the power of perseverance. Setbacks, disappointments, and failures are inevitable—your response to them is optional. If you don't give up, you can turn your stumbling blocks into stepping stones . . . and you should.

GOD'S FORGIVENESS

Let us, then, feel very sure that we can come before God's throne where there is grace. There we can receive mercy and grace to help us when we need it.

Hebrews 4:16 NCV

When we genuinely repent from our wrongdoings, and when we sincerely confess our mistakes, we are forgiven by our Heavenly Father. But long after God has forgiven us, we may continue to withhold forgiveness from ourselves. Instead of accepting God's mercy and accepting our past, we may think long and hard—far too long and hard—about the things that "might have been," the things that "could have been," or the things that "should have been."

Are you troubled by feelings of guilt, even after you've received God's forgiveness? Are you still struggling with painful memories of mistakes you made long ago? Are you focused so intently on yesterday that your vision of today is clouded? If so, you still have work to do—spiritual work. You should ask your Heavenly Father not for forgiveness (He granted that gift the very first time you asked Him!) but instead for acceptance and trust: acceptance of the past and trust in God's plan for your life.

Once you have asked God for His forgiveness, you can be certain that your Heavenly Father has given it. And if He, in His infinite wisdom, will forgive your sins, how then can you withhold forgiveness from yourself? The answer, of course, is that once God has forgiven you, you should forgive yourself, too.

When you forgive yourself thoroughly and completely, you'll stop investing energy in those most useless of emotions: bitterness, regret, and self-recrimination. And you can then get busy making the world a better place, and that's as it should be. After all, since God has forgiven you, it's about time that you demonstrate your gratitude by serving Him?

★ ★ ★ ★

The pardon of God deletes past, present,
and future sins—completely!

Franklin Graham

There is only One who can cleanse us from our sins—He who made us.

Corrie ten Boom

Mistakes offer the possibility for redemption and a new start in God's kingdom. No matter what you're guilty of, God can restore your innocence.

Barbara Johnson

To be righteous means to be in right standing with God because your sins have been taken care of!

Kay Arthur

No man ever loved like Jesus. He taught the blind to see and the dumb to speak. He died on the cross to save us. He bore our sins. And now God says, "Because He did, I can forgive you."

Billy Graham

A TIMELY TIP

You cannot do anything that God can't forgive. Accept His forgiveness today.

PRAISING THOSE WHO SERVE

But he who is greatest among you shall be your servant.

Matthew 23:11 NKJV

The future of our nation depends, in large part, upon the sacrifices made by those who serve and protect us.

Jesus made it clear: We achieve greatness through service to others. But, as weak human beings, we sometimes fall short as we seek to puff ourselves up and glorify our own accomplishments. And sometimes, we fail to do our part to serve others. Jesus commands otherwise. If we seek spiritual greatness, we must first become servants.

Today, our nation needs our prayers and our service. May we, as Christians, offer both. Let us begin by offering our prayers to God, and then, let us work courageously to fulfill His kingdom's work here on earth.

No life can surpass that of a man who quietly continues to serve God in the place where providence has placed him.

C. H. Spurgeon

Have thy tools ready; God will find thee work.

Charles Kingsley

In the very place where God has put us, whatever its limitations, whatever kind of work it may be, we may indeed serve the Lord Christ.

Elisabeth Elliot

We are only fully alive when we're helping others.

Rick Warren

If doing a good act in public will excite others to do more good, then "Let your Light shine to all." Miss no opportunity to do good.

John Wesley

A TIMELY TIP

Wherever you happen to be—whatever your age, whatever your losses—you can find people to help and ways to serve. And the time to begin serving is now.

THE RIGHT KIND OF ATTITUDE

For God has not given us a spirit of fearfulness, but one of power, love, and sound judgment.

2 Timothy 1:7 Holman CSB

Are you fearful, angry, bored, or worried? Are you pessimistic, perplexed, pained, and perturbed? If so, God wants to have a little talk with you.

God created you in His own image, and He wants you to experience joy, contentment, peace, and abundance. But, God will not force you to experience these things; you must claim them for yourself.

God has given you free will, including the ability to influence the direction and the tone of your thoughts. And, here's how God wants you to direct those thoughts:

"Finally brothers, whatever is true, whatever is honorable, whatever is just, whatever is pure, whatever is lovely, whatever is commendable—if there is any moral excellence and if there is any praise—dwell on these things" (Philippians 4:8 Holman CSB).

So, the next time you find yourself dwelling upon the negative aspects of your life, refocus your attention on things positive. The next time you find yourself falling prey to the blight of pessimism, stop yourself and turn your thoughts around. The next time you're tempted to waste valuable time gossiping or complaining, resist those temptations with all your might.

And remember: You'll never whine your way to the top . . . so don't waste your breath.

We are either the masters or the victims of our attitudes. It is a matter of personal choice. Who we are today is the result of choices we made yesterday. Tomorrow, we will become what we choose today. To change means to choose to change.

—

John Maxwell

We shouldn't deny the pain of what happens in our lives. But, we should refuse to focus only on the valleys.

Charles Swindoll

Pain is inevitable, but misery is optional.

Max Lucado

Attitude is more important than the past, than education, than money, than circumstances, than what people do or say. It is more important than appearance, giftedness, or skill.

Charles Swindoll

The greater part of our happiness or misery depends on our dispositions, and not our circumstances.

Martha Washington

A TIMELY TIP

If you're a Christian, you have every reason on earth—and in heaven—to have a positive attitude.

DOERS OF THE WORD

But be doers of the word and not hearers only.

James 1:22 Holman CSB

I t's stressful to believe one thing but do something else. And as Christians, we must beware: Our actions should always give credence to the changes that Jesus can make in the lives of those who walk with Him.

God calls upon each of us to act in accordance with His will and with respect for His commandments. If we are to be responsible believers, we must realize that it is never enough simply to hear the instructions of God; we must also live by them. And it is never enough to wait idly by while others do God's work here on earth; we, too, must act. Doing God's work is a responsibility that each of us must bear, and when we do, our loving Heavenly Father rewards our efforts with a bountiful harvest.

In times of stress and adversity, it's always best to keep busy, to plow your anger and your energy into something quite positive.

Lee Iacocca

Action springs not from thought, but from a readiness for responsibility.

Dietrich Bonhoeffer

The church needs people who are doers of the Word and not just hearers.

Warren Wiersbe

Let us not be content to wait and see what will happen, but give us the determination to make the right things happen.

Peter Marshall

A good plan executed now is better than a perfect plan executed next week.

George S. Patton

A TIMELY TIP

Because actions do speak louder than words, it's always a good time to let your actions speak for themselves.

TEAMMATES IN NEED

Each one of us needs to look after the good of the people around us, asking ourselves, "How can I help?" That's exactly what Jesus did.

Romans 15:2-3 MSG

Sometimes we would like to help make the world a better place, but we're not sure of the best way to do it. Jesus told the story of the "Good Samaritan," a man who helped a fellow traveler when no one else would. We, too, should be good Samaritans when we encounter people who need our help.

The words of Jesus are unambiguous: "Freely you have received, freely give" (Matthew 10:8 NIV). As followers of Christ, we are commanded to be generous with our friends, with our families, and with those in need. We must give freely of our time, our possessions, and, most especially, our love.

Today, take God's words to heart and make this pledge: Wherever you happen to be, be a good Samaritan. Somebody near you needs your assistance, and you need the spiritual rewards that will be yours when you lend a helping hand.

The truest help we can render an afflicted man is not to take his burden from him, but to call out his best energy, that he may be able to bear the burden himself.

Phillips Brooks

Make it a rule, and pray to God to help you to keep it, never, if possible, to lie down at night without being able to say: "I have made one human being at least a little wiser, or a little happier, or at least a little better this day."

Charles Kingsley

Do all the good you can. By all the means you can. In all the ways you can. In all the places you can. At all the times you can. To all the people you can. As long as ever you can.

John Wesley

A TIMELY TIP

Someone very near you may need a helping hand or a kind word, so keep your eyes open, and look for people who need your help, whether you're at home or on the front line.

WHERE IS GOD LEADING?

Consider it a great joy, my brothers, whenever you experience various trials, knowing that the testing of your faith produces endurance. But endurance must do its complete work, so that you may be mature and complete, lacking nothing.

James 1:2-4 Holman CSB

Whether we realize it or not, times of adversity can be times of intense personal and spiritual growth. Our most difficult days on the front line are also the times when we can learn and relearn some of life's most important lessons.

The next time you experience a difficult moment, a difficult day, or a difficult tour of duty, ask yourself this question: Where is God leading me? In times of struggle and sorrow, you can be certain that God is leading you to a place of His choosing. Your duty is to watch, to pray, to listen, and to follow.

When times are tough, the Lord is our only security.

Charles Swindoll

A tried Christian grows rich by his losses, he rises by his falls, he lives by dying, and he becomes full by being emptied.

C. H. Spurgeon

The only way to learn a strong faith is to endure great trials. I have learned my faith by standing firm amid the most severe of tests.

George Mueller

God does not help us by removing the tests, but by making the tests work for us.

Warren Wiersbe

A TIMELY TIP

When you experience tough times (and you will), a positive attitude makes a big difference in the way you tackle your problems.

A BOOK UNLIKE ANY OTHER

For I am not ashamed of the gospel, because it is God's power for salvation to everyone who believes.

Romans 1:16 Holman CSB

The Bible can be a powerful tool for defeating stress. George Mueller observed, "The vigor of our spiritual lives will be in exact proportion to the place held by the Bible in our lives and in our thoughts." As Christians, we are called upon to study God's Holy Word and then apply it to our lives. When we do, we are blessed.

The Bible is a priceless gift, a tool for Christians to use as they share the Good News of their Savior, Christ Jesus. Too many Christians, however, keep their spiritual tool kits tightly closed and out of sight. Jonathan Edwards advised, "Be assiduous in reading the Holy Scriptures. This is the fountain whence all knowledge in divinity must be derived. Therefore let not this treasure lie by you neglected." God's Holy Word is, indeed, a priceless, one-of-a-kind treasure. Handle it with care, but, more importantly, handle it every day.

God gives us a compass and a Book of promises and principles—the Bible—and lets us make our decisions day by day as we sense the leading of His Spirit. This is how we grow.

Warren Wiersbe

I am certain that the Bible is the Word of God. Either it is or it isn't, and either all of it is the Word of God, or we never can be sure of any of it. It is either absolute or obsolete. If we have to start changing this verse, toning down that, apologizing for this and making allowances for that, we might as well give up, so we must take it as it is or leave it alone.

Vance Havner

The Bible is the one Book to which any thoughtful man may go with any honest question of life or destiny and find the answer of God by honest searching.

John Ruskin

A TIMELY TIP

Take a small Bible with you wherever you go. When you're serving on the front line, you never know when you'll need a quick look inside God's book.

IT'S POSSIBLE TO HEAL

Is anything too hard for the LORD?

Genesis 18:14 KJV

When you find yourself caught in the emotional quicksand called grief, you may wonder if you'll ever recover. When the feelings of sorrow are intense, you may think—mistakenly—that the pain will never subside. But the good news is this: while time heals many wounds, God has the power to heal them all.

Ours is a God of infinite power and infinite possibilities. But sometimes, because of limited faith and limited understanding, we wrongly assume that God cannot or will not intervene in the affairs of everyday life. Such assumptions are simply wrong.

God is busily at work in the world, and your world. Your job is to ask Him—fervently and often—for the things you need.

Have you sincerely asked God for His help as you begin the healing process? Have you asked Him to lead you on the first step back to recovery? Have you prayed for the peace that passes all understanding? If so, you're on the right track. If not, it's time to abandon your doubts and reclaim your faith in God's promises.

God's Holy Word makes it clear: absolutely nothing is impossible for Him. And since the Bible means what it says, you can be comforted in the knowledge that the Creator of the universe can do miraculous things in your own life and in the lives of your loved ones. Your challenge, as a believer, is to take God at His word, and to wait patiently for Him to bless you with peace that flows from His miraculous healing touch.

God can heal the brokenhearted if all the pieces are given to Him.

—

Warren Wiersbe

When we face an impossible situation, all self-reliance and self-confidence must melt away; we must be totally dependent on Him for the resources.

Anne Graham Lotz

I believe that the Creator of this universe takes delight in turning the terrors and tragedies that come with living in this old, fallen domain of the devil and transforming them into something that strengthens our hope, tests our faith, and shows forth His glory.

Al Green

The grace of God is sufficient for all our needs, for every problem and for every difficulty, for every broken heart, and for every human sorrow.

Peter Marshall

A TIMELY TIP

When you're hurting, it's up to you to find people who understand your pain and are willing to talk about it. Even if you're a person who usually keeps things bottled up inside, you'll be wise to talk about your feelings with trusted friends, with family members, with mental health professionals, and, most importantly, with God.

WHEN OUR PLANS DON'T WORK OUT

Haven't I commanded you: be strong and courageous? Do not be afraid or discouraged, for the Lord your God is with you wherever you go.

Joshua 1:9 Holman CSB

Some of our most important dreams are the ones we abandon. Some of our most important goals are the ones we don't attain. Sometimes, our most important journeys are the ones that we take to the winding conclusion of what seem to be dead-end streets. Thankfully, with God there are no dead-ends; there are only opportunities to learn, to yield, to trust, to serve, and to grow.

The next time you experience one of life's inevitable disappointments, don't despair and don't be afraid to try "Plan B." Consider every setback an opportunity to choose a different, more appropriate path. Have faith that God may indeed be leading you in an entirely different direction, a direction of His choosing. And as you take your next step, remember that what looks like a dead-end to you may, in fact, be the fast lane according to God.

The difference between winning and losing is how we choose to react to disappointment.

Barbara Johnson

Often God has to shut a door in our face so that he can subsequently open the door through which he wants us to go.

Catherine Marshall

Every achievement worth remembering is stained with the blood of diligence and scarred by the wounds of disappointment.

Charles Swindoll

The amazing thing is that God follows us into the blackened ruins of our failed dreams, our misbegotten mirages, into the house of cards that has collapsed on us in some way and he speaks, not with the chastisement we feel we deserve, but of all things, with tenderness.

Paula Rinehart

A TIMELY TIP

As you face uncertain times, make sure to build your future on a firm foundation: the unshakable foundation of God's eternal promises.

WHEN PEOPLE BEHAVE BADLY

Bad temper is contagious—don't get infected.

Proverbs 22:25 MSG

Sometimes, people can be discourteous and cruel. Sometimes people can be unfair, unkind, and un-appreciative. Sometimes people get angry and frustrated. So what's a Christian to do? God's answer is straightforward: forgive, forget, and move on. In Luke 6:37, Jesus instructs, "Do not judge, and you will not be judged. Do not condemn, and you will not be condemned. Forgive, and you will be forgiven" (Holman CSB).

Today and every day, make sure that you're quick to forgive others for their shortcomings. And when other people behave badly (as they most certainly will from time to time), don't pay too much attention. Just forgive those people as quickly as you can, and try to move on . . . as quickly as you can.

We are all fallen creatures and all very hard to live with.

C. S. Lewis

A keen sense of humor helps us to overlook the unbecoming, understand the unconventional, tolerate the unpleasant, overcome the unexpected, and outlast the unbearable.

Billy Graham

Bear with the faults of others as you would have them bear with yours.

Phillips Brooks

From what does such contrariness arise in habitually angry people, but from a secret cause of too high an opinion of themselves so that it pierces their hearts when they see any man esteem them less than they esteem themselves? An inflated estimation of ourselves is more than half the weight of our wrath.

St. Thomas More

A TIMELY TIP

If you can't find it in your heart to forgive those who have hurt you, you're hurting yourself more than you're hurting anyone else.

A SERIES OF CHOICES

But seek first the kingdom of God and His righteousness, and all these things will be provided for you.

Matthew 6:33 Holman CSB

Your life is a series of choices. From the instant you wake up in the morning until the moment you nod off to sleep at night, you make countless decisions—decisions about the things you do, decisions about the words you speak, and decisions about the way that you choose to direct your thoughts.

As a believer who has been transformed by the love of Jesus, you have every reason to make wise choices. But sometimes, when the stresses of the daily grind threaten to grind you up and spit you out, you may make choices that are displeasing to God. When you do, you'll pay a price because you'll forfeit the happiness and the peace that might otherwise have been yours.

So, as you pause to consider the kind of Christian you are—and the kind of Christian you want to become—ask yourself whether you're sitting on the fence or standing in the light. The choice is yours . . . and so are the consequences.

The greatest choice any man makes is to let God choose for him.

Vance Havner

Every step of your life's journey is a choice . . . and the quality of those choices determines the quality of the journey.

Criswell Freeman

Life is pretty much like a cafeteria line—it offers us many choices, both good and bad. The Christian must have a spiritual radar that detects the difference not only between bad and good but also among good, better, and best.

Dennis Swanberg

Every day, I find countless opportunities to decide whether I will obey God and demonstrate my love for Him or try to please myself or the world system. God is waiting for my choices.

Bill Bright

A TIMELY TIP

Little decisions, when taken together over a long period of time, can have big consequences. So remember that when it comes to matters of health, fitness, stress, and spirituality, there are no small decisions.

PRAISE HIM

Praise the LORD. Give thanks to the LORD, for he is good;
his love endures forever.

Psalm 106:1 NIV

Sometimes, in our rush to get things done, we simply don't stop long enough to pause and thank our Creator for the countless blessings He has bestowed upon us. After all, we're busy people with many demands upon our time . . . and we have so much to do. But when we slow down long enough to express our gratitude to the One who made us, we enrich our own lives and the lives of those around us.

Thanksgiving should become a habit, a regular part of our daily routines. After all, God has blessed us beyond measure, and we owe Him everything, including our constant praise.

So today, pause and count your blessings. Then, give thanks to the Giver. God's love for you is never-ending; your praise for Him should be never-ending, too.

Be not afraid of saying too much in the praises of God; all the danger is of saying too little.

Matthew Henry

Stand up and bless the Lord, ye people of his choice; stand up and bless the Lord your God with heart and soul and voice.

James Montgomery

Nothing we do is more powerful or more life-changing than praising God.

Stormie Omartian

Our God is the sovereign Creator of the universe! He loves us as His own children and has provided every good thing we have; He is worthy of our praise every moment.

Shirley Dobson

A TIMELY TIP

The appropriate moment to praise God is always this one.

BEYOND ANGER, BEYOND GUILT

If we say we have no sin, we are fooling ourselves, and the truth is not in us. But if we confess our sins, he will forgive our sins, because we can trust God to do what is right. He will cleanse us from all the wrongs we have done.

1 John 1:8-9 NCV

Life on the front line is often accompanied by the emotions of anger and guilt. We are understandably angry about our losses, and we may feel guilty about the things that we might have done to prevent them. But please beware: prolonged feelings of anger or guilt have the potential to do you great harm.

Anger, left unchecked, tends to invade every aspect of life, eventually transforming itself into bitterness. Irrational guilt, especially over past events that cannot be changed, creates an environment of self-doubt and self-recrimination.

If you are ruled by feelings of anger, guilt, jealousy, fear, or any other negative emotion, understand that these emotions are part of the grieving process. But understand too that hurtful feelings should never become a permanent part of your emotional makeup. God has better things in store for you!

Spiritual life without guilt would be like physical life without pain. Guilt is a defense mechanism; it's like an alarm that goes off to lead you to confession when you sin.

John MacArthur

If God has forgiven you, why can't you forgive yourself?

Marie T. Freeman

Let's take Jesus at His word. When He says we're forgiven, let's unload the guilt. When He says we're valuable, let's believe Him. When He says we're eternal, let's bury our fear. When He says we're provided for, let's stop worrying.

Max Lucado

Satan knows that if you live under a dark cloud of guilt, you will not be able to witness effectively or serve the Lord with power and blessing.

Warren Wiersbe

A TIMELY TIP

If you've asked for God's forgiveness, He has given it. But have you forgiven yourself? If not, the best moment to do so is this one.

GENUINE CONTENTMENT

The LORD gives strength to his people; the LORD blesses his people with peace.

Psalm 29:11 NIV

On the front lines of life, contentment may seem fleeting and incomplete. Yet even amid the inevitable battles of life, God offers contentment that is all encompassing and everlasting.

Happiness depends less upon our circumstances than upon our thoughts. When we turn our thoughts to God, to His gifts, and to His glorious creation, we experience the joy that God intends for His children. But, when we focus on the negative aspects of life—or when we disobey God's commandments—we cause ourselves needless suffering.

Do you sincerely want to be a contented Christian? Then set your mind and your heart upon God's love and His grace . . . and let Him take care of the rest.

God is most glorified in us when we are most satisfied in him.

John Piper

The secret of contentment in the midst of change is found in having roots in the changeless Christ—the same yesterday, today and forever.

Ed Young

Contentment is something we learn by adhering to the basics—cultivating a growing relationship with Jesus Christ, living daily, and knowing that Christ strengthens us for every challenge.

Charles Stanley

Contentment is not escape from battle, but rather an abiding peace and confidence in the midst of battle.

Warren Wiersbe

A TIMELY TIP

God offers you His peace, His protection, and His promises. If you accept these gifts, you will eventually discover the peace that passes understanding.

THE POWER OF PATIENCE

And we exhort you, brothers: warn those who are lazy, comfort the discouraged, help the weak, be patient with everyone.

1 Thessalonians 5:14 Holman CSB

L ife on the front line demands patience . . . and lots of it! We live in an imperfect world inhabited by imperfect people. Sometimes, we inherit troubles from others, and sometimes we create trouble for ourselves. In either case, what's required is patience.

Lamentations 3:25-26 reminds us that, "The Lord is wonderfully good to those who wait for him and seek him. So it is good to wait quietly for salvation from the Lord" (NIV). But, for most of us, waiting quietly for God is difficult. Why? Because we are fallible human beings, sometimes quick to anger and sometimes slow to forgive.

The next time you find your patience tested to the limit, remember that the world unfolds according to God's timetable, not ours. Sometimes, we must wait patiently, and that's as it should be. After all, think how patient God has been with us.

Our challenge is to wait in faith for the day of God's favor and salvation.

Jim Cymbala

God never hurries. There are no deadlines against which He must work. To know this is to quiet our spirits and relax our nerves.

A. W. Tozer

As we wait on God, He helps us use the winds of adversity to soar above our problems. As the Bible says, "Those who wait on the LORD…shall mount up with wings like eagles."

Billy Graham

Two signposts of faith: "Slow Down" and "Wait Here."

Charles Stanley

A TIMELY TIP

When you learn to be more patient with others, you'll make your world—and your heart—a better place.

COUNTING YOUR BLESSINGS

Blessings are on the head of the righteous.

Proverbs 10:6 Holman CSB

O n the front lines of life, it's easy to become preoccupied and distracted. And it's easy to overlook God's gifts.

Have you counted your blessings today? And have you thanked God for them? Hopefully so. After all, God's gifts include your family, your friends, your talents, your opportunities, your possessions, and the priceless gift of eternal life. How glorious are these gifts . . . and God is responsible for every one of them.

So today, as you faithfully serve your country on the front lines, pause and give thanks to the Creator. He deserves your praise, and you deserve the experience of praising Him.

God's kindness is not like the sunset—brilliant in its intensity, but dying every second. God's generosity keeps coming and coming and coming.

Bill Hybels

When you and I are related to Jesus Christ, our strength and wisdom and peace and joy and love and hope may run out, but His life rushes in to keep us filled to the brim. We are showered with blessings, not because of anything we have or have not done, but simply because of Him.

Anne Graham Lotz

Do we not continually pass by blessings innumerable without notice, and instead fix our eyes on what we feel to be our trials and our losses, and think and talk about these until our whole horizon is filled with them, and we almost begin to think we have no blessings at all?

Hannah Whitall Smith

God is more anxious to bestow His blessings on us than we are to receive them.

St. Augustine

A TIMELY TIP

God gives us countless blessings. We, in turn, should give Him our thanks and our praise, even in the midst of battle.

DEFEATING NEGATIVITY

Let angry people endure the backlash of their own anger; if you try to make it better, you'll only make it worse.

Proverbs 19:19 MSG

From experience, we know that it is easy to criticize others. And we know that it is usually far easier to find faults than to find solutions. Still, the urge to criticize others remains a powerful temptation for most of us.

Negativity is highly contagious: We give it to others who, in turn, give it back to us. This stress-inducing cycle can be broken only by positive thoughts, heartfelt prayers, encouraging words, and meaningful acts of kindness.

As thoughtful servants of a loving God, we have no valid reason—and no legitimate excuse—to be negative. So, when we are tempted to be overly critical of others, or unfairly critical of ourselves, we must use the transforming power of God's love to break the chains of negativity. We must defeat negativity before negativity defeats us.

Winners see an answer for every problem; losers see a problem in every answer.

Barbara Johnson

We never get anywhere—nor do our conditions and circumstances change—when we look at the dark side of life.

Mrs. Charles E. Cowman

To lose heart is to lose everything.

John Eldredge

Do not build up obstacles in your imagination. Difficulties must be studied and dealt with, but they must not be magnified by fear.

Norman Vincent Peale

A TIMELY TIP

Negative thinking breeds more negative thinking, so nip negativity in the bud, starting today and continuing every day of your life.

FINDING AND SHARING ENCOURAGEMENT

Timely advice is as lovely as golden apples in a silver basket.

Proverbs 25:11 NLT

Life is a team sport, and all of us need occasional pats on the back from our teammates. This world can be a difficult place, a place where many of our friends and family members are troubled by the stresses and challenges of everyday life. And since we cannot always be certain who needs our help, we should strive to speak helpful words to all who cross our paths.

In his letter to the Ephesians, Paul writes, "Do not let any unwholesome talk come out of your mouths, but only what is helpful for building others up according to their needs, that it may benefit those who listen" (v. 29 NIV). This passage reminds us that, as Christians, we are instructed to choose our words carefully so as to build others up through wholesome, honest encouragement. How can we build others up? By celebrating their victories and their accomplishments. As the old saying goes, "When someone does something good, applaud—you'll make two people happy."

As a faithful follower of Jesus, you have every reason to be hopeful, and you have every reason to share your hopes with others. When you do, you will discover that hope, like other human emotions, is contagious. So do the world (and yourself) a favor: Look for the good in others and celebrate the good that you find. When you do, you'll be a powerful force of encouragement to the world...and a worthy servant to your God.

☆ ☆ ☆ ☆

The secret of success is to find a need and fill it,
to find a hurt and heal it,
to find somebody with a problem
and offer to help solve it.

Robert Schuller

God is still in the process of dispensing gifts, and He uses ordinary individuals like us to develop those gifts in other people.

Howard Hendricks

He climbs highest who helps another up.

Zig Ziglar

No journey is complete that does not lead through some dark valleys. We can properly comfort others only with the comfort we ourselves have been given by God.

Vance Havner

You can't light another's path without casting light on your own.

John Maxwell

A TIMELY TIP

On the front lines of life, you should seek out encouraging friends who can lift you up. And you should strive to be an encouraging friend to others.

RELY UPON HIM

Humble yourselves therefore under the mighty hand of God, so that He may exalt you in due time, casting all your care upon Him, because He cares about you.

1 Peter 5:6-7 Holman CSB

Do the stresses of the front line threaten to overwhelm you? If so, you must rely not only upon your own resources but also upon the promises of your Father in heaven.

God is a never-ending source of support and courage for those of us who call upon Him. When we are weary, He gives us strength. When we see no hope, God reminds us of His promises. When we grieve, God wipes away our tears.

God will hold your hand and walk with you every day of your life if you let Him. So even if your circumstances are difficult, trust the Father. His love is eternal and His goodness endures forever.

God can do all that we need.

Juliana of Norwich

God calls each of us in secret to make certain sacrifices which always involve a risk, even though it may differ from person to person. He does not promise us success, or even final victory in this life. God does not promise that He will protect us from trials, from material cares, from sickness, from physical or moral suffering. He promises only that He will be with us in all these trials, and that He will sustain us if they remain faithful to him.

Paul Tournier

I was learning something important: we are most vulnerable to the piercing winds of doubt when we distance ourselves from the mission and fellowship to which Christ has called us. Our night of discouragement will seem endless and our task impossible, unless we recognize that He stands in our midst.

Joni Eareckson Tada

A TIMELY TIP

God can handle it: Bill Hybels writes, "Pour out your heart to God and tell Him how you feel. Be real, be honest, and when you get it all out, you'll start to feel the gradual covering of God's comforting presence." Enough said.

GOD CAN HANDLE IT

I will lift up my eyes to the hills. From whence comes my help? My help comes from the Lord, Who made heaven and earth.

Psalm 121:1-2 NKJV

It's a promise that is made over and over again in the Bible: Whatever "it" is, God can handle it.

Life isn't always easy. Far from it! Sometimes, life can be very, very difficult, indeed. But even when the storm clouds form overhead, even during our most stressful moments, we're protected by a loving Heavenly Father.

When we're worried, God can reassure us; when we're sad, God can comfort us. When our hearts are broken, God is not just near; He is here. So we must lift our thoughts and prayers to Him. When we do, He will answer our prayers. Why? Because He is our Shepherd, and He has promised to protect us now and forever.

Either we are adrift in chaos or we are individuals, created, loved, upheld and placed purposefully, exactly where we are. Can you believe that? Can you trust God for that?

Elisabeth Elliot

God is in control, and therefore in everything I can give thanks, not because of the situation, but because of the One who directs and rules over it.

Kay Arthur

The choice for me is to either look at all things I have lost or the things I have. To live in fear or to live in hope. Hope comes from knowing I have a sovereign, loving God who is in every event in my life.

Lisa Beamer

God is God whether we recognize it or not. Nothing about that can change, except us.

Lisa Whelchel

A TIMELY TIP

As you establish priorities for your day and your life, God deserves first place. And you deserve the experience of putting Him there.

THE LESSONS OF TOUGH TIMES

If you hide your sins, you will not succeed. If you confess and reject them, you will receive mercy.

Proverbs 28:13 NCV

Have you experienced a recent setback? If so, look for the lesson that God is trying to teach you. Instead of complaining about life's sad state of affairs, learn what needs to be learned, change what needs to be changed, and move on. View failure as an opportunity to reassess God's will for your life. And while you're at it, consider life's inevitable disappointments to be powerful opportunities to learn more—more about yourself, more about your circumstances, and more about your world.

Life is difficult at times. And everybody (including you) makes mistakes. Your job is to make them only once. And how can you do that? By learning the lessons of tough times sooner rather than later, that's how.

Truth will sooner come out of error than from confusion.

Francis Bacon

Mistakes offer the possibility for redemption and a new start in God's kingdom. No matter what you're guilty of, God can restore your innocence.

Barbara Johnson

We become a failure when we allow mistakes to take away our ability to learn, give, grow, and try again.

Susan Lenzkes

Keep your face to the sunshine, and you cannot see the shadows.

Helen Keller

Lord, when we are wrong, make us willing to change; and when we are right, make us easy to live with.

Peter Marshall

A TIMELY TIP

When it comes to repairing mistakes, sooner beats later. So ask yourself, "If not now, when?"

TRUSTING GOD

It is better to trust the Lord than to put confidence in people.
It is better to trust the Lord than to put confidence in princes.

Psalm 118:8-9 NLT

Sometimes the future seems bright, and sometimes it does not. Yet even when we cannot see the possibilities of tomorrow, God can. As believers, our challenge is to trust an uncertain future to an all-powerful God.

When we trust God, we should trust Him without reservation. We should steel ourselves against the inevitable stresses of the day, secure in the knowledge that our Heavenly Father has a plan for the future that only He can see.

Can you place your future into the hands of a loving and all-knowing God? Can you live amid the uncertainties of today, knowing that God has dominion over all your tomorrows? If you can, you are wise and you are blessed. When you trust God with everything you are and everything you have, He will bless you now and forever.

God delights to meet the faith of one who looks up to Him and says, "Lord, You know that I cannot do this—but I believe that You can!"

Amy Carmichael

It helps to resign as the controller of your fate. All that energy we expend to keep things running right is not what keeps things running right.

Anne Lamott

Sometimes the very essence of faith is trusting God in the midst of things He knows good and well we cannot comprehend.

Beth Moore

God is God. He knows what he is doing. When you can't trace his hand, trust his heart.

Max Lucado

A TIMELY TIP

When life seems unfair, try spending more time trusting God and less time dwelling on "the unfairness of it all."

CONQUERING EVERYDAY FRUSTRATIONS

A hot-tempered man stirs up conflict, but a man slow to anger calms strife.

Proverbs 15:18 Holman CSB

Life on the front line is full of frustrations: some great and some small. On occasion, you, like Jesus, will confront evil, and when you do, you may respond as He did: vigorously and without reservation. But, more often your frustrations will be of the more mundane variety. As long as you live here on earth, you will face countless opportunities to lose your temper over small, relatively insignificant events: a traffic jam, a spilled cup of coffee, an inconsiderate comment, a broken promise. When you are tempted to lose your temper over the minor inconveniences of life, don't. Turn away from anger, stress, bitterness, and regret. Turn instead to God. When you do, you'll be following His commandments and giving yourself a priceless gift . . . the gift of peace.

When something robs you of your peace of mind, ask yourself if it is worth the energy you are expending on it. If not, then put it out of your mind in an act of discipline. Every time the thought of "it" returns, refuse it.

Kay Arthur

Anger is the noise of the soul; the unseen irritant of the heart; the relentless invader of silence.

Max Lucado

Doomed are the hotheads! Unhappy are they who lose their cool and are too proud to say, "I'm sorry."

Robert Schuller

Take no action in a furious passion. It's putting to sea in a storm.

Thomas Fuller

A TIMELY TIP

Angry words are dangerous to your emotional and spiritual health, not to mention your relationships. So treat anger as an uninvited guest, and usher it away as quickly—and as quietly—as possible.

ACCEPTING YOURSELF

My dear children, let's not just talk about love; let's practice real love. This is the only way we'll know we're living truly, living in God's reality. It's also the way to shut down debilitating self-criticism, even when there is something to it. For God is greater than our worried hearts and knows more about us than we do ourselves. And friends, once that's taken care of and we're no longer accusing or condemning ourselves, we're bold and free before God!

1 John 3:18-21 MSG

Are you your own worst critic? And in response to that criticism, are you constantly trying to transform yourself into a person who meets society's expectations, but not God's expectations? If so, it's time to become a little more understanding of the person you see whenever you look into the mirror.

Being patient with other people can be difficult. But sometimes, we find it even more difficult to be patient with ourselves. We have high expectations and lofty goals. We want to receive God's blessings now, not later. And, of course, we want our lives to unfold according to our own wishes and our own timetables—not God's. Yet throughout the Bible, we are instructed that patience is the companion of wisdom. Proverbs 16:32 teaches us that "Patience is better than strength" (NCV). God's message, then, is clear: we must be patient with all people—including ourselves.

The Bible affirms the importance of self-acceptance by exhorting believers to love others as they love themselves (Matthew 22:37-40). Furthermore, the Bible teaches that when we genuinely open our hearts to Him, God accepts us just as we are. And, if He accepts us—faults and all—then who are we to believe otherwise?

The great freedom Jesus gives us is
to be ourselves, defined by His love
and our inner qualities and gifts
rather than by any kind of show
we put on for the world.

—

Leslie Williams

As perfectionists we find it difficult, if not impossible, to believe that God could completely accept, love, and long to be with us in this unfinished state.

Susan Lenzkes

Yes, we need to acknowledge our weaknesses, to confess our sins. But if we want to be active, productive participants in the realm of God, we also need to recognize our gifts, to appreciate our strengths, to build on the abilities God has given us. We need to balance humility with confidence.

Penelope Stokes

Being loved by Him whose opinion matters most gives us the security to risk loving, too—even loving ourselves.

Gloria Gaither

A TIMELY TIP

You were wonderfully made by a loving God who knew exactly what He was doing. Accept it.

BEYOND DISCOURAGEMENT

When you pass through the waters, I will be with you; and through the rivers, they shall not overflow you. When you walk through the fire, you shall not be burned, nor shall the flame scorch you. For I am the Lord your God, the Holy One of Israel, your Savior.

Isaiah 43:2-3 NKJV

We Christians have many reasons to celebrate. God is in His heaven; Christ has risen, and we are the sheep of His flock. Yet sometimes, when life on the front line bears down hard upon us, we may become discouraged. After all, expectations of service men and women can be high and demands can be even higher.

When we fail to meet the expectations of others (or, for that matter, the expectations that we have for ourselves), we may be tempted to abandon hope. But God has other plans. He knows exactly how He intends to use us. Our task is to remain faithful until He does.

If you become discouraged with the direction of your day or your life, turn your thoughts and prayers to God. He is a God of possibility, not negativity. He will help you count your blessings instead of your hardships. And then, with a renewed spirit of optimism and hope, you can properly thank your Father in heaven for His blessings, for His love, and for His Son.

Bravery is the capacity
to perform properly even when
scared half to death.

—

Omar Bradley

A TIMELY TIP

When things go wrong, it's easy to become discouraged. But those who follow Jesus need never be discouraged because God's promises are true . . . and heaven is eternal.

TEMPTATIONS EVERYWHERE

No temptation has overtaken you except what is common to humanity. God is faithful and He will not allow you to be tempted beyond what you are able, but with the temptation He will also provide a way of escape, so that you are able to bear it.

1 Corinthians 10:13 Holman CSB

If you stop to think about it, the cold, hard evidence is right in front of your eyes: you live in a temptation-filled world. The devil is everywhere, hard at work, causing pain, stress, and heartache in more ways than ever before. Here in the 21st century, the bad guys are working around the clock to lead you astray. That's why you must remain vigilant.

In a letter to believers, Peter offered a stern warning: "Your adversary, the devil, prowls around like a roaring lion, seeking someone to devour" (1 Peter 5:8 NASB). What was true in New Testament times is equally true in our own. Satan tempts his prey and then devours them. As believing Christians, we must beware. And, if we seek righteousness in our own lives, we must earnestly wrap ourselves in the protection of God's Holy Word. When we do, we are secure.

Do not fight the temptation in detail. Turn from it. Look ONLY at your Lord. Sing. Read. Work.

Amy Carmichael

In the Garden of Gethsemane, Jesus went through agony of soul in His efforts to resist the temptation to do what He felt like doing rather than what He knew was God's will for Him.

Joyce Meyer

Temptation is not a sin. Even Jesus was tempted. The Lord Jesus gives you the strength needed to resist temptation.

Corrie ten Boom

The devil's most devilish when respectable.

Elizabeth Barrett Browning

A TIMELY TIP

Because you live in a temptation-filled world, you must guard your eyes, your thoughts, and your heart—all day, every day.

KEEP PRAYING!

Is anyone among you suffering? He should pray.

James 5:13 Holman CSB

Life on the front line is a marathon, not a sprint—it is a journey that unfolds day by day. And, that's exactly how often you should seek direction from your Creator: one day at a time, each day followed by the next, without exception.

Daily prayer and meditation is a matter of will and habit. You must willingly organize your time by carving out quiet moments with God, and you must form the habit of daily worship. When you do, you'll discover that no time is more precious than the silent moments you spend with your Heavenly Father.

The quality of your spiritual life will be in direct proportion to the quality of your prayer life. Prayer changes things, and it changes you. So today, instead of turning things over in your mind, turn them over to God in prayer. Instead of worrying about your next decision, ask God to lead the way. Don't limit your prayers to meals or to bedtime; pray constantly. God is listening; He wants to hear from you; and you most certainly need to hear from Him.

We must leave it to God to answer our prayers in His own wisest way. Sometimes, we are so impatient and think that God does not answer. God always answers! He never fails! Be still. Abide in Him.

Mrs. Charles E. Cowman

When you ask God to do something, don't ask timidly; put your whole heart into it.

Marie T. Freeman

God delights in the prayers of His children—prayers that express our love for Him, prayers that share our deepest burdens with Him.

Billy Graham

It was the darkest hour of my life; relief came in prayer. God heard my cry, and enabled me to say, from the depth of my soul, "Thy will be done."

Dwight L Moody

A TIMELY TIP

Prayer changes things—and you—so pray.

SHARING YOUR BURDENS WITH GOD

If God is for us, who can be against us?

Romans 8:31 NKJV

The Bible promises this: tough times are temporary but God's love is not—God's love endures forever. So what does that mean to you? Just this: From time to time, everybody faces hardships and disappointments, and so will you. And when tough times arrive, God always stands ready to protect you and to heal you. Your task is straightforward: you must share your burdens with Him.

As Corrie ten Boom observed, "Any concern that is too small to be turned into a prayer is too small to be made into a burden." Those are comforting words, especially in these difficult days.

Whatever the size of your challenges, God is big enough to handle them. Ask for His help today, with faith and with fervor. Instead of turning things over in your mind, turn them over to God in prayer. Instead of worrying about your next decision, ask God to lead the way. Cast your burdens upon the One who cannot be shaken, and rest assured that He always hears your prayers.

We are not called to be burden-bearers, but cross-bearers and light-bearers. We must cast our burdens on the Lord.

Corrie ten Boom

When you're enjoying the fulfillment and fellowship that inevitably accompanies authentic service, ministry is a joy. Instead of exhausting you, it energizes you; instead of burnout, you experience blessing.

Bill Hybels

God knows what each of us is dealing with. He knows our pressures. He knows our conflicts. And, He has made a provision for each and every one of them. That provision is Himself in the person of the Holy Spirit, dwelling in us and empowering us to respond rightly.

Kay Arthur

No matter what we are going through, no matter how long the waiting for answers, of one thing we may be sure. God is faithful. He keeps His promises. What He starts, He finishes...including His perfect work in us.

Gloria Gaither

A TIMELY TIP

God will most certainly keep His promises to you. Your job is to keep your obligations to Him.

LET JESUS GUIDE THE WAY

I have come as a light into the world, so that everyone who believes in Me would not remain in darkness.

John 12:46 Holman CSB

Is Jesus the cornerstone of your life . . . or have you relegated Him to a far corner of your life? The answer to this question will determine the quality, the direction, the tone, and the ultimate destination of your life here on earth and your life throughout eternity.

Thomas Brooks spoke for believers of every generation when he observed, "Christ is the sun, and all the watches of our lives should be set by the dial of his motion." Christ, indeed, is the ultimate Savior of mankind and the personal Savior of those who believe in Him. As His servants, we should place Him at the very center of our lives. And every day that God gives us breath, we should share Christ's love and His message with a world that needs both.

The dearest friend on earth is but a mere shadow compared with Jesus Christ.

Oswald Chambers

When we are in a situation where Jesus is all we have, we soon discover he is all we really need.

Gigi Graham Tchividjian

In your greatest weakness, turn to your greatest strength, Jesus, and hear Him say, "My grace is sufficient for you, for My strength is made perfect in weakness" (2 Corinthians 12:9, NKJV).

Lisa Whelchel

Tell me the story of Jesus. Write on my heart every word. Tell me the story most precious, sweetest that ever was heard.

Fanny Crosby

A TIMELY TIP

Jesus is the light of the world. Make sure that you are capturing and reflecting His light.

FINDING FOLKS WHO WILL LISTEN AND HELP

A wise man will hear and increase learning, and a man of understanding will attain wise counsel.

Proverbs 1:5 NKJV

If your world has been turned upside down—or shattered—you should reach out to folks who have truly walked in your shoes—men and women who have experienced your particular pain and lived to tell about it. And then, when you've recruited a small team of friends and counselors, it's time for you to talk (about your feelings) and listen (to their advice).

God doesn't intend for you to suffer in solitude, so He inevitably places counselors and comforters along your path. But when you're hurting, it's tempting to lock the door, and to sit, alone, in your self-pity. Tempting, but unwise. A far better way to deal with your feelings is to share them with the people whom God sends your way.

So, the next time you're tempted to wall yourself off inside an emotional prison of your own making, resist that temptation. Instead, find a compassionate friend you can talk to, or pray with, or even to cry with. Consider that friend to be God's gift to you—a precious gift you can use to guide your path and hasten your healing.

The glory of friendship is not the outstretched hand, or the kindly smile, or the joy of companionship. It is the spiritual inspiration that comes to one when he discovers that someone else believes in him and is willing to trust him with his friendship.

—

Corrie ten Boom

God specializes in taking tragedy and turning it into triumph. The greater the tragedy, the greater the potential for triumph.

Charles Stanley

Though our pain and our disappointment and the details of our suffering may differ, there is an abundance of God's grace and peace available to each of us.

Charles Swindoll

No one stands taller in the climb to success than when he bends over to help up someone else.

John Maxwell

We need to learn to set our course by the stars and not by the lights of every passing ship.

Omar Bradley

A TIMELY TIP

Other people have experienced emotions that are similar to yours, and they are willing to help. Your job is to let them help.

THIS IS HIS DAY

This is the day that the Lord has made. Let us rejoice and be glad today!

Psalm 118:24 NCV

God gives us this day; He fills it to the brim with possibilities, and He challenges us to use it for His purposes. The 118th Psalm reminds us that today, like every other day, is a cause for celebration. The day is presented to us fresh and clean at midnight, free of charge, but we must beware: Today is a non-renewable resource—once it's gone, it's gone forever. Our responsibility, of course, is to use this day in the service of God's will and according to His commandments.

Today, treasure the time that God has given you. Give Him the glory and the praise and the thanksgiving that He deserves. And search for the hidden possibilities that God has placed along your path. This day is a priceless gift from God, so use it joyfully and encourage others to do likewise. After all, this is the day the Lord has made....

All our life is a celebration for us; we are convinced, in fact, that God is always everywhere. We sing while we work... we pray while we carry out all life's other occupations.

St. Clement of Alexandria

The church is the last place on earth to be solemn . . . provided you have lived right.

Sam Jones

Some of us seem so anxious about avoiding hell that we forget to celebrate our journey toward heaven.

Philip Yancey

Celebration is possible only through the deep realization that life and death are never found completely separate. Celebration can really come about only where fear and love, joy and sorrow, tear and smiles can exist together.

Henri Nouwen

A TIMELY TIP

If you're too stressed out to celebrate life today, start thanking God for the gifts He has given you. Try counting those gifts one-by-one.

USING YOUR TALENTS

Do not neglect the gift that is in you.

1 Timothy 4:14 NKJV

God gives each of us a unique assortment of talents and opportunities. And our Heavenly Father instructs us to be faithful stewards of the gifts that He bestows upon us. But we live in a world that encourages us to do otherwise.

Ours is a society that is filled to the brim with countless opportunities to squander our time, our resources, and our talents. So we must be watchful for distractions and temptations that might lead us astray.

God has blessed you with unique opportunities to serve Him, and He has given you every tool that you need to do so. Today, accept this challenge: value the talent that God has given you, nourish it, make it grow, and share it with the world. After all, the best way to say "Thank You" for God's gifts is to use them.

You are the only person on earth who can use your ability.

Zig Ziglar

Not everyone possesses boundless energy or a conspicuous talent. We are not equally blessed with great intellect or physical beauty or emotional strength. But we have all been given the same ability to be faithful.

Gigi Graham Tchividjian

The Lord has abundantly blessed me all of my life. I'm not trying to pay Him back for all of His wonderful gifts; I just realize that He gave them to me to give away.

Lisa Whelchel

It is the definition of joy to be able to offer back to God the essence of what he's placed in you, be that creativity or a love of ideas or a compassionate heart or the gift of hospitality.

Paula Rinehart

Almighty God created us, redeemed us, called us, endowed us with gifts and abilities and perceptions. To demean the gift is to insult the Giver.

Penelope Stokes

A TIMELY TIP

It's both stressful and futile to squander God's blessings. You possess a unique set of talents. These gifts are from the Creator—use them while you can.

GOOD DECISIONS MEAN LESS STRESS

Now if any of you lacks wisdom, he should ask God, who gives to all generously and without criticizing, and it will be given to him.

James 1:5 Holman CSB

Life presents each of us with countless questions, conundrums, doubts, and problems. Thankfully, the riddles of everyday living are not too difficult to solve if we look for answers in the right places. When we have questions, we should consult God's Word, we should consult our own consciences, and we should consult a few close friends and family members.

Perhaps Søren Kierkegaard was stating the obvious when he observed, "Life can only be understood backwards; but it must be lived forwards." Still, Kierkegaard's words are far easier to understand than they are to live by.

Taking a forward-looking (and stress-conquering) approach to life means learning the art of solving difficult problems sensibly and consistently . . . and sooner rather than later.

No trumpets sound when the important decisions of our life are made. Destiny is made known silently.

Agnes DeMille

Life is built on character, but character is built on decisions.

Warren Wiersbe

The Reference Point for the Christian is the Bible. All values, judgments, and attitudes must be gauged in relationship to this Reference Point.

Ruth Bell Graham

Successful people make right decisions early and manage those decisions daily.

John Maxwell

A TIMELY TIP

If you've got a decision to make, the first thing you should do is slow down and check it out with God.

FOLLOW HIM

Then Jesus said to His disciples, "If anyone wants to come with Me, he must deny himself, take up his cross, and follow Me. For whoever wants to save his life will lose it, but whoever loses his life because of Me will find it."

Matthew 16:24-25 Holman CSB

Jesus walks with you. Are you walking with Him seven days a week, and not just on Sunday mornings? Are you a seven-day-a-week Christian who carries your faith with you to work each day, or do you try to keep Jesus at a "safe" distance when you're not sitting in church? Hopefully, you understand the wisdom of walking with Christ all day every day.

Jesus loved you so much that He endured unspeakable humiliation and suffering for you. How will you respond to Christ's sacrifice? Will you take up His cross and follow Him—during good times and tough times—or will you choose another path? When you place your hopes squarely at the foot of the cross, when you place Jesus squarely at the center of your life, you will be blessed.

Do you seek to fulfill God's purpose for your life? Do you seek spiritual abundance? Would you like to partake in "the peace that passes all understanding"? Then follow Christ. Follow Him by picking up His cross today and every day that you live. When you do, you will quickly discover that Christ's love has the power to change everything, including you.

You who suffer take heart. Christ is the answer to sorrow.

Billy Graham

Jesus Christ is not a security from storms. He is perfect security in storms.

Kathy Troccoli

In the midst of the pressure and the heat, I am confident His hand is on my life, developing my faith until I display His glory, transforming me into a vessel of honor that pleases Him!

Anne Graham Lotz

A TIMELY TIP

You don't have to be perfect to follow in Christ's footsteps. Jesus doesn't expect your perfection—He expects your participation.

TIME FOR RENEWAL

I will give you a new heart and put a new spirit within you.

Ezekiel 36:26 Holman CSB

The demands of life on the front line can sap our strength and rob us of the joy that is rightfully ours in Christ. When we find ourselves tired, discouraged, or worse, there is a source from which we can draw the power needed to recharge our spiritual batteries. That source is God.

God intends that His children lead joyous lives filled with abundance and peace. But sometimes, abundance and peace seem very far away. It is then that we must turn to God for renewal, and when we do, He will restore us.

Once the fog of emotional exhaustion begins to lift, it's time to reengage with the world. The willingness to take action—even if the outcome of that action is uncertain—is an effective way to combat hopelessness. When you decide to roll up your sleeves and begin tackling the challenges that confront you, you'll feel empowered.

The advice of American publisher Cyrus Curtis still rings true: "Believe in the Lord and he will do half the work—the last half."

So, today and every day, ask God for these things:

clear perspective, mountain-moving faith, and the courage to do what needs doing. After all, no problem is too big for God—not even yours.

Are you tired or troubled? Turn your heart toward God in prayer. Are you weak or worried? Take the time—or, more accurately, make the time—to delve deeply into God's Holy Word. Are you spiritually depleted? Call upon fellow believers to support you, and call upon Christ to renew your spirit and your life. When you do, you'll discover that the Creator of the universe stands always ready and always able to create a new sense of wonderment and joy in you.

God specializes in things fresh and firsthand.
His plans for you this year may outshine those
of the past. He's prepared to fill your days
with reasons to give Him praise.

—

Joni Eareckson Tada

He is the God of wholeness and restoration.

Stormie Omartian

In those desperate times when we feel like we don't have an ounce of strength, He will gently pick up our heads so that our eyes can behold something—something that will keep His hope alive in us.

Kathy Troccoli

Repentance removes old sins and wrong attitudes, and it opens the way for the Holy Spirit to restore our spiritual health.

Shirley Dobson

A TIMELY TIP

God can make all things new, including you. When you are weak or worried, God can renew your spirit. Your task is to let Him.

ONE NATION UNDER GOD

Blessings are on the head of the righteous.

Proverbs 10:6 Holman CSB

The American dream is alive and well because of those who serve us and protect us. America owes its undying gratitude to the men and women who serve in the military, in government, in health care, and in the helping professions. Without them, the promise of this great nation would remain unfulfilled.

Since its earliest days, America has truly been "one nation, under God." And, the Word of God instructs us that service to others is one way of fulfilling His purpose here on earth. Romans 12:10 reminds us, "Be devoted to one another in brotherly love." Thankfully, Americans of every generation have heeded these words.

If you have chosen a life of service, and if by doing so, you've placed yourself on the front line of conflict, please accept the profound thanks of a grateful nation.

Americans everywhere appreciate your service and your sacrifice.

We highly resolve that this nation, under God, shall have a new birth of freedom, and that government of the people, by the people, for the people, shall not perish from the earth.

Abraham Lincoln

We must be ready to dare all for our country. For history does not long entrust the care of freedom to the weak or the timid.

Dwight D. Eisenhower

We hold these truths to be self-evident, that all men are created equal, that they are endowed by their Creator with certain inalienable Rights, that among these are Life, Liberty, and the pursuit of Happiness.

Declaration of Independence

This will remain the land of the free only so long as it is the home of the brave.

Elmer Davis

A TIMELY TIP

America remains a shining light to the world. As Barry Goldwater correctly observed, "This nation and its people are freedom's models in a searching world. We can be freedom's missionaries in a doubting world."